Contents

1. Chapter 1   1

2. Chapter 2   8

3. Chapter 3   17

4. Chapter 4   23

5. Chapter 5   29

6. Chapter 6   39

7. Chapter 7   44

8. Chapter 8   54

9. Chapter 9   59

10. Chapter 10   66

11. Chapter 11   72

12. Chapter 12   78

13. Chapter 13   84

14. Chapter 14   91

15. Chapter 15   99

16. Chapter 16   105

17. Chapter 17   110

18. Chapter 18   115

19. Chapter 19   120

20. Chapter 20   130

21. Chapter 21   136

22. Chapter 22   140

23. Chapter 23   144

24. Chapter 24   154

25. Chapter 25   164

26. Chapter 26   176

27. Chapter 27   182

28. Chapter 28   194

29. Chapter 29   200

30. Chapter 30   206

31. Chapter 31   213

32. Chapter 32   218

33. Chapter 33   224

34. Chapter 34   228

35. Chapter 35   233

36. Chapter 36   239

37. Chapter 37   244

38. Chapter 38   250

39. Chapter 39   256

40. Chapter 40   262

41. Chapter 41   266

42. Chapter 42   273

43. Chapter 43   280

44. Chapter 44   283

45. Chapter 45   286

46. Chapter 46   288

47. Chapter 47   292

48. Chapter 48   295

49. Chapter 49   305

50. Chapter 50   310

About the author   314

Chapter One

August 1945

The letter slipped to the floor through Lanya's trembling fingers. A letter from the Communist Party. Lanya could feel the tension rising, her fingers tight. What could the Communist Party want? She was not in trouble, was she? Again? Her chest tightened and her breathing was shallow. What could they want? She reached down carefully and picked up the letter. She leaned against the wall as she opened it with a nearby kitchen knife and tore open the envelope. Official letterhead, official paper, an invitation? To what? The Communist Party was inviting her to an awards ceremony next weekend, anyone who survived the siege of Leningrad. They were called the *blokadniki*, the survivors of the siege. They were to be given the Order of Lenin, the highest Soviet honor, for their service and sacrifice in the Great Patriotic War. Lanya focused on slowing her breath. She knew to be careful. An award for surviving? Lanya smiled a weak smile, thinking it was better than the alternative.

As she folded the letter, her history with the Communist Party came back. Eight years ago they had taken her father, and then one year later her mother for "Anti-Soviet" activities. There was no explanation and no public trial. She had never seen either of them again. Her heart still had a huge hole. During the war, she had been accused of being a spy for the Germans, spent three weeks in jail and was only released by a friend who worked for the Party. She would never love the Party like many seemed to and she wished the Party did not know she was alive.

The war was over, finally. It ended in May, and now it was August. But the war was still everywhere in Leningrad. There was still rationing, but not like it had been. The city was not demolished by the Nazis, but it might as well have been. Not one building was untouched. Not one life was untouched. Shelling, bombing, fires and the worst winters on record scarred the city so badly it might never recover. Leningrad was no longer the elegant, beautiful city it was before the war. Only determined perseverance could bring a stalwart beauty from the inside. A million Leningraders had died, many from starvation and cold, and quite a few from air raids. Of the ones who did survive, many would never be the same. Now, there was some food available, gas for cars, restaurants were open. People who had left the city came back. The trees were lush with branches and birds and squirrels were making their noisy chatter for the first time in four years. People were proud that the Hermitage was open again and full of the art it was famous for. Visitors could come and go from the city. Locals were hopeful for the first time in years. Those who wished for death now wished for normalcy. And it was coming.

She decided they would make a day out of the unexpected ceremony. Lanya and her brother Mikhail would go together. Lanya would ask her best friend Maru and her mother to join them. Lanya and Maru had been best friends since they were teenagers, Maru was crazy about Mikhail and only he did not see it.

Lanya and Maru went shopping for new dresses to wear for the outing. Clothes were coming into the city since the war was over and it was like a breath of fresh air to have something new. Lanya looked at the rows of dresses in soft colors, glad to be rid of the drab browns and grays of war time. Lanya chose a new pair of white sandals that had been made at the factory where she worked. She picked a light blue dress with flowers on the front because it felt summery and light. The belt would wrap around her slender frame well. Maru chose a dress that was gold with navy trim, she had more curves than Lanya, and the dark color would show those off. Maru always cared how she looked. Maru added a little hat, a classic look, but Lanya did not like hats on her straight brown hair. With Maru's blonde curls though, it would be a cute look. Lanya picked up a shirt and trousers for her brother, since he hated to shop.

The day before the ceremony, Lanya was surprised at a knock on the door to the apartment she shared with Mikhail. Their previous apartment had been bombed and they had few visitors so she wondered who it would be. She opened the door and it was Josef, the friend who had gotten her released from jail. Josef worked for the Party, so Lanya immediately felt some trepidation that she quickly tried to hide. "Josef, good to see you. Won't you please come in?" She waved her arm to invite him in. She joined her hands to keep her fingers from drumming. Josef had a small smile and pushed his thick eyeglasses up as he entered. The glasses enlarged his eyes but the rest of his face was almost child-like. His clothes looked new but were crumpled and wrinkled. Since the war ended he had filled out a bit, but he would never be a big man. The only lively thing about him was his brown hair that swirled across his forehead. As soon as he came in, Lanya squeezed her fingers together, wondering if this was official business.

"Lanya, um, sorry to just come by, but, but... will you be going to the ceremony tomorrow? I will... and I hope to see you there." Josef was a gentle soul who had gotten her out of jail and brought food when she was hungry so she wanted to be good to him.

"Josef, yes, we will be going. Mikhail and Maru will go, too. Where will you be at the ceremony?" They had not taken a seat in the front room and Josef was shifting his weight from one foot to the other so Lanya could tell he was nervous. He was always nervous around her. He held one hand in the other as he talked. His thick brown hair refused to stay combed and Lanya smiled at it. His glasses were perched on his nose and she wondered if they might slide off any second as they usually did. He was not a handsome man but Lanya knew he had a good heart.

"I will be at the entrance, guiding people to their seats. Can I save you seats? You will see me in my Party sweater." Every member who worked at a Party office had a brown sweater they wore for official functions.

"That would be wonderful, thank you. It will be a big crowd."

"The *blokadniki* will sit in the front and there will be guests near the perimeter." His eyes shifted from her face to the floor. "I, I, I will get you seats near the front. There will be speeches and a band will play."

Lanya focused on stilling her fingers. "I would like that Josef. Thank you again for offering. We will see you at ten then."

"Yes, Lanya, I will look for you at ten. I need to be going. See you tomorrow."

Josef quickly turned and went out and Lanya closed the door. He was a kind man. Lanya smiled at his nerves but never mentioned it to him. In truth, she would like to avoid any Party functions but she was afraid someone would notice. Being near the front would remove any concerns about her. Good of him to suggest it.

Saturday morning was bright and warm. Lanya woke up slowly, enjoying the quiet. The war had been so noisy at night. She did not have as many nightmares as she did during the war and was sleeping much better. Lanya was glad that hope was slowly seeping back into her blood. There were days during the war when death would have been a relief. Leningrad was still a beautiful city even though buildings were piles of rubble and broken glass. People wore genuine smiles that had been missing. Theaters were opening and Lanya wanted to try out for a new show. She had only been onstage for a few weeks in a small show at the beginning of the war, but she knew the stage was her place in life. She missed singing to a crowd and loved the applause. New shows were coming in from Moscow and Lanya thought she could find a part. Her old fears were fading. For the first time ever, she was looking forward to what the world might offer.

As she prepared to leave, Lanya started singing an old folk song that she learned from her grandmother Babu. She remembered singing during the war in the food lines and the smiles that broke out. They sang along and that made Lanya smile too. As she brushed her fine hair she remembered how singing always perked people up. Even a sad song could get people singing along and bring their own memories. Singing was powerful.

Lanya and Mikhail got off the tram after taking the long way to the Admiralty, where the ceremony would be held. Maru was there with her mother, a small woman with a quick smile. They went the long way, to avoid the part of town most heavily bombed since that was still hard to see. The Admiralty was at the center of Leningrad and parts of the building had been bombed, but the golden spire was still intact. It was the center for the Soviet Navy now and the room they were going to was spacious and not too bad. The Admiralty was near the Winter Palace and the gardens in town, and Leningraders loved their city so much that no one had chopped down the elm trees that lined the gardens. Even when people were freezing to death, these majestic trees stayed, defiant like the *blokadniki*. The crowd was big and people were smiling and laughing. The long summer day was warm and the birds were everywhere. Lanya and Maru felt pretty in their new dresses. Lanya wore a small necklace that had been her grandmother's. Her Babu had been with her all her life except the last three years. Babu's age meant she did not make it through the war but Lanya wanted to bring her, in some way.

"Mishka, you did not tell me you like my hat, do you?" Maru stalled and forced Mikhail to look at her. Her eyes sparkled as she looked at him in his new outfit. He did not care how he looked but she certainly did. He nodded and had a silly smile on his face. Maru always flirted with him and kept him on the hook. Lanya and Maru's mom smiled, both knowing what was happening.

"Almost as pretty as you, Maru" he said. She flirted better than he did. Lanya was always glad to hear his deep voice. During the war he was hurt and could not talk for more than two years. Lanya was glad he could talk now, though he never said too much. After he returned from chasing the Germans out of Soviet territory and she was glad he made it home.

The crowd filled into the auditorium and Lanya looked for Josef. There were many brown sweaters and finding him might be tough. Lanya bit her cheek to check the bile that came from seeing those sweaters. She saw Josef, along the side and waved to him. He rushed over with his smile as wide as could be.

"Right up here, See, I have your names here."

"Thanks Josef, this is perfect." Lanya smiled and Mikhail went to join the soldiers. They sat near the front and the stage had seats for plenty of the leaders. The ceremony began with a rousing song by a chorus of children and the mayor stood up to speak. Then the Party leader spoke, then another official from Moscow. A general was next, and Lanya did not listen to any of it. She knew that their words were not important, only their actions. Even though she could see that no one in a sweater was looking for her, her hands were tight on the chair and she looked at her feet to calm her breathing. She found Josef and he saw her and smiled so she gave a weak smile in return. The speeches were finally over and they began a queue to receive a certificate almost like a graduation. Lanya held hers tightly. Even though it came from the Party, it felt good to be a survivor. When the certificates were all handed out, a band played a song that had the tune of a march, and the crowd stood and began filing out. As they got to the door, Josef appeared at Lanya's elbow. "Thank you again Josef, that was just right. Such a nice day."

"Lanya, can I talk to you?"

"Josef, we are going to lunch now. Can we talk tomorrow?"

"Yes, um, can I come by?"

"Yes, around noon?"

"Yes, Lanya, see you at noon." He disappeared into the crowd and Lanya watched him go. She wondered what he wanted to say. She never really knew what was going on inside his head.

Lunch was at a small restaurant on Nevsky Prospekt, the main thoroughfare in town along the Neva River. They got a table on the sidewalk and most of the customers had certificates in their hands too. As they sat down, Lanya noticed that Maru kept her hand on Mishka's arm and smiled up at him. The food was good and Lanya had fruit with her meal. It was so good to have fresh food again. Lanya might never eat one of those rusk biscuits again. As they left the table and separated to catch their trams home, the good bye hugs were a little longer than normal and Lanya smiled. When would her brother see it all?

At home, Lanya put the certificate on top of her dresser. One day only, she thought. Then tomorrow, in with the socks. Even if it was from the Party, it felt good to be noticed. She realized her tension had dissipated and hoped it would stay gone for good.

Lanya was straightening the kitchen after lunch the next day and humming a new song in her head when she heard the knock on the door and knew it was Josef. Mikhail got to the door first and greeted Josef, then went back to his room. Josef came into the front room. "Josef, good to see you, would you like some tea?"

"No, Lanya, thank you. I am glad we can talk. Can your brother hear us?" Josef looked down the hall towards the bedrooms, hoping Mikhail was far enough away. Lanya watched him, seeing his tension.

"No, he shuts his door and does not hear me, even when I sing."

"Lanya" he said as he pushed his glasses up his nose, "Lanya, I wanted to have a, a personal talk. I have known you for a long time, and I think we are friends." They stood just inside the door and Lanya was glad she had the towel to wipe her hands on and keep her fingers still.

"Yes, Josef, I think we are friends." Lanya searched his face, but he quickly turned his eyes as he looked at her. She did not want to be too direct.

"Lanya, I want..." Josef paused almost like he was choking. "Lanya, I want us to be more. I think you are beautiful and talented and I enjoy being with you. I got news from the Party in Moscow this week, and they want me to work there. In the main office, working under people who work under Stalin. I leave next month." He reached out and took Lanya's hand, letting the towel fall to the floor. "Lanya, I want you to come with me. I know we could have something. I know we have never talked about... us...." He seemed to choke on the words. "But I think we could have something. I could see us together many years from now." His eyes searched her face. Her knees were going to buckle and she held tightly to his hands to remain upright. Her brain was a mash of things but Josef kept going. He released her hands and stepped back, like she was too hot to touch.

"I have shocked you. I am sorry. This has been on my mind for months. I could not tell you when the enemy was at the gates. No, that was not it, part of it. I was..." He looked here and there, glanced around the room, looking at anything but her face. He looked at his shoes. "I was scared. I was not man enough to talk to you about this before. I was sure you would laugh at my face." He brought his eyes back to hers. "Again I am sorry to be so blunt. I could have found a better way. Please think about this and let me know your decision. Give me an answer when you can." He took her hands again and she felt the warmth of his fingers. "I love you Svetlana. I want to be with you for a long time. Let me know. Goodbye my Lanya." With that, he jerked to the door and threw it open, nearly running outside. Lanya fell into a chair. He loved her? Wanted her? Moscow? She buried her face in her hands and tried to breathe.

Chapter Two

The sun was bright and the sky a clear blue on this 22nd of June 1941. No one could foresee that by midnight it would all change. Summer was a wonderful time to be in Leningrad. Days were long and warm and the nights were short. It was daylight well into the night, and 10 pm was a comfortable walk with plenty of light. Lanya and her friends would sometimes go out at night, just for fresh air and some ice cream. Leningrad did not sleep much in summer, and there was always something going on at night. There were street musicians, vodka and plenty of people. On every street the food hawkers had their kiosks, the sizzles of the pierogies as they fried and the smell of the sausages as they turned crisp were tempting. Old women with their yellow kvas barrels handed out drinks for a coin. Nobody ever got drunk off homemade kvas, but everyone drank it. Evenings were magical. Sometimes Lanya took her younger sister Valentina out after her bedtime; the little girl thought it was so exciting to be up late and act so grown up. Being up at eleven pm on a Saturday evening when you are thirteen years old is quite an adventure! This was the longest day of the year, and the only problem was the nagging talk about war. This talk had been around for quite a few months, but nothing had really come of it. The Red Army had taken over part of Poland a few years back, but that did not disturb Leningrad. There was no bad news about Poland. A few men had gone, but those were the regular army. No one felt threatened, it was all so far away. She knew they had signed a peace agreement with Germany a few years back. The Nazis had taken over Western Europe and Lanya heard there had not been a lot of fighting. Then the Germans had a long fight with England, but the Soviets and the Germans had an agreement, that they would not fight each other. Everyone felt it would work out. Maybe the generals had different ideas, but it was not apparent that warm, bright evening in 1941.

But as Lanya woke up on June 23rd, it was all different. Cars and trucks buzzed by on the street and the market had more people milling about. Their bags were not full,- they were shopping for news, Some shouting drew Lanya's attention. Germany had attacked the Soviet frontier! People were asking questions and the older men were cursing about the vile Germans. The younger men looked dazed; they would be the ones to fight. Women clutched their children close, hoping to protect them from bad news. Lanya wondered what would happen as she hurried by on her way to catch the tram to her job at the shoe factory where she ran a sewing machine. At the factory, no one wanted to sit and work quietly. They clustered and asked question after question. Would the Germans come to Leningrad? Or would they go straight to Moscow? Were they strong enough? Would the Red Army be ready? Could Stalin and his generals keep them safe? One word that was often used was "betrayed". The Germans broke the earlier agreement, to not attack each other. Stabbed in the back. All day long her coworkers were irritable and tense.

As Lanya returned home at the end of the day, her grandmother was in the kitchen with a dour look on her face. "Babu, what is going on? Have you heard?" She heard the radio on in the other room and was sure her grandmother knew what had happened.

Babu looked up from preparing dinner and her eyes were sad, remembering the Great War and the Revolution of 1918, Lanya could see. "It is war. We will need to get ready." Her look did not change.

"What do we do?" Lanya's voice felt small, full of a tense fear shrouded in uncertainty.

"Let's see what happens, what the Party does." Lanya did not have confidence that the Party would fix things. Babu did not offer more information and Lanya did not feel at all confident.

Mikhail, Lanya's older brother, came into the kitchen covered in the dirt from his welding job. His clothes always had the dust and debris from working with metal bits and he took his hat off and hit it against his other hand while Babu frowned at him. The smell of the metal shavings mixed with sweat, so Mishka never snuck up on anyone.

"Do that outside before you come in here!" Babu said this to him every day but Mishka never listened. Any time Mishka smiled, he got away with things. It was that kind of smile.

"Babu, Lanya, did you hear? There is a war! We are going to teach the Nazis a lesson!" He tossed his hat onto the table where more dust fell off.

Babu replied, "I hope so, but it will not be easy. Go get cleaned up." Mikhail left to wash up and Lanya wondered when answers would come. Valentina breezed into the kitchen with bows in her hair and some makeup on her eyes. Lanya realized again that her baby sister was pretty. A delicate kind of beauty, but she had a lot of fire inside her.

"War? Ha- it will not touch us. They do not want Leningrad- they want the capital. That is what my friends say."

Lanya wondered how much the friends of a 13 year old would know about the working of the world but did not say anything.

"Be ready for dinner in twenty minutes girl, go on!" Babu shooed her out of the kitchen as she stirred the cabbage in the pot. "Silly girl." Lanya left the kitchen and went to her room that she shared with Valentina. She picked up a magazine on the nightstand. It was about agricultural production with a smiling farmer and his family on the cover. Lanya looked at it and was glad she lived in the city. Her grandparents had been farmers years ago and she remembered visiting their farm when she was a child. She preferred the city with the variety of foods, clothes and people. Even without a clear plan for her future, Lanya was sure that city life was for her. There was always something to do here in Leningrad. And they had theaters. Lanya loved going with Maru to the theater, especially for musicals. She had been in a school show and the bug bit her hard. Lanya dreamed of being on stage one day, where she felt like she was valuable. She loved the attention. She should try out for a show. Maru would help her.

Dinner was quiet; no one wanted to ask questions without answers. Lanya was glad, she did not think war talk would make dinner go down well. It was too soon to know anything anyway. Maybe Germany would just skip Leningrad. Maybe they only wanted the capital like Valentina said. That would be best for them.

After dinner, they crowded around the radio in the front room. There was no music or stories tonight, only talk about war.

Every segment said again how despicable the back stabbing Germans were and how the Red Army would take care of themselves. Lanya bit her nails as the stories came in. She would never have nice nails. Her stomach was tight and she wondered if dinner would stay down. Valentina was having trouble sitting and listening and did not stay long. Mikhail was quiet but Lanya could see a lot was going on in his head. Babu's teeth were clenched and she absorbing every word. War might bring something new to Leningrad and Lanya wondered if it might change her dreary existence. How bad could it be? The war with Finland a few years back had not been too bad. Babu had told a few stories about the hardships of the Great War, starvation and rationing. Lanya had no idea what it would be like but was glad that Babu could handle it. Lanya knew that Mikhail would have to go. As a welder, he might be able to work here in town but Lanya dreaded the thought of life without him. She would have to lead the family and she was surely not ready for that.

The Party was quick to get things going. The next day, announcements came out that all young men needed to register with the Party office to be called up. There was talk of rationing already, but food was plentiful now. Citizens were asked to find ways to contribute. There was night watch work, looking for bombers; packing up the Hermitage and making sandbags and other choices. There were work teams to go outside the city to dig trenches in case the Germans came this way. Lanya thought they should see where the Germans were going before they went to dig trenches, but she knew she would have to do her part.

The trench digging started within a week. Every able-bodied citizen went outside the city and dug to keep tanks outside the city. Germans were known for their tank power and trenches were the best way to stop them. This was back breaking and Lanya had no energy to go out in town in the sunny evenings. She flopped into bed every night. Mikhail dug, too. Valentina was put to other tasks like delivering notes on bicycle. Babu stayed home since she would not be considered productive. Soviets were always efficient. At the factory, they were no longer making nice ladies sandals, but now they had heavy duty leather for sewing boots. An army needed good boots.

The Party made announcements and put big speakers up through the city at major intersections. Everyone needed to hear all the news, even if it came only from the Party. People quickly started to cluster around these for news.

Mikhail got called to go for training. Lanya was devastated. He was told to report Monday morning at the army center on the other side of town to be enlisted. Lanya felt like her world was falling apart. But Mikhail laughed, and did what many young men did that weekend, drink with their friends, eat too much and wish they had women to miss them.

Lanya could not understand her brother's cavalier attitude. "You could get hurt! What will we do without you? When will you come home?"

Mikhail put his hand on his sister's head like she was a child. Lanya hated that but did not move away this time. "I have to go. We all do. The only men left will have good reason to stay. We have to fight the Nazis. You will fight at the factory. You will work long hours making things for us. I might even get boots made by you! Anything is better than losing to the Nazis. I will fight with a gun and you will fight with a sewing machine. We will each do our part." Babu had entered the room and stayed back, but Lanya saw her nodding.

"How will I live without you? Without you calling me 'little Lanya'- which I hate, by the way! I am not six anymore! Without you eating that stinking herring that smells up the whole house!" Lanya wanted to wrap her arms around him and lock him up but part of her knew that would be pointless. Mikhail did not say more but his gentle smile said enough.

"I got money out of the bank. All of it. Use it. Feed the family, keep the apartment warm. Buy a coat for Valentina, nothing fits her right. She is growing too fast! I will also give you my rabbit coat, you will need it at the factory, and a ring that father gave me before he left. It will be yours. When I come back, give back what you can. You need this more than I will. I will be fed and have clothes." Lanya could not say anything more. Tears were ready to spill from her eyes. Her heart was broken like a teacup smashed to the floor.

Monday morning came too fast. The family was in the kitchen and Lanya could not eat. Her stomach was in knots. Even Valentina was quiet. Babu was sipping tea. Mikhail came in with his duffel bag on his shoulder. Lanya opened her mouth but nothing came out. She closed it feeling silly. Valentina started crying and snuffling as she asked "Why does Mishka have to go? When will he come back? When will we see him again?" No one answered. Lanya could see that Babu had tears too and Lanya decided not to hide hers anymore as they streamed silently down her face. Mikhail gave each a quick hug then left the room, ready to be off. Lanya rushed to the window with an arm around her sister as they watched Mikhail walk away. Lanya's breath was shallow and she wondered when she could ever breathe easy again. Lanya wished for the numbness she so often felt but had none of now. Now it was all loss.

As she got to the factory, people were settling in to work. Maru came running over to her machine. She had tears in her eyes too. "Did he go? Already? What are we supposed to do?"

Lanya saw her pretty petite friend who looked like she had been hit by a truck. *Hope I look better*, she thought to herself. "Yes, he left. He seemed okay. Almost in a hurry to get going. Pretty sad. Valentina was crying like crazy."

"This is so wrong. Damn Germans!" Maru did not curse often, but Lanya echoed the thought. *Damn Germans.*

The day went by slowly with no interruptions. Back home, the house seemed empty. Sitting down for dinner without Mikhail was impossible. The empty chair seemed to fill the room. Lanya remembered the empty chairs after her parents left. She was sure Valentina and Babu were thinking the same. Lanya asked Babu what they could expect in war. Not that she really wanted to know but the silence was too much.

"It is hard. It will be hard. They will ration food. They may ration firewood. If they attack Leningrad it will be worse. I do not know what that would be like." Babu paused, going somewhere else in her mind. Lanya watched, wondering what was next. "I do not know." There was sadness in her face and Lanya mirrored it. Perky Valentina was quiet but her eyes were as big as her face. There was terror there. All of them were scared of what would come. "We will do our best." Babu closed the conversation and picked up her empty plate. "Valentina, you do dishes tonight." Dinner was over and that was a relief. Babu turned the radio on looking for answers. The Germans were moving eastward and the Soviet Army was fighting. Nothing more yet.

Lanya went out. The apartment without Mishka was stifling and she wanted air. The sun in the sky at seven pm looked like midafternoon, the summertime nights were so short in Leningrad. That was one of the things Lanya loved best. But, the cost was the longest nights in the coldest times. Lanya only thought about the sunshine now. She needed to find some way to deal with all this. Germans were coming, and Mishka was gone and might never come back. Food would get thin. A song popped into her head, an older song that she remembered her mother singing when she was a child. "It looks tough now, but you will win! Put a smile on and get right in!" Lanya sang softly as she walked, and she remembered her mother's gentle smile as she used to sing in the kitchen. Lanya missed her mother badly. She had no idea why her mother was taken or what really happened to her. People who Party came for were put on "trial" and sent away to prison camps, sometimes in Siberia. There was no communication, no letters, no visits. Just gone. This left a black hole in Lanya.

As she walked in the evening sunshine, Lanya noticed there were no young men out in the evening sun. They were all at the army center, like her brother. She wondered if she, her sister and grandmother could get out of Leningrad. Where would they go? They had some family near in the Ukrainian farm area, but that did not seem any better. No matter where the Germans didn't go, Leningrad was certainly on their list. Would they be allowed to leave? Babu was old but not too bad, but what were the rules? She wondered how to find the answers. She was sure she could find a job anywhere they went. Probably a job she liked better than the sewing factory, too, that was tedious. Could they just get on a train and go? Valentina would hate being away from her friends. How would Mishka find them? She could not go if it meant any problem for her brother. As she walked, her brain was racing. If she was going to be "in charge" in the family, shouldn't she have a plan?

Leningrad was often called the "Venice of the North" because of the canals. There were streets, but Leningrad had numerous canals linking the Neva river and the sea. Lanya had never been to Venice so she could not compare. But many of the older homes had been built in the last century when Leningrad was the capital and the wealthiest town in Russia, before the Bolshevik Revolution. Lanya often felt like these stately mansions were grandmothers, looking at her and judging her. Silly. But the beauty of the city was no solace now.

Lanya decided to join a sewing group that met nearby on Wednesday evenings, to do her part. They would work on sewing things the soldiers needed. Lanya wanted to help in some small way. She was not sure she would know any of the women but maybe a neighbor would be there. And new voices might be good, might get her out of the rut she saw herself in. Her first Wednesday night was the second week of the war. They met at the home of an older woman, Lidia, who had tea and cookies, and they set down to work on parachutes. Lanya looked around and she was the youngest woman there. They all introduced themselves and had some small talk about weather. One older woman with silver hair named Nadia talked about her son leaving to fight. Another talked about her aching back after digging trenches. Another asked a question about ration cards since she had not used them before. The hour passed quickly and Lanya felt she would fit in well.

As she left, she decided to walk around the city on her way home. She lived just three blocks away but she was not ready to be done and locked up in the apartment for the night. She walked along the banks of the Fontanka Canal towards the Neva river. The Neva was the lifeblood of Leningrad, pouring into the Gulf of Finland. Along the Neva was the Hermitage museum, which used to be a royal palace that Leningrad was so proud of. Lanya had been there once or twice but did not spend many hours at the museum. There were trucks at the entrance, looking like they were being loaded. Were they emptying the museum, just in case? Nearby was St. Isaac's Cathedral that used to be the center of church life in Leningrad but was now a museum. Lanya could see that the gold dome was being covered in some sort of mud. Were they worried about air attacks? That thought made her nervous. She turned and walked the other way. She came to the Church of the Spilled Blood with the famous onion domes, built where Alexander II was killed in a car bomb long ago. That church always made her feel good, like Leningraders themselves, strong and standing loyal. It was another museum now, but a beautiful one. The Bronze Horseman statue of the city's founder Peter the Great had sandbags at the base, maybe they were going to cover it to protect it. Lanya wondered why she came this way. Too many reminders that they were in danger. Time to go home. Damn Germans.

As she got home from the factory the next day, Babu was in the kitchen with flour on her hands and her apron. "What are you doing Babu? Making a cake?" Lanya loved the Russian cake medovik layered with honey and cream. Babu's was the best.

"No, I am making rusks. Lots of rusks." Rusks were like biscuits that would not go bad. They could stay in the cupboard for months as they dried. Not so good, but they were better than nothing, and edible if dipped in coffee. "We will need these, I am afraid." Lanya did not say anything. Rusks were not tasty, but Babu knew how to live in tough times, so Lanya said nothing. Another dreary thing in her life.

The announcements came through the city speakers every day, while Lanya waited for her tram, and while she walked back to her tram after work at the factory. The announcements were expected. Grain harvests were good. Winter was coming. Germans were advancing, Soviets were fighting back. The Soviet navy was barricading along the Gulf of Finland, an important entry into Leningrad. The Finns, who the Soviets had beaten in 1939, attacked just north of Leningrad. Lanya wondered when there would be good news. Where was Mishka? Would they tell her if he was hurt? Lanya, like most citizens, went about her work quietly. Nothing she could do, she had no control over things. Ever.

Chapter Three

July felt dreary. Not on the surface. The parks were full of children playing, the sun was warm, birds were singing and there was plenty of food. But further down, it was dark. Men were missing. There were few left at the factory and not many around town mostly older men, tottering around with canes or with physical problems. Disturbing. Depressing. The talk of war was every day, everyone had some comment about how tough it would be when the Germans got to Leningrad. No one had answers yet. The Party said nothing. Mishka was gone and that alone was enough to depress Lanya and Valentina. Troops would sometimes march through town and Lanya always stared, hoping to see her brother with her heart in her throat. Trucks and military things moved through town so no one could deny things were different.

One night, Lanya had trouble sleeping, a nightmare. She got them sometimes, often about her missing parents or some monster coming after her to kill her. She was sure the monster was the Party but she did not dare say that to anyone. This time, it was not her being chased but Valentina. The monster was green and brown and very loud. Lanya woke up with a scream. She was up first in the morning and when Babu came in, she saw Lanya's state.

"What happened?" Babu was not always gentle.

"A nightmare, but not like most. They weren't after me, they were after Val."

"What happened?"

"Just a monster, all green and brown, very loud. Like explosions."

"Hmm. Wonder what it means."

"Me, too." She put her head on her arms on the table. Babu got up to make breakfast, but turned around.

"I think it means something. I think it is real."

"What?" Lanya was too tired to think hard.

"I think it is war. Coming after all of us. Especially Valentina."

"Could be. Why her?"

"I think we can do something."

"Like what?"

"When you go into the factory today, ask around. See what people are doing to get out of town. I hear they did some of that in England. They sent the children out of town."

"That is frightening. Are you sure? I can ask around." After breakfast, Lanya dressed and dragged herself to work. She asked some of the moms she knew what they were going to do. One of them who was a mom to one of Valentina's friend Betina, said she was thinking about sending her away to children's camp to the west, out of the path of the Germans. No one knew that path, but this would be out of a direct line from Berlin to Leningrad. Lanya wanted to ask more questions but waited.

"Babu, Betina's mom is talking about sending her to a children's camp in the west, where the Germans will not bother her. What do you think about that?" Lanya asked as Babu started chopping cabbage for dinner.

"A camp? Where?"

"I am not sure yet. But I can ask. Do you like the idea?"

"I will need to think on it. But if it will keep our girl safe, yes, I like it. What do you think Val will say?" Lanya had not yet thought how her sister would react to being sent away, to a place she did not know, to people who were not family.

"I never know what she will say." She smiled a weak smile, but that was true. Valentina was not predictable. How many 13 year olds were? "Maybe if I tell her about my dream it will convince her."

"We will see, find out more if you can." Babu continued cooking and Lanya could see they were done for now. Lanya wondered what Mishka would say. Would he say send her away? Too bad she could not ask him.

Over the next few days, Lanya listened and asked a few questions. Yes, parents were talking about sending their children to these distant places that the Germans would never bother. Lanya liked the idea more and more.

Babu agreed it was time to talk to Valentina, so Lanya took her out after dinner for an ice cream. Valentina ordered strawberry, like always, Lanya had fruit sherbet. Lanya decided to dive in, though her stomach was tense. Val was so much stronger, so she would need to hit it hard.

"Val, this war is frightening, don't you think?" Valentina looked at her, knowing there was more. She slurped at her cone before she answered.

"I don't think so. It is not even here. The Germans want Moscow, they will not even bother us. We will be fine!" Lanya knew this was wishful thinking. She paused before going on.

"I do not know where the Germans will go. No one does. And yes, they want the capitol, but who knows. Babu and I think it would be better if you were not in the city." She looked at Valentina, who had a dumbfounded look. "We want to send you where Betina is going, to a camp in the west." She expected an immediate response and was surprised when Val was quiet. So she went on. "You will be safer there. Lots of kids are going." Lanya herself was not completely sure it was better, but she knew there was not much she could do. This seemed like the best.

"I do not want to go. You and Babu are always in charge of me! I want to make my own decisions! I will not go!"

Layna was relieved when she heard this, she had expected it. This was the fight she anticipated. "In two days, I will take you to the train station. You will go, and some of your friends will go too. You will be safe. I need for you to be safe." Lanya felt tears come into her eyes and the thought of Valentina going away or being hurt.

"I will be as safe as you are. I want to stay here!" She threw the last bit of her ice cream into the trash can and jumped up. Lanya got up, and Val stormed off. Lanya followed. She was not surprised at this reaction. But she had to keep her safe.

Two days later, Lanya and Valentina walked to the train station in silence. Valentina was sullen and her silence was the key. Her hands were closed tightly on her bag and Lanya could see her teeth almost clenched the whole way to the station. To be torn from home in a time of such upheaval was not easy. At least she would be with her friends. That should be a comfort for her. The trains were waiting and they found the right platform and bought the ticket. One way. Valentina nodded to some of her friends who were in line also. Each carried a small bag and some were crying. This was tough. The train engine fired up and the conductor was beginning his rounds. Lanya put her hand on Valentina's shoulder. "This won't be for long. This war will be over soon and you will come right home." She paused. "I am going to miss you. Babu will miss you. We will see you as soon as we can. I love you Sissy." She did a small push with her hand on Valentina's shoulder, to prompt her to get on the train.

Valentina twisted so Lanya's hand brushed off her shoulder. "I am not going! I am not getting on that train! I am not scared of everything, like you are! I am staying!" And she dropped her bag and ran from the platform into the crowd. Gone. Valentina disappeared. Lanya was stunned. Where did she go? What would she do? Panic gripped Lanya. Valentina had to leave Leningrad; it was safer to get out! If she stayed here... Lanya could not think. She searched the crowd, looking for her sister. She was quick, that girl! She picked up her sister's bag and dragged out of the station, with her heart at her feet. What was Valentina talking about? Like she would fight the Germans herself? And who was scared? Lanya stopped at that and leaned on the station wall for support. Was Lanya scared? Of what? Her feet started moving towards home but her mind was all over. What was Lanya scared of? She was not as bold and feisty as Valentina, that was sure. But was she scared? Her brain was on full speed. Yes, she was scared of the Party, for what they did to her parents. Took them away with no explanation and no defense. Sure, even Valentina was probably scared of the Party. Of the Germans? Yes, but they were still a distant problem it seemed. What else? She could get on stage and sing, Valentina could not. She wasn't scared of the stage. She was scared that she had no purpose, no control in her life, but many 19 year olds felt the same way, didn't they? She had no skills and the only gift she had was her voice. But that was not worth much until she got onstage.

"She ran out of the train station Babu. She did not get on the train!" Lanya explained to her grandmother what her sister had done. Lanya felt like she lost. "Is she here?"

"I have not seen her." Babu said and looked at Lanya to judge her response. Babu's face did not give anything away, she could be stoic. Lanya could not. Valentina was strong willed and there were fights, and Babu knew these were hard on Lanya. "She will come home." Lanya nodded, but felt like she wanted to fall into a heap on the floor, powerless.

"I hope so."

The day passed and no word from Valentina. At the factory, the mother of one of Valentina's friends worked with Lanya, and Lanya asked about her sister, but this woman had not seen her. She found Betina's mom and was told that Betina did not go away to camp yet. Betina's mom had not seen Valentina. At break, Lanya could hardly eat, she was so tense. She told Maru what Valentina did and Maru laughed. "What a little fox she is!" Maru said with a smile on her face. How could she laugh when her baby sister was missing? Dinner passed and no word. Lanya went out later and walked around a few blocks, with a half-hearted search. Lanya was sad, but resigned. Her sister would come home when she was ready. Hopefully.

When she got home, still no word from Val. Rations had begun and food was available but might get tight. Babu had stocked up on food before the rationing started so the cupboards were full. Lanya was glad they had a cupboard full of the rusks as well. Maybe she would help Babu make more.

As Lanya came towards the apartment on Kazanskaya Street the next day, she watched the squirrels as they scampered here and there. They made her laugh, even on tough days. This time, Valentina was sitting on a park bench, watching the rodents. Her head was hanging low. Lanya squealed and ran to her sister with a big hug. Valentina hugged back. "Where have you been? Are you okay?"

"I am fine. I went to Ilya's, she is staying in town too. I could not leave you."

"Were you hiding?" A small nod. "We will see. What are you going to tell Babu?"

"Well, that I am sure the camp food would not be as good as hers! That will do it!" Valentina had a big smile but her eyes were not smiling. Lanya put her arm around her sister and they went up the stairs.

"You go first, I want to hear this." Lanya stayed back so Valentina could enter first. They went to the kitchen where Babu always was.

"Babu, I am here!" Valentina said in a sing song voice. Babu hurried over and gave her a bear hug. "I could not go and eat camp food Babu. No one cooks like you do!" Babu had not yet let Valentina go.

"You gave us a scare! What are you thinking?" Valentina did not answer. "Will you please set the table?" Babu made it feel like it was no big deal, so Lanya just bit her tongue. It already felt like a normal night.

As Lanya settled in bed for the night with her sister in the bed near her, she thought about this war. *Will the Germans come to Leningrad? This is a major industrial city and the home of Communism, but not the capitol. Do they want Moscow? Do they want it all? Can they ever conquer the Soviet Union, as vast as it was? Maybe they only want the grain from Ukraine and the capitol. Maybe they will leave Leningrad alone.* With that hopeful thought Lanya drifted off.

Chapter Four

The Germans were pushing closer to the city. Lanya quaked in her bed at night as she could hear the bombs in the distance. The Germans were bombing the Soviet trenches nearby. They made such an ugly sound, the *brrrrhummmm* of the German planes, the horrible smash sound as the bombs hit. Each neighborhood in the city was assigned an air raid shelter, so Lanya, Valentina and Babu found theirs with undisguised fear. The war was so real now. According to the daily reports, the Germans were along the Luga river, just a few miles outside the city. That was awfully close. Could the army keep the fascists out? The Luga was the last stretch right outside the city. If the Germans conquered this part of the river crossing, would they reach the gates? Lanya wondered daily where Mikhail was. Was he there, on the Luga line? Was he further out? Or had he gone east, to protect Moscow? Lanya did not get any letters so she had no idea where he was.

Rationing was real. Transport into and out of the city was cut, so not much was going out and even less was coming in. Fresh fruits and vegetables were rare. People no longer could come and go, there were no trains moving. The Party was rounding up people accused of spying for the Germans and there were rumors everywhere. Every day the loudspeakers on the streets and in the factory made announcements, Soviets were advancing, Germans were weak, leadership was making plans, all designed to control what people thought. Lanya listened to the daily announcements and wondered how much was true. The Party told you what they wanted you to know. Were the Soviets fighting back? Was the Navy on the offensive? No one had talked about letters home. Maybe those were being held? There was no way to know since there was no other source of information. Lots of talk, lots of nationalist music, and speeches to inspire you. The poetry was the best. Leningrad had many artists and poets and they were often featured. Lanya's favorite was Anna Akhmatova, a Leningrad local, who always seemed to hit right in the heart.

Lanya felt largely safe from attack. She felt naïve when she hoped that the war was short, everyone said it would be. She wanted to believe it. She knew the Red Army was going to stop the Nazis. She knew they would fight to the death. She knew her brother Mikhail was brave, and they would keep them safe. She had helped dig those trenches, endless trenches. She had seen the barricades on the outskirts, and she especially liked the ones called "hedgehogs." These were made of concrete and steel with barbed wire across the top. These were at every entrance. She had heard talk about the pillboxes of antitank guns. She knew the Leningrad factories were turning out munitions by the train load. Her factory was already in overtime, making boots and bags for the soldiers. With the trains out, supplies only came by truck, so things were thin. She was not worried about Germans walking the streets of Leningrad. She was sure that would never happen.

In early September the first bombs dropped on the city. It was night time and blackout was required. Heavy curtains covered the windows and no outside lights were on. No cars went up and down streets at night. Lanya felt it was eerie. The sirens went off while Lanya was in her room looking at an old magazine and Valentina was reading a school book. Lanya jumped up with a squeal and put shoes and her jacket on. She ran to the front room. "Babu, Babu, are you ready? Valentina?" Her grandmother was coming into the kitchen, with boots on her feet and her coat. Babu was worried she would get cold. "Valentina, we need to go now! Do we have everything? Let's go!" Lanya grabbed her grandmother's arm and made Valentina go first so she could keep an eye on her. They ran outside with all the neighbors. The stairway was crowded but people were being polite as they hurried down the stairs. Lanya's mind was racing- would they get hit? Would it hurt? Would she die? Who would care for Babu and her sister if Lanya died? She did not speak these concerns, but every new thought created new fears. The air raid shelter was two blocks down the road. Lanya recognized many people, some from her building some from the park or the tram. She held onto Babu's arm, trying to protect the older woman but more to keep herself calm. She could hear the whistles of the bombs as they thudded in town. What would it be like? Super loud? Would she know which one was coming for her? They crowded into the basement of an older home that had an agriculture office on the first floor. Lanya had checked this out a week ago but it felt different with fifty people in it. People were milling about, looking for friends and finding a spot to sit. Many people were smoking and some brought food. Lanya could see a bottle of wine here and a bottle of vodka there. She wished she had remembered the vodka. How could these people be so relaxed? They could hear but not feel the bombs so maybe they were not too close. The electric lights were on so it was not too cave-like. Valentina, Lanya and Babu sat in a corner next to a file cabinet. Lanya kept her hands wrapped with Babu's, and with every explosion, Lanya shook. Valentina was shaking and put her head on Lanya's shoulder. Tears ran down her face and she did not even try to stem them. A shudder turned into shaking arms and legs, till Lanya just put her head between her knees to contain her terror. Between bombs, Lanya did not want to talk to anyone. Silence was her best defense. The smell of people packed so closely was sickening and the new smell of urine made it worse. The air was not moving so Lanya had to push down nausea. Lanya wondered if they would sleep down here. She did not bring any blankets or pillows, maybe next time. How could anyone sleep with all those bombs going off? It was good that the building did not shake from being hit. Lanya was sure that if the building got hit they would all be dead in an instant.

She did not feel clear headed. Her mind was so full of questions it hurt. *If we get hit, what will it feel like? Will I be dead all at once or will it take time? What if just my legs are hit? Will I bleed to death? What if Babu got hit? If the whole building is bombed who will come and bury us? Or will we already be buried?* Lanya did not pray but this was the first time in her life she considered praying, if there was a god.

After about an hour that felt like forever, the bombs slowed down and then stopped completely. At the end of two hours, the all clear bell sounded and everyone began to filter out. Lanya decided she loved the sound of the all clear bell and hoped she would not have to hear it often. It took a few moments to get her strength enough to stand and walk up the stairs. Lanya was embarrassed since her skirt was all wet, she had wet herself in fear. She looked to see if anyone else had the same problem and was glad to get out of the shelter onto the dark street. Lanya's eyes darted around the street to see what was hit. She couldn't see much but she saw broken windows in one building and there was dust everywhere when her foot hit the ground. "Are you okay Babu?" Lanya asked with a show of false bravery. Babu knew Lanya and silently nodded. But her eyes watched Lanya carefully. Lanya was a wreck and Babu hoped that Lanya would be able to accept this new part of the war. Babu wrapped her arm around Valentina as she glanced at Lanya. She knew of Lanya's frequent over thinking, how it always created stress for her. The streets were deathly quiet now. How many Leningraders had died tonight? Was her brother alive? Lanya always hated when she had no choices and no control and tonight was the worst ever. Lanya wished Valentina had gotten on that train and left the city.

As they walked back two blocks to the apartment, Lanya had old safe memories flooding her brain. Days when she was a child and had no worries. When her parents would take them to the park for a summer picnic, when they would go ice skating on the Neva. When school was her biggest concern. When she did not worry that all her choices were stripped from her and she was a puppet in someone else's game. She grabbed Valentina's hand as they walked, Babu on the other side. What was this war going to do to them?

In the apartment, no one slept. Lanya laid in bed and tossed and turned. She sensed Valentina do the same. After a few hours it seemed that Valentina settled and Lanya heard her steady breathing. This brought Lanya some calm. For years she had slept with her sister's regular breaths and it was calming. Maybe this would bring her sleep, too.

As she went to work the next morning, Lanya saw what the air raids hit. Buildings had broken windows and demolished walls. People's belongings were thrown out into the streets, clothes, pans, blankets. Where were those people? Lanya felt like throwing up, seeing this hellish scene. As the tram crossed the city, no one spoke as they saw emergency teams pulling people out of smashed buildings. One body had a blanket over them. She did not try to hide her tears. Good decent people ruined by war. *Damn Germans.*

At the factory, people did not rush to their machines. They wanted to share their experiences. Not everyone was in the raid. Many were in shock. Lanya could see it in their eyes, the unbelievability of it all. One of the men was venting about his home being hit and windows broken and his daughter so scared that she screamed all night. Lanya watched and saw the fear and the anger that overrode rational thinking.

In the sewing group that week there was a lot of news. One older woman who seemed to know Party leaders announced that Leningrad was cut off. "They have enclosed the city. They will attack soon. I worry that our days are numbered. Does anyone here speak German?" She looked around, as if anyone would admit to that. It was not funny. No one spoke immediately, but within a few minutes the general talk began again. Lanya listened. She had nothing to add. Another said she was told the train lines to Moscow had been cut. Another said something that made Lanya stop, needle in hand, feeling numb all over. She said that the Germans had come through the Baltic states, north after conquering Poland, instead of straight through to Moscow, as was expected. The Baltic people welcomed the Germans because they hated the Soviets for their takeover years back. Lanya froze because that was where her little sister was supposed to have gone to camp. Maybe it was better that Valentina was so stubborn. Lanya thought her not leaving was the worst thing that could happen but maybe she was wrong with the Germans cutting through the Baltic states. Lanya was quiet through the rest of the group time.

"Babu! Babu!" Lanya almost screamed as she opened the apartment door. Babu was not in the kitchen but Lanya bumped into her in the hallway. "Babu, did you hear? The Germans came through Latvia and Lithuania, right where Valentina would have been! Valentina, come here!" Babu moved into the kitchen where Valentina joined them.

"Did you hear? The Germans came through Latvia and right where your camp is! I heard it tonight at sewing group. You would be in grave danger!" Lanya grabbed Valentina and gave her a huge hug. She had tears starting. "You were right sister, you were right not to go! I was wrong. I wanted you safe but you would be exactly in the way of the Germans if you had gone."

"My friends? Dmitri and Olga? Are they in trouble?"

"We do not know, but probably. I am sorry. I am so glad you are stubborn! I may never say that again!"

"Oh no!" Valentina ran from the kitchen with tears in her voice repeating the names of her friends.

"Svetlana, you could have done that better. You did not have to dump all that on a young child. Her friends are so important to her. If you had told me first I would have prepared her. Now her heart is broken." Lanya felt awful, she had not thought of it that way. She just wanted to share what she heard. Now she would go to apologize to her sister. This war was too much.

Lanya waited a while before going into her room and Val was on her bed, face down. Why did Lanya not have more control? This would be tough. "Val, I am sorry. I should not have blurted that out. I know your friends are important." She took a deep breath. "I do not know if the camp is in the German path. They could have gone around it. I do not know. I am so sorry." She sat on the edge of the bed and smoothed a hand on Val's back. Should she do anything else? Valentina rolled over and Lanya could see the tear stains.

"I hate this war! I hate every German! I want to kill them myself! If my friends are gone, and my brother, I will join the army!" Lanya knew that was a long way off but still she dreaded it. And she understood the anger.

The official announcement came days later. The Germans had crossed the Luga river, which was the last barrier to Leningrad. The Party admitted that the city was enclosed and demanded citizens rise up and do everything they could. Leningrad was surrounded by Germans on one side, the Gulf was circled by German ships on the other, the Finns were to the north and broken train lines to the east. There was no way out. The Germans were just at the city perimeter. Everyone could hear German planes and Soviet planes going back and forth. Nighttime bombings came more often, so everyone blindly rushed into the air raid shelters when the sirens went off. So far this was only now and then, once a week. No one knew when they would break into the city. The feeling of dread was ever-present. Lanya wondered if everyone had a stomach as tight as hers. Was vodka enough to keep them all functioning?

Chapter Five

The war was real. About once a week, Germans planes bombed the city. The bomb shelter was more comfortable now. Lanya and Babu brought food, blankets and an oil lamp. And vodka. Valentina found her friends there. Lanya wished Maru was there but she was more than a mile away in her shelter. Babu was a rock, always quiet, always sure. Lanya was glad to have her. Nights were dark with total blackout, the birds had all flown south and the squirrels Lanya loved to watch were busy hoarding nuts. Winter was coming, but Lanya was not worried. Winters were tough but not impossible if you were ready. Squirrels needed food, Russians needed food and firewood.

On her way to the tram station for work, Lanya walked past the Mariinsky Theater, a small, local showhouse. She had been there many times for the shows. She had dreams of being on stage, singing to a full house. As she walked, shows came back and Lanya found herself singing quietly. Singing was the only thing that gave her great joy so she sang often. Not that anyone could hear, usually in her own head. She wondered how the war would affect the shows she loved. Could people perform while raids were going? Would they just halt the show and come back in two hours? It was almost laughable, she decided.

At the factory, everyone was clustered around supervisor Grigory who was on a chair so everyone could hear him. Lanya got as close as she could. "Yes, they bombed the Badayev warehouse last night. The granary warehouse where they kept all the grain. Tons of sugar and wheat, enough to last us weeks, is now gone. God help us." Grigory got down and was swarmed with people. No grain? How would they eat? Could they bring more in on the train? No, the trains were cut off. Maybe just a week of trouble and they would bring in more, stored somewhere else. Lanya felt her heart sink. She had never been without food before. She did not eat that much but Babu and Valentina needed food too. And how would they feed the troops? Mishka? He loved his food. Lanya trudged off to her machine with her brain full of worry and fear.

After work, Lanya moved with a small crowd down to the warehouse area, following the heavy smoke from fires still burning. The air was dark and she could smell the burnt sugar. She could almost feel the stickiness of burnt food on her skin. The crowd grumbled and cursed. Back-stabbing Germans was the most frequent grumble she heard. No one questioned the defense of the Red Army, not out loud anyway. How these planes got into the city was a mystery, since Soviet troops were all around. Some children were darting in and out of the fire area carrying buckets of dirt. Why would anyone want dirt? She watched one mother as she took her son's bucket and handed him another empty one. "Go sweet child, do it again. Now we will have sugar." Sugar? In a bucket of dirt? Lanya could see the dirt was clumps with some shine to it. Was there burnt sugar in the dirt? Could that be saved? *I will never eat dirt,* Lanya thought with her nose in the air. *Nothing could make me rinse the dirt off those clumps.* As she turned to go, another thought came in, and it sounded like her mother's clear soft voice "maybe if you were really hungry girl, you would."

At sewing group, they had tea and cookies like always. There was much chatter about the bombing. As everyone started to work, the hostess Lidia got their attention by tapping on a teacup. "Ladies, as you have heard, the grain warehouse was bombed and burned. Rations will be cut for sure. Enjoy these cookies because I do not know when more will happen! She raised her single cookie in a toast and they all chimed in and toasted with her.

"We are in trouble!"

"They will bring more in, just watch."

"I do not know, the rail lines are closing. Not much is coming in to town anymore."

"That smoke will last for days."

"What do we do?" Lanya did not say it, but she could have.

"Rusks!" A murmur of agreement went through the small group.

"Yes, rusks! I have a few put away and tomorrow, I will make more!" Lanya felt good that Babu had already made quite a few and appreciated her grandmother's forward thinking.

"Some were carrying buckets of dirt that had burnt sugar inside. I saw that today when I went down there."

"I saw that, too" Lanya offered. "There were children scooping it up. It was very hot."

"How bad are we doing to eat burnt sugar coated in dirt?" That made everyone quiet.

Lanya felt like a small child among these older women, many of whom had seen so much. She wanted to absorb their experience and understanding to make her own life a bit easier. That was why she did not speak much, but listened.

Rations were cut and Lanya wondered how they would make it. Trainloads full of food would be most welcomed. She knew they had to feed the troops first, so she ate her portions and tried to be grateful. She noticed the sparkle leaving her sister, and her skirt was a bit looser.

At lunch, she approached Maru about the theater, asking if they could go soon. Maru was excited "Of course we should go! What is playing?"

"*Volga, Volga*, about the amateur group that is trying to get to Moscow to perform but everything goes wrong for them- we saw the movie a few years ago- remember?" Maru rolled her eyes back trying to remember. "They got stuck behind a truck on the highway and almost fell out of the car. That one!" Maru laughed.

"Oh yes- that was fun! Let's go!" Both wanted something to do that was not all wrapped around this ugly war. "Friday- let's go Friday!"

"Okay- let me make sure with Babu, she likes to know where I am." Lanya was excited to get to the theater, she loved the music and the energy. Maru went more often to look at the men, not the show. But Maru was cute and men liked her. Lanya felt a touch of envy, but she wanted to see the show no matter.

Friday came, and Lanya prepared for the night. She put on her dark red skirt and gray sweater that she thought made her look good. She pulled her belt a bit tighter. She brushed her brown hair until it shone then pulled it back with a ribbon. Her straight hair did not curl, ever, like Maru's did but it looked healthy.

The breeze from the Gulf on Friday was cool but not cold. Evenings were darkening and fall was in the air. Lanya was excited to forget about this war and the lack of food and go to the theater with Maru. She arrived at Maru's apartment with her eyes sparkling and a newer pair of boots on her small feet. "Are you ready? Let's go!" Lanya buzzed. Maru was not yet ready, still in her slip with no make up on.

"Just a minute, sit down!" Maru ran back into her room to prepare, while Lanya looked around. She could not help it, she burst out in song. There were so many good songs from the movie, Lanya knew every one of them by heart. "Do you think we will see Nikolai and Vladimir there? They were at the last show. They probably are in the army now, but I hope we see them." Maru was almost dancing with expectation at seeing the men. She liked them tall and dark. Lanya was not sure that any men would be at the show since most were fighting now.

"I will be surprised it any men are there. But, let's go!"

As Maru grabbed her things, they rushed to the door. The tram picked them up just at the corner. At the theater, they were early so there was no line yet. Maru was looking for some of the actors, sometimes they came out to greet the audience, but Maru was already looking at men. "Lanya, look over there, in the green jacket! He has a nice, trim mustache and black hair! Do you see him?" Lanya peeked over and saw the handsome man with the green jacket and his friend who was a blond. Nice pair, she thought. Maru was already smiling and tugging Lanya's arm to bring her to the other side of the lobby. Maybe these were Party men, so Lanya resisted a bit; she did not want to seem overeager. The girls found themselves at the concession stand and Lanya ordered a weak coffee for both of them. They got their cups and stood nearby talking and looking around, trying not to spend too much time staring at the men. The other men at the show were older, so Maru did not even acknowledge them. Lanya thought men were okay, but she was not as boy crazy as Maru. No one was as boy crazy as Maru. With the drinks finished, they went to their seats. Maru quickly noticed that the two men were near the front while the girls were farther back. "If no one checks, we should move up!" Maru whispered. Lanya smiled, a smile she often used for Maru's crazy ideas.

The lights dimmed and Lanya was swept away by the show, the singing and dancing. She sang every song in her head and had to work to not get up and sing with them. Maru was humming along. The story told of the traveling performers trying to make their dreams, a story everyone could identify with. Lanya thought it was a classic timeless theme, it had been around for many years.

At the intermission, Lanya and Maru saw the attractive men in the lobby. Maru walked past them, hoping to give them an eyeful. They were talking with each other and Lanya thought that the talk suspended a bit while the girls walked by. Maybe not, but it seemed that way. Maru kept up a mindless chatter to try to be unobtrusive, but Lanya understood where her brain was. The two pairs did not talk to each other, but when it was time to go back into the theater, Maru again grabbed Lanya's arm and brought her to a seat two rows behind the men and off to the left. She was sure the men knew where they were. The dark haired one turned around to see them just as the show came back on and smiled at Maru. Maru almost melted into her chair. "Did you see that? He smiled at me! I hope it was me- maybe he was smiling at you!"

"It was you, I am sure of it." The second half of the show was as good as the first, and Lanya reveled in how completely she was engrossed. Nothing else was happening in the world while she was at the theater. There was no war, no bombing, no lack of food. Just a great show. The show ended too soon, and Lanya and Maru clapped so long their hands hurt. People stood up for an ovation and so did the girls. The performers came out for an encore and the applause went on and on. Finally, the actors went behind the curtain and people began to gather their things. Lanya picked up her purse and Maru put on her sweater. They turned to go and saw the men coming up the aisle. A deep voice broke in, "What a wonderful show. Did you both enjoy it?" Maru stopped and Lanya waited. The dark haired man waited for an answer. His mustache was perfect. His hair was dark and so were his eyes. His smile was quick and Lanya could feel Maru almost melting.

"Oh we did, immensely!" Maru replied with a brilliant smile. She always loved talking to handsome men. They came out of their aisle and the men walked them up towards the lobby.

"What was your favorite part?" dark hair inquired again.

Maru chimed in "The songs! I always love the songs!"

Lanya added, "Me, too!"

"The songs were great- such emotion they had, great show!" Dark hair was the talker it seemed. "Would it be too much to ask if we can take you ladies for coffee?" Maru almost tripped over her feet at that. Lanya held her up as she stumbled.

"Lanya, that would be nice; would you like to?" Lanya could see that Maru would kill her if she said no, so Lanya agreed with a small nod of her head.

"That would be lovely. We will be happy to join you!" If Maru was a balloon, she would have left the building!

"Well, to be proper, I am Leonid Vasilevich and my friend here is Ivan Sivkov." Leonid had more than a perfect mustache, thick dark hair with a wave here and there but not quite a curl. He was tall and slender and his fingers were long like a piano player's. The blond man flashed a huge smile at the girls and Lanya noticed it. Ivan had a nice smile and sparkling blue eyes. Maru was looking only at Leonid, so this was good.

"I am Maru Nevetsky and this is my best friend Svetlana Zhudanov. Where can we go?"

"I know a little place just around the corner. May I?" He held out his arm for Maru, she floated over to him as they turned to go. Ivan turned his hand for Lanya who came to his side.

Lanya was excited, but it was not as easy to see as Maru's excitement. But she felt like good things were happening. Like most young women, Lanya liked the attention of a good looking man. She was tired of boys. Some men were not good, but Lanya thought this might be a worthwhile distraction for now. Now, if these were Party men, it would be a quick visit.

The cafe was only a three minute walk around the corner. They walked carefully in the almost dark streets but they could hear the conversations from outside the building. They opened the door into another dark room, so no light could leak out, and quickly went into the bright, warm café. Lanya had been here before once or twice before the war when they could sit outside. They took a seat along one wall, Lanya and Maru on one side of the table, Leonid and Ivan on the other. There were quite a few customers, most probably from the show. Lanya smiled thinking this was great fun. A show then coffee in a lively place! Coffee and pastries were all that was on the menu, so that was what they ordered.

Leonid opened with "At least there were no air raids tonight, right?" Maru nodded and Lanya murmured a yes. She had not thought about air raids in hours, until she came outside to the dark streets.

"Would we have just left the theater, gone to the shelter and come back when it was over? Resume the show?" Ivan had a smirk on his face and a playful look in his eyes. It was a good question. No one answered.

Leonid asked, "So you liked the singing, so did I. And the acting was good, don't you think?"

Maru quickly answered, "Oh, very good."

Lanya did not want to be left out, so she added "The costumes were believable, too."

Ivan nodded and said, "Yes, I have seen a suit like that one character, the one with the blue. Leonid, do you remember that one man in Minsk, outside that church, with the blue suit that was so funny?" Leonid nodded and chuckled.

He continued, "Do you two come to the show often?"

Maru again grabbed the spotlight with "We come now and then. Sometimes Lanya's brother Mikhail comes but he is away at the front." No one commented on the front, so they let it pass.

"We like the shows, more than the opera" Lanya commented. "Do you like the opera?"

Leonid answered "No opera for me, too stuffy. Ivan here is new to Leningrad so this is his first show here. I am glad he got a good one."

"Where are you from?" piped Maru. She was born near Moscow but had been in Leningrad since her teen years.

"I am from near Minsk. I wanted to see Leningrad so my friend Leonid invited me. Have you ever been to Minsk?" Neither girl had ever been to Minsk, and Lanya had only been outside Leningrad a few times. "It is beautiful there. Maybe you should visit."

"That would be nice" Lanya said. She liked the tone of his voice, and his slight accent was charming. His eyes had a liveliness that was appealing. It seemed Maru would want to know Leonid more, and Lanya could get to know Ivan.

"Do you like Leningrad, Ivan?" Maru asked, sipping her coffee.

"I do, it is a beautiful town. The grand homes, the canals and the cathedral. Minsk does not have those! And the beautiful churches! The Spilled Blood is imposing, amazing how it looks!" Everyone nodded. Every Russian knew it was tragically beautiful.

"Will you go to another show soon?" Leonid asked, with a trace of a smile.

Maru again spoke first, "I hope so. No one knows what will be open." She had a pout on her lips that was cute, Lanya could never be that cute. "This one is open for another week, and we will see what comes next." She smiled at Lanya for confirmation and Lanya nodded. "Do you know what the next show will be?"

Lanya shook her head "I am not sure."

Ivan added "I have been to shows all over Europe. Paris, Moscow, Berlin, Prague, Munich. This may be the best!" The girls giggled a bit and Leonid smiled. This was going well.

"Have you ever been in a show?" Leonid asked. Maru drew in her breath, she would never be on stage. But Lanya had been on stage a few times, in school shows. She loved it.

"I would not be up there, but Lanya would." Maru pointed at Lanya and Lanya shrunk a bit. She did not want to be in the spotlight right now. "Lanya can really sing and was in a show a few years ago at school. What show was it Lanya?"

"It was a Party musical, if I remember." The Party selected movies and musicals to promote their agenda, and these were everywhere. This show was before her father was taken, back when Lanya almost trusted the Party.

"You were so good!" Maru gushed and Lanya could feel her face turning red.

To change the subject, Lanya asked the men "Have either of you been in a show?"

Leonid looked at Ivan, and replied "I have done a bit of acting, but Ivan produces shows now and then."

"You produce them? Hire the actors, design the sets and all that? Wow!" Lanya tried to contain her excitement.

Ivan tried to brush it off, "Well, it is a lot but when it comes together, it is really good."

"Don't be silly Ivan!" Leonid said. "He was talking about doing one here in Leningrad this fall!"

"No, here? That is exciting!" Maru and Lanya both felt the tingles. Lanya was wondering if she might be able to be a part of it. She had always wanted to perform.

"There is a lot to look in to, but I could probably do it right here, where we saw tonight's show. The location and size are right."

"Do you know what show?" Maru asked.

"I am not sure, Leonid and I were just talking about that. Maybe something new. Unless you have a favorite?"

"Oh, I love them all!" Lanya gushed. She held one hand in the other so her fingers did not dance. She was always nervous about her wiggling fingers when she was anxious.

"Does the Party have a say in what gets produced? Sometimes they do." Leonid asked thoughtfully.

Maru replied "I do not know. Maybe you have to ask them." Lanya was sure this was true.

"No matter, we will figure it out as we go. A toast!" said Ivan, "to shows that make people smile!" Everyone lifted their glasses and clinked and took a sip. The coffee was cooling off. "Ladies, I think it is time for us to depart. How can we see you again?" Ivan had a slight grin and a tiny dimple in his cheek, and seemed to listen to every word Lanya said, like she was the center of his world. That was heady.

Maru squeaked as she said quickly, "We both work at the shoe factory near the river. Maybe you could come by?"

"That would work fine, expect us soon!" They all got up and collected their things. Leonid walked near Maru with his head tilted towards hers. Ivan waited for Lanya to leave the table and gently touched her back as she walked in front of him. "I look forward to seeing you again." he said gently. Lanya was grinning. At the door of the cafe, Leonid took Maru's hand and kissed the top of it and Ivan followed the example with Lanya's hand. "Adieu then" Leonid said and Ivan nodded. The men turned to walk away and Lanya and Maru nearly swooned as they left.

As they walked down the street preparing to go home, Lanya turned to Maru. "Why were they here? Not fighting?"

"I do not know. Maybe since they are from Minsk, it is different?" Maru was not going to worry about finding a handsome man.

"I do not know either. I hope they are not Party men, that would be awful."

"You worry too much Lanya!" Maru wrapped her arm in Lanya's arm. "Too much!"

The day after the show, Lanya and Maru could hardly keep still. They hugged when they saw each other at work, and at break all they talked about was meeting Leonid and Ivan. "Will we see them again? I hope so!" Maru chattered.

Lanya added "Of course, we will see them soon. They sure seemed interested."

"Did you think he was cute?" Maru asked. Lanya knew she meant Leonid, since she hardly talked to Ivan all night.

"Yes, he is cute, with that dark look. He has nice hair." Lanya preferred the blond of Ivan's hair, but Maru was smitten.

When work was over, the girls split up to get home, and Maru again asked, "When will we see them?" Lanya did not know. Who knew what would happen. Maybe the Germans would be singing in Leningrad soon.

Chapter Six

Lanya had her sewing group soon and she went dutifully, even though she let the talk run through her head time and time again. She overthought everything constantly. After one of these sewing sessions she felt caught up on all the gossip in Leningrad. These ladies knew everything. The big question tonight was what was next? The city was cut off from everything and no one could predict what would happen. These ladies had ideas though. How bad would rationing get? Few men were left in Leningrad, the only ones left had some problem like bad eyes or a limp. This made her wonder again about Ivan and Leonid. Would the Germans invade Leningrad? What about Moscow? Surely they would attack the capital. How long would the war last? Most of the women believed it would be short. They knew the Soviet army was top notch, since they had beaten the Finns just a few years ago. These ladies knew people in every sector and Lanya did not add anything, but again listened a lot.

"Did you hear the announcement today? It was the best!" The older woman, Lidia, who seemed to be the leader was always "in the know". Lanya listened to every word. Lidia was small but her dark eyes were quick and her smile seemed to hide a lot. Lanya had not heard the announcement today but she heard many of them. She paused in her sewing and she could see most of them waited anxiously to hear the news. "It was Anna. You know, our Anna Akhmatova? Our poet? She is amazing. She read one of her poems today and I wrote it down. She fumbled with a small sheet of paper that she opened and straightened on her lap. "This is what she read today and it is perfect. Anna is always perfect." No one was talking or moving. Anna spoke for all of them. Lidia read:

"The enemy threatens the city of Peter, the city of Lenin, the city of Pushkin, of Dostoyevsky and of Blok with death and shame. I, like all of you, live with an unwavering belief, that Leningrad will never be fascist."

The quiet in the room was as solid as an iceberg. Lanya realized she was holding her breath. Someone sniffled, and then someone else made a peep. The woman to Lanya's left reached out and took her hand, and Lanya was part of the warmth as it grew throughout the room. She reached out and took the hand of the woman on her right, and the chain went around the room. Women who were bonded by war, loyalty, patriotism and poetry. Someone let their breath out slowly and Lanya could see the smile Lidia had. A slow steady smile. "Do we all agree? Leningrad will never be fascist!"

"Not as long as I live!"

"No German will get in with us here!"

"I will use the gun myself!"

"Lenin can count on me!"

Lanya cheered and said "Me, too!" She felt what they felt. If Lanya saw a German on the way home she was sure she would kill him herself.

Five days later as Lanya and Maru left the factory into the late September chill, the golden and brown leaves were already falling from the trees. Snow was not expected yet but Lanya knew it was not far off. They separated to get to their trams when Lanya looked up and right there, leaning on a lamppost, was Ivan! Lanya stopped and shook her head. He was here! Where was Leonid? Lanya only saw Ivan. He stood straight and moved towards her.

"Good evening, Svetlana. How are you?" Lanya faltered. No one ever called her by her proper name. Maybe she did not give her nickname the other night. Still, was he Party? She clasped her small purse with jittery hands. She looked over her shoulder to see if Maru was already gone. She was.

"Hello Ivan. It is nice to see you."

"I thought you might say that. I wanted to see you. Do you have a minute?"

Lanya gave a weak smile and wondered how she looked. Her hair was pulled back and her skirt was an old, plain one. Her sweater had a hole in the front from the dog chewing on it last year. She never wore makeup to work. She was sure she was a mess. Ivan was polished and sharp in a crisp dark jacket and wool cap.

"Yes, I have some time. I did not know you would come Ivan."

"I wanted to see you. Do you have time for a cocktail now?"

Lanya stepped forward but caught herself. No need to stumble. She could have a cocktail with a nice man. A handsome man. "I do." They turned towards the industrial street to find a place.

"I know of a place down on the Prospekt. Shall we?" Nevsky Prospekt used to be so busy, where restaurants, shops and all kinds of offices stood. Lanya wished for a second that she was Maru, who could endlessly chatter about nothing. They walked in unison, neither talking. The streets were almost empty since gas was getting tough to find. The sun was lowering and soon the nights would be so very long. They found a small place that was open, since many had closed for lack of food. They went to sit and he brushed past her as he pulled her chair out. A small jolt went through her and she tried to focus.

"I hope you do not mind me just showing up. I am sure it is a surprise." Ivan looked at her directly and Lanya blushed a bit.

"It is a surprise. Please, call me Lanya. No one calls me Svetlana."

"Lanya, I like that." His smile was charming and Lanya warmed up. He said her name with a slight accent, and she liked the sound of it. He ordered a dark beer. Lanya usually had something with fruit juice but wondered if that was available so she ordered a beer also. Ivan asked a few general questions about how long she had lived in Leningrad, did she like her job, what else he wanted to know. Simple small talk that was easy for both of them. "I did not want to waste time so I came to find you." He leaned his head in over the table. "Lanya, you enjoyed the show so much. Can you sing?"

Lanya choked on the foam of her beer. She set the glass carefully on the table. Boy, was he direct!

"Well, I have sung some in school. Nothing professional." *Yet*, she added in her head. She pressed her toes down in her shoes to keep herself from running out. He was staring right at her!

"Well, you said something about singing and I want to produce a musical. Would you be willing to try out?" Lanya felt like the air was being sucked out of her lungs! He wants me to try out? For a real show? On stage? With an audience? It took a moment before thought came back to her and she realized he was waiting for an answer.

"Yes, I would love to." She tried hard to sound collected and calm though it was completely an act.

"This would be next month sometime, I need to work on the dates." He seemed at ease, though Lanya was a bundle of nerves.

"Let me know." Lanya was feeling a bit stronger. She would show up to that audition. Even the German army could not keep her away! After a few more pleasantries and the end of the beers, Ivan stood and escorted her back to the street.

"Thanks for this unexpected meeting. I know you were not expecting to see me." Ivan spoke carefully, wanting to be clear. "Can I see you again in a few days? I will meet you at the same place."

Lanya thought that she was calm and then this. Her head was floating. He wanted to see her again? Ivan reached out and touched her arm and his touch burned through her sweater. "Sure, I will look for you." She looked around him, not wanting to catch his eye. He was direct and she wanted to run.

"I need to go. See you soon?" The question mark was unnecessary and Lanya nodded her head. Ivan turned and walked the other way. Lanya froze then slowly turned and headed back towards the tram. He wanted to see her again and wanted her to be in a show? Could this be a dream come true? Maru. She needed to get to Maru!

Lanya ran up the steps to Maru's apartment and pounded on the door. Maru's mother rushed over and opened the door quickly and smiled when she saw Lanya. "In her room" as she waved to invite Lanya in. Lanya almost ran to her friend's room and threw the door open, "Ivan came by- we went to get a beer! He is going to come by again! He wants me to try out for a show!"

"Wait, what? Ivan did what?" Lanya collapsed on the edge of Maru's bed as Maru sat at her mirror.

"Ivan was outside the factory when we came out. You went your way and I looked up and he was there!"

"Wow- and then what?"

"He said he came because he wanted to see me, we went to the Prospekt and had a beer. We talked for a minute and he asked me if I could sing and if I would try out for a show!

"Of course you told him you would, right?"

"Yes, I did. He said it will not be for a while yet, but I was so nervous! I hardly touched my beer!"

"This is so exciting! You are going to be a big star! Your voice is like angels singing!"

"I don't know. Maybe I won't make it. But I have to try out, don't you think?" With that thought, Lanya's stomach clenched some. *What if I don't make it? What if I am not good enough?*

"Yes! Yes!!" Maru reached over and gave Lanya a big hug.

"Thanks. I had to tell you. I have not even been home yet."

"You had to tell me first! Yes you did! I am glad you came by! Anything else?" Maru had a gleam in her eye and Lanya knew she was asking if there was anything more personal to share.

"No, I would not even have noticed I am so excited about this! But he did say he will come by again in a few days."

"That is so good!" They talked for a few minutes more and Lanya knew she needed to get home or Babu would be worried. She left Maru's with a huge smile all over her face and songs running through her head all the way home.

Lanya burst into the front room when she got home. "Babu, sorry I am late. Babu, I met a man who wants me to try out for a show!" Babu was in the front room, darning an old sock. She looked up at Lanya with a gentle smile.

"He wants you to try out? Wonderful news. Once he hears your voice you will win him over!"

"Thank you Babu. It will be in a few weeks. I need to decide what song to sing!" Lanya floated off to her bedroom. Valentina was at a friend's house so she was alone. Song after song came to her mind and she racked her brain trying to decide which one was best. Lanya wanted to share this with her brother. She sat down and wrote him a letter like she did every other day. She told him about meeting Ivan and their beer on the Prospekt. And about trying out for a show. Her hands were trembling as she wrote and her handwriting looked like a child's. As she finished, her nerves came on. *What if I can't sing? What if I freeze up and cannot even croak? What if I get scared and can't go?* Lanya could feel the tension flooding through her, though only thirty minutes ago she was on cloud nine. *Why do I have to overthink all this? How am I going to handle all this?*

Chapter Seven

Lanya could not stop singing. While she was on the tram, sewing at her machine in the factory, waiting in line for food, trying to sleep at night, songs went through her head. Which one was the right one? Which one would show off her range, her skills, her depth? She sang the songs from the show she had just seen, ones from her school years, ones that were in other shows, party songs, even some old ones her mother and father used to sing. Usually, she sang in her head, but sometimes she hummed. If anyone looked at her, she looked around pretending it was someone else. Singing was like breathing; she could not stop. At home, sometimes Valentina joined in but usually, Lanya sang to herself. When she was singing, there was no war, no rationing. When she was singing there was no tension. Even her fingers were still.

The air raids were once or twice a week. No one knew when the Germans would break through and enter the city. Daytime shelling happened now and again. The city had camouflaged landmarks, and anti-aircraft guns were in neighborhood centers. Life was certainly an uproar. One of the women at the factory did not come in one day last week and the story was she was killed when a bomb hit her house. No one was reassigned to that machine and people had placed small trinkets there, sometimes a flower in remembrance. Lanya did not know the woman well, but her absence was acknowledged by everyone.

At the sewing group, it was confirmed that the city was completely surrounded. No way in and no way out. No trains, no cars. The only way new products could get in was via Lake Ladoga, just north of the city. But that got bombed too. And there was not much available. As September drew to a close, things looked dismal.

And then it got worse. One cold, clear night, Valentina wanted to go to a friend's house and Lanya was sure they would take care of her. An hour later the air raid sirens went off. Valentina would go with her friends to a nearby shelter. Lanya was sure about that, but her stomach was not calm. Again she felt like she had no control over things. Lanya and Babu gathered their escape bag and went to their neighborhood bomb shelter. It was not as bad as before and Lanya recognized a few faces. They had their little corner again by the file cabinet. No one knew how close the bombs would be. Tonight they were close and the power went out. Some had brought oil lamps so they were not completely in the dark. The dust and the smell were stifling but it was better than being outside. Lanya was glad she was more comfortable than in the early days. She and Babu held hands and Lanya hummed old songs that Babu knew. Babu squeezed her hands. After a few hours, the glorious all clear rang and they trudged out into the dark night. Lanya was glad she had not soiled herself again. Debris was everywhere and bricks were all over. People tripped in the dark so it was with great care they made their way back to the apartment. Lanya peeked out the heavy curtains and saw the bright night. How could they do this? *Damn Germans.*

After settling into her bed, Lanya relaxed, feeling safe that they had made it through another attack. Sleep came quickly. Then a loud banging on the front door with screaming. "Come here, come here!" Lanya jumped out of bed. Babu was still snoring so Lanya did not wake her. "Come here!" The pounding continued. Lanya pulled open the door and saw a man covered in grime, His hair was sticking out and his face had dirt in every crease. "Come here, come with me. Your sister! Now!" Lanya grabbed a jacket and shoes and followed.

As they ran, he explained he was the father of Valentina's friend Ilya. The father's name was Omar, and they lived a few blocks away. The streets were filled with rubble and they ran as carefully as they could in the dark. As they ran, Lanya's brain was in the worst of places. Where was Valentina? Was she okay? Ilya's house had been hit and Valentina was missing. Omar's wife was hit but not too bad, however both girls were buried in the mess.

The apartment building was a mound of wood and brick. Two walls were completely gone and there was no roof. Bricks and boards covered the ground. Lanya could hear moaning and crying. People were really hurt. Lanya was sickened. Somewhere in here was her baby sister, probably hurt, hopefully only trapped. Omar lived on the third floor, so there could be seven floors on top of her. Omar let go of her hand and went to see his wife. Lanya began crawling around, as others were doing. City rescue was coming, Lanya could hear the bells. Would they be in time?

"Valentina, Tina, can you hear me?" Lanya cried this over and over. There was no answer. Others were calling out for their missing ones. Once in a while someone would shout back "Here" but nothing from Valentina. Lanya moved boards and kicked bricks. Her pajamas were thin for this cool night but this did not stop Lanya from moving debris and calling out. Rescue arrived and were removing the boards and broken furniture to clear space. Now the street was littered even more. One person was uncovered and Lanya rushed over to see if it was Valentina. It was an older gentleman who was pretty badly hurt. His legs were crushed, Lanya wondered if he would live. Another person was pulled out but not Valentina.

Daylight crept through the dust as dozens of people moved materials and searched. All were groggy with exhaustion and chill. Another person was found and Lanya went over- not as fast as before. It was a girl, Valentina's friend Ilya! She was dead, her body smashed and blood everywhere. Omar ran over and wailed at the sight of his daughter. Lanya cried out, feeling his pain. Omar told them to keep looking right there, there should be two girls. The rescue workers kept moving beams that took two men. "Hey, hey, we have her" a worker shouted. Lanya ran over and pushed in. She recognized the long hair right away.

"Valentina!" she yelled out. She grabbed for her, hoping she was awake. She got her hand on Valentina's arm, still warm. A glimmer of hope surfaced. The rescue team pulled away boards and bricks until they finally got to Valentina. Lanya went to hug her but was pushed aside.

"Let us get her over here." They carefully picked her up and put her on a nearby table. Lanya heard her grunt and her hope grew as she realized Valentina was still breathing. The rescue chief was running his hands over her, arms, legs, stomach. "Broken leg, maybe neck." Lanya was still kept away but hankered for every word. "Not sure what else, there is blood on her neck." That did not sound good. Valentina had not moved.

"Can we get her to the hospital?" Lanya asked, hoping they would move her immediately.

"The hospital is full. We just left there. Too many soldiers and too many hurt in the bombing. She cannot go to the hospital." Lanya was stunned. How could they not take her to the hospital? Weren't they supposed to fix things? The rescue worker turned to her, "I would take her home. Maybe the hospital will have room later."

"I can take her home?" Lanya hoped that would be enough. She and Babu would do everything they could to help Valentina. "Can you help me get her there? It is only a few blocks."

"Ask me in thirty minutes. Then we will be done here." He went back to the building looking for more survivors while Lanya moved right in and took Valentina's hand.

"Tina, Tina, I am here. We will do anything we can to make you all better. You are not alone. Can you squeeze my hand?" Nothing. But Lanya held on speaking gentle and soothing words. She tried to talk through the tears. Lanya looked carefully now that the sun was coming up at the injuries. Blood was on her neck and face. The leg was certainly broken since it was at an unnatural angle. Valentina had broken her leg as a child while skating but it had not been like this. Lanya took her face in her hands and carefully rolled it left and right. Something was off. Maybe her neck was broken as the man had said. Lanya took off her jacket and put it over Valentina to keep her warm. She knew that was what rescue always did, keep them warm. She had no medical training, but she had seen a movie where they did this.

The rescue chief came back after a while and took another look at Valentina. "Any change?" he asked Lanya.

"Nothing. She has not said anything nor moved."

"That is not good."

"Are you sure we cannot get her to the hospital?"

"I am sorry, but they are closed. I can get her to your house if it is close as you said."

"Yes, just a few blocks away."

With that, he slowly gathered Valentina up in his arms, turned to Lanya and said "Let's go." She walked him quickly down the street and turned towards her apartment. Lanya was angry they moved so slowly but the streets were full of all kinds of rubble. Was Babu awake yet? This would be a shock.

As they got to the apartment, Lanya opened the door and called out "Babu?" Babu came running, knowing that if Lanya was coming in this early something was wrong. The rescue chief brought Valentina into the house and put her on the sofa.

"Do not move her. Keep her warm and give her liquids if you can. She may develop a fever so take care of that. Check with the hospital later in the day, they may have room in the afternoon."

"Thank you so much, this means a lot." Lanya was already looking away from him at her sister on the couch and he quietly left the apartment without another word.

Lanya turned to Babu. "The house where she was got bombed. Ilya was killed, it was awful. I saw her. Valentina has a broken leg and maybe a broken neck. The hospital is too full to take anyone else so I thought here was best." She grabbed Babu's arm. "What do we do Babu?"

Babu was quiet. Then she knelt on the floor beside the couch and took Valentina in her hands. She ran her hands over her, like Lanya had done, picking up limbs and turning her neck. "There is not much we can do, Svetlana. We will keep her comfortable and see if the hospital can do more later." She went to the closet and got out a blanket then went to the kitchen to make tea. Feodor, the little brown dog that Valentina loved, sniffed around. He wanted to be a part of this.

In the kitchen over weak tea and a biscuit, Babu went on. "In a case like this, even the hospital cannot do much. It is out of our hands." She looked like all the life had been drawn right out of her, she was pale and her hands were shaking a bit. Lanya took her hand in hers and squeezed. She rested her head on Babu's hoping to give her strength. In her life, Babu had lost so much. Maybe Valentina would come round.

Lanya went into the front room and sat near her sister on the couch. Valentina's breath was calm not labored and that was good. She did not move. No wiggles, no twitches. *Maybe she is not in pain*, Lanya thought. She touched her forehead. It was a bit warm, so Lanya decided to check often. She washed Valentina's face and neck as gently as she could, to remove the blood. It was too hard to look at. The dog sat near Valentina's feet, quietly, like he could feel the tension. Babu was in the kitchen as she often was. A quiet day, it seemed. Not peaceful, but quiet.

Around noon, Valentina had a fever. Lanya got a cold cloth and put it on her forehead and cheeks. The fever rose as the afternoon went on, and Lanya asked Babu to come see.

"A cold cloth is all you can do unless we can get some aspirin in her. But I do not think that will work. Has she moved?"

"Not at all."

"Just keep the cool cloths coming. Do you want to go check the hospital to see if they have room for her?" Lanya decided that would be good. She hated sitting here watching her sister's life fade away. Maybe a walk to the hospital would help her, anyway. As she rushed, she hoped that her sister would still be alive when she got back.

On the street, Lanya went to the trams and waited. But the trams were late. Really late. No, the trams were not running. Lanya had never seen this before. Was there not enough fuel? So Lanya almost ran to the hospital on the other side of town. This took over an hour.

At the hospital, Lanya came in the front entrance. There were people everywhere, doctors, nurses and patients even in the hallways. This does not look good, Lanya thought. There was a nurse there with a clipboard in her hand who seemed like she was in charge.

"I have a question- my sister was in a house that was hit by a bomb last night, can I bring her in? She is badly hurt." The nurse looked around as if she could not answer that question. She went to a nearby doctor and spoke with him. He shook his head.

The nurse came back. "We cannot take any new patients. We are filled- overfilled. I am sorry."

"She needs to be seen. What can I do?"

"I am sorry. Pray." The nurse quickly moved away. Lanya was shocked. *Pray?* That was all that was offered? *Pray?* Lanya walked out the front door with her heart in pieces. Her sister might die because too many people had been hurt by the Germans and no one could help. The tears streamed down her face as she started the walk home.

Her parents were gone, because of the Communist Party. Her brother was gone, because of the Nazis. Her sister was also almost gone because of the Nazis. *How do politics ruin people so much? How can one idea over another kill good people?* As Lanya walked, she was convinced that her life was worthless. Why bother. What good would it do? How long before she was the next one lying there breathing her last breath? The tears kept coming and Lanya did nothing to stop them. People looked at her but no one tried to comfort her. They all knew what she felt. They all knew loss, or would.

After rushing back home, Lanya thanked Babu and took her seat. The fever was rising and the cool cloths seemed to do nothing. But every few minutes, Lanya went and put fresh cool water on the cloth and brought it back. Valentina's breath sounded worse, like she was struggling for air. *How long*, Lanya thought. *How long will she hang on? How long will I hang on?*

Lanya fell asleep in the chair, holding her sister's hand. She woke later and found that the cloth on Valentina's head was cool, Babu must have brought it. Her breathing was a struggle, Lanya could hear. Valentina shivered and Lanya brushed her hair away again. *I am glad she is not in pain,* Lanya thought. There was no way she could drink or eat so Lanya did not even try. Lanya did not pray, she had never prayed. Never even thought about it. There were no churches in the Soviet Union they were all museums now but no one went. But this would be a good time to start praying she thought. She had no understanding of God but she got on her knees because that is what she heard people did, and whispered the first prayer of her life.

"God, I do not know you, but my beautiful sister is hurt. Can you please heal her, keep her alive and healthy? I have nothing to offer you except gratitude. If you can do this, I will pray often and honor you." Tears were again pouring out of her eyes. She checked the cloth on Valentina's head and it was cool. Then she put her fingers on Valentina's forehead and it was not feverish, even cool.

"Babu, Babu come here!" Lanya looked for breathing and did not see any. Babu came rushing in and Lanya said, "Her skin is cool. Is she breathing?" Babu went away and Lanya wondered what she was doing. She could not feel a pulse or see her chest rising. Babu came back with a small mirror She held the mirror in front of Valentina's nose to see if air was coming in or out.

"If she is breathing, it will show on the mirror." Babu held it there for a few minutes but it felt like hours. There was no moisture on the mirror. Babu put her hand on Lanya's shoulder. Lanya rose and grabbed Babu tightly. "She is gone." Lanya sobbed heaving sobs and Babu did the same. They held each other up. Lanya sat back down on the chair using her sleeve to wipe her face.

"She is gone? My baby sister? Gone?" Lanya grabbed Valentina's cool hand and brought it to her forehead. She put her hand on her face stroking her soft cheek. Lanya looked at Babu who had sat in the other chair with her head in her hands. Her world was completely destroyed.

Lanya was numb. *How can this be? What kind of world is this?* She stroked her sister's hand until the coldness of it made her stomach sick. She gently put it down, afraid to leave her sister. This young girl who Lanya fondly remembered as an infant in diapers. Was cold. What else could go wrong? Lanya was afraid to ask that. She still had Babu. She got up from the chair and rushed from the room to retch. That seemed like the perfect response. She went to the kitchen to make some tea and made two cups. Babu came in after her.

"What do we do?" Lanya asked, afraid again of the answer. Swallowing the tea was impossible so the cup sat untouched. Babu did not drink either.

"Let me think. Let's just wait for a bit. This is too hard." Babu was obviously in great pain, as Lanya was.

"Valentina's friend Ilya was killed too. Immediately. I hated it." Lanya remembered the scene just a few blocks away. She now better understood the trauma that Omar was going through, losing his daughter.

"I am sorry for them. I know what it feels like." Babu whispered, as if to speak at normal level would upset the world. Lanya laid her hand on Babu's and squeezed. They sat in the kitchen, unable to move or drink their tea. No reason to do anything.

Time passed, and night came. There were no sirens tonight, the Germans had done enough yesterday. Lanya moved to the cabinet where the bottle of vodka was and threw out the cold tea and filled both cups with vodka. It went down quickly, the first sip. Lanya knew she would finish the cup. She had to if she wanted to sleep. Babu sipped at hers, which was unusual for her but she seemed to need help tonight as well. As she could feel the vodka seeping in, Lanya rose and went back into the front room where Valentina lay. She pulled the blanket over her face and sobs came quickly. She did not touch the hand again it was too disturbing. After just a few minutes, she went back to her bedroom, that she shared with Valentina, and sunk onto her bed. She hoped to quickly fall asleep. It came, thanks to the vodka. But so did the nightmares. Lanya had had nightmares since her mother was taken a few years ago. This night was one of the worst. The noise of the bombs, the shelter, the debris and broken buildings and glass on the road, the shriek of the planes as they dropped their evils, and death. Dead people all over, the road, the building, the apartment. Lanya was afraid in her dream that she was next. And who knows? She turned and woke and went back to sleep for more dreadful dreams. At one point she decided just to stay awake to avoid the nightmares. She turned on a light and picked up a book. She did not really read but she knew that sleep was not working.

When the sun peeked through the heavy drapes. Lanya got up. It was a new day but she had no energy to face it. In the kitchen, her stomach grumbled as she made tea. She was not brave enough to go into the front room, so she went to Babu's room to peek and make sure Babu was alive. She was, and Lanya went back to the kitchen. If she lost Babu, she would want to die too.

Lanya went back to her bedroom and opened Valentina's drawers. She had never done that before and she saw an assortment of trinkets. Would any of these be important enough to bury her with? Lanya found it hard to see as tears filled her eyes again. A small ring with a stone on it, probably glass but Lanya remembered her sister wearing it now and then. A small stuffed doll from her childhood that was dirty and worn from years of love. These would do. Lanya did not want to change Valentina's clothes, that would be too hard. She brought these into the kitchen and put them on the table. Babu came in, looking like she had not slept much either.

"I see what you did. This is good" Babu offered. She fondled the ring, remembering it too.

"Didn't she get that with Ilya? They had matching rings I think." The thought of her sister being young and silly brought tears again.

"Did you sleep last night? I thought I heard you struggling." Babu looked with concern at Lanya's tired face.

"I did not sleep well. Normal for me. Did you sleep well? Maybe my nightmare from a few weeks ago was real? The brown and green that sounded like a bomb? And now..." Babu looked at her with a grim face.

Sadly, Babu said "Maybe." Babu sipped her tea slowly. "Now we must prepare her." For burial was implied, but Lanya's heavy heart knew what she meant. Babu probably had done this before, but Lanya had not. She had never seen a dead person before, and this was all new to her. "We can take her to the Arshavin house a few blocks away, they are setting up for burials there." Lanya had nothing to add, so she left the kitchen to take a shower. The shower was good but what Lanya needed was strength. She had none. Back in her bedroom it was depressing since Valentina's belongings were there. The front room was depressing since Valentina was there. The kitchen was the only safe place in the house.

The day passed slowly. Lanya opened the heavy curtains thinking sun would help to restore her. Around noon, Babu said she was ready to take Valentina away, Lanya was not sure she could take her sister away forever. She lay wrapped in a blanket on the sofa with a scarf across her face. Babu lifted her legs and Lanya got her head. They went out the door and carefully down the steps. There was a cart downstairs that the whole building shared and they gently put Valentina it. Lanya pushed and Babu walked alongside. The Arshavin house wasn't too far, even though the walk seemed like it took years. There was another family outside, with a bundle on a wagon. *A line for the undertaker* Lanya thought. *This was what war does.*

When they went in, they handed over money and were told to put Valentina in a back bedroom. They would get a letter saying where she was buried sometime next week. There were three other bundles in there, but Valentina was laid alongside another small bundle. Before she could leave, Lanya pulled the scarf away and touched her sister's cheek one more time. Babu looked on. The tears came immediately and Lanya stumbled as she walked out. On the road, Lanya took Babu's hand while she pulled the cart with the other. They needed each other. As she returned to the apartment, Lanya decided that she would do anything to hurt those damn Germans. Anything she was asked to do, she would do. Revenge would give her some peace. Maybe she should join the army. She knew she could not leave Babu so that was pushed aside. She would find a way.

Chapter Eight

The singing stopped. There was not a song inside her so none came out. Lanya felt no joy, no pain. Nothing. She was numb. She heard someone say once that this was normal. She did not care. She did not think. Vodka was her best friend. She went to work. She tried to avoid Maru, but could not put her off. Maru had to know.

"Maru, can you come over here?" Lanya called her aside on her second day back at work. Maru came over with a smile on her face.

"Lanya, where have you...wait. What is wrong? You look awful!" Maru sat on the seat where Lanya patted.

"It is Valentina. She is gone." Lanya choked on the words and the idea.

"No! Valentina, the cutest kid on earth?"

Lanya did not try to stop the tears and Maru was sobbing soon. "She went to Ilya's house the other night, you remember... the air raid?" Maru nodded and wiped her nose. "Ilya's house got hit and Valentina was hurt too. Ilya died right away. We brought Valentina home but she did not make it." Lanya tried to go on, but couldn't. Maru wrapped her arms around her and they cried together.

"How are you? How is Babu?" After a few minutes of sobbing, Maru cleared her head a bit.

"We are a mess, but we keep going. I am going to hurt those Germans if I can. I hate Germans!"

"I will help you!" After a few minutes, the bell sounded and they returned to their machines. Lanya was glad for the mindlessness of it. Nothing to think about. Good for a numb soul.

Lanya had to walk home since the trams were no longer running. It was not too bad now but in January that would be tough. It was cold but not biting. As she walked, Lanya saw littered pieces of paper on the ground. She picked one up. It was in Russian, but something was not right. This was small sheet about the size of her hand. It had a picture of a broken building and said 'This will be your city. The German Reich will make it beautiful. Surrender now!' Lanya's stomach twisted. The Germans were threatening the city, not rebuilding it. She crumpled the sheet, threw it on the ground and stomped on it for effect. The Germans wanted Leningrad to surrender? That would never happen. Not as long as there was one walking Russian in town. Never. Lanya was angry. Maybe that was better than numb.

At home, Lanya told Babu about the leaflet. "They want us to surrender! That will not happen!"

Babu looked at Lanya and said, "No. we will not surrender. But, what if it means fewer people die? Would that be better than what we are going through?" Lanya was shocked. Babu said that? Would Babu want the Germans in town? Or was Babu just tired of death? Lanya left the kitchen thinking about both sides of that. *What would be better? Not just for palaces and factories but for people? Would fewer people die if the Germans came into the city? They would bring food and gasoline.* Food was not tight yet and rations were rather small, but Lanya could see that might change. She did not know what their government was like. Fascism is a word someone used. Lanya was sure it would not be worse than the Communist Party she knew.

Lanya hated nighttime. Sleep did not come every night. The dark, the chill and the raids. Every four or five days, another air raid. Lanya had some safety in the shelter and was coming to know these neighbors. But back in the apartment, the nightmares did not let up. Lanya hoped for a pill that would put her to sleep. If Babu had anything she would share, but nothing yet. Maybe she could ask someone.

At sewing group, she shared that she had lost her sister. Every woman there was sympathetic and many of them told their stories. Lanya asked the woman next to her about sleeping and she did not offer a suggestion. Lanya decided to ask the older ladies before she left. Older women had all kinds of remedies from years of experience. As Lanya dawdled at the end of the evening, she asked one older woman whose hair was as white as snow what she could suggest for her lack of sleep. Chamomile tea was recommended and was agreed upon by the remaining ladies.

"That tea is best. Very soothing. I have some here if you like. You may have it. My husband used to use it and I do not need it." She went into her tiny kitchen, brought a small canister and placed it in Lanya's hand. "Good luck my dear. Many of us are having trouble now." Lanya thanked her gently and went on home. She wondered if this would work and if she could get more of it somewhere.

Babu was already asleep when Lanya got in. Feodor met her at the door. It was getting dark so early and felt so late. She heated the water and put some tea in her cup. She had nothing to lose she thought. A small bit of sugar and Lanya relaxed on the kitchen chair. When Mikhail left, she had felt empty. With Valentina gone now, could it get any worse? How could she tell Mishka about Valentina? She felt so powerless, unable to help her sister or her brother. At least she had Babu. She decided not to tell Mishka in a letter, he had enough to worry about so she would tell him when this was all over. The tea was warm and soothing so she made a second cup. She pulled one of the rusks out of the cupboard and dunked it in the tea. She remembered her mother dunking biscuits in coffee. Maybe she was becoming her mother. She began to feel drowsy. Could it be the tea? A miracle in a cup.

While at her machine a few days later with the weak October sun coming in through the windows, Lanya remembered that Ivan was going to have her try out for a show. She felt a bit of a bright spot in her heart, the first in over a week. A song came into her head, one from the radio last year, about a man who had lost his lover. Lanya went through the lyrics and the tune began to form. She surprised herself when she realized she was singing. She felt great relief. She could sing, even a sad song. Another sad song came in, and she sang that in her head as her hands pushed the boot leather this way and that. A stream of sad songs came through her mind that morning and Lanya felt each word and thought about her sister. Tears came but they were gentle tears. Lanya felt some peace and the beginnings of healing.

Valentina had been gone three long weeks and Lanya and Babu stayed quiet. Lanya did not think about Ivan much and she spent more time with Feodor the little dog. He had always been Valentina's dog and spent every minute he could right next to her. But Lanya sensed he needed her now, so he sat near her on the sofa most nights.

October came in gently with a cold breeze. Cold rain had fallen and Lanya was beginning to worry about getting to and from the factory by when things got to freezing. But then, one evening she began her trek home and a voice called out "Lanya". She stopped and looked around. Ivan! Ivan was standing right where he was the last time and he wanted to see her! Lanya had not realized she had frozen up and he walked up to her. "Lovely Lanya, I wanted to see you. Sorry I have not been here for a few weeks. Things have been busy." He reached out his hand and touched her arm. "How are you?"

Lanya faltered, but the words came out immediately. "Not good. The bombings... killed my younger sister ...Valentina." It hurt to say her name. She tried to stop the tears but could not. "I hate this war." She said nothing else and he put both arms gently around her.

"I am sorry. War is ugly." It was a quick hug but Lanya felt better. "Can I walk you home? I was going to suggest a drink but a walk home will do."

"That would be nice." They began an easy stride through the cold darkening night.

"Feels like snow may be coming. Isn't that early?"

"I think you are right. We often get snow in October, sometimes even September. We are so far north it does come early. I hear this could be a really tough winter."

"Oh no. I hope I am ready!" Ivan's voice was light but Lanya thought it felt a bit false. Maybe she needed false. She was not worried about the cold. She had never been to the south so cold long winters were normal for her. The winter would match her heart.

The walk continued with Ivan asking about work and Babu who he had not met. As they got to her street, Lanya stopped and faced Ivan. "Thanks for the walk home Ivan. It was very nice of you." Ivan put his hands on her arms and leaned in.

"I am really sorry about your sister. I hope this war is over soon, too." Lanya nodded and did not want to say anything or he would hear her voice waver. "I will see you soon Lanya. It won't be so long." Lanya nodded again then turned away, glad she did not have to say goodbye. She could hear Ivan's footsteps as she turned towards her apartment.

It was so nice of him to come by and walk with her. Ivan was a bright spot in another dreary day.

Chapter Nine

There was a banging on the door. It was early morning and her breakfast of brown bread and "coffee" was on the table. Banging again. Babu turned, but Lanya got to the door. The little dog barked and rushed to the door as protection. A big man was there, and behind him- was Mikhail! Lanya opened the door and the man pushed Mikhail into the room. "I have a report for you if you are Svetlana Zhudanov?"

"Yes, I am, what is the report?"

"This is Mikhail Zhudanov, your brother?" Lanya stumbled as Mikhail tottered into the room. Babu moved forward but not in time.

"Yes, this is my brother, we have not seen him in months!"

"Well, he is home now, to stay with you. One shell went off near him out on the Luga line and his brain is damaged. He does not know how to do things. We cannot have him on the line. He is your responsibility now."

Lanya had mixed feelings. Mikhail was home, the best possible news! But damaged? What did that mean? The big man hurried away and Lanya tried to follow him to the hallway but he barreled out into the street. She had questions for him but she choked on them as he hurried away. She went back and looked at Babu and at Mikhail. Mikhail was sitting in a chair in the front room slumped over. Babu was already asking him about a drink and a bite to eat. Babu was asking him if he was okay, if he was hurt. Mikhail did not answer. Lanya was sick. He looked around, and a look came over him of relief. He got tears in his eyes. Babu hugged him tight, murmuring that she was so

happy to see him. Mikhail was quiet and put his head in his hands.
What was wrong?

Lanya put her arm on her brother's shoulder and looked at her
grandmother. Babu was good at caring for people, but she had a blank
look in her eyes. Mikhail was home and in one piece, but what else?
Her brother was hurt, but not in a normal way. A gunshot, you knew
what to do. A broken bone, easy. But this? What would a doctor do?

Lanya got right in front of Mishka and tried to look in his
eyes. There was nothing there. "Mishka, you are home. Are you okay?"
Still nothing in her brother's beautiful dark eyes. Lanya ran her hands
over his arms, his back, neck and sides. She could feel nothing out of
place. No bumps, no damage and he did not react like he was hurt.
Babu came in from the kitchen with warm tea and a slice of bread. She
put them down in front of Mishka because Babu thought snacks fixed
everything. He did not pick them up. Lanya looked at Babu again and
rolled her eyes to the kitchen, beckoning Babu. Babu followed her into
the kitchen.

"What do we do? What is wrong?"

Babu took her time answering. "I saw this once. A man was
hurt like this after the factory he worked in had an explosion. He hurt
his head. He came back after a few weeks. Maybe Mishka will also.
Let's keep him comfortable and see." Lanya had no better ideas. She
went back into the front room and carefully pulled off Mishka's coat.
It was clear from the smell of his clothes that Mishka had been in the
trenches for some time. A bath and some clean clothes were in order.
He had plenty of clothes in his room so that was not a problem. Babu
went to draw a bath while Lanya worked to get him undressed. His
coat came off and then they took his uniform shirt off. Mikhail had
been a beautiful man and now he was not. Tears welled in her eyes and
she did nothing to stop them. She was glad he was alive, both she and
Babu had worried over and over about that. Here he was, but not the
same. Finally in his underwear they pulled him into the bathroom and
pushed him into the tub. He settled in well since it was warm. Lanya
did not want to wash her big brother so she left Babu to do it. She
put his uniform in her room where the dirty clothes were and hoped
Babu would wash soon so she did not have to smell this for long. The
uniform had small rips and tears here and there but no big gashes.

Lanya tried to be grateful that he was home, but this was bittersweet news.

In a little bit, Lanya heard Mishka come out of the bathroom and his bedroom door open. Babu went in and got him dressed. Lanya came to see. Babu laid Mishka down on his bed, and sat near him. She took his hand and sang an old song quietly. It did not take long and Mishka was asleep. He must have been exhausted. Lanya went back to the kitchen and Babu followed.

"I think you are right. This is the best we can do for now." Lanya had no other ideas. Babu nodded.

Lanya went off to work, with snow coming down in a wet soggy mess. She was wrapped up in her coat, scarf and gloves. The boots on her feet were a few years old; maybe she needed some new ones. Hoping she could find some. As she walked, Lanya thought about her life as it was now. Parents gone, sister gone. Brother home, but probably only a shell. Would he come back, like Babu had said? Or would he be like this for years and Lanya would have to care for him? She would, but she was not ready to be anyone's mother. Her heart sunk as she slogged through the snow. Her town was blocked off from everything and her brother was broken. If she had to care for him, would that keep her off the stage? Would Ivan even offer her a role if she had to be close to Mishka? There were a lot of questions and few answers.

At work, there was an answer. The power was out. People clustered around the supervisor.

"How am I going to run my machine without power?"

"Where will we get boxes for finished boots?"

"How can we ship these out with no mail? Will we have to deliver them to the front ourselves?" That one got a few chuckles from the back.

The supervisor got on a chair like he always did and put his hands out to quiet them. "I was told by the Party that this is a short term problem. We will probably get power back in a day or two. But, until it comes back, two things. One, we will use the old czarist machines in the back." A huge groan went out.

"The hand crank ones? Those are awful!"

"I had to use those once, killed my arms!" The supervisor scowled to enforce order.

"Two, we are going down to three days a week. Every one of you will now work only three days. Your immediate boss will tell you your schedule." More grumbling. The supervisor called some men forward to go into the warehouse in the back to retrieve the older, heavier machines. Lanya had never even seen a hand crank machine. Did they work the same? Her boss came over and told her that her days would be Monday, Tuesday and Saturday. Lanya offered to work more days but was cut off. Today was Monday, so she went to the machines coming in to see what was next.

Lanya had to wait for her machine so she took the time to go find Maru at her spot. She was waiting too.

"Can you believe it? We have to use these ancient machines! This is awful!" Maru acted like she was angry but Lanya could tell from the tone of her voice it wasn't too bad.

"Shhh- I have to tell you" Lanya tried to whisper- "Mikhail is home!" Maru's eyes lit up.

"How is...," After seeing Lanya's face, she stopped.

Lanya cut her off. "Not good." Maru froze and listened carefully. "He was near an explosion and he cannot talk. He is like a child." Maru grabbed Lanya's arm and looked at her pleadingly.

"Our Mishka? Broken?"

"Yes, he is broken. My handsome brother who is so strong. Broken." Again the tears came and she was powerless. She could see tears in Maru's eyes too. Lanya dropped her head to Maru's shoulders. "Babu says maybe his brain will come back. We need to wait and see." Maru said nothing. Lanya had nothing more to add and went back to wait for her machine.

The older hand crank machine arrived after a while. It was heavy. Lanya sat at the same chair but it was not the same. Who had used this old thing? She put her hand on the crank on the right side near the wheel. The knob was cold but swirled easily. She turned the knob while her right hand stayed near the needle. Yes, she could operate this but it would be slow. She found the thread and carefully threaded the old machine. As she turned the crank, there was a small squeak. This would be the new noise, no electric hums, just squeaks. Lanya got her material together and started. It did not take long to become fatigued. Near her were pedal machines where your foot pushed down on the pedal to work. That looked like it would be faster but wear you out even quicker. Lanya thought to herself that the days would be feeling longer. Maybe three days was enough.

As she returned home, Lanya thought about her brother. *What was really wrong? What can I do, and how can I help him?* Babu was in the kitchen, preparing dinner. "Any news? How is Mishka?" Lanya was afraid of the answer but asked anyway.

"He has been sleeping but he has come in. Ate a little."

"Did he talk?"

"No, just a few grunts." Lanya went down the hall to his room. He was on his bed with some small trinket in his left hand. She came into the room and sat at his chair.

"Hello Mikhail. Good to see you. How do you feel today?" Lanya did not expect an answer. He looked at her and then away. It seemed that he did not even recognize her. The brother who had pulled her hair, called her names and acted like her father anytime she had a boyfriend, did not recognize her. She gave him a weak smile, trying to comfort him. She got up and touched his leg as she walked out. She was empty.

"Babu, we need to get him a ration card. I can do it on Wednesday. I am only going to be working three days a week now. We have no power, so they brought out the old machines with hand cranks. I used mine but my arm is tired and it will be slow."

"I remember those machines, I used to have one when I was younger." Babu smiled lightly, remembering the days of her youth. "My arms got tired too." The kitchen was lit only by candles since the power was out all over the city.

"I will try on Wednesday to get him a ration card. If his appetite comes back we will need two for him!" They had just returned Valentina's card but kept it until the end of the month, as long as they could. The penalty for abusing ration cards was high and they knew the undertaker would report it so they understood they had to return it. Now Lanya had to go ask for another one.

When dinner was ready, Lanya had the table set for three. She remembered buying this small table two years ago, and selling the bigger one that fit all six of them. With her parents gone, the big table was too much. It was good to have three plates out and Lanya remembered when Valentina died and they did not set a plate for her. But Mishka was here and three plates looked good. She went to get

Mishka for dinner. She stood at the door and asked "Mishka, it is time for dinner. Can you come please?" He saw her but did not seem to understand her words. She motioned with her arm that he should come towards her and again he did not move. She went in and touched the back of his shoulder and gestured like to get up. He sat up and she took his hand as if to pull him to standing. He stood. The look in his eyes was blank and Lanya could not see any emotions. She made the motion of putting food in her mouth, as with a fork, and pulled his hand for her to follow. He came along and they went to the table. She pulled out a chair that he sat in. There was food on his plate and he put his fingers on it. It was hot and he yelped and pulled his fingers back. Lanya sat and picked up her fork, looking at him. He picked up his fork. Lanya had to show him how to eat. Like a baby. Her beautiful older brother was a baby. Lanya lost her appetite and ate very little. Mikhail ate his portion and seemed content. Lanya knew this would be a long journey.

Lanya was grateful to be working three days a week. Nights were getting longer and the walk to and from work was tiring. Limited food meant she had less energy and her clothes were getting loose. She never had much extra anyway and often was envious of Maru's curves. Maru was excited about Mishka being home and wanted to come over and see him. That would happen soon. Mishka spent his days like a child, playing with trinkets and keeping to himself.

On Wednesday, Lanya went to the Party office to get him a ration card. While waiting in line, she could feel the familiar tension from being near the Party. Her stomach tightened and she worked to control her shallow breathing. When she got to the counter, she tried to explain.

"I need a new ration card for my brother please. He came back from the front."

"Why did he come back from the front? We need him out there! Send him back."

"He is injured."

"Is he in the hospital? They will feed him and send him back." The clerk was making this tough and Lanya wanted to scream. She just wanted to take care of her brother.

"He is not in the hospital. His brain is not working. He is like a child." For the first time, the agent looked at Lanya. She reminded

Lanya of a mouse, small and without color and it seemed her nose twitched as she spoke.

"I need proof that he is here. You could be telling me a story. I need to see him."

"I am not sure that would work. He is scared of everything."

"If you want the ration card" the mouse said, "You bring him in here." Lanya turned and felt like the whole world was on her shoulders. As she trudged home her brain was deep in thought. The Party was making this ridiculously difficult. The Party always talked like they were taking care of people but Lanya could not see it. She knew better than to provoke the Party. She was not lying just to get more food. She was sure some people did. She just wanted to get enough food to keep him alive.

Chapter Ten

Lanya wondered what it would be like when she took her brother to the Party office to get a ration card. She had never taken children anywhere and wondered what would happen if Mishka got upset, or if he got angry. Lanya took a pen and wrote their address on the sleeve of his coat, in case they were separated. She knew he would not be able to give the address to anyone so she wrote it carefully in big block letters, just in case.

Dressing warmly, they went down the stairs into the cold morning. She kept her arm on his. He did not do what he used to, like commenting on the birds, the weather or other people. He kept his head down and walked silently. Lanya tried to engage him now and then but after fifteen minutes she gave up.

At the office where she was yesterday, she stood in line again waiting her turn. Like all Soviet lines this took forever. Finally they were called up.

"What is your business?" The man at the desk was small and his hair was combed sideways to cover a bald spot.

"I need to get a ration card for my brother here, Mikhail Zhukanov."

"Doesn't he have one? Why not?"

"He just got back from the front two days ago. He is injured."

"Why is he not in the hospital? They would feed him." The man had not looked up yet.

"His brain is damaged. He cannot understand. He cannot talk." The man looked Mishka up and down weighing Lanya's words.

"What do you mean?" Lanya sighed. She hated having to explain this, but she was sure she needed to.

"He cannot talk. He does not move much. He cannot communicate. I do not know more."

"He does not talk? How can that be?"

"His sergeant brought him back to our apartment and said that there was an explosion and he is not the same."

"I am not sure I believe you."

"I came here yesterday and the lady said I needed to bring him to prove he was real, so here he is. We just need a ration card for him." Lanya looked around for the mousy woman from yesterday but did not see her here.

The man looked at Mishka and said in a gruff voice, "What are you doing here? Why aren't you fighting?" Mishka did not respond, did not even look at the man. The man grunted, grabbed his pencil and stabbed it at Mishka's middle. "I am talking to you!" Mishka reacted to the pencil coming at him and pulled his hand up in a fan spreading it wide over his torso. The man backed off, startled.

Lanya quickly said, "I am sorry, he does not understand you." She turned to Mishka and laid her hands on his arm and spoke soothingly to him. His eyes darted from side to side but came to Lanya's face. She looked at him and smiled, trying to pacify him. He settled down. The man had a confused look on his face. He had never seen this before and wasn't sure what to do. People did not just show up in at the Party office looking for ration cards.

"I'll be right back." He turned away and went to a desk at the back. The man at the desk had a hard face and it looked like he never said yes once in his life. He got up and came forward to where Lanya and Mikhail were standing.

"What is the problem here?" He looked them both up and down. It was an inspection. Her already tense stomach got even tighter, and Lanya hoped she would not choke for lack of air.

"My brother just came back from the front. His sergeant brought him. A bomb went off and it damaged his brain. He is like a child." She looked at both men again. She was angry through her tension. Could they not see what the problem was? She very carefully said "We need a ration card for him please."

The hard man thought, then turned to the balding man but kept an eye on Mishka. Ignoring Lanya, he said "I could use a big bowl of borscht now. Maybe with some sausages on the side. And apple cake. Wouldn't that be great?" The balding man looked like he was going to slobber, the food sounded so good. Lanya thought he was just being cruel. No one had food like that now. The hard man watched Mishka. Mishka did nothing. He did not look at the man, he did not cock his head, did not sound interested in the food.

"Nothing? That did nothing for this man? He must be damaged! Go ahead then. If that did not get his interest he really is hurt. Give him a fresh ration card." He then returned to his desk at the back. The balding man rolled his eyes, and prepared the papers and a moment later handed Lanya a crisp new card, good till the end of the month and an identification card so he could get new cards each month. Lanya tucked those into her inside coat pocket and breathed a sigh of relief. She tugged on Mishka's arm and they left the building. As she walked out she could feel some tension ease in her stomach.

During the quiet walk home, Lanya wondered about life. *When would it be good? When would she get what she wanted? Why were things so bad? Was it the war?* Yes, the war killed her sister, and caused her brother to be almost killed and ruined. They were all tired, scared and hungry. Lanya was not asking for too much. A comfortable life with family and friends and time singing on stage now and then. That was not too much. Plenty of people got what they wanted, why not her? The feeling again that she had no control was depressing. Maybe vodka would help.

At the sewing group, there was a new idea that was outrageous. "Did you hear what they did? It is crazy but maybe it will work!" The sewing circle was a big one tonight; Lanya never knew who would be there. When Lidia said that all talk stopped. This woman always had news that was brand new. All eyes turned toward her as she put her needle down and adjusted her glasses, looking around. "One of the generals, I do not know which one, came up with this. He went to a theater show here in town and in the show, they had tanks made out of cardboard. He said they were very realistic, especially from a distance! And so he ordered some made! He ordered the prop men in the theater to make these tanks out of cardboard, and had them taken to the front, to fool the Germans! Is that the craziest idea you have ever heard?" Talk broke out throughout the room, and Lanya heard many voices.

"Really?"

"Crazy."

"Remove him."

"This will never work."

"Cardboard against steel?"

Lanya thought it was the craziest thing, but she knew the prop men could do strong construction work. She wondered what would happen.

One voice said, "What if it works? What if the Germans believe we have more tanks? The factories here could make them if we could get steel. What if?"

"Maybe they will not attack?"

"I cannot believe it, but it can't hurt."

The talk went round and round and Lanya listened carefully so she could report to Babu later. What if it did fool the Germans? It could not hurt.

The next day at work she was reminded of the horror of the war when the machine next to her was empty. Nikola did not miss much work and Lanya hoped she was not ill. Or too weak from lack of food. At lunchtime, she asked Maru where Nikola was and Maru froze in mid-step. "You did not hear? Oh my, her house was bombed last night. Nikola was hit, Lanya. She was killed." Maru searched Lanya's face. Lanya froze too. Sweet Nikola with the giggles and sense of humor? She remembered when Nikola teased the foreman with a pretend sandwich last month and how mad he got when he realized it was not real, before he laughed. Sweet Nikola. Lanya felt the anger inside her. *Damn Germans.* They all deserved to be blown up, every single one of them. She hated them before but now she hated them even more. To take a soldier out at the front was different- they knew what was going on and they could defend themselves. But Nikola asleep in her bed? Lanya gritted her teeth and returned to her machine. She would stay late today for a while to do extra work to make up for Nikola. She would do more to defeat the damned Germans.

As she left the factory that evening, Lanya had a heavy gray cloud on her shoulders. Nothing felt good, nothing felt right. The sky was dark gray with night time coming soon. "Lanya" she heard from

a short distance. She looked up, and there in front of her was Ivan!
A warmth coursed through her heart. He was dressed in slacks and a
warm sweater with a long coat over it all. Lanya was tired of her baggy,
tired clothes. But Ivan was here! "Lanya" he stepped closer. "I wanted
to see you."

Lanya smiled and forgot her depression. "Ivan, I did not expect
to see you. How nice." He put his arm out and gave her a one arm hug
with a squeeze. Lanya liked that.

"Can I walk you home again? It has been a while since I saw you,
but I wanted to see you again."

"That would be nice, if you have time."

"I have time for you. How are you doing?" Lanya paused. Should
she tell him of Mikhail's return? Would he see it as too much effort
on her part and not want to come by? She decided to wait on that for
now.

"As well as can be expected I guess. How are you?" They walked
through the darkening night. Lanya wanted this to last.

"I am doing pretty well. An apartment near mine was hit last
time, but they are cleaning it up. Not having power is tough though."

"Yes, it is. We have some small oil lamps that are really old but
they work fine."

"That is nice. Maybe I should get some." Lanya wondered if he
was going to bring up the tryout he offered but was too scared to ask. "I
went back to that theater where we met, and they have nothing going
for the next few months. So, I booked it!" Lanya stopped walking and
looked over at Ivan, who was grinning like a child.

"You what? Booked it?"

"Yes, I booked the theater. For three weeks of rehearsals and two
weeks of a show. Would you like to be in it?"

Part of Lanya was frozen to the ground and part of her was high
in the sky floating. "I would love to be!"

"Well, we will do a try out. Do you know anyone else who can
sing or act?" Lanya shook her head, no.

"Have you decided what show you will do?"

"I am still working on that. Maybe something with a patriotic
theme, that would be good now, wouldn't it? Not something down
or sad."

"That would be good. No one wants sad now, I agree." They had come to Lanya's corner and stopped.

"I will come back to see you in a few days when I have a schedule worked out and a few more people to audition. It is nice to see you, made me smile." He wrapped both arms around her for a quick hug. Lanya wanted to melt.

"It was good to see you, too, Ivan. Hope to see you again soon."

"Will do, Lanya." He turned and left. Lanya did not move and watched him walk. After a few moments, he stopped and turned back. He waved when he saw Lanya still there. Lanya did not need her coat, so she took it off and ran the last few steps into her apartment building.

Chapter Eleven

After a small dinner, Lanya went to her room. It was not really her room, she was reminded of Valentina every time she came in here. She had not touched her sister's things, so it was easy to feel she would be right back. Lanya put her eyes on her own bed. She wanted to think about Ivan. Who was he? Why was he here in Leningrad? Why didn't he leave? Why would someone want to be in such a city, with little food and bombings? Why wasn't he fighting? Because he was from Minsk maybe? Did he come here just to say he did a show in Leningrad? What kind of man was he? She was intrigued. He was exciting to be around. Did she want a boyfriend? Did he want a girlfriend, or was this all about the show for him? Were boyfriends even worth it? There were few men in town, since the army took almost all of them. So if she was looking for a man, there were few choices. Maru always had choices, Lanya not so much. But she had known young men before and enjoyed their company. None whom she wanted to keep, at least not yet. What would her mother say? Her mother would offer advice, usually before Lanya even asked, but there were some good nuggets there, Lanya remembered. Her mother always gave a bit of advice and a pat on the back. Would Lanya want Ivan as a boyfriend? It might take her mind off losing Valentina. Or Mishka's problems. Or the frequent bombings. If she did not let her heart get involved, it could be good. She smiled as she thought about this. Ivan could be a handsome diversion.

It took a week before Ivan returned. Lanya had been looking for him every day, and Maru even waited with her once. The snow was coming soon, rain had come yesterday and the air was crisp and cold.

Lanya remembered as a child the excitement of the first snow, how they made special treats and spent hours outside. Lanya was looking at the sky wondering if the snow would be tonight when she heard Ivan's voice, "Lanya".

She jerked her head to the side, irritated that she looked away. She would like to see him first for once! "Ivan, good to see you!" He was dressed in a sweater and his long coat again with leather gloves. Lanya had gloves, that Babu had crocheted for her years ago. Ivan reached out and took her hands and gave them a squeeze.

"You were looking up- are you searching? For planes?" The sky was nearly dark, so that would not be unexpected.

"No, I was wondering when the snow will begin. It is coming. It does not wait for winter here."

"Snow, this early? It is October."

"Yes, sometimes even in September in Leningrad."

"Well then, I have to get ready. I might need a new hat." He did not have one yet, and Lanya tried to picture him with one. "I have a date for a try out, would you like to hear?"

Lanya looked right at him, "Yes, oh yes!"

"Next week, on Thursday. At three in the afternoon. Here is the address." He handed her a small piece of paper that was neatly folded. "At a different theater, just for auditions. What are you going to sing?"

Lanya was dumbfounded and faltered. "Um, I do not, know." Her brain was racing. What should she sing?

Ivan took her hands again, "I cannot walk you home tonight. I have to go see about the auditions. Will I see you next Thursday?"

"Oh yes, of course." She was disappointed that he would not walk her home, but she knew he had things to do. Ivan reached to touch her cheek, then turned and walked off. Lanya could not move right away, but her feet finally broke from their roots and she began to walk towards her route. She was going to try out for a real show? Was she good enough? Everyone told her she was good. Were they just being nice? What if she did not make it? Would Ivan want to see her if she could not sing well? Or, she changed her direction, what if she did make it? What if she got into the show? Her feet were like wings now, and she hurried up the street. Songs came into her head and she hummed this and hummed that, searching for the one best song.

The air sirens went off as soon as she got home, so she and Babu guided Mishka into the shelter down the block. It was crowded but not too cold. They brought some snacks for dinner. This usually only lasted three hours until the all clear, and they huddled together in their own little spot. Lanya was singing in her head and hummed, too. Mishka looked at her when she hummed but did not join. Babu noticed but talked with another older lady, about how the rationing was going. Lanya was in her own world.

By breakfast, she was down to three songs, and wanted Maru's input. She walked to her apartment, and Maru was happy to see her. Lanya told her about the audition, about Ivan's short visit, and asked her to help her decide.

"You have to remind me which songs these are- you know them better than I do." Lanya went through the songs, and which shows they were from. "Sing a bit of each for me." Lanya sang the chorus of each and Maru was delighted with them. Maru liked the last one best, which was about a girl recovering from heartbreak. "That one! The last one!"

"Do you think my voice is right for it?"

"It's like it was written for you!" Lanya hugged Maru and hurried home, the song circling in her head. When she got home, she wrote out all the words, just to make sure she had them. Babu noticed her light mood and asked about it.

"Babu, I have an audition for a show! A man I met, at the theater a while back, is doing a show and asked me to try out! Maru said I should do this song." She sang the chorus but knew Babu would not know the song. And I am trying out next week!" Babu's eyes lit up and she smiled.

"You will do beautifully. Your voice is like an angel, and we could use some angels now." Lanya hugged Babu and went into her room to practice.

Sewing group on Wednesday night was better than it had been in a long while. They had quite a few oil lamps going so it was easier to see than nights with only candles. Today they were repairing parachutes that had been used and torn. Lanya spent most of the evening in her own head, singing until one of the older women announced that her daughter was in the hospital, after surviving a plane crash.

"Really? A woman on the plane?"

"Yes, she was the pilot!"

"Pilot? What?"

"Yes, there are many women pilots now. They have all been trained in the last few months. Stalin said train them and my daughter signed up. She loves flying!" The women were all caught up in this idea, that women could fly! "They are flying over German camps right outside town, dropping bombs on the Germans!" A hurrah went up as women paused in their sewing. "They have quiet planes and they shut off the engine and glide, and the Germans do not even know they are there! So they drop their bombs and come back quickly. She got shot at, but she will be okay in a few weeks. She wants to go again!"

"Such courage!"

"A hero!"

"Brave!"

"Crazy, I think!"

"The Germans," the mother now added "have a name for these women. 'Night witches!' Since they cannot hear them or see them at night, the Germans hate them!"

"Wow- wonderful!"

"Your daughter deserves a medal!"

They were universally thrilled that this young woman, Lanya's age, was bombing Germans. Lanya felt that she was not doing enough to hurt the Germans. So at the end of the night, she took extra parachute work home.

"I just want to do a bit more." Lidia gladly gave Lanya a bag full of more parachutes to be repaired. Lanya decided Babu would help. Anything to hurt these Germans.

At work, Lanya sang in her head. She worked on the range, the trills, the pacing. Walking to and from work, she sang out loud, stopping only when she saw someone nearby. In the apartment, she sang as she sewed, cooked or folded laundry. Mikhail looked at her but did not interrupt. When he was near, she sang songs he knew, from their childhood or radio songs he might recognize. He never let on that he was aware, but she thought it would not hurt.

Thursday morning came, and Lanya was petrified. Babu wished her well, but Lanya wanted Maru to help. She walked through the city to Maru's apartment building. The streets were not what they were six months ago. They were torn up and filled with potholes and rubble.

With the light snow, it was difficult to keep your footing. There was no ice yet, but that would come soon enough. But Lanya did not worry about that now. At Maru's house, Maru insisted she sing the whole song.

"The whole thing? Are you sure?"

"Yes, just like your tryout. You can do this." Maru was a gem. Lanya began, and her voice became like liquid silver as she reached full tone. The song poured out, filling the room and even the house. Maru's mom came to the door way and watched. As Lanya finished, she applauded. Maru jumped up and hugged her tightly.

"That was perfect! He will love you!"

"I hope so. I have done nothing else for the week, you know it."

"You got this, you will be in the show!"

"I hope so." Lanya repeated herself. But that was all she had.

"Now go on out, and do this. I am sure you will be on stage soon!"

Lanya turned to go and left the apartment. Was Maru being kind or did she really believe Lanya had a gift? Too late. Lanya walked quickly to the address she had, coiled tight as a spring. It was an older theater but rather run down. She found the door and went in. Dark inside but she went to where the lights were glowing. Ivan was there.

"Lanya! Good to see you. I am glad you are here. Are you ready?"

Lanya nodded, afraid her voice would break. She had a woolen scarf around her neck and she twisted it in her hands. She twisted it so tight her fingers were white.

"Take a minute to warm up while I check something." Ivan walked into another room and Lanya began her warm up, a scale and a chorus. She was too scared to sing loudly just yet. Ivan returned and sat in a wooden chair near the desk.

"As soon as you are ready. I am dying to hear this." He had a pencil in his hand and a notepad. Lanya wondered what he was going to write. He was alone, so Lanya knew he would make the decision. She looked at her shoes to gain strength. She began, this song she had been practicing for a week, and the words came out, like an angel. Her voice was clear, her range was perfect and she put the force into it that she had been saving. She imagined she was on a stage and raised her face to get the full extension of her throat. As she stopped, Ivan jumped out of his chair.

"That was fabulous! A dream! You are in the show for sure! Maru was right, you really can sing!" He crossed the room in three steps and put his arms around her. She was dazed, with the singing and his closeness. She moved to sit because she thought she might fall over. He went to his notepad and wrote for a minute and came back to her. "That was so very good! That song was the perfect piece for your voice. A perfect match. I do not know what part you will get, but you are in the show." Lanya recovered a bit and stood up.

"Thank you. I worked really hard on it.""It showed. Very well done." He went to show her out and she carefully followed. She was still a bit light headed. They got to the door, and Ivan said, "I have other auditions all day today. I will see you soon."

"Thank you, Ivan." Lanya turned to go, but he put his hands on her arm and pulled her to him. His lips came down hard on her lips and she trembled and was glad the door was right behind her. The kiss was quick but powerful. Ivan turned and walked back into the theater. Lanya would have fallen over if she was not leaning. It took a minute to get her thoughts and feet together, but she was able to walk after a moment. She walked home in the cool air, singing in her head, but this was a different song. Something about kisses and hopes. She got home so fast she hardly remembered the walk. Babu saw her as soon as she came in and without a word, questioned Lanya with her knowing eyes. She raised her eyebrows and Lanya burst out "He loved it! I have a part!"

Babu came and gave her a squeeze with a huge smile. "Of course. I am glad for you. I am glad he could tell what a gift you have." Lanya sank into a kitchen chair and her heart glowed. How much from the tryout and how much from the kiss? It did not matter.

Chapter Twelve

The next day, just past noon, there was a solid knock on the front door. Lanya looked at Babu, who raised her eyebrows but did not get out of her chair. The little dog yipped and moved towards the door. Lanya followed, thinking it was probably Maru coming to visit. She opened the door to see two young men in uniform, dirty and unkempt who looked eager to see her.

"Is this the home of Mikhail Zhukanov?" asked the smaller of the two, who had dark hair and a quick grin. Lanya hesitated and looked back at Babu.

"Yes, why?" Lanya wondered what was going on. Was the Party coming to check on him? Did they not believe his ration card was real?

"We know him, from the front" the man continued. "My name is Aleksander Sidorov and this" he pushed his friend closer to the door, "is Boris Vasiliev. We were with Mikhail when the bomb blew up. Can we see him?" Lanya was scared. Was this real? Were these men really with him. They saw she was hesitant and Boris spoke up.

"We were next to him. We saw it all happen." Boris was a bit bigger than Aleksander with a ruddy face and dark blond hair. His arms were thick and covered in blond fuzz..

Babu called Lanya, who told her to invite them in. Lanya waved her arm to invite them in. They crowded through the door.

"How is he? Did he recover?" Aleksander seemed concerned for his friend. Lanya waved them to chairs.

"He is healthy." She said guardedly.

"But how is he?" Boris butted in, anxious for an answer. Babu got up and caught Lanya's eye. What was she up to? She nodded her head towards Mishka's room. Lanya gave a slight nod but was not sure what would happen.

"He has problems. He does not talk. He cannot understand simple things. We do not know what is wrong. We do not think a doctor would help." The men were quiet, unsure of how to respond. There really was no right response. A sound came from behind and Lanya jumped out of her chair. The men jumped up, too.

Lanya moved towards Babu, who was leading Mishka. She looked confident that he would be calm. Aleksander and Boris moved towards him, happy to see him up and about.

"Mikhail!"

"Brother!" They moved towards him, their arms reaching for him. Mishka recoiled a bit. They moved closer.

"How are you?" A clap on the arm from Boris.

"Good to see you!" An attempt of an embrace from Aleksander. Mishka pulled back, raising his arms in defense. A loud moan came from him and he swung his arms around him as he seemed to fight back. Boris and Aleksander backed off, alarmed. Mishka turned and bolted back to his bedroom, with a moan that came from down low.

Lanya was thunderstruck. She did not expect this. She was embarrassed. They only wanted to greet him with a hug.

"I am so sorry. I did not know he would do that. He has not seen many people since he came home." She felt bad that he was so damaged. Her poor brother.

"No, I am sorry. We should have handled that differently. He does not remember us and has no idea what we were doing." Aleksander put his hand on Lanya's arm, trying to soothe her.

"He is pretty bad." Boris sounded disturbed by what he had just seen. He was acting like a caged animal.

Aleksander moved to get his coat from the back of the chair, and Boris did the same.

"I am sorry we bothered him. You were good to let us in. Maybe we can come back in a few weeks and see if there is a difference. Would that be okay with you?" Aleksander sounded like a gentle soul.

"Yes, yes, that might be good." Lanya was not sure what had really happened or how to work on it. They moved to the door, Boris opened it and turned back.

"I hope he gets better. We saw it all. We were such great comrades at the front."

"Maybe he needs more time. I heard that sometimes it is all that is needed. We will see you again, I hope?" Aleksander looked at Lanya as he went through the door. She looked up into his eyes, and Boris was already walking down the hall.

"I hope so. Thank you for coming by. Maybe he will get better." Aleksander left with those kind words.

Lanya turned to go back into the apartment and shut the front door. She sank into the nearest chair, feeling exhausted. What just happened? Was Mishka okay? She was glad he did not hurt anyone. Babu came back in the room.

"He is alright. He settled down on the bed. He will not remember this tomorrow."

"What happened?"

"I am not sure, but I think they were too much for him. Maybe he cannot handle things that are different or loud."

"Yes, they were loud and boisterous. Not what we see here. But I think they meant well, don't you?"

"Yes, they probably did. They are not used to things that are quiet and calm."

"They said they may come back in a few weeks. Will that be a good idea?" Lanya did not want to see a repeat of this.

"Yes, I think they saw what they did wrong. Maybe if they came one at a time it would be better."

"Yes, that might be better." Lanya got up from her chair and went to check on Mishka. He was asleep, looking peaceful and perfect. A tear graced her eyelashes. Her wonderful brother was reduced to a child. Her heart broke a bit more, if that was possible.

Work went by slowly. The factory was usually cold and Lanya knew it would get worse as winter came. Without lights it was dark so they only worked mid-day. It was getting tough to get the leather needed for the boots. Now and then, they had something else to sew but boots were still the main product. Every day as Lanya left the factory, she looked for Ivan. Snow and wind kept her from staying long, but she did a quick look up and down the street, with her hopes high. On the fourth work day, there he was, looking dashing and dapper. He did have on a new hat, with fur on the edges. He had on a

longer coat and a scarf, ready for winter. Lanya rushed across the street
to him and he held out his hands to welcome her.

"Ivan, so good to see you!"

"Lanya, the same. How are you?"

"I am okay but a bit tired. We are using the hand crank machines
and my arms get really tired each day."

"Oh my, that sounds tough. No power at the factory either?"

"No, it has been off for a few weeks. They said it will come back,
but who knows. How are you?"

"I am good, adjusting to this cold. Can I take you to dinner
tomorrow?"

Lanya faltered. Tomorrow? She had no plans. Were there any
restaurants open?

"I will pick you up at your house, and take you out. Will six
work?"

"Sure, that sounds nice, Sorry, I was thinking about something."

"I cannot stay tonight, but I wanted to see you and ask
about tomorrow. What is your address?" He took out a small paper
and pen and prepared to write. She gave him her address but worried
about Mishka. Would he react? Hopefully, if Ivan was not there long,
Mishka would not even come out of his bedroom. They separated and
Lanya could not help but be excited. A dinner with Ivan! She pulled
her woolen hat down over her straight hair and hurried home.

Ivan showed up at six, looking sharp as always in a dark sweater
and a long brown coat. He did not have that haggard look from lack
of food that everyone else had. Maybe he found a better way? Lanya
welcomed him in, and Babu was right there in the front room.

"Ivan this is my grandmother, we call her Babu." He leaned
forward and tipped his hat at her.

"A pleasure to meet you. You must be so proud of Lanya. She
will be in the show."

"We are very proud of her. Her singing lifts us up."

"I can see that! Her audition was superb!" Lanya moved in to
break this up, she wanted to get him alone.

"We will be home before too late Babu." Babu made a noise that
was not really a word. She did that often Lanya usually understood
them. As they got to the street, Ivan took Lanya's gloved hand as they

went down the street. She could feel the warmth in her fingers spread to her arms. This was exciting!

They came to a restaurant that was mostly concealed because of the blackout. Ivan knew the place. They were seated and Ivan ordered a bottle of wine. The menu was severely limited so it was written by hand on paper. Lanya chose sausage and Ivan decided on fish. Lanya had to focus on her conversation, she was so excited about this dinner and the show. She asked about when auditions would be complete, where the show would be, what show it would be and when rehearsals would start.

"Hey there, slow down! I just want to have a nice dinner with a pretty girl! I am still working on all that but when I am sure, I will tell you!" Lanya felt childish, barraging him with questions, but these questions had been running around her brain for days and she was hoping for answers! The food arrived and the portions were tiny as expected. The bread brought to the table was dark and not very soft. Lanya still was happy to be eating something that was not cabbage, herring, or rusks, so she did not say anything.

They left the restaurant and the street was absolutely black, as was necessary. There was a small moon so they could walk the street without stumbling. As they got to Lanya's apartment, Ivan slowed down and brought her into his arms. "Lanya, this has been very nice, as I hoped. Thank you for this. It is hard to find nice times during a war like this. Thank you." With that, he brought her closer and kissed her deeply. She struggled to breathe but did not want it to stop. When the kiss ended, she worked to put her feet back on the sidewalk.

"Thank you, Ivan. I have enjoyed myself. You are right, it is hard to find a nice time now." He gave her one more quick kiss and sent her up the stairs. She was floating.

She came into the apartment and Babu was on a chair in the kitchen. Lanya came in, and Babu was all eyes.

"Did you have a nice time?" From Babu's flat voice, Lanya knew something was not quite right.

"Yes, we went to a little place not far from here. They did not have much. I have baked sausage and Ivan had fried cod."

"Nice. Will you see him again?"

"Of course- he is the producer of the show so I will see him often. Why, Babu?" Babu did not normally get involved in Lanya's dating.

"Something about him is not good. He will cause problems. I feel it."

"Oh Babu, that is silly. You always believe the worst. Goodnight." Lanya left the kitchen without any worries. Babu was just old and forgot what it was like to have a man interested. Silly old woman. Though her gut feelings had been right, more than once. Lanya settled into bed feeling warm and content. She tried not to think about Babu's warning. Lanya could not see anything wrong with Ivan. Nothing. And the kiss made up for a lot of problems. How could a kiss from a handsome man cause problems? Lanya realized she did not think about bombs or boots or ration cards when she was with him. Maybe he was magic?

Chapter Thirteen

Lanya loved Leningrad, even in war. What other city could brag so much? What other city was created out of marshes by a tsar, and was home to the most beautiful, cultured people? What other city could claim the beauty of canals and homes that were like royal palaces? What other city could boast of scientific institutes and museums? What other city was where the arts were like the lifeblood of the people? Where writers and poets flocked? Even now, in this area of bombings and starvation, poems were being written and symphonies composed. What other city could compare?

Lanya tried to remember this as she hurried to work on this cold morning in the beginning of November. The skies were gray and there was snow here and there. The ground was not yet frozen and the river was flowing so it was not that bad. February was usually the worst and that was a long way off.

Maru caught her before she sat down at her machine.

"Lanya, I have a date tonight!" Lanya looked up to see Maru grinning like a child with their fingers in the cookie jar.

"Really? With whom?"

"Leonid, of course. No one else is around now." Her mouth turned down a bit. "I had a drink with him last week. This time we are going to dinner."

"Nice! A few restaurants are open." Lanya knew they were usually filled with Party officials. "Anything else?" Lanya gave her a side eye, wondering what might be in Maru's plan.

"I am not sure. He is cute, don't you think? And he likes me."

"Yes, he does, You are a lucky girl!" Lanya was a bit envious, as she often was with Maru's love life. Though her own budding relationship with Ivan was worth a smile.

"Who knows?" Again, the grin.

"Tell me everything!"

"You know I will!" They hurried off to their separate areas to start work. Lanya was excited for Maru. Maru liked to have men around and usually found one. Work went slowly and Lanya was getting better at the hand crank machines though she missed the power ones. She could get so much more done with electricity. Every few days, the suits from the Party came through the factory. Lanya tried to ignore them and become invisible. She had never attracted attention, keeping her eyes on her materials and machine. Today, as usual there was no problem, but with her family history, Lanya knew it could change at any time.

As Lanya left the factory for home, she saw Ivan waiting. Her heart skipped a beat and she smiled. It was good to see him again and her hopes were high. What was up today?

"Ivan." She greeted him first like she wanted to. It made her smile.

"Lovely Lanya." A quick hug that warmed her more than it should. "I only have a minute. I scheduled rehearsals, are you sure you want to do this?" Lanya's heart went through the roof.

"Oh yes, more than anything!"

"Well we start at six pm next Tuesday at the Mariinsky Theater, where we met. Will you be there?"

"Even a war would not keep me away!" Ivan turned to go, then came back for another hug. This one was slow and promising.

"See you Tuesday, beautiful girl. Keep that voice warmed up!"

"Goodbye Ivan. Thanks for coming by." Ivan turned and walked quickly into the evening air. Lanya watched him walk. It was smooth and confident. Would she ever have such confidence? She quickly set out for home. Babu would want to know!

At her sewing group, another woman was missing. She was alive but too weak to come. The lack of food was taking its toll. There was talk about what they were putting in the flour but Lanya did not want to know. Another woman brought up an announcement from the Party today that seemed hopeful.

"I heard this today. Stalin said it in July, but they repeated it today and it stayed with me. He said 'History shows that there are no invincible armies.' So we can be sure that even the Germans cannot last forever. We will win."

"Oh yes."

"I hope so. This is hard."

"I wish it was over already."

"Our army is good, so I want this to be done." All the women agreed on this, that the Germans could not last forever. Lanya left feeling a bit bolstered, and that there might be light at the end of this dark tunnel.

The first rehearsal was a whirlwind. Lanya met Andre, the director, who was a small man with a limp, which would explain why he was still in town. There were fifteen people clustered around, waiting to hear their roles and get scripts. No one was familiar, so she was just part of the crowd. Were they all singing parts? She did not see Ivan anywhere. Where was he? Andre cleared a path and with a stack of papers, and he got everyone quiet.

"Here we go. I will read your name and your spot. Take your script; look it over. If you have any questions, ask someone else before you ask me. You will be expected to memorize these by next Tuesday...you have a week. The orchestra will join us in two weeks. They are working on their own for now. Ready?" The tension was tight. Lanya realized she was holding her breath. Did she have the lead? Andre read names and titles, finally getting to Lanya. She grabbed her script and quickly thumbed through it. Not the lead! She had a good part, quite a few songs, but she was not the major role. Her heart crumbled. Ivan did say she might get it, not a guarantee. For a moment, she considered walking out. But then she reconsidered-this was a professional stage role! She calmed herself and decided to stay. This was a dream. Andre came up to her when he was done and handed her a second script.

"Svetlana, I have not heard you sing but Ivan raved about you. I want you to be the understudy for Natalya the lead. Do you know what this means?" He handed her a second script. Lanya shook her head. "This means that you learn her role, and if something happens and she is not here, you will play lead. It is important, so you must learn two roles. Can you do this?" Lanya was shaking. Two roles? Was this because she was good? She nodded her head but did not look Andre in the eye. She was so mixed up!

In a corner, Lanya looked at the script. This story was good, it was about a small-town girl who goes to Moscow to make it herself known. She has trials, but the Party recognizes her work and she moves up. It would go over well. The Party would approve. *Good call Ivan*, she thought. She did a quick search for him again but he was nowhere to be seen. Andre was running the show. After an hour, Andre told them to go home and come back Thursday night, then Friday. Three days of rehearsal each week. Three weeks of rehearsal then the show would happen in late November. With that realization, Lanya's heart again fluttered. She would be singing on stage in three weeks? A dream come true!

Babu and Mishka were asleep when she got home, but she probably would not sleep easily with all the excitement of the show. She made some of the soothing chamomile tea and sipped it at the table. She read the script, her role and the lead. She did not read music but the lyrics were simple and rhymed some so they would be easy to learn. Lanya was comfortable with the whole thing. Even without the lead, she could do this.

Ivan met her after work the next day. He greeted her with a big hug and a kiss on her forehead.

"I heard from Andre that the rehearsal went well. How do you feel?" Lanya was not sure how to respond. She wanted the lead, but was happy to be included. She decided to go neutral.

"It is a lot to learn and there is a lot of energy there. Will you be there next time?"

"Yes, I had something come up. I will be there and would love to hear to hear you sing again." Lanya nodded. Ivan came closer and put his hand on her arm. "Lanya, would you like to have dinner again?" He could see the warm glow in Lanya's eyes. She turned her head to look closely at his face. "At my apartment. I will cook for you." Lanya caught her breath, and her lips parted in a smile. "We have rehearsal for the next two nights. Saturday?"

"I would like that." Lanya smiled a bigger smile as Ivan wrapped her in a hug and kissed her forehead.

"I have to go now. See you tomorrow." Ivan turned and left, leaving Lanya unable to keep her feet on the ground.

Rehearsal on Thursday was more collected, with Andre telling people where to be, Ivan in the back, and Lanya going where she was told. The songs were coming along, and the lead Natalya did have a wonderful voice. Andre made sure to tell everyone where the air raid shelter was in case a bombing happened while they were there. Lanya hoped that would not happen. She almost liked her own shelter since she knew the people there now. She had some of her lines learned and was still working on the rest. She sang along with the cast on three shows and had one duet. She was beginning to feel like she was part of something and enjoyed the camaraderie of it all. At the end of the night she looked for Ivan but did not see him so she walked home quickly.

Friday rehearsal was the same with Andre yelling at people who did not know their lines and pushing people here and there with the blocking, trying to fill the stage during the songs. Without power, the theater would be lit by special oil lamps and candles, just like from a hundred years before. Lanya thought that could be fun. She saw Ivan, but he did not go out of his way to talk to her. He was almost distant. She wondered if it was because he was so busy. She watched him when she could. Did he spend too long talking to the lead girl? Was there something there? Lanya tried to push away a pang of jealousy.

Saturday came and Lanya was excited. Ivan was going to fix dinner at his apartment. Would there be more? Lanya could feel the tingles on the back of her neck as she thought about this. A few kisses did not mean more. But at his apartment? Lanya had been with a boyfriend here and there but nothing too serious. Mikhail always seemed to be watching over her. But he wouldn't now. Ivan said he would pick her up at six and she was ready early. Babu knew something was going on since Lanya had washed her hair and put makeup on.

"I am having dinner again with Ivan. We have a lot to talk about with the show." Lanya did not explain more, there was no need. Ivan knocked on the door at three minutes before, Lanya quickly said good bye and they rushed off. Babu could see what was coming. Babu always seemed to know things.

As they walked down the dark streets, Ivan held her hand lightly. They talked about the cast, the songs and the show in general. Lanya wanted to ask questions about his home but did not want to pry.

They came to a gray apartment block that had not been hit. Many had but somehow this one was still sound. They went upstairs and Ivan opened the door.

"I live alone here. Leonid may join me soon, but not yet. So tonight, its just us." He slid Lanya's coat off her shoulders and took her in his arms. He kissed her in a way that was filled with longing.

"I need to finish up in the kitchen, come on in." As she went in, Lanya looked around. Two chairs, a small sofa, and a few tables were all the furniture he had. A small figurine here, a simple postcard in a frame. Nothing too personal, like any man would have.

In the kitchen, a pot was cooking at the back of the stove, Lanya could smell onions. Ivan was opening the oven and putting in rolls! How did he get rolls? Flour was hard to get!

"I have been saving flour for weeks so I could do this for us. I wanted you here a long time ago." There was something else on the stove but Lanya could not tell what. It had been a long time since she'd a full meal. This would be wonderful!

When it all came together, they sat down to a meal that Lanya loved, fresh warm rolls, but without butter, klopse meatballs, with a sauce made of sauteed onions and a bottle of wine.

"The klopse do not have much meat in them, sorry. Mostly beans I am afraid. And the wine came from a trade I made with a neighbor." That explained it. Meat was almost unheard of except for fish from the Neva. The food went down well and Lanya felt spoiled. They did not talk much during dinner, but Lanya wanted to hurry, in anticipation.

As they finished, they moved the plates to the sink and Ivan again took her in his arms. "Lanya, lovely Lanya, I want you. I have wanted you since we first met. I love the look of you, your sweet face. So innocent. It has been hard not to rush you. I told Leonid to stay away, he can have your friend, I wanted you. Do you want me?" His hands were on her back and her shoulders and she could feel the warmth of them. Of course she wanted him! She did not talk, but kissed him back with passion. "Let's go." He grabbed her hand and led her out of the kitchen into his bedroom, where the oil lamp was already burning. It was not much light, but enough to see what was going on. His hands moved again and Lanya put up no resistance and went right along. The kissing and the stroking went on, and soon they were undressed and toppling onto the bed. Lanya got lost into the moment and did not think again for some time.

Lanya woke up and looked around, wondering where she was. Then Ivan moved and touched her arm and she remembered. She had a warm glow in the cool room. But she needed to get home. Babu would be upset if she did not return. So she began to get up and gather her clothes. She quickly dressed and saw Ivan lying there unmoving. She tried not to wake him. When she was dressed, she went to get her coat and came back.

"Lanya, do not go. I want you here."

"Ivan, I need to go. My grandmother will be upset if I do not come home She is a worrier."

"I would love to have you come back soon."

"I think that could happen. Thank you, Ivan for a fantastic night, the dinner, your time. I am glad you asked."

"See you soon lovely." Lanya walked out and slipped out the front door. Her brain was singing songs as she walked home, thrilled that Ivan wanted her. Even in her thin, frazzled shape, he wanted her. She had to work hard to not take this too far. *This does not mean marriage and babies, calm down.* She had to tell Maru! At work, she would.

Chapter Fourteen

It was clear to Lanya, and everyone else, that this war would not be short. Earlier they had said it would be over before Christmas, but that was unlikely. The Germans surrounded the city and bombed it at least once a week. She did not know how it went in the rest of the Soviet Union; all she had to go on was the announcements over the loudspeakers every day. And those came from the Party, so no one believed them completely.

At lunchtime, she told Maru about her night with Ivan.

"Really? He did? Dinner? And then?" Maru was almost as excited as Lanya.

"Dinner was meatballs made of beans and rolls. Dessert was, well I told you!"

"Lucky Lanya! We have not said that in a while!"

"Yes, I feel lucky. I am not sure if it will affect the show; he hardly notices me at the theater. I don't know why he is not at the front, but I am pretty happy now!"

"Yes, neither of us feels truly attractive but you still got it girl!" They split and went to their machines, and Lanya felt like she was glowing. Could anyone else tell?

Later that week, on her way to work, she pondered the things that Babu had said a while back. *What would happen if the Germans took over the city? Would it be awful? Would they bring food? Would they turn the power back on? Would the men who left come back? Would living under the Nazis be so different? Would they kill people straight up?* The thoughts were repulsive. The Germans killed her sister and ruined her brother. She would never quietly live under Nazis. She would die to be rid of them. As she thought that, she hoped it would not happen. She wanted to sing. And see Ivan again.

She saw Ivan at rehearsal on Thursday. She hoped he would take her in his arms again but he was busy with other people. She was doing well with her lines and the songs were good so she was sure she was in the right place. She liked the other cast members, though she was not crazy about the lead girl Natalya. Once, she saw her talking to Ivan. A pang of jealousy shot through her. She needed to see what was here. Ivan owed her nothing. But Natalya was still a bitch. She tried to catch Ivan once or twice, but he quickly turned away. At the end of the night, she stayed late, on purpose, so he could not get away. Everyone else was gone.

"Lanya, why are you still here? You should have left."

"I wanted to see you. You have been busy all night."

"Um yes. I like what we did Lanya, I really did, but I do not want anyone here to know about it. They would talk and they would say ugly things about you. Or me. You got this role because you can sing, not because of something between us. They would say otherwise." Lanya heard this, and her heart fell into her stomach. She wanted the world to know! But, as she thought, she knew he was probably right. They would talk. And it would be catty.

"You are right. I did not think of that. Goodnight Ivan." He came over at that point and gave her a tight hug and kiss. Since no one else was there, why not?

"They can't see that!" he said with a twinkle in his eye. He turned to go into the office and she went out the door.

Her worries were getting the best of her. She asked herself the same questions over and over in different forms. *What did she want? Did she want Ivan? Or just anyone who could make her feel desirable? Would he have cast her if she was married, or older, or heavy?* She knew her voice was good, but was it good enough? *Did he only put her in the show hoping to get her into his bed?* Was time the only way to answer these questions? *And what about him? Why was he here in Leningrad, living a much easier life than the men at the front? Was there more?* She enjoyed herself, so maybe it was enough. And no matter what happened, this was experience that she did not have before.

By the time she got home, the questions in her head had exhausted her and she quickly climbed into bed. Sleep came quickly, but the nightmares did too. It had been a few weeks since she'd had them. It wasn't always the same thing. Some people saw the same nightmares over and over. Being chased, on fire, being shot. No, hers were random, but she was always an inch from death, screaming when she woke up. Tonight, she woke up with her covers clenched in her hands and Mikhail was standing there, as he used to. He put his hand on her arm but did not say a word. Lanya was comforted anyway. It was good to have him come in. Babu had learned to sleep through it. Maybe he understood more than she knew. Mikhail left as soon as he saw she was calm, and she said a quick good night as he left.

Rehearsals in the next week went quickly. Ivan was friendly but not too much. He did not invite her over again. She was a bit lost. At home, there was an air raid on Wednesday so she did not go to sewing circle. This was not the biggest one, and it did not feel as if the bombs were right on top of them this time. A relief.

Maru had updates about Leonid. They had a date, and things were going along but they were interrupted. No intimacy yet, but Lanya knew it would come. But she loved hearing Lanya's story about Ivan.

"He has not asked me back yet but I think he will. I hope this grows. Don't you?"

"I hope he can see what a treasure you are!"

October faded, and the bombings continued. Another empty machine at work. Rations were cut again. Lanya was beginning to feel weaker every morning. Her skirts were very loose and she was wearing a belt now. How long could this go on? She was not sure she wanted to know the answer.

At rehearsal, Andre was tense, He yelled at everybody.

"Don't you realize we are live next week? Next week?" Lanya worked hard to be perfect but the stress of it caught her now and then and Andre even yelled at her. Why didn't Ivan tell him to ease up? Ivan came and went. Lanya tried to smile when she saw him and he sometimes smiled back. At the end of the rehearsal, he caught her in a corner.

"I have missed you. Can you come back tomorrow?" Lanya looked up and saw the need in his eyes.

"Yes, I would like that. Five o'clock?"

"Yes, that will be good. I am not making dinner, so eat first if you can. You will be dessert!" His arm went around her waist quickly and he placed a kiss on her temple before rushing away. Lanya felt her heart go straight up into the stage lights! *He wants me back*! She would not miss it!

Five o'clock did not come fast enough. Lanya went from room to room checking the time. Babu watched her but did not say a word. Finally she left, bundled up but warm on the inside. When she got to Ivan's door, she was early by fifteen minutes. He was thrilled to see her.

"I am so glad to see you! This show is making me crazy!" He wrapped her in a big hug before he even closed the door.

"I am glad to be here. I have been hoping for this for a week!" They kissed, and both knew exactly where this was going. No worry about food or formalities. They were quickly in the bedroom and undressed. His hands were everywhere and Lanya reciprocated. It was over quickly and Lanya wondered if she should have done something different, but Ivan explained.

"Sorry, I was in a hurry. I missed you so much it was too quick. But do not worry, give me a few minutes and we can start over." He kissed her again and her concerns evaporated. She felt beautiful. At this minute, she felt worthwhile and valuable. *Do not think too much* she told herself. *Just stay calm*. She knew her brain would go racing but she did not want that. She should have brought some vodka. Next time, we will warm up with a few shots. She was glad vodka was not rationed!

They had some time and true to his word, Ivan had more duration the next time. Lanya acted brazen but she ate it all up. As she got up to go, she glanced around his bedroom. A bed, a small dresser and an armoire. Papers here and there, with a book on top. Ivan fell asleep and she quietly dressed and snuck out of his room. She let herself out of the apartment and went out onto the street. She faced the cold night and a thought came in *I forgot to ask him why he is not at the front. Oh well, we did not do much talking tonight*, she remembered with a smile.

She got home after a brisk walk and the apartment was quiet. She got into her own bed and knew things were good for her. Except for this war, she was fine. She was on stage and had a man. Then she saw her sister's empty bed and the bubble burst. The weight was back on her chest and her heart was heavy. She felt guilty just thinking that she was fine. Tears came in and she did not try to stop them. *Damn Germans*!

Opening night was a thrill. Lanya was a bundle of nerves and could hardly speak. The other cast members were, too. Natalya seemed calm, but she had been in a show before. Lanya hated her a bit more for that. The theater was almost full, and Ivan came out to explain in case of a drill where the shelter was. The crowd nodded grimly. With that, the stage candles were lit, the orchestra began and the show was on! The singing was fantastic, Lanya and the whole cast gave it all they had. Lanya sang with real purpose and real passion. She sounded good, like she was born to this. She was in her right place at the right time along with the others. The applause warmed her veins. Intermission had Andre crowing about how well they were doing.

"Fantastic, on cue, in tune! Good job!" Ivan was at the back, watching everything. The second half went just as well, and Lanya knew this was her dream. One of the men slipped up but Lanya covered for him, and he sent her a sly smile as thanks. She wanted this forever. When the curtain finally came down, the applause went on and on. The cast hugged and squealed and all came together on the stage. The applause went on, and the curtain came back up. They bowed as a group and the lead bowed separately, and the curtain came down again. The applause died slowly and the first show was over. Lanya was exhausted but fulfilled.

As she was in the dressing room taking off her makeup and changing clothes, Ivan came in.

"How do you feel? You did a fabulous job tonight." She smiled at him.

"I feel good. Tired, though. I did not know it would wear me out."

"Yes, that it does. Two more nights this week. If the theater stays full, we can extend a week. Would you like that?"

"Yes, of course. Would you?" she asked while her brain was saying *I would do this every day if I could!*

"Yes, it is a great honor to extend. It means things are going well."

"Great. I enjoy this so much."

"I am glad. I knew you would. You were born for this." He came into the room with a small notebook in his hand. "Can I put this here?"

'Sure, just over there by my shoes." He put the notebook by her shoes and patted her on the shoulder.

"See you tomorrow, beautiful."

"Yes, see you tomorrow Ivan." He left and she finished cleaning and clearing, wondering what the notebook was. Other people came and went as they changed their clothes, and all were jubilant over the success of the show. Lanya got her things and left the theater. She looked back on the cast doorway as she left thinking about how she loved this show.

Babu was waiting up when Lanya gone home though it was long past her bedtime. As soon as Lanya opened the door, Babu rushed to greet her.

"How did it go? Did you sing well? Did they love you?"

"Babu, it was perfect! Everything I have dreamed about! I sang well, and so did everyone. We got an encore, they clapped and clapped! I loved it Babu!" Lanya gave her grandmother a hug and did not want to let go. Babu had always believed in her.

"Great, of course you did well. When is the show over?"

"We have two more weeks, then maybe more if the theater stays full. We could be extended."

"Oh, that is good. I hope you get extended then. I am going to bed now but I needed to know how it went!" Babu shuffled off to her room.

Lanya knew that sleep would not come quickly so she made some chamomile tea and sat at the kitchen table, reflecting on her day. The show was everything she wanted, the applause was magic to her ears, and Ivan came to see her. *This is the life I want*, she thought. *If I could be on stage I would not need to be making boots.*

The second show, the next night was the same, but Maru was in the audience. After the show Maru rushed into Lanya's changing room and gave her a bear hug.

"You were wonderful! The best! Your voice was better than any! I love you!" Lanya was touched by her biggest cheerleader.

"Thank you, it went well. I am happy with it. Did you see Ivan?"

"Not yet. I am here with Leonid, and we are going for a drink after. Maybe more... is Ivan around? If I cannot find him, Leonid will."

"He is around somewhere."

"Lanya, this is what you were born to do!" Maru turned to go.

"I hope so!" Lanya let her out and began changing. This still felt so good. She looked at her shoes and saw Ivan's notebook. She wanted to look at it. She picked it up and turned it over. It was a small notebook, not much bigger than her hand, with a plain cover. Inside, she saw words but no pictures. Words. She looked them over. Some were in Russian, but they made no sense. Were these real sentences? Some were not in Russian. It was not the Russian alphabet, but the Western one. Was it German? Polish? French? Lanya had never seen any other languages so she could not identify which language it was. She heard a noise and jumped, quickly tucking the notebook back where it had been. It was Ivan, coming in, with a broad smile on his face.

"Lanya, you were fantastic, again. I just saw Leonid and Maru, they are going for a drink. Would you like to go?" Lanya knew they did not want others around.

"No, not tonight. I am a bit tired, so I am going home. This wears me out."

"Oh, okay. I am not sure I want to go either. I will see you for tomorrow's show, Lanya. Goodnight beautiful." Ivan turned to go, but stopped and came back for the notebook. "Do not want to leave this." He left the room. Lanya was glad she was not looking at it when he came in, but glad she had taken a peak at it a moment ago. What did it mean? Jumbled words and other languages? Lanya was too tired to think much about it. She gathered her things and started home.

Babu was not up, but Lanya again made some tea. She knew she would not be up long. Being on stage was exhausting, because she put so much energy into every move and song. Sleep would come quickly tonight.

The nightmares started almost immediately. Lanya's head hit the pillow but the banging in her head started quickly with bombs going off and blasts of light had Lanya in her dream running for cover. Valentina was there too, and Lanya grabbed her hand to pull her to safety. But Valentina's hand dissolved and Lanya could not hold on. The bombs kept coming and Lanya woke up with a scream, feeling like the next sound would blow her to bits. She had sweat on her forehead. She lay still afraid to move. Slowly she began to breathe, unsure of what was going on. Nothing was going on she realized as she carefully inhaled and exhaled. Nothing going on. Another bad dream. Lanya tried to remember the last time she had a good dream, pleasant and pretty. She could not think of one. Certainly none in the last few months. These nightmares always woke her up. The tea did not stop the nightmares. It did help her relax, but did not stop the nightmares. Lanya rolled over and started singing in her head, to distract her from the ugly war scenes she could not get away from.

Chapter Fifteen

November rolled on with gray sleet and a brisk wind. The days were short and Lanya really missed the street lights that lit her way home after work. But she knew this route well so she was not confused. How long could this war go on? She remembered that every winter she yearned for long warm days, walking along the harbor. Winter always felt longer than just a few months. Tonight was sewing group and then three more nights of the show this week.

At sewing group, things were quiet. They sat down near an oil lamp and picked up their needles. Tonight, they were repairing sleeping bags. These were so dirty. Lanya went with another woman to the other room to wipe them with towels and clean them a bit before repairs were made. As Lanya touched them, she wondered who had slept in them and if they would they want them back? Or were they gone, in worse shape than the bag? This made the war so real. Almost personal. Mishka had slept in one of these, and his friends Boris and Aleksander. Her heart was heavy as she wiped.

The show on Thursday opened with a full theater, and Lanya loved the applause. The cast was friendly, one older man was being a bit more than just friendly but Lanya brushed him off, he was old enough to be her father. She did not want any complications. She did not have any agreement with Ivan, but she did not need anyone else involved. Ivan was friendly but not obvious. Lanya worried that she was just a "when I have a need" thing. That did not feel good, but it was okay for now. Maybe that is how she should feel about him, too.

There was no encore tonight, but the crowd did love them. Lanya wished Babu could come to see her, but she was not getting around very well lately. Lanya was not sure how old her grandmother was, but her age and her size and the cold kept her home. Lanya knew she would have to start doing the shopping and ration card renewals. She had time. At the factory they were only working during the brightest parts of the day, since there was no power for seeing the work.

In bed, Lanya tossed and turned, a lot of things rumbling inside her head. Mikhail and his disability. When would he "come back"? Ever? Would Lanya have to care for him into his old age? Would he ever be able to marry and have kids? Would he ever be a welder again? And Babu, would she make it through this winter? She was moving slowly but did get around. But winters were tough, and food was hard to get. They got enough to survive but not to thrive. Everyone was looking gaunt. And Ivan. Lanya knew she had churned this one over many times. Would they have more than occasional visits? Would it be more than physical? Would he help her to go on and do more shows? Or was this almost over? Would it end when the show ended? Would he ever have to go fight? With little food, intimacy was not a priority as it could be in peaceful times. These ideas went round and round until Lanya finally succumbed to sleep.

At the theater on Friday, Lanya was met by a rushed and irritated Andre.

"Lanya- you are it tonight. That worthless Natalya did not show, so you are the lead! Get ready!" Lanya caught her breath. She was lead tonight? Could she do it? She went into her dressing room and spent a few minutes hoping to be alone. The songs, the blocking, the costume. She could do this. Cast members went in and out and a few tried to speak to her but she focused on her show. When the curtain rose, Lanya was as ready as she could be. The songs came easily, the blocking needed a bit of improv but it worked. The second act opened fine and Lanya stumbled on one or two words trying to keep her other songs out of her head. Overall it was a great hit and the applause again had Lanya beaming. There was no encore but when the curtain came down, Lanya had tears in her eyes. Ivan was nowhere to be seen but cast members came up and congratulated her.

"That was fantastic!"

"The best!"

"Better than last night. You should be in the lead every night!" Lanya thought this was better than an encore and she smiled and enjoyed it all. As she went into the dressing room she wondered where Ivan was. Was he even here? Were they together? Her heart, after flying high just a moment ago, sunk. They must be together. Natalya could sing but she was a snake. Oh well. This kind of stuff happens to me all the time. As she walked home in the dark, she spent more time on Ivan being gone than one her success on stage. Babu was asleep so she could not share till tomorrow.

At breakfast, Babu saw Lanya drag in from her bedroom.

"Some coffee, girl, best we have." Lanya accepted a cup and was grateful for the warmth of it in her hands. "Tonight I want us to sleep here in the kitchen near the stove. We cannot keep the whole apartment warm, but the stove will work. I will sleep here," she pointed to a spot right near the stove, "and you sleep there. We will put Mishka over there." She pointed around the kitchen. They would move the dinner table into the other room so there would be more room. Lanya nodded.

"Babu, last night the lead girl did not show up, so I got to do the lead part! Remember I told you I was the understudy? Well...last night I was the start. I got the best songs! Isn't that great?"

"You got to do the main? That is wonderful." She looked deeply into Lanya's eyes. "How did you do? How do you feel?"

"I feel very good. I did well, not quite perfect but good. Many said I did better than she did. I wonder what will happen tonight."

"You will do fine. Your voice can make up for small mistakes. No one sings better than you." Lanya almost blushed. Her grandmother was her biggest fan.

"Thank you Babu. I will let you know. I need to get a bath." Without power, that meant draw and heat the water like the old days, pour it into the bathtub and wait. They would leave the water in until it was cold. But this was a lot of work and took some time. As she filled the bucket, Lanya remembered fondly turning the shower knobs and hot water cascading out. But it had to be done.

Babu was no longer comfortable going to the market or getting ration cards, so Lanya had to do it. It was a good thing she was not working five days a week anymore. After her bath, she dressed and bundled against the November cold. The ration cards were at the Party office and she hated going there. But that was the only place to get them. The Party office was the place Lanya dreaded most in the world.

Surrounded by Party loyalists she was afraid to say the wrong thing, afraid to make eye contact. She wanted to sink into the floor. She was scared, she realized, of the Party. Of what they could do to a person. She thought about her parents. Was Valentina right? Was she scared of everything? As she waited she realized she was justified in being scared of the Party. Most people were but no one said it out loud. She had to show identification for the three of them to get the cards. The process took about three hours since there was always a line. She could not get groceries the same day, the lines were too long. One day for cards and one day for groceries. But she needed to do these things. So, like so many others, she waited in line outside the door, braving the cold and snow, then waited inside. It was not so bad with oil lights now. The people at the desks looked more human, with oil lamps. As she waited in line, Lanya fought her anxiety and tension by reviewing the songs from the show. She sang her songs in her head, then she went back and quietly sang the lead songs. She found herself humming. The woman next to her looked at her and Lanya swallowed. 'Do not attract attention!' she said to herself and stopped humming. She kept her eyes on the floor mostly. Her right hand was going fast, her fingers drumming. Her time at the counter was quick and without any trouble and she left the building as soon as she had the ration cards in her hand. When she got outside she gulped a whole breath of air, glad to be done for the day. The knots would leave her stomach as she walked. Such a relief to be out of there. In ten days she would be back.

Lanya left for the theater early that night, wondering if the lead girl would be back. She hoped not, so that she could sing lead again. She took care with her hair and stage makeup and put on her original costume. The cast showed up and Lanya looked around for Natalya. There she was, coming in a bit late. She was smiling. She really was awful. Was Ivan the cause of that smile? She left the dressing room looking for Ivan, and found him near the office. He was smiling too. Lanya almost turned to go the other way but he reached out and caught her arm.

"Hey, I heard you did a great job last night, when you got called to play lead. Congratulations."

"Thanks." Her heart was zigging and zagging, wondering what he meant. Was he happy she got to play lead? Was it a test to see if she could handle it?

"I am glad you got that chance." He paused. "Lanya, can I see you again? Can you come to my place tomorrow night?" She again wondered what he really wanted but gave in to the magic of being wanted. She let go of the jealousy.

"Yes, I can come."

"Thanks. Six again will be good for me." She nodded and turned to go. He did not say anything else so she quickly went back to the dressing room. As they gathered to raise the curtain, Andre asked everyone to meet after the show, that he had an announcement. There was some talk about a party after since it was the last night of the show.

The show went well and Lanya sang her supporting part with as much brilliance as she could. The rest of the cast were almost deferential to her, knowing she had played the lead. Natalya avoided her. Natalya stumbled on a line and was out of place once, almost like she was drunk. Lanya actually tried to get close to see if she could smell anything on her breath. If she was drunk she would be fired and Lanya would be the lead. No, too late. Lanya had a crazy idea about hiding a bottle of vodka in her things to make it look like she had been drinking before the show. Lanya stomped her foot- why did she not think of these things before the last night? The second act went off without a hitch. They all enjoyed the applause, and tonight there was an encore. They crowded the stage together and took a group bow. Lanya had some relief that it was all over. They left the stage but did not disperse, as Andre came in and hushed them.

"Attention, attention!" he called, his voice firm. For a small man he had a captivating voice. "I have an announcement!" The group got quiet. Lanya looked for Ivan and saw him at the edge. "This show has done so well. I applaud you for your time and efforts. This is hard to do when you are cold and hungry. But I have good news!" The cast looked around to see if anyone would spill the news first. Lanya had no idea what this could be. "We have been extended! We get another week! Ivan made this happen. Thank you Ivan!" The cast started clapping and cheering. Andre came back with "So, next Thursday I want everyone here on time, just like this week! Any questions?" No one had questions so the group broke up and splintered into smaller groups. Lanya nodded and congratulated people as she went to change and leave. She folded her costume and packed her bag. She wanted to leave. Two weeks of putting all her energy out on stage three nights a week had worn her out. The cold and lack of food made it worse. She drudged home through the cold dark streets and was happy when she saw her building.

At the dining table in the front room, she made a cup of tea and tried not to wake Babu and Mishka laying in the kitchen. She went to her room to put her night clothes on and realized Babu was right. The kitchen was much warmer. As she sat, new ideas came. Being on stage was a dream. While she was singing, there was no war. There was no loss. There was no missing sister, no damaged brother. All she knew were lights, music and applause. This was a dream. She sighed contentedly. This was what she wanted. All her life. And, she realized, on stage she had a purpose. For the first time ever. On stage, she was not that slim, plain girl who worked at the shoe factory. On stage, she was part of a crew, something bigger than herself. On stage, she could be a star, the center of attention! Her heart warmed with that. She had struggled for years to find a purpose. What was Svetlana's purpose? She knew, now.

Chapter Sixteen

Lanya walked to the factory in the rain. Or sleet. She was not sure, but it was cold. She missed the trams, but she needed to get to work. When she got there, things were as usual. People clustered at the time clock until the hour hit. She found some coffee on the counter and took a sip. This was not coffee. But she did not put it down because it was warm. She sipped as she got to her seat. The boot pieces were right there, the thread all ready to go. She put her hands on the machine and began singing in her head. The machine did as she needed, joining edges and tops. She knew there were only a few days left in the show. Then what? Would there be another show? Would Ivan do it? Or would someone else come in? Would they look for Lanya? She hoped so. She wanted to spend every night on stage.

Lunch with Maru was full of news. Maru and Leonid had spent time together at his apartment and become intimate. Maru was smiling.

"It was good, you know? Of course you know. I do not know what is next, but he was very nice to me. That is enough for now. There is not much that is nice right now." Lanya nodded and understood. That was how she felt with Ivan.

"Will you see him again?"

"Yes, I think so. I don't know when. Will you see Ivan again?"

"Well, we have extended the show for another week. So, we have that. Not sure about anything else. Yet." Maru nodded. They did not go any further than that.

Ivan was waiting outside the factory when she got off work. His smile was genuine. Lanya rushed to greet him with a hug. He wrapped his arm around her and they walked slowly.

"I wanted to see you. We have been so busy, it feels like we hardly know each other."

"Yes" she said, muffled into his coat.

"Can you come by tonight?" Lanya thought about that. How should she tell Babu?

"I need to tell my grandmother first."

"If you would, I would like that. I need some time with you." Lanya knew what that meant. This was physical, nothing else.

"Let me go by the apartment, then I can come by."

"That would be great. I will have something for dinner but not sure what it will be." Lanya decided to grab something at home. No reason to strain his rations. They split at the corner and Lanya walked home feeling happy.

At the apartment, she went in and traded one coat for a larger one. If she was going to be out late, she would need the warmest one for this. As she grabbed her wool scarf, she saw Babu watching her going from room to room.

"Are you going out?" Babu always had judgement ready.

"Yes, Babu. Ivan is offering dinner. But I am going to grab something here first. I am not sure he can cook. And I am sure he does not cook like you do." She grabbed small oladyi, a small buckwheat pancake that was left over from breakfast. Babu wished her good night as she closed the front door. She creased the pancake and snacked as she walked.

The walk to Ivan's was quick, as quick as could be in the November near dark on broken roads. She knocked at his door and he took a moment before opening. He gave her a bear hug as she came in and she hugged him back. The kiss was long and deep.

"I have something here if you are hungry." He pointed to the kitchen.

"No thanks, I ate something from home." That was the signal for him to toss her heavy coat on a chair and grab her hand to lead her to the bedroom. He had one oil lamp burning in the bedroom but there were papers all over. She saw more than one little notebook like the one he had left in the dressing room, but she was not prepared to think about anything but his hands. For a while. For some time, Lanya did not think, did not worry, did not bother with anything outside this room. Ivan fell asleep quickly. Lanya stretched. Now she was hungry. She got up. put her clothes on and went to his kitchen to see what she could find. He had some things in his cupboard and it was better stocked than hers. She wondered how he did that. But maybe he just did not eat much. She grabbed a piece of bread and some jam and quickly ate it, feeling guilty as she did. As she ate, she looked around the apartment. It was small, two bedrooms, with a table in the kitchen and a small front room. The bathroom was between the bedrooms. She looked at him sleeping. What were all those papers? She silently went in to take a look. Yes, she was snooping. But she wanted to know more about him. She picked up one set, then picked up another. These were maps of Leningrad. No problem, he was not a local and he would need a map. These were not in Russian and she tried to decipher which language they were. Many people in Leningrad spoke more than one language. Was this a dialect from Minsk, his hometown? No, the alphabet was not Russian. He had traveled. French? Slavic? German? Why would Ivan have German words? There were some numbers as well. On the map? This map was of the city and the surrounding area. No one was coming and going, except soldiers now and then. What was all this? She decided not to touch the notebook. This time. But now she was curious. Ivan stirred and she jumped and put her hands on her hips.

"I need to go now, Ivan." His eyes fluttered open and she could tell it took him a second to remember who she was. Her heart dipped.

"Thank you for coming over lovely Lanya. I will see you tomorrow at the show."

"Yes, tomorrow at the show. Good night Ivan." She could hear his deep breathing before she left the room. He would not miss her.

As she walked home, she worried. Ivan had a room full of papers that looked like a jumbled mess, but they made no sense to her. *Maps, numbers, but not in Russian? Is there more to Ivan than I can see? Is he really Russian? He has an accent when he speaks and she thought that was just because he was from out of town. Is there a problem here? What was going on? Was he more than a show producer?* The Party was always looking for spies and troublemakers; maybe Ivan was one? How could she be sure? She sure could not ask someone. She decided to study him a bit more as she worked with him.

At the theater, she looked for Ivan. She could not find him. She did not want to ask or people would be suspicious. So she just looked around. Andre was tense, yelling at people. She heard him cursing at Ivan and listened carefully for why.

"He is not here again? Two nights? What is wrong with him? I guess I will have to get this going." More curses. Lanya looked to see if the lead was here and she was. Lanya admitted to being saddened about that. No spotlight for her tonight. But no Ivan?

The show began perfectly and things sounded good. Lanya could see how they got an extra week extended. Nothing went wrong and the applause was like food, never enough. At the end, Lanya gathered her things and found Ivan's notebook in her corner. Was this the same one? Or did he put this here recently? She looked at it. She wanted to know what was in here. On the inside cover was a chart of some sort, substituting this letter or symbol for that. A code? Lanya's stomach tensed. The words on the pages were gibberish, but again not in Russian. What was Ivan doing? She left the dressing room and the notebook behind and began her walk home. *What might the Party think about these notebooks? Should I talk to the Party? What would happen then? With my family, would they believe me? Or would they suspect me, too? Would Ivan disappear? Will I be in trouble too?* She could not imagine offering information to the Party. That would make her look bad. They would ask where she got the notebooks, so Lanya shut that idea down. Her brain was wrapped in questions and air raid sirens went off. She was not near home, and she saw people coming out of their buildings. They did not seem to be in a hurry. Maybe people were just ready to give up. No rush. When it's your time, it's your time. She followed them into the closest shelter and huddled down with them. She did not recognize anyone. She stayed silent and to pass the time, she hummed songs that she knew. Maybe she should start writing songs. She decided to give that some thought when she got home. After about an hour, the all clear rang and she padded to the door and into the street. She was home within 20 minutes and was happy to get into her warm apartment. She made some tea and sat down at the table. Could she write a song? Would she have to learn to write music or would that just come? She put her head in her hands and thought about stories that songs would tell, stories about love, heartbreak, loss, death and loyalty. Living though wartime there had to be lots of songs ready to be created. She pushed the idea aside, for another day.

In the food line the next day, she hummed songs she knew and began with little bits that were new in her head. A few people looked at her, but she hummed anyway. If she was humming or singing, her brain was not obsessed with Ivan.

The final night of the show came too quickly. Lanya was as ready as she could be and gave her role an extra push. She was on top of the world. The applause was raucous and filled her soul. There was an ovation and the cast joined hands for the final bow. As they split up to change, Ivan came by the dressing room and popped his head in.

"You were exceptional tonight Lanya." He smiled at her but did not touch her. "Are you going to the cast party?"

"Yes, I want to go. I will be there soon." Ivan left with a quick nod. Lanya changed and pulled on her coat. The party was at Andre's apartment and Lanya wondered what food they would have, but she was sure they would at least have vodka. She even had a small bottle in her bag in case they were short. The whole cast was there and the oil lamps made it almost magical. Everyone was friendly and in good spirits. Even in a war, there could be good. Ivan went from group to group. Lanya heard someone ask him about the "next" show.

"Haha- I am not sure. This war makes things tough. No one will have any energy to be on stage unless food comes through." This made sense. Lanya was weak many nights. The cast was enjoying the little food and the vodka, singing and laughing. She hoped Ivan would come over to her and treat her like she was special but he gave nothing away. Lanya did not stay too long. The cold was enough that she did not want to be out too late. She said her goodbyes and hit the road. At least there was a moon out tonight and she could see the street as she walked home. She worried about sliding on ice with the broken roads. The warm apartment welcomed her and she made a quick cup of tea to settle down. This apartment in some ways was like an old friend, and always a comfort. Her first live show was over and she did very well. She wanted more of this. If Ivan was going to do another show, she wanted in.

Chapter Seventeen

With the show behind her, Lanya got back to normal life. She gave herself a minute to ponder on what "normal" even meant. Her city was being bombed every week, her baby sister was dead and her brother was like a baby boy. What did normal even mean? For Lanya that meant getting up to go to the factory to sew, eating what was available, having nightmares often, visiting with Maru at lunchtime and not much else. She had not seen Ivan since the last night of the show and was not sure she would again. She did not know what his plan was... if he had one.

Wednesday night sewing circle was somber. One of the women shared that her son was killed near Moscow. Everyone understood her pain. Another woman offered a ray of hope about food.

"Lake Ladoga- you know Lake Ladoga?"

"Oh yes, we went there as a child."

"Of course, who doesn't?"

"Well, the lake is almost frozen over, just like every year. In fact, a bit earlier."

"Yes, it always freezes. We went across it by carriage one year."

"I heard from someone at the Party that they hope to use it as a road."

"What? How would that happen?" The chatter began and everyone wanted to know what this would mean.

"What I heard was that when it is frozen completely, they will send trucks across it to get food. Or to evacuate people. The railroads on the other side are working, the Germans did not get to that." The chatter exploded.

"That could save us!"

"A blessing!"

"When will it start?" There were no answers but every woman present looked forward to this. Food was scarce, November was cold and people were dying. Bringing food in would save them, for sure. And gasoline and medicine. Lanya had a tiny spark of hope.

When she got home, she shared with Babu.

"Babu, did you hear about Lake Ladoga? When it freezes, they will bring in food and evacuate people. Won't that be good?" Babu got a sparkle in her eyes and Lanya realized she had not seen that in her grandmother in a long while.

"That will be good. We need it to be sure."

"Yes, we do. I would sell my soul to get some ham and potatoes right now." Babu smiled. Lanya went to her room with a smile.

As Lanya hurried into the cold after work the next day, she stopped in her tracks to see Ivan waiting at the street light, like always.

"Lovely Lanya, I have come to see you. How are you?" Lanya was not sure she should but she hurried into his outstretched arms.

"Ivan, it is good to see you." she said with her mouth against his wool coat.

"Yes, good to see you, too. Do you have some time? I would love to have you come over tonight." Lanya let that idea run in her head quickly and nodded.

"Yes, but I need to tell Babu."

"Of course, can you come over right after? You know where."

"Yes, thanks. I will see you soon then." Ivan walked away with a smile and Lanya almost ran all the way home.

"Babu, I am going to see Ivan tonight, he is making dinner." Lanya knew Ivan had not mentioned dinner, but knew also that this would work for Babu.

"Again? See if he has any extra ration cards will you? If he is feeding you he must have something." Babu did not smile and did not look up from the needlepoint she was doing.

"I will let you know Babu." A kiss on the cheek and Lanya left the house in a flash.

When she arrived at Ivan's place, Lanya quickly removed her heavy coat, hat and gloves. It was not warm in there but better than outdoors. Ivan grabbed her hand and without pretense, moved her into the bedroom. They came together as they had done before and for a short while Lanya believed she was attractive and desirable.

"Lanya, thank you for coming tonight. I wanted to let you know that I will be going away for a few weeks. I did not want you to think that I was abandoning you. I will see you when I get back, if I can." Lanya did not dare ask where he was going or why. She held onto him but he began to get up.

Ivan was getting dressed so Lanya began putting her crumpled clothes on too. When she was all together, she went towards the kitchen. Her heart dropped a bit when she did not see dinner going. Her stomach rumbled a bit but she was used to that now. Ivan helped her put her coat and gloves on. He gave her a big hug with an extra squeeze.

"I will be back in just over two weeks. I will meet you outside the factory again, okay?"

"Okay, that will be nice. Be careful out there." She walked out the door. Bells were going off in her head. *Who is he? What is going on? Why is he going away? Where is he going? Am I in trouble?* Maybe she should not be involved like this. She knew she needed no incentive to get the Party looking at her. When she got home she was grateful that Babu was already asleep. Lanya changed into her layers of pajamas and went back into the kitchen to her little spot on the floor near the oven. She was glad to be here in the kitchen. Babu was snoring in a comfortable way and Mishka was curled up with the little dog Feodor, so Lanya quickly fell asleep.

December came in quietly but Lanya was sure that it would not stay that way. December was usually full of storms and snow and sleet and ice. She remembered cars sliding across the black ice and running into the heaps of snow at the sides of the roads. The trees had been bare for a long time and the squirrels in the park were all hidden away for the next few months. No life in the park in December. Lanya was not looking forward to walking to and from work for the next three months, if she made it.

As she walked to the factory along roads she knew well, she saw an older man pulling a sled. The sled carried a wrapped bundle- was that a body? Lanya tried not to stare. Was this old man bringing a body out on a sled? She remembered taking Valentina wrapped up like that. Where were they going? This was not the way to the undertakers where they took her sister. Lanya slowed her walk so she did not disturb him. The ground was frozen and there were no burials now. Winter was too cold and they had to wait until spring to bury people, all over the Soviet Union. Was he taking the body to the cemetery? There was a huge cemetery a few miles down this road, which was where Valentina had been buried. Lanya felt some guilt that she had not been to her sister's grave. Maybe this was his wife or his child and he had to take them to the cemetery. Did they starve or get killed in a bombing? Would the cemetery just store them? The old man continued and Lanya's heart sank with each step of the old man.

At work, someone was coming around to collect leather scraps. Lanya handed her all the bits. Why was this happening? At lunch, she asked Maru.

"Why was that woman gathering the leather scraps? What is she going to do with them?"

Maru looked around and spoke quietly "She is going to cook them." Lanya's mouth dropped.

"Why?"

"Well, what I heard is that there may be some protein in the broth. If you make some broth, soak them in hot water, it may give you some protein." Lanya had never heard of this, but she decided to give it a try. From this moment on, she would collect leather too. She had to feed her brother and he was wasting away. By the end of the day, she had a small bag of leather bits.

At home, she brought the small bag to Babu.

"Babu, I know this is ridiculous, but I heard this is a good idea. If you can boil these scraps, there might be some protein in the broth. Do you think you can do this?" Babu peered into the small bag and Lanya could see a tear in her eye.

"Svetlana, I have done this before. After the Revolution there was no food anywhere. People were starving. People cooked their own boots hoping to survive. I had forgotten about this. I have done this before and will do it again. It is necessary." Lanya gave Babu a hug and was grateful that her grandmother had seen so much of the world.

"Thank you Babu. You always make it work." Lanya left to go to her room. What a miserable time, when leather scraps became dinner.

Each day was harder. The rations were so small it was unbearable. Not even a handful a day. The flour for bread was not all wheat and she knew it had a stretcher, but she thought maybe they were past just the stretcher mark. Fresh fruits and vegetables were rare. An onion here, a potato or cabbage there. In December, things were always a little tough, but when the trains were running food came into the city. Sometimes it came from the Black Sea area where they still grew food in December, but now, fresh was a miracle. Maybe this road over the frozen lake would make a difference. It surely would not hurt.

Chapter Eighteen

Lanya again fought with her stomach as she went to the Communist Party office to get ration cards. She tried to breathe slowly and deeply. She was not convinced that it worked but she tried it every time. Of course she would hate the Party who took her parents. Who wouldn't? But she had to be here so she tried. Every ten days. She would even face the German army for ration cards. She remembered a game she used to play with her mother and Valentina about a magic dining table that would create whatever dish you spoke of. She used to dream of roasts and sausages while Valentina used to talk on and on about cakes and cookies. That girl loved sweets for sure. Lanya thought about this now. What would she dream of for this table now? Simple things like vegetable filled soups and fruit tarts. Yes, roasts, too. Lanya stopped herself. *This is dangerous. This is not going to happen soon, not while the Germans are at the gates. Just be glad we have anything* she told herself. Easy to say, hard to do.

At the counter, she gave her identification cards and the woman slowly processed the papers. This woman had helped her before. She looked something like a beaver, with a scrunched up face and whiskers here and there. She was never kind, just mechanical with paper shuffling. Lanya looked around. Mostly women, with flat gray hair. These women would have been thick and round if there was no war, but today they were all flat. None of these people had a spark in them. Lanya saw a new face now and then and today she saw a young man looking from a corner. He was young and slight with wavy brown hair that fell over his eyes and glasses that looked like they were thicker than canning jars. Lanya wondered if his bad eyes were the reason he was not at the front. He eyes scanned the room and she quickly looked away. She did not want anyone here to notice her. As soon as she had her ration cards she quickly left this prison of an office.

The leather scraps she collected were made into a broth and Babu put some cabbage in with an onion if she could get one. There were still rusks in the cupboard, Babu had made so many of them they might last forever. The rusks could be dipped into tea or coffee or leather broth. Lanya would eat almost anything now.

After breakfast the next morning, Lanya was shocked by a knock on the door. Babu was not in the front room, so she opened it, hoping it was Ivan. It was not. She looked at the young man trying to remember if she knew him.

"Svetlana, I am Aleksander, Mikhail's friend. I came by a few months ago to see how he was. Can we talk please?" Lanya nodded and stepped outside the door and closed it. She did not want her brother to see him again, remembering his outburst last time. Aleksander continued. "Is he better? I want to apologize for last time. Boris and I did not know what to do and it seems we startled him. I am sorry for that. Please forgive us." Boris was not here this time.

"Did you come alone?"

"Yes, Boris had to do some work. They let us come into town now and then to visit family. My family is too far away. But I wanted to say I am sorry."

"That is okay. He has not done it again. I think you did startle him. We did not know what to expect with him." She looked around at the hallway clenching her hands together so Aleksander would not see her fingers twitching. "He is unchanged. Still like a child." The thought brought her down as it did every time she thought about her charming vivacious big brother turned into an idiot.

"I am so sorry." He reached out and touched her hand. "This must be tough on you."

Lanya looked at him and was touched by his thoughtfulness. "It is."

"Is there anything I can do to help? This is not what you expect of your big brother. He is like my brother too, the Mikhail I knew. Always made me laugh." Lanya decided it might be all right to bring him in. He seemed calm, more calm than Boris.

"Come on in." She opened the door quietly. "Please sit here." She pointed to the kitchen table in the front room. "Would you like some tea?"

"That would be nice, thanks." Lanya moved to the kitchen to make tea and saw Babu at the sink.

"It is Mikhail's friend- he came back. I brought him in because he is calm. Will you make us some tea?" Babu nodded and peeked into the front room, spotting Aleksander. Babu assembled a tray with two tea cups and two rusks and brought it to the table. She did not say a word as she set it down and went back to the kitchen. "That is our grandmother. She has cared for us since our parents were taken." As she said it, Lanya hoped this was not the Communist Party setting her up, trying to get her to talk so she would be next.

"How is he?" Aleksander asked keeping his voice low. "Any changes at all?"

"He is okay I think. He spends his days quietly playing in his room. He has toys if you can believe that. Sometimes he goes with me to get groceries but he just stays in there by himself."

"Do you think he would recognize me if he saw me?" This question saddened Lanya. Probably not. She was not sure Mishka even knew who she was.

"I do not think so. He seems to understand simple things, like come here or sit down, but not much else." At this point their little dog jumped onto Aleksander's lap and tried to lick his face. Aleksander laughed and petted Feodor, while Lanya realized that her brother was like the dog. Follow simple instructions, eat and sleep. She was sorry Aleksander was here, her heart was heavy.

"Well, how are you?" Aleksander looked into Lanya's eyes like a lover would. A small tingle went down her neck. She turned her eyes away.

"I am ok. Babu and I stay home. It is too cold to go anywhere." She decided he did not need to know about the show and how it charged her up. She looked at him again. "How are you?"

He grabbed her hand on the table. "I am doing okay. The Germans are doing their best but we are still there fighting back. We do a lot of trench digging. Every time they bomb we need a new trench. My muscles are getting big!" He held up his arm but Lanya could not see any shape through his sweater. "I got a letter from my mother the other day, she lives outside of Moscow now, though she used to live here, when I was small. She is struggling too. I feel as prepared as I could be to fight." Lanya took a moment and remembered the sleeping bags they had repaired and the boots she was making.

"I make the boots you use, in a factory down by the river."

"The shoe factory? That old thing? I used to run around there when I was a kid."

"I have been there for a few years now. We are using the old hand crank machines now and it is a pain. My arms are getting big, too!" She held up her arm. "But we are still making boots."

"That is a good thing. Ours get so messed up from mud and cold." Lanya wanted a friendship with Aleksander and wondered why. Maybe he was like Mikhail.

"You did not bring your friend with you, Boris."

"No, I actually wanted to see you and Mikhail without him. He is easily agitated and creates chaos sometimes." Lanya gave a small smile. *Very thoughtful, Aleksander.* "And, I wanted to see you again." Aleksander broke into a gentle grin and her heart reached out to this kind man. Her smile grew.

Babu came back through the room, holding socks she was darning.

"Babu, do you remember Aleksander? He came by a few weeks ago with another man to see Mikhail?" Babu nodded. "He came alone this time, said that Boris gets excitable. Should we bring Mishka out?" As Lanya said that, she heard a noise in the hall and Mishka was walking towards them. Lanya rushed to him. "Mishka, come here." She grabbed his hand and pulled him towards Aleksander. Aleksander dropped the rusk in his hand, barely breathing. "Mishka, do you remember your friend Aleksander?" Lanya watched closely as Mishka looked up and down at Aleksander. She wondered what might happen. Another outburst? Nothing happened. Mishka looked at Aleksander and opened his palm to show a small wooden cart that he held. Aleksander quietly took it, turned it over and rolled the wheels with his finger then put it back in Mishka's hand with a very gentle thank you. Mikhail smiled and turned away. He trudged into the kitchen.

"Well, that was better." Lanya said, though she was sad for Mishka. She sipped her tea and picked up her dry rusk.

"I feel so sorry for him, he was always such a great guy. I should be going." He rubbed his fingertips together to remove any crumbs. He stood and turned to the door and Lanya followed him out. As she closed the door, he faced her.

"I am sure this makes you sad, too. If it was my brother, I would be sad." She looked at him trying to read his face. "I may be forward, but may I write to you? It would be good for me to have something to think about, and a pretty girl like you thinking about me would brighten my day." Lanya caught her breath as she squeezed her hands together. She did not expect that!

"That would be nice. I would like that. But we have no mail now, no fuel for the trucks." His smile dimmed.

"Well, at the front we still have mail. I will write you a note when I can. Thank you Svetlana." He touched her hand and gave it a light squeeze. She squeezed back and he headed down the hall to the stairs. Again he looked back before he left the hall and smiled at her. Suddenly, she was not thinking about her brother. She was thinking about Aleksander. What a kind, gentle man who asked nothing of her. Who liked her. She was smiling from ear to ear as she went back into the front room.

"A nice young man." Babu said, noticing Lanya's smile.

"Yes, he seems it." Lanya walked down the hall to Mishka's room to check on him. She did not bother to ask him if he recognized Aleksander, she knew he had no memory. She smiled at him, sadly, and went to her bedroom.

Chapter Nineteen

December's cold brought a false sense of peace. The nighttime bombing had not happened for six days and everyone was sure it would be back with a vengeance. The days were gray and the nights were quiet. Did storms cut down on the bombings? Maybe she would wish for more lightning and snow. *Like every December*, Lanya thought as she trudged to work. Except her sister was gone and her brother was like their dog. *When would life be normal again? Could life be normal?* That thought weighed on Lanya as she came into the factory. Things looked normal in here, if oil lamps and hand crank machines could be normal. She passed by an empty machine that had small mementos on it. Another worker gone, dead. Starvation? Probably. People were dying every day. Food was hard to find. Pets were scarce, people were eating them. Lanya thought about their little dog. Could she eat him? They were starving. Or could she find another way? With a heavy heart, she sat down at her machine. Probably. Valentina's dog was cute, but they needed to live. She decided to talk with Babu about it tonight. Babu would know what to do. They still had a small box of rusks that they had baked in the fall. It was enough to get through December but what then? Lanya was tired of being adult.

At Wednesday night sewing group, people were quiet. There was tea to share but it was little more than warm water. Lanya had come to value these women and their understanding of the world.

"The lake is frozen and I hear they are bringing in flour and ham!"

"I would kill for a slice of ham!"

"Real flour would be good. I am not sure what we are eating now, but real flour would be heavenly." They all commented on the food dreams they had. Lanya interrupted.

"When I was a child, I played a game with my mother, where we imagined a table full of food, and what outrageous foods we would put on it." She looked around and every woman was watching her. She went on, "Anything we imagined would appear on our table and we spent hours imagining what we would put on it." She paused, wondering if anyone would join in. "If it was today, I would start with coffee, real, dark coffee." The talk began immediately.

"Coffee? No, I would start with sausage."

"Sausage? How about roast beef? With potatoes and gravy?"

"Oranges! Just plain oranges!" Oranges were a delicacy this far north. The women went on for almost an hour listing every edible dream they had. The night went more quickly than most. Lanya wondered if it was wrong to build up this feast in their heads but her imagination was strengthened by it. Not such a drudge.

As they gathered their coats, one older woman came to Lanya, and said, "I remember that game with my own kids years ago. We spent hours doing the same. You brought back good memories, Svetlana." Lanya nodded and let the guilt wash away. She did something nice today.

The next day at the factory, there was a crowd just inside the door. People were irritated and angry.

"They bombed it?"

"The road of life is gone?"

"I thought this road was going to save us!" Lanya tried to piece together what had happened. The Germans had bombed Lake Ladoga, the frozen road that was bringing in supplies. The lake was in an area to the northeast of Leningrad that the Germans had not touched so no one believed they would bother it. There was a grimness in the air. Everyone was looking forward to the frozen lake saving them from starving or freezing.

"I am sure it will freeze again."

"Yes, the ice gets to be a foot thick."

"Many trucks have gone down, and even some horse drawn carts went down at the start."

"I pray it will come back. I wanted to go across it and out of this town." Lanya knew that some people were abandoning Leningrad to get to somewhere safer. She wondered if that would be good, but was she sure that Babu would not do it. Any evacuation required doctor's orders and Babu was too frail. And too stubborn. As she sat at her machine, Lanya wondered if they would all starve or freeze in Leningrad. Damn Germans.

As Lanya left the factory, she was wrapped in her own brain. She jumped when she heard someone call her name. She looked up and Ivan was there leaning on the dark light post. She smiled and hurried to him. He wrapped his arms around her.

"Lovely Lanya, how are you?"

"Ivan, I am okay. No change. How are you?"

"I only have a few minutes today. Can I see you tomorrow?" Lanya thought she would see him anytime he asked.

"Yes, of course. After work?"

"Yes, will you come to my apartment? Or do I need to come get you?" Lanya did not want him to be out walking if he did not have to, since he was not as used to Leningrad in December as she was, so she agreed to come to his place. "Thanks Lanya. I am talking with Leonid about the next production and we are trying to figure out what show would be best." He stopped walking at the corner. "I need to go but I am glad I got to see you. Tomorrow?" He hugged Lanya again as she nodded, then Ivan turned away.

Lanya savored Ivan's visits and her time at his apartment. But it was becoming clear in her head that her heart was not part of this. Yes, Ivan made her feel desirable when she looked like a twig with straw for hair. And yet, there was some value to that in this ugly time when no one looked good. But he did not make her feel good about herself. She was sure he had no intention of this being more than bedroom visits. She knew she wanted more, offered more. And he came with risks, that she was beginning to worry about. She did not see this affair lasting beyond the next show. As she thought about her heart, Aleksander's face popped in her mind. His gentle grin and his concern with her, even though her brother was broken. Aleksander would be worth getting to know. She did not know when she would hear from him again. But as she walked, there was a tiny warm spot inside her that did not have Ivan written on it.

Later, after their small dinner, Lanya sat near Babu in the front room.

"Babu, I want to talk to you about something." As she sat, the dog came up and sniffed her hand. She put her hand in his short hair. Even the dog was skinny now. Babu leaned in to watch Lanya. "Babu, what do we do with the dog?" Lanya had trouble even finishing the sentence. Her hands clenched together. Babu looked at Lanya then down at the dog.

"You mean, do we...? Ohhhh... We need food." Even Babu could not say it. Lanya could not look at the dog. She had tears in her eyes and knew that if Valentina was here no one could touch her dog.

"I am not sure. I do not think I could... Could you?" Lanya choked on the words. The picture in her mind almost wrenched her stomach.

"Let me think on this. Maybe we can find something else." Babu got up and went into the kitchen. Lanya still could not look at the dog. but she watched Babu's back, and the way her dress hung loosely on her thin shoulders. Babu and Mishka were more important than a dog. She would think of something else. Vodka would help.

The air raid came late that night, and Lanya stumbled out of her bed on the kitchen floor. She got Babu and her brother, gathering them and their shelter bag as they put on their coats. Lanya grabbed a blanket off the couch, as they would need it in the basement. They never took the dog with them, no one wanted animal accidents in the shelter. They hurried down the steps and into the night, They could see the lights on the planes and hear the explosions as they crowded into the shelter. Would this be a big bombing? Would it hit them? The building shook as they huddled in their corner by the filing cabinet. Lanya pulled the blanket around them, Mishka on one side and Babu on the other. She remembered their first night here months ago and how frightened she was. She did not feel that scared now. Sure, they could get hit. But that might be better that how they lived now. She hoped if they did get hit she would die, and not just be injured. She did not want to lose an arm or leg or have some injury. The hospital had almost no medicine and people went there to die.

The building shuddered again and Lanya heard glass breaking close by. She did not sense a direct hit. She wondered if their apartment would be hit. The planes were close. Her body tensed with each squeal of a bomb, then the explosion. She looked at Mishka to see if the explosion would disturb him but he was asleep, like a child. Part of her wished for that simple set of needs. The last bomb shook the building hard and she heard crashing sounds like walls breaking. This could be it. She found herself holding her breath. She tried to relax. The bombs sounded a bit farther away, then farther. Maybe it was over. The sound of dropping bombs faded more then disappeared altogether. Okay, the raid was over and they had lived through it. Again. Soon, the all clear bell went off. They plodded to the door but people were not really going out. She saw over someone's shoulder that the street was full of chunks and boards and broken glass with thick dust. They needed to help each other get out the door from all the bricks and broken boards at the doorway. As she got on the street, she saw the building they were in. Two walls were toppled, not from a direct hit but from the thunderous noise of the bombs. The building next door was a shell. They had almost gotten hit. Her knees buckled but she caught herself before she fell. She leaned on Babu like always but tried to remember that Babu might need to lean on her. Slowly, they walked towards their apartment with dread. What if it was gone? They rounded the corner and saw it,- still standing. But the windows were all broken and the entry doors were shattered. The line of people entered and carefully walked up the stairs. *What would the inside look like?* They opened their door and looked around. One window was gone and cold air was present throughout. The back part where the bedrooms were did not look too bad.

"Babu, I am going to get a blanket for the window. Will you get the nails and hammer? They parted each to their own task. Lanya guided Mishka to his corner in the kitchen and directed him to lie down. He obliged. Lanya grabbed a blanket from the back closet and hoped one would be enough. She would need to get some wood tomorrow. She hammered at the edges trying to seal the broken glass and keep the cold out. One blanket would not do much but it was all she had tonight. As she finished, she got more wood and put it in the oven to keep the kitchen warm. As she lay down next to Babu, she hoped the oven would give off enough heat to keep them warm. They could all get closer like a pack of dogs if they needed. She drifted off to sleep hoping the dreams tonight would be gentle.

Finding wood for the stove was not as hard as it used to be. Usually, men with carts or trucks drove through town and would bring the wood up and stack it along a wall. Not this year. No one was going through town since no one could get in and out to get the firewood. Lanya and Babu had already used up everything left over from last year. This year though, since so many buildings were bombed, there was broken wood everywhere. Broken tables, chairs, beds, cupboards. It was not enough to keep them toasty, but it was enough to keep them from freezing. Lanya went in search of some wood the day after their windows were shattered, hoping to find some boards also which would certainly work better than a blanket. She took Mishka along, just to get him out of the house. They aimed for the bombed buildings that no one would be living in. They entered carefully hoping no one was lurking in the shadows. Lanya hoped she would not see anyone who had been killed. That would be creepy. They gathered a few pieces of a shattered table, Lanya showed Mishka which pieces were better. She also took a few items of clothing to help start the fire. No boards were there this time but she would look again another day. They brought their trove into the apartment and Babu silently nodded, approving of what they did. Lanya did not feel bad. With this war going on, survival was the key. They were not hurting anyone.

After dinner, Lanya walked to Ivan's house. This time of year, the sun was only bright for a few hours in the middle of the day. The sun was dark gray until mid-morning, less gray throughout the lunch period and gray again into the afternoon. Many days, there was no sun at all, just clouds. Snow was frequent; war did not change that. Winter in Leningrad could bring people down without war. How people were going to get through this Lanya was not sure. How she was going to get through this she was even less sure. Ivan's apartment, while not warm, was welcoming. Ivan offered hot tea and Lanya accepted. She wanted a moment to warm up before they went into the bedroom. As she sipped, she knew this was a short term thing and wondered how it would end. *Will he stop coming by? Will I be too busy to visit? If there is another show, will it continue?*

The bedroom beckoned, and they held hands as they went down the hall. This was not as exciting as the first time but she still felt wanted. As she walked down the short hallway, she understood that for now she was not filled with fear. That was one reason she continued this. She undressed herself as he did and they lay on the bed. There was not much talk, there was no need. It was over quickly and they spent some time curled up together. She glanced down his body. Like everyone, thin but healthy. His attractive face had deeper cheeks than before, but he was doing as well as any. Before she left she looked to see if he had any food in his refrigerator. She saw something and grabbed it. She did not care. He would be okay. She snacked on this gob of food as she went down the stairs. Potatoes. It was potatoes. She liked potatoes and she smiled, not just for the food, but for the fact that she stole it from him. In her mind she was taking care of herself.

At lunch the next day, Maru asked how things were with Ivan. Lanya paused. Should she tell her everything? Lanya always shared with Maru and could not see any reason to change.

"To be truthful, I do not feel anything for him. I feel pretty when I am with him." She ran her hand down her skirt to show Maru that she obviously was not pretty, "But my heart is untouched. Does that make me bad?"

Maru reached and covered Lanya's hand with her own. "No, no, no! You are pretty. And if you do not feel anything, do not worry. None of us are at our best now, with this war and no sleep and no food. I do not even have any lipstick! And you know I love my pink!" Maru paused and licked her dry lips. "If he makes you feel pretty, you can spend time with him. But, if you feel guilty, let him go. If you will be at true peace without him, let him go." Lunch ended and they went back to their machines.

As she sat at her machine, Lanya was a mess. This thing with Ivan had some good points but now it had more bad points. *Good points, he distracts me. From war, from being hungry and cold, from worry about bombing. The bad, who is he? Is he helping Leningrad? With those notes that made no sense? Why is he even here? Can I get into trouble being with him? What if he was married?* As she left the factory, she decided to follow Maru's advice. Maru knew more about men than Lanya ever would. And breaking it off with Ivan would not be too hard. She would not see him again. If he showed up, she would be too busy to come by. With that in her mind, Lanya relaxed as she plodded home through the streets.

Christmas in Leningrad was usually magical. There were lights in the houses, lights on the street, and carolers walking from house to house. They had a Christmas carnival on the frozen river, where people would have a bonfire right in the middle of the ice-covered river. Lots of food, vodka and singing. There was skating and food kiosks on weekends. But not this year. This year it was dark. Lanya could see a few decorations in the windows, showing the world their cheer. But no lights, no snacks and nothing else going on near the Neva. Dark and cold. What a dreadful Christmas this would be.

In the ration card line the next day, Lanya knitted her fingers together as she always did in this building that she hated so much. She looked at the floor, She looked at the walls. Why was this building not bombed? It would be appropriate if it was, with what the Party did to people. But here it was, as good as it was in 1940. There were pictures of Comrades Lenin and Stalin up on the bland beige walls. Lanya could not imagine working in here every day. There was no life in here, her breath was shallow. As she got to the counter, the same mousy woman who helped her an earlier time helped her again. Same lack of personality, same hair, same flat face. Lanya wanted to scream or shriek just to stir things up. But, this was not a stage. She would get arrested for that. So she meekly got her stamps and her cards. At the door, a young man was waiting. Did he need something? She put her head down and went to slink out but he stopped her.

"Can I see your papers please?" He put his hand out and she gave him her papers. It was the young man she had seen last time, with thick glasses. He looked over her papers, said thank you and sent her on her way. *What was that about? Did he stop anyone else? Just me? Why? Does he know about my parents? Would he cause trouble for me because my parents were taken?* Her hands got even colder as she went into the street. He did not ask any questions. He did not stop anyone else leaving the office. *What does he want?* Lanya found herself taking tiny steps so she did not slip. The ice on the street made walking difficult, and her boots were old, but good enough for it. She admitted that she did not know how the Party worked. She wished they did not know she was alive.

A few days later, Lanya left the factory and saw Ivan before he saw her. She tried to remember Maru's advice. She walked to him as his head turned. He put papers into his pocket.

"Good afternoon Lovely Lanya."

"Good afternoon Ivan." Her throat was constricted, a lot of things running through her head.

"I hear more snow is coming. This is more than I am used to. How do you all do this every year?"

"This year is colder than I can recall. Many say it may be the coldest ever."

"It might not be so bad if the power was on and the trams were running."

"That is true." Lanya did not feel like she had much to say.

"Leonid and I are working on another show. We will do tryouts after the first of the year, when the holidays are over. Will you try out?" Lanya caught her breath, she had forgotten about another show.

"I hope so. If I am still here. We never know."

"True. Are you free tomorrow night? I would love to see you."

"I am sorry, I have to say no. My Babu is not feeling well and I want to stay home. You understand." She was not sure he understood but expected it.

"Of course. It is good of you to take care of her. Another time then?" He put his arms out for a hug and she slid in, where it was warmer and felt good. At that minute, she did not care where her heart was, he was warm.

"Thank you, another time." She turned to go first, walking away. He did not walk just yet but watched her. She could feel his eyes on her. She had never walked away from him before. *Things change,* she said to herself. *Things change.*

Lanya arrived at work the next morning, and people were standing at the entrance, some cursing,some crying. Lanya's heart sunk.

"What happened" she said as she got close.

"The roller coaster. It is burned. They bombed the roller coaster!" She heard more cursing and people talking about the wreck of the roller coaster. Lanya had fond memories of the roller coaster near the river. She had many rides on it as a child and many more with Valentina, who simply loved that old rattletrap. Valentina would go around and around, squealing each time.

"The roller coaster? Why would they destroy that? It had nothing to do with this war!"

"Damn Germans!" Lanya went into the factory to her machine with a bleak heart. *If they destroyed fun, why bother living?* After her shift was over, she caught Maru and asked her to go see the burned down roller coaster. They walked down to the river and they could smell it before they saw it, the burned rubber from the joints and the leather seats. The metal heap still had some flames and was still smoking. There was a small crowd looking. Lanya could feel tears coming to her eyes. Such good times here. There was only one in town and no other until you got to Moscow. Such happy times here. *Damn Germans.*

At home, she told Babu about the roller coaster She did not bring up Valentina, Babu would know. She saw a stack of wood near the fireplace and raised her eyebrows, Babu nodded.

"Your brother. He went out and picked up some wood like you showed him. He brought some in and there is a bit more in his room." Lanya was thrilled! She did not have to do all the work! Babu could not really leave so Lanya was doing all the ration cards, shopping and any errands. If Mishka could collect the firewood needed, that would be a weight off her shoulders. She walked into Mishka's room and sat on the edge of his bed. He smiled. She touched his arm.

"Mishka, thank you for the firewood. It means a lot. We need it to stay warm. I appreciate it." She leaned over and kissed his forehead. She saw the extra wood in a corner of his room. Enough for a few days at least. He did not say anything, and she wondered again if he would ever come back to normal. He smiled after the kiss and she got up. They might not freeze. This might work.

As she woke up the next morning, Lanya's stomach wrenched. As it twisted she jumped up from her corner of the kitchen to make it to the restroom before she threw up. Not much came up, since she had so little to eat at dinner. A million thoughts entered her head. *What is making me sick? What did I eat that was bad?* She could not think of anything different. *Will throwing up lead me closer to starvation? Will this come back?* She did not work today so she decided to go lay in her bedroom away from Babu and Mishka just to settle. She was not sick often, so this was a surprise. On her bed, she fell back asleep quickly, her stomach calm.

Chapter Twenty

CHAPTER TWENTY

Lanya again approached Babu about the little dog. Feeding him put a small strain on their food allotment. He did not eat much, but Lanya knew that all their food should be used to keep them alive.

"Babu, I think we have to do this, I hate it but I would hate it more if one of us starved."

Babu nodded and looked at the little guy asleep near the stove. "Yes, you are right. It is necessary." She had a sad look on her face. Since Valentina died little dog had become her close companion.

"I cannot do it and I know you cannot. I will find someone who will trade us. Get some ration cards." Babu nodded silently.

At work, Lanya hoped for a gentle soul. She knew these people. She knew who might help her. At lunch, she found a man who worked in a different department named Oskar.

"Oskar, I need a little help and thought you might be the one to help me." He turned to her. They had spoken before but only in passing. Oskar had a questioning look on his face.

"Lanya, our little singer. What can I do for you?" Oskar was a hearty man who looked frail, since his pants were held up with a rope now. He had on a heavy coat, the factory was barely heated. His smile was genuine and Lanya hoped she had made a good choice.

"As you know, the rations they give us are not enough." Oskar nodded and kept looking at Lanya. "I want to make a trade. We need more food. I want someone to trade me ration cards for..." Lanya paused since she choked up with what she was going to say. Oskar raised his eyebrows, since no one was trading ration cards. For

anything. Lanya cleared her throat and continued. "My dog." Oskar
jerked his head and stared at Lanya.

"Your dog?"

"Yes. I cannot eat him. He is a small dog and I am sure someone
else..." She gagged again. It was too hard to say. Oskar reached out and
covered her hand with his big one.

"You think that someone will trade your dog for ration cards.
Hmm. Any meat is better than no meat I guess." They both knew that
meat was rare with rationing.

"But, Oskar, I hope it is not you, I do not want to think of the
dog every time I see you." Oskar patted the hand he held and nodded.

"So, you want me to find someone you do not know, to trade
your dog for ration cards." Lanya nodded now, unable to complete
a sentence. She had tears in her eyes and hoped they would not run
down her face. "This is tough. On you, on me, on all of us. I will see
what I can do." He got up and patted her shoulder as he walked back
into the factory. Lanya let the tears come. She was not a devil. She was
hungry.

Christmas was coming but there was no reason to celebrate.
Lanya knew this and Babu said nothing. There was a rumor that they
were going to get a bit more rations for the holiday but Lanya was not
sure what was true. Every day as she walked to and from work she saw
people pulling sleds laden with wrapped bodies or dragging them atop
the snow and ice. They all went to the cemetery where Valentina was
buried but the ground was too frozen to dig holes. She was afraid to ask
what they did. Usually, bodies were stacked until the spring melt then
buried. That was probably what happened now. Such devastation,
when you could not even bury your loved ones. *Damned Germans.*

At the sewing group on Wednesday, Lanya listened as the
older ladies talked about their holiday memories. She grew misty again.
Seemed like all she did these days was cry or almost cry. She tried to
remember the last time she laughed. She tried not to think about the
old days when she was a child. Christmas was her favorite. There were
festivals, presents, all kinds of foods and both her parents singing and
hugging. With her parents gone, Babu tried to make it still festive.
They would decorate the house and cook special foods. But this year,
there was no festive. It was dreary. The women around her mentioned
that this year they were not cooking like they usually did, no one

could. Some still decorated the house. As they quieted, Lanya began singing a song she remembered from her childhood. A song about a little girl and the magic of the holiday. They all joined in and the group brightened a bit. Maybe there was some Christmas, even without cookies. One woman started a second song and the whole group shared. Christmas was not about food.

At the factory, Lanya sat at her machine and was surprised when Oskar walked up. She smiled but he did not.

"I found someone who can help. He will give cards from his brother who died last week, in exchange for the dog, if you can." He patiently waited for her response. She stopped the machine and lowered her head.

"Thank you, that is the best news I guess. When shall we do this?"

Oskar nodded and said "Do you work tomorrow? I can meet you right out in front of the factory tomorrow for the trade."

"Yes, that will work." Her heart sank as she said it. Oskar tapped her hand and told her to meet him at 10 am right out front. She did not work but would meet for the trade. Lanya begrudgingly nodded. The afternoon seemed to last for a week as she tried to control what was in her head. She was sure she was a beast.

At home, she was not sure what to say to Babu. She decided to say nothing and just sneak the dog out. That would hurt less than goodbyes. So the next morning, Lanya gathered a big bag, grabbed the little dog, stuffed him in it, told Babu she was going to get food, and hurried out of the house. As she got onto the stairs, the dog scuffled and made little noises and Lanya was glad he did not do that in the house. She wanted to pat him as she walked but knew that meant she would turn around.

At the factory, sunlight was creeping up as Lanya arrived, just at ten. Oskar was there and greeted her warmly.

"Lanya, you know you have to do this. Do not feel bad. Lots of people do this. This is how you keep your family alive." Lanya said nothing. Oskar reached into his pocket and pulled out an assortment of ration cards. Lanya's eyes lit up. They would eat for more than a week on these! Her heart felt lighter. She went to pull the dog out but decided to just hand over the whole bag. She did not want to see him. She pulled the bag off her shoulder and offered it to Oskar. He took it, and she took the ration cards. "This is right. Your family will stay alive." Lanya had no words so she just turned and left. She stopped at the grocery store on her way back and bought some extra flour and some butter and she found a potato that might work.

At home, she brought the groceries into the kitchen where Babu was working. She looked at Lanya and the extra food and did not ask. She knew. Lanya started to cry again and made a quick exit to her bedroom.

Christmas was in a few days and today was the shortest day of the year. Lanya had mixed feelings about this day. Of course it had fewer hours of sun than any other. The longest night. And here in Leningrad, that was a really long night. Lanya remembered one year they had less than two hours of sunlight and she did not even see the sun much because of clouds. Gray everywhere. In years past there was a party for this long night, where people came, sang and drank. But, Lanya knew that tomorrow would be a tiny bit brighter. And the next day. Spring would come, if she lived that long. But she had to get through today.

The bombing this night was intense. It wasn't enough for the Germans that today was dark and freezing cold, they had to make it worse. Lanya and Babu and Mishka hurried to the shelter through the ice and piled up snow, as soon as they heard the sirens. A few people were missing, and Lanya wondered if they were dead. Probably. Maybe they were too sick to come. Or too weak to move from their apartment. People were starving and freezing. Their neighbor died three days ago and Lanya expected the wife would go soon. She could not help. How long could this go on? The building shook and glass shattered. Lanya wondered what glass was left to shatter. Would their apartment still be standing? They had repaired the last broken window, but who knew what this would do. The bombing went on and on. Lanya closed her eyes and wondered if she could sleep. How could she with all these explosions and kaboom sounds? It took hours for it to stop. The Germans were just messing with them. They expected the Leningraders to just come out with their hands up. Lanya knew that would never happen. Leningraders were proud and stubborn. Really stubborn.

Back at the apartment, Lanya lay down in the kitchen with the small fire going in the oven. Babu was quickly snoring and Lanya was a bit jealous. Babu could sleep anytime. Mishka was soon deep in slumber. Lanya tossed and turned. She was not too cold, but her heart was cold. This was wearing on her. *Can I die from this hell? Not from injury, cold or starvation, but this horrible existence?* If she was Babu's age it would be torture. The cold, the dark and the lack of food. That is why Babu did not leave the house. Lanya had to leave the house. Eventually, Lanya fell asleep. The dreams came but she did not scream as the bombs went off in her head. She simply rolled over and tried again.

In the morning, announcements came as she went to the grocers that the Party had given everyone an extra ration of flour and oil for the holidays. So it did happen. Was it really for the holidays or were enough people dying that they had a bit more? *What a sick thought*, she said to herself. *Couldn't it just be the holiday?* No, she was sure the holiday was only a symbol. She quickly changed plans and went to the Party office to get the new cards first. The line was longer and out the door, since everyone wanted the new cards immediately. The office was still gloomy and dark. The people at the counter were lifeless. She waited in line with her stomach in knots. She wondered if she would ever get over this. Probably not. At her turn she went and collected the cards, said a quick *spasibo* and turned to leave. As she got to the door, the young man with the thick eye glasses waited for her again. She faltered wondering what he wanted. Her hands tightened around her papers. Again, he asked for her papers as she prepared to leave. He looked over her papers and the ration cards, and as he handed them back, said "Thank you Svetlana." She jumped. He noticed her name. Now, he would probably go look up her family. They might come for her now. Her fear raced through her whole body and she had trouble taking steps to get out. *He knows my name and address. This is why I hate coming here. I would never in a million years come here if we were not in a war.* As she got out of the building she opened her mouth to gobble in air. It was too cold so she quickly pulled her scarf around her face and breathed through her nose. *The Party knows me. They will be keeping an eye on me now. What about Ivan?* Her feet were heavy like lead as she kicked the snow aside to stay on the sidewalk.

Christmas came and was no different than any other cold December day. This was the new Christmas, though plenty of people still celebrated holidays according to the old Julian calendar. Babu did not like the new calendar, but she went along. She always celebrated twice. Maybe the Christmas next month would be better. Lanya laughed at herself. Too much of an optimist? She wondered if there would be bombing tonight, or if the Germans would celebrate and give them some peace.

When Lanya came home from the factory a few days later, Babu was taking a nap in her bedroom. Lanya looked for Mishka but he was not in his room. Not in the front room, not in his bedroom, not in the kitchen. Where would he go? Lanya began to get anxious. Her brother might have gone out? She was glad she put their address on the arm of his coat since he had no idea how to tell anyone if he was found. She was putting her coat on again getting ready to go out to find him when the door opened and he walked in! Relief flooded through her. *Where had he been? What was he doing?* Then she saw his hands, he had a package in his hands. He held his package out to her. She carefully accepted. It was cold. She moved aside the flannel it was wrapped in, it was a fish! Mishka had brought home a fish! Lanya was too excited to talk.

"Mishka, how did you get a fish? Did you take it from someone?" It did not look like the kind at the grocers. Mishka was grinning. He then reached into his back pocket and pulled out what looked like a short fishing pole. "You what? You caught this? With the pole?" She hugged her brother. When Mishka was younger he was a great fisherman and would go to the Neva often. But the Neva was frozen over; how had he done this? "Did you break the ice? Ice fishing?" Lanya had done ice fishing as a child and knew it meant hours of sitting in the cold waiting for a bite. Mishka knew that too. But here was a fish that he caught! Her brain raced with ideas about Mishka- would he come back? Was he getting better? Would he do this again? Lanya was so excited she took the fish into the kitchen, knowing that Babu would make a feast out of it. Meat in Leningrad was rare. Tonight would be special.

Schastlivogo Rodhdestva. Merry Christmas.

Chapter
Twenty-One

Christmas was behind them and Lanya was happy for that. No point in celebrating when people were dying every day. Eventually, spring would come. Lanya slogged through the snow and ice going to work and coming home. It was easier if she did not think. Easy to say. Hard to do. She had not seen Ivan for more than a week and was sure that their affair was over. She was okay with that. He was a puzzle, and she did not have the energy to unwrap a puzzle. She had not heard from Aleksander, though he said he would write. Lanya smiled, thinking that if the mail was running he would send letters.

At sewing group, Lidia was almost jumping up and down.

"The wallpaper! Wallpaper will save us!" They looked at her like she had lost her mind. How could wallpaper save them?

"What are you talking about? How?"

"Have you been getting into the vodka?" A chuckle here.

"Not the wallpaper- the paste!" No one understood. "I heard today that the paste may be made with potatoes! We could scrape it off!"

"And what?"

"Hold on- I remember as a child putting wallpaper up. I tried to help but my father sent me away because I made too much mess. But the paste was made from boiled potatoes. Mushy and like a glue."

"Oh yes, I remember that."

"Potato glue?"

"So, what if we scrape it off?"

"Could we get some potato starch from the back of the wallpaper?"

"If we scraped it off, then boiled it, maybe." There was talk about how to get to this paste and what to do with it when they got it off the wall. Lanya decided it was worth a try. Better than starving.

When she got home, she went into her bedroom to start. She took a kitchen knife and went into a corner. If it did not work she would not ruin the whole room. Babu was asleep so Lanya worked quietly. She cut the wallpaper into a strip and tore it off the wall. It did not come off in big chunks, but small pieces. *This will take forever* she grumbled as she gathered bit by bit. *All I need to do today is to see if anything feels like paste.* She had never put wallpaper on or taken it off. So she was not sure what to expect.

She got a few pieces in her lap and touched the back of them. Crispy and firm. But there was some gunk stuck to it. She licked it to see if it tasted like a potato. No taste. But it was not disgusting. She took these pieces into the kitchen and laid them on the counter. She would talk with Babu in the morning.

Lanya had nightmares again. She woke up screaming and Babu spoke gently to her. Mishka rolled over to her corner and patted her arm. These dreams were different. Usually, she had bombs dropping. But in this one, as she ran from the bombs, some big black monster was chasing her, with gnashing teeth. What was it? A bear? Feodor, their dog? She could not tell but to her mind it looked like death. So she ran. What a way to wake up. Mishka patted her arm till she sat up. He smiled. She gave him a weak smile in return and he went back to his corner. How awful that she had to be comforted by her child-like brother. She rolled over and tried to sleep but it did not come. But laying here not sleeping was better than being chased by a monster and bombs. So Lanya waited. After some time, she slept.

When she woke, Babu was already making coffee. It wasn't real coffee, but it was almost coffee, and it was warm. As Lanya poured her cup, she remembered the smell of rich dark coffee. She liked hers black because she did not want anything to mess with the flavor of the coffee. But this is what would have to do.

"Babu, do you see these strips?" She pointed to the wallpaper from last night.

"Yes, what is this?" Babu was not smiling. She knew this was wallpaper and her tone was asking why Lanya was destroying a perfectly good wall.

"At sewing group last night, one woman said that the wallpaper was put on the wall with a paste made from potatoes. Do you know about that?" A gentle smile came over Babu's face.

"Oh yes. I remember putting some on the wall of my home years ago. Such a mess but it held the paper well. Why? What does this mean?"

"Well, you will know more then. One of the women said that we could scrape the paste off and use it to cook with."

"Hmm. Interesting." She picked up the strips and looked them over carefully. She ran her finger along the back side to feel the paste. "There is some thick paste here."

"I licked one to see if it tasted like potatoes." Babu picked up one and licked the back side, as Lanya had done. They both smiled.

"Maybe. So let me see what I can do. Can you get more?"

"There is wallpaper in every room. I can scrape it off. Mishka can help."

"Well, get me a stack and I will see what I can do. I will soak it first then see."

"I do not work today so I will spend today scraping. After I go get food." Babu nodded as she fondled the wallpaper strips. Lanya could see her brain running.

Lanya hurried out the door to get some food. She was relieved she did not have to go to the Party office for ration cards today. After last night she was hoping for simple tasks. Groceries and wallpaper. Yes, that would be enough. She got to the grocers early and there was a line. There was always a line. Even before the war there were lines, but then there were more stores. With the war, only a few stores were left that could handle the ration cards and difficulties of them. She knew this would take a while, it always did. She was glad to finally get to the front and see potatoes and cabbages and onions. These must be coming across Lake Ladoga. That was good. No meat but these would give her something to work with. She was glad Babu did the cooking since she could only make three or four meals with these items. But Babu could make a week's worth of food with some variety.

Back at the apartment, she asked Mishka to join her in her bedroom. She carefully peeled wallpaper and showed him how to do it. It was simple so she was not worried that he would do it poorly. And if it came off in small pieces, if Babu was going to soak it and scrape the paste off, the size of the piece did not matter. They spent most of the afternoon working on the bedroom walls and had a nice stack to take to Babu. The other rooms would come later. Unless Babu decided there was no point to it.

Babu smiled as Lanya brought the stack into the kitchen. She gathered them up and put them in her stock pot and covered them with hot water, hoping the heat would help release the paste. Lanya left the kitchen knowing this was in good hands.

For dinner, Lanya was surprised to see pancakes with sauteed onions on top. Babu explained, "I soaked them and scraped them and got quite a bit of paste off. Then I treated it like flour and made these pancakes. Topped them off with that onion you brought home today. I hope they are good. I used all the strips today. If I added some flour that we have it might do more." Lanya looked at the plate. They seemed fine. She added a bit of oil since there was no butter now and a touch of salt. Not too bad.

"Babu, this is pretty nice. I am glad you knew how to do this."

"Well, I did not know but I gave it a shot. They taste ok."

"They do taste okay. Not much taste. But free pancakes!" Mishka was eating well and finished his plate looking for more. Babu had another small stack on the counter and he quickly put those on his plate. Wallpaper for dinner. Who would have thought?

Chapter Twenty-Two

January was brutal. The storms were relentless and the sun did not shine for over a week. The cold and the gray was enough to make anyone go crazy. But, that was not all. The bombing continued. Every week at least once, sometimes more, Lanya and Babu grabbed Mishka and ran to the shelter through the snow or sleet, slipping as they hurried into the shelter basement. Inside it was better, Lanya felt somewhat protected. Now and then the building shook. More than once, Lanya wondered what would happen if this building got hit. Would they all be blown to bits? Or would they be smashed with debris and bricks? She remembered the huge mess when Valentina was buried and how long it took to get her out. As Lanya walked to work the first week of 1942 she looked around her beautiful city. There was nothing beautiful now. Buildings were broken and falling. Trees were split, and people were hobbling in the cold. Every day, she saw a family taking a bundle on a sled towards the cemetery on the other side of town. Sometimes families did not make that walk, they had no energy. They just kept the family in the apartment. It was too cold to become smelly, so there was no worry. Maybe they thought they would go next and kept the windows open to hurry it along. Lanya thought about that. *Would it be easier to freeze to death than to starve?* If she did not have Babu and Mishka, she would consider it.

Did Lanya expect to die from this horrible war? This thought stayed in her mind all day as she sewed and snipped. *What will death feel like?* The only one she had ever seen die was her sister and she did not show much pain. There was no blood. Movies always showed death with blood and guts, but not here, not now. Death here was silent and cold.

Lanya left the factory with these grim thoughts. She did not see Ivan as he stood outside. He called her name and Lanya froze. Ivan? Was that Ivan? She looked for him and there he was, with a smile on his face.

"Lovely Lanya, how are you?" He crossed over to her and opened his arms. She snuggled in.

"Ivan, I did not expect you. What a treat." Ivan grabbed her face and looked at her closely.

"Are you free tonight? I can share dinner?" This was temptation-for dinner she might do anything.

"Yes, I am free. If the Germans leave us alone." Ivan smiled and took her hand.

"Let's go." They walked towards his apartment, avoiding the most slippery parts of the street. They did not talk much but Lanya had butterflies in her stomach. *Food and sex with Ivan? Count me in!* She remembered Babu, and put that away; she would be home before too long. She remembered that she had decided against intimacy, but then again, for dinner, she would. She knew women who traded favors for food at the factory. It might be the only way to stay alive.

At his apartment, she could smell something in the kitchen. Ivan walked in and checked the stove, a pan was on the stove. As he lifted the lid, Lanya recognized the smell-ukha, a fish soup. Ivan found fish! Lanya was sure it could be done because her brother caught one in the frozen river a few weeks back.

"You have ukha- how nice!" Lanya's mouth was watering at the idea.

"Yes, I think it is ready. Shall we?" Ivan prepared the table while Lanya took off her coat and wrap. Ivan put the bowls on the table with a small cracker for each. Ivan must know people, Lanya thought. Her family was eating wallpaper paste and leather soup, but he has fish and crackers?

Lanya ate slowly, enjoying the taste and the texture on her tongue. It was not as good as Babu's but she would not say it. She was glad to have this.

"I am working on another show. Would you like to hear about it?" Lanya stopped eating to listen carefully.

"Yes, oh yes!"

"Well, I am thinking that we will perform in February, when everyone needs something to look forward to. I bet February in Leningrad is awful." Lanya nodded, it was freezing for days on end in February. "That means we need to get tryouts going now and practices started. Will you try out?"

"Of course I will!" Lanya began to feel some tingles running through her. Would she have the lead this time? Maybe she would be stage front! She did not take a moment to wonder how she could perform without energy and food to keep her standing hours at a time. That was a problem for another day.

"Well, I am working now on the theater. I have found another that is not so expensive to rent. I will talk to Andre so he knows when to have people show up." Lanya had finished her soup, and Ivan saw it. He took her hand again and led her to the bedroom, which again was lit only by a candle. The bedroom was cold, but she knew they would heat it up. She promised in her mind to thank him properly for telling her about the new show, so she did.

Soon after they were done, Lanya could hear Ivan's steady breathing; he was already asleep. *He sleeps like a dog*, she thought, and she wished she could fall asleep so easily. She left the bedroom and went back to gather her coat. She peeked into the kitchen to see if there were any more crackers but did not see them. Oh well. She walked out and down the stairs into the cold dark. But inside, her ego kept her warm. As she walked, she put aside the small glow and remembered her recent decision, to cool things with Ivan. *Was it guilt?* She just ignored her own decision. She knew this would go nowhere good. *And Ivan was trouble*, but she was not sure what kind of trouble. But, there was a new show, so again she focused on what was easier to think about.

Ivan was waiting two days later after work. Lanya smiled and he seemed in a hurry.

"Lanya, I cannot stay. Sorry." His smile broke but he kept going. "I want to tell you when tryouts are. Can you come by next Wednesday? I need to finalize the location, I can give it to you another day."

"What time?"

"Hopefully around dinner time. We are scheduling some for morning, but you can do after work.

"I will be there."

"Great." He bent down and kissed her cheek and turned to go. "See you then lovely Lanya." He hurried off. Her smile faded but remembered their time a few days ago and was not too heartbroken.

Tryouts next week! As Lanya scurried home she racked her brain thinking of a song to work on. Should she use the same song as last time? Or, if Andre and Ivan were there should she use a new song? Should she use a song from the last show? There had been no new songs in Leningrad since the war started seven months ago so it had to be one from earlier.

She got home fast and burst into the front room.

"Babu, there is going to be another show soon! I am going to try out!" Babu looked up from her knitting and smiled. Lanya understood that Babu worked hard in the candlelight trying to make things to keep them warm.

"Good, you will get a spot for sure. Do you want to do this?" Babu knew the answer to that question as she said it. Even starved, Lanya wanted to be onstage.

"Yes, yes, yes!" Lanya danced to her bedroom where she threw her coat to the bed. *What song will I sing?* Songs came in and out of her mind and she started singing quietly. She wanted the lead, so this tryout would be her most important!

Chapter
Twenty-Three

Lanya took Mishka out the next day to gather firewood. Again, they went to bombed buildings looking for broken furniture. It was not tough, as every building had some broken pieces. They gathered armfuls and returned to their apartment. Lanya decided that they would come back another day to scrape the wallpaper. The day was gray and cold. It was too cold to snow and usually this just meant they stayed inside baking cookies and sipping tea. But today, they just stayed inside. The opened the heavy drapes because even gray light was better than no light. Lanya wondered if this would ever end. Winter, death, this war. It was endless.

At work, another empty machine had small tokens. Lanya did not spend time looking at it, it was too painful, too close. *If she was killed will they do the same for me? What will they put on my machine? A program from her show, maybe some trinket from school?* Lanya was glad to collect the leather scraps, this was a small way to help. They had already boiled Valentina's shoes and the boots left by her dad years ago. And the dog was gone, so they could eat what they would normally give him. Babu was weak but Lanya was not sure if that was age. Babu ate as much as Lanya did, but she was not as stout as she used to be. Neither was Lanya. She had never been big or curvy, but now, she was like a twig. Her clothes hung on her. She wished she had some fat to keep her warm. But she usually wished for that this time of year.

Sewing group was somber. The women were all irritable tonight.

"They bombed it again! I hope they go to hell!"

"What did they bomb this time?"

"The Road of Life!"

"Again? They bombed the road across the frozen lake?"

"How will we get food and medicine now?"

"It will freeze again I am sure." Lake Ladoga was completely frozen over and some supplies and food were coming across. And the Germans bombed it. How inhuman could they be? There was some comfort in the idea that ice always comes back. Reason said it would be as good as ever after one January night and Leningraders hung onto any hope they were desperate for. Not sure what would happen in March as thawing began, but for now it was a sliver. The women settled into their sewing, Again it was sleeping bags, and the talk turned to family and gossip. Another Wednesday of hell.

Ivan was at the lamppost after work, huddled against the cold. Lanya could not help the small warmth that surged in her.

"Lovely Lanya, good to see you. Can I walk you home?"

"Ivan, very nice. That would be nice." Lanya was going to be grateful for the walk; it was better than alone. But she knew there was more.

"I have tryouts ready, are you free on Wednesday, as I said?" Wednesday was sewing night, but Lanya knew she could miss.

"I will be, what time?"

"Around five in the afternoon, at the theater near St. Ivan's- you know the one?" Lanya had seen it. It was small and intimate as theaters go.

"Yes, I will be there. Do you have any favorite song you think I should do?"

"No, I trust your judgment, you know so many songs." Yes, she did. She started again searching in her head for the right song. Ivan kept going.

"I have a new show in mind, about a young couple that wants to make it big but has trouble. Do you remember that one?" Lanya went back into her memory but it did not come.

"I am not sure. But once I hear a song I am sure I will."

"Great. I may come by next week to ask you for dinner again, if I may." He stopped, as they were at Lanya's street. He put his arms around her lightly, but she could feel the notebook under his coat.

Again she wondered what it was for. Probably the show, she figured. She hugged him back quickly, then Ivan pecked her cheek as he said goodnight. "See you on Wednesday if not before."

"Goodnight Ivan." Her heart was a bit lighter than when she came out of the factory. She got to the apartment and handed Babu her small bag of leather scraps and Babu put them aside. She liked to wait until there was a bowl full before she cooked them up, if that is what you called it. She hurried off to her room to work on song choice.

On the way to work the next day, she was humming and singing lightly. In line for groceries she was humming. It was hard for her to put the songs away. She still could not think of the show Ivan mentioned or she would be practicing a song from that one specifically. But she wanted to be sure she was at her prime.

At the factory in the morning, there was a cluster of workers near the supervisors desk. Lanya gathered with them.

"She had a whole drawer full of them!"

"How did she get them?"

"Was she going to sell them?" One worker in the Party office who was in charge of the ration cards had been found with a whole stack of cards. While people were dying without food, she was hoarding them! That was evil!

"I heard she took a few home every night."

"Probably after telling families they could not have more!" These people were angry, and rightfully so!

"They will send her to prison camp." That thought brought fear to Lanya, after her parents were taken like they were. But Lanya did not know why her parents were taken.

"No, an announcement was made yesterday that any fraud of ration cards would mean execution." Wow. This woman was going to be killed. But she killed others it seemed. *Sounds like harsh justice,* Lanya thought.

"I hope she goes straight to hell." Lanya was not sure exactly what hell was, but the person who said it seemed to have a picture.

"If we did not have enough to worry about being bombed and starved, this woman, this Leningrader, steals more! They should shoot her. I will do it myself!" This was an older man who probably saw fighting in the Great War twenty five years ago. Lanya had never heard him speak before.

The crowd wandered off and Lanya went to her machine. *How can people be like this? We are all hungry. That woman probably had put on a few pounds during the war,* Lanya thought. She cinched her belt a bit tighter and was angry at this woman. *Maybe I would shoot her too.*

Another bombing that night, and Lanya and Mishka helped Babu down the stairs and into the shelter. They found their little corner, like always and wrapped their blankets around themselves. Lanya clasped her hands together to control her fingers that never stopped. She should work on that, finding peace for her fingers. Lanya had the vodka. She offered Babu some and she took a sip. She did not offer any to Mishka because she was not sure what he would be like. He used to be fine with liquor and enjoyed vodka now and then. But if he was like a child, it did not seem right. Lanya tried to sleep but the bombs kept her awake. She knew she would not sleep when they got home. She always had nightmares after a bombing raid.

The day of the audition, Lanya was up early and could not sit still. She had songs running through her head but had still not made the final decision. Maybe she should just sing one from the last show, from the night she played lead? That sounded good. At lunch, she told Maru about the tryout, and Maru, as usual was thrilled.

"Go get 'em! You have a fabulous voice! You will get the lead!" Lanya loved having such a cheerleader.

On her way to the theater, Lanya had to go through a different section of town. She had been there before so it was not foreign, though she had never spent much time there. As she turned a corner, a man was standing at the edge of a shop that had no signs.

"Hey come here" he said as Lanya came around. He was a small man with dark hair streaked with gray and a tired looking coat. "I have something you want." Lanya paused. How would he know what she wanted? "Come inside. I have meat." Lanya stopped cold. He had meat? But this was not a grocery store. He was looking at her intently. "No ration cards needed."

Lanya did not have her ration cards, so that was good. But she did not have any money, either. She did not carry money since there was not much to buy. Something about him sent shivers down her spine.

"No, not today. Sorry." She crossed the street end kept going, hurrying a bit to get away from him. *How can he have meat?* This was not a true shop. And no ration cards? Something was not right.

"You know you are hungry. We all are." His voice followed her down the road. Shivers.

When she got to the theater, there were a few people about. She recognized Andre, the director, and Ivan in the back. She waited for them to call her and she walked onto the stage. They were using oil lamps so there were not spotlights at this time. When is was her turn, she hummed for a second, then burst into song. Her voice was full and strong and she hit every note just right. She did all the extra bits she had practiced and when she finished, there was no applause, she did not expect it. But she felt good. She breathed a huge relief sigh and left the stage. As she went to the door, Ivan appeared.

"That was as good as I have ever seen you. You impressed me Lanya." She glowed at his compliment. She had been good. "Dinner tomorrow? Six?"

"Thank you Ivan. Tomorrow sounds good. See you at six." She hurried out into the cold night, glad that was over. She knew it would take a few days to get the results. Ivan might even tell her tomorrow.

When she got home, Babu was still up. Lanya started to make their weak tea and sat at the kitchen table.

"Babu, I went to my try out. I will find out soon." Babu covered Lanya's hands with her own. Lanya continued. "I had to go to a different theater, over by St. Isaac's. You know that neighborhood?" Babu nodded.

"Not nice place" she said in a low voice.

"No, it was... um... different. A man came up to me and what he said gave me chills. I am not sure why. He said he had meat. No ration card needed. Do you know what that means? How..." Babu squeezed Lanya's hand hard.

"Never go by that place again! Never go to that place!" Lanya was shocked. Babu never raised her voice but she was angry.

"What, Babu, what is it?" Lanya had no idea what had made her grandmother so mad.

"Those people, those people should all go to hell!" Lanya waited for an explanation and sipped her tea. This was not normal for her grandmother.

"Do you know what this is? What they are doing?" Lanya shook her head.

"It is not pork or beef or fish." Lanya tried to understand. *Not pork, beef, fish, was it mutton?* She had eaten mutton years ago.

"It is people!" Babu yelled and jumped out of her seat. People? What people? Lanya was confused. "They wanted you to eat dead people!" Lanya finally could picture what Babu meant and her stomach wrenched. *People? They were selling people? To eat?* Lanya pushed her teacup away. "Do not ever go there again. Or they will get you next!" Babu left the room and Lanya had pictures running through her head of the man she saw. Now she understood why she had the creeps when he was near. *He was sizing her up.* She would never go back to that street again. Her stomach cramped thinking about it. Sick. She had nightmares again, without the air raid.

At six o'clock the next day Lanya was at Ivan's door. She hated to be late. And she was hoping for another good meal. Ivan smiled and hugged her and brought her into the kitchen. She smelled sausage. *How can he get sausage?* But she was anxious. Lanya looked to be sure the sausage was round with casing on it, so she did not worry about what kind of meat it really was. She did not want to discuss her disgusting adventure with Ivan. Too gruesome.

He had plates ready and loaded them up. Not loaded, but there was enough food to make Lanya salivate before she even sat down. Having Ivan around was good for her. *Or is he? Was she trading bedroom time for dinners? And stage time? As she ate, these questions rumbled in her head. I have no backbone. Or I would be at home with Babu. Hungry.* They ate quickly with little talking. The only thing they had to talk about was the show and it was too soon for answers. He put the empty plates in the sink and took her hand, leading her into the bedroom. They undressed quickly and got into the bed. It was over quickly and they relaxed after. As Lanya got up to leave, Ivan got up too.

"Will you hold onto this for me?" He handed her a different little notebook with a brown cover. She nodded and took it from him. *What is in these notebooks? And why does he want her to hold them? Should I ask him?* He saw the doubt in her eyes and added "There are people who are trying to cause trouble for me and they do not need to see this. Thank you again." *People? Who?*

Lanya finished dressing and put her coat and gloves on. She put on her wool hat and pulled it over her ears as she shoved the notebook in a pocket inside her coat. She would try to read this one again tonight. Would Babu understand this? She let herself out after a quick kiss and sludged through the January night to get home.

She did not see Ivan the next day, but on Saturday there he was at the light post. He had a smile on his face and her heart jumped. Would he tell her she got the part? A warm hug and and she stepped back, looking at his face.

"I have good news, lovely Lanya." Her breath stopped. "You, lovely, have the lead!" Lanya wanted to jump up and down but she did not have the energy.

"Really? The lead?"

"Yes, and I have here the script for you. The songs are in here as well. Do you read music?" She did not, but she took the folder and squeezed it with both hands. The lead! She really could be a star! "I cannot stay; I have other cast members to meet tonight. Rehearsals start Monday at five, in the same theater where we had tryouts. I look forward to coaching you!" With that, he gave her a kiss on the cheek and turned to walk away. Part of her was frozen. This was her big chance! She hugged the folder then started her quick walk home.

"Babu, Babu, I got the lead! I have the script right here!" She hurried in to the kitchen where Babu was soaking leather bits.

"The lead? That is wonderful. You will be the best!" Babu turned and gave Lanya a big smile. Lanya had noticed she did not walk much, only from the kitchen to the front room and bathroom. Babu was slowing down. But Lanya was not worried about that, she wanted to go into her room and study this script! She had a lot of work to do!

As she got into her room, she saw the brown notebook she took from Ivan's house on the table. She put the script aside and opened the notebook. Again, some Russian, some other words in a different language. She knew it was not Cyrillic, it was the alphabet they used in the West. *Does Ivan speak another language? What if this is German?* Could Babu help?

She took the notebook into the kitchen and laid it down. Babu looked up. "Babu, can you help me for a second? I cannot read this and thought maybe you could." Babu slowly came to where the notebook was and opened it. She turned a page and another.

"Where did you get this?" Lanya wondered if she should tell.

"Someone asked me to hold onto it. What does it say?"

"This has Russian in it, but it also has German." Lanya's heart stopped.

"Can you read it?"

"Yes, in my youth I could read German. It has been a long time, so I am not sure I can understand this."

"What does it say?"

"I am not sure. The Russian seems to be a random mix of words..."

"Yes, I saw that. I have never seen anything like that."

"Hmm. The German seems to be random as well. Where did you get this?" Again, Lanya wondered what she could say. *Why does Ivan have a notebook with random mixed up Russian and German?* She decided to be discreet.

"I do not want to say, Babu. Because I do not know what this all means."

"Well, Lanya, we are in a war. With Germans. And this notebook makes no sense. If it was something that was not a problem, it would not be all mixed up, right?" Lanya nodded, and Babu went on. "I think this is suspicious. I wonder if it has to do with the war. Why both languages and we cannot read them either of them?" Babu closed the book. "You need to think about why you have this. Whoever gave it to you could be in trouble." Babu moved away from the book and went to the stove. She said no more.

Lanya picked up the book and went back into her bedroom. She opened it again, studying the Russian words. *Can this be a code? Why does Ivan have a book with a code in it?* She looked at the words carefully. *Is Ivan in trouble?* The Russian words were in a jumble, but Lanya saw a few words repeated. Over and over. *Campfire, rosebush, cigarette. What is this? Do these words substitute for something?* She spent more than an hour trying to decipher it. She looked at the German words too. Again, some words were repeated. *This has to be a code! What is Ivan doing with a book full of codes? Do his other notebooks have codes too? Is this Ivan's handwriting? Is he in Leningrad for more than a show? Can he be a spy?* She had never seen his handwriting so she could not say. This was a mystery. *Should I tell Babu?* She was exhausted after all this turmoil and fell into a light sleep.

As she went to get groceries the next day, everything was chaos. There was no bread. At all. Anywhere. Lanya knew that bread was hard to get, but none? The crowd was angry and Lanya could understand. She listened to the commotion trying to discern the problem.

"No bread!"

"Nazis must have something to do with this!"

"I thought we got some wheat from the Road of Life!"

"I heard it was all the bakeries."

"No water."

"No water? The bakeries need water?"

At this point, a Party man came out, you could tell he was a Party man by the brown sweater, and he said "Calm down. We are working on it. With no power, the bakeries are out of water. They need water to bake and clean." The chaos got louder and Lanya got pushed to the side a bit. "We are going to the river to get water." The Neva was frozen over completely though water was running below the ice line, and it would take a lot to break it. Lanya could hear the roar of a truck of some sort. People backed off as the truck came near. Another rumble was from some earth mover thing with a big crane. Was this how they were going to break the ice? "Will you all help? If we get buckets, will you all help bring the water up?" The Party man looked like he was begging. The Party needed to look like it was in control and keep these people from an uprising. Lanya backed off so she could see what was happening. The truck and heavy equipment moved slowly down the street as the crowd parted. The Party man came out, lining people up in two lines. Telling them to go down to the river where he took the buckets. They wanted a human chain? To bring water up? Would they have a tank for it? She looked farther down the road and saw a large round water tank coming and it stopped near the bakery on the corner. So, they wanted to make a human chain, everyone fill a bucket and then all fill the tank. Lanya decided she had nothing to lose, and if this was the only way to get bread, she would.

So she got in line with the other women, the few men were closer to the river and she took the bucket as it was passed to her. There were some people who shifted to the other line, and Lanya moved to the full bucket side, helping the older ladies go to the empty bucket side. These older ladies had it tougher than she did.

This went on for two hours, in the January cold. But Lanya wanted bread. So she quietly handed buckets down the line. While she did, she sang the songs from the new show in her head. Someone down the line was singing a patriotic song and Lanya joined in. Soon the whole line was singing. Lanya could think of worse ways to spend a day. She did not have much energy and could not do much more, as she was feeling weak. She saw the older women and could see they were feeling a bit worse. The Party man walked towards them. "Soon we will be done. The tank is almost full. You have saved the day!" He said that as he went down the line and Lanya was ready to stop. She heard a call and they all stopped getting water and passed the last of the buckets. The crowd talked and a few laughed. How long before bread? At least another hour, she was told. The crowd began to disperse, as some were going home first. Lanya gathered her things and went to see what else she could buy today. She never knew what would be available at the stores so it was always a grab what you can situation.

With one loaf in her hand, Lanya climbed the steps to the apartment. The bread was warm, so she kept it in her hands. Babu noticed the smell right away and Lanya told her the story of the bucket brigade. Babu raised her eyebrows but was glad to have the bread. Mishka had brought in some more broken furniture for the stove today so the house was warm. Lanya was exhausted again so she went to her room and crashed on the bed. As she rolled over, she saw Ivan's notebook again. She needed to take it back to him. If this was something sneaky, she did not want it here in her house. The Party would crucify her.

Chapter
Twenty-Four

As Lanya woke up in her bedroom the next morning, she was freezing. The kitchen was much warmer. Why didn't she go to the kitchen? She sat up, and was hit by the urge to vomit and stood up trying to get to the toilet. She made it, but after she threw up she sat down. What was that? She had dinner at Ivan's, was there something that made her sick? She stood up but felt weak and went back to her bed. After a short period of time, her stomach settled so she got up and dressed. She was not ill often, so this was a surprise.

In the kitchen, she had weak tea and a biscuit. She saw the pan with the leather scraps simmering on the back of the stove. Mishka was there, lying on his side. Babu was turning and coming awake. Lanya looked at her grandmother. *What do I know about her?* She was her mother's mother and her first name was Natasha. *What was her name before she married?* Lanya remembered being told that her husband, Lanya's grandfather, had died in the civil wars after the Revolution around 1920. So Lanya never met him and her mother had no memories of him. She had never heard Babu talk of anyplace else, so Lanya was sure she was born and raised here in Leningrad. *Did she ever have a job? Or was she always a housewife or caretaker?* Lanya could not imagine her in an office; that did not work. Probably at home all the time. And she was a good cook, even with simple foods. Like leather and wallpaper paste, Lanya thought with a wry smile. *How old is she?* At least 60, plenty old. Maybe older? She got around the house without too much effort, but she could not easily go up and down the stairs anymore. *It is time I to listen more to Babu,* Lanya decided.

Lanya's stomach was quiet now, so she washed up and got ready for work. She had a show to prepare for! Work went by slowly because Lanya was going over the script in her head. She had not finished it and was excited to get to the songs. When she got home, she huddled down and read and re-read the script. The story was a good one, and the audience would love it. Lanya wondered how big of a hit it would be. Would people even come?

At dinner, Lanya wanted to ask Babu some questions and listen.

"Babu, I have never asked before, but what do you miss? About your life from years ago?" Lanya thought this was a fair question to ask an older person; they all had memories. Babu did not answer quickly but Lanya could see the thoughts buzzing around. She looked directly at Lanya.

"Church. I miss going to church." This was not what Lanya expected to hear. She thought it might be dancing, boyfriends, or new clothes.

"Tell me why."

"In church, you were part of something. Something that would make you better, make the world better." Lanya had never been to church. All churches were closed now, and called museums.

"Did you go to St. Isaac's?"

"Yes, a few times for holidays. It was so big, with all the natural light and the high ceilings. So grand." Babu smiled as she reminisced. "We usually went to a small church about six blocks from here. It is now the Ministry of Transportation." Babu's face had a smirk. Lanya knew the building, not your typical office building, but she had no idea it was originally a church.

"If churches were open now, would you go?"

"Oh, yes. I liked the people and the faith, caring for what was inside me. Now we have nothing. The Party does not care for what is inside you. Would you go?" Lanya did not know how to answer. She did not know what that even meant.

"I do not know, Babu. I do not know what church is like."

"And you probably never will. That is sad." Babu got up and cleared the plates and rinsed the dishes. Lanya decided to go back and start memorizing her parts.

As she got up the next morning, Lanya again was sick. She made it to the bathroom and went through her head to see what she had eaten. She could find nothing abnormal. She decided that tonight, she would take a few sips of vodka and see if that would make a difference in the morning.

Rehearsal the first night was chaotic, as was usual. Andre was here and there, yelling and scolding. Ivan was in the background. Lanya knew a few of the other cast members and the girl who was lead in the last show was not here. That was okay with Lanya. It was her turn to be the star! They worked through the first act, with blocking and prompting. Lanya liked this feeling. The songs came easily. As soon as she heard them she was sure this would work. She sounded good, and had some energy while on stage, better than she had in a long time. After the rehearsal, Lanya used every ounce of energy she had to get home.

Lanya woke up with a violent stomach and rushed to get to the bathroom again. What was wrong with her? The vodka sips had done nothing. She had fallen asleep quickly since she had been so tired after rehearsal. She was not usually so tired. As she came out of the bathroom, Babu was up and starting tea. Lanya felt like she had to explain.

"I do not know what is wrong with me. I have been so sick." Babu looked at her. She handed Lanya her tea.

"You do not know?" Her voice was full of disbelief.

"No, it is not like me to be sick." Babu was still looking at her and Lanya was beginning to feel uncomfortable. What was the old woman thinking?

"No, it is not. I do not think you are sick." Babu stopped what she was doing and looked at Lanya. Lanya looked back.

"Of course I am sick. You saw me rush to the bathroom."

"Yes, your stomach is upset; that is normal." Normal? Lanya was confused. She did not want to eat the oat cake Babu offered. Her stomach swirled again. She pushed it away. Babu sat down.

"When is the last time you had your cycle?" Lanya looked up and tried to remember. Since the war, without food, she had not been regular. It had been a few months. Maybe once since the last show ended in November. Not since Christmas, for sure. Lanya began to understand.

"You think I am..." She trailed off, unable to express the dawning realization.

"You tell me. Your stomach is upset in the mornings. Are your breasts swollen at all?" Lanya ran her hands down the side of her pajamas. Yes, her breasts had a tiny swell, but she thought nothing of it. "Are you tired? More than normal?" Lanya nodded, remembering how tired she was last night. "I think you might be pregnant." Lanya was glad Mishka was not here listening. *Can I be pregnant? How? Ivan? Oh no, this is not good. I have a show!* And Ivan would not be a good father. He was too wrapped up in himself. They had never prevented it. Lanya thought back and realized she had not spent any time thinking about the risk. But her cycles had been off, probably due to the lack of food. And stress. Oh, no. Lanya put her arms on the table and laid her head on them. Babu put her hand on Lanya's shoulder. "There, there, we will make it work." Lanya wanted to cry but couldn't.

At the factory, Lanya could not get the idea of pregnancy out of her mind. *What if I am? How will I handle that? Will I be able to be on stage? Will I still work? Will Babu watch my baby while I am at the factory? Will I tell Maru?* She would have lunch with Maru. *No, don't tell her yet. Make sure. Will I tell Ivan? What will he do?* Lanya was sure he would not welcome a child. No, this would be Lanya's problem. *As if I need another problem. This will ruin my chance to be a big star. I will not be able to travel and go to Moscow or Kiev for shows. I am not ready for this.* She hated herself for not planning ahead.

At rehearsal, things went as they usually did. Lanya tried to keep her mind on the stage, not the bathroom. She could feel herself getting tired. She hoped this would not make her too tired to perform. They had four weeks of rehearsal and the show was supposed to open at the beginning of March. Maybe by then, she would be better. Would she fit into her costume then? Or could she just wear her own clothes? She pushed these thoughts away. She saw Ivan as they finished and gave him a weak smile. He did not come over to speak so she did not approach him. When she got into bed, she had a feeling of dread thinking about waking up. She skipped the vodka.

As she awoke, again she dashed for the bathroom. She decided not to eat again, since she was sure it would not stay down. *How do women go through this, time and time again? My mother did it three times, I can do it once.* Did she want a boy or a girl? She had not yet even imagined what would come. She had no pictures in her head, no names. Definitely not Ivan. No work today so she went into her room and curled up and slept again.

The next few mornings were ugly. Lanya hated herself. She hated Ivan. She hated everyone except Babu. Babu was gentle and fed her carefully. When the bombs came, Babu guided Lanya instead of the usual way. The shelter was almost comfortable now. Lanya had nightmares afterward, as usual. *Will the nightmares hurt the baby? Is the baby getting enough food, if Lanya threw up so much?* Honestly, not much came out since so little went in. *Will I starve to death from lack of food or from the pregnancy?*

Rehearsals were three nights a week and sewing circle one. Lanya was exhausted. As soon as she got home she flopped onto her mattress in the kitchen. Mornings were dreadful but she learned how to manage. If she could eat a soft rusk, the nausea subsided. Breakfast came later. She would get used to this. She tried to figure out how pregnant she was. If she had her last cycle in November, and it was late January, she could be almost three months. Maybe. When would she show? She did not want to be carrying a baby around since she was so frail already. That would be impossible.

The next morning, she woke up and rushed to the bathroom. As she was done vomiting, she felt cramping. This did not bother her since her stomach was wretched. But the cramps did not let up. She curled up on the bathroom floor. She was not sure she could walk to work today. She forced herself back to bed again. After an hour, the cramps shifted and she felt something break. What? Then she her thighs were warm. And wet. What? She looked at her lap and saw blood. She called for Babu.

"Babu, can you come here please?" Her weak voice hardly carried. She tried to wipe the blood using her shirt nearby. She saw it all over her legs and her crotch area. The cramps were getting worse. She folded over in pain. "Babu!"

Babu came tottering in and raised her eyebrows as she saw the mess. She went out and came back with warm wet rags.

"Let me get this. You lay back." Babu went about, wiping her and saying soothing words. Lanya wondered what was going on. She felt like she was on her period, but ten times stronger. The cramps came and went. She was light headed. *Loss of blood?* She lay back and wondered if she was losing this baby. Was she hoping that she was losing this baby? She was afraid to think that. Babu seemed to finish and gathered all her rags to take to the kitchen.

"Babu, what is it?" Babu looked at her gently.

"I am not sure. But...." She paused and turned her head away. "You may not be pregnant anymore. Stay in bed. I will bring you some tea. And vodka." Babu went out and came back later with a cup of steaming hot tea and a small bottle of vodka. "Drink both of these and try to relax. I will bring you some food in a while. Try to sleep." The cramping had lessened, Lanya drank the tea and followed it with two shots of vodka. Two may not be enough she thought. Sleep came. When she woke up, Lanya stumbled to the bathroom. More bleeding but no more cramping. *How will I know if I am still pregnant?* She had no answers.

When she woke up the next morning, she was not sick. That is good, she thought. She got up to use the bathroom and wiped away a small amount of blood. Is this over? She left early for work, knowing it would take longer to get there in her weakened condition. She made it to the factory and slumped at her machine. *How am I going to operate this thing today?* She missed the power machines. She tried all day to do her best but was very glad when the day was over. She had rehearsal tonight and rushed home to get a nap in.

The nap was needed and welcome. She almost overslept but Babu came in and woke her. She knew she needed to leave early to be sure to get there in time, still weak. Would she have the energy to sing? She pulled on her warmest coat and gloves and made it to the street. It was not too dark so she could make out the street. When would spring get here? She stumbled into the theater and looked for the cast. There were a few people around, no one on stage. She found Andre.

"What is going on? Where is everybody?" She turned her head and could not find Ivan.

"We are not having practice tonight Lanya. Ivan is not here and the Party came to look for him. Do you know where he is?" Andre gave her a look, without saying he knew about them.

"I do not know. I have not seen him." She had a bad feeling nagging at her. She still had his notebook. She did not bring it today since she did not want any extra weight. She turned to go. She saw two cast members leaving and followed them. *Is Ivan in trouble? If the Party is looking for him, this is very bad.* They had practice again tomorrow and that might reveal the truth. She hoped Ivan was not in trouble. She knew, better than most, that the Party would spare no one in their hunt.

She dragged herself home in the dark. She wondered why she even came tonight. She could have missed practice, but hated to think that they could not count on her. It was better that practice was cancelled. *I will be better tomorrow.* She stumbled up the stairs and jerked the door open and almost fell into a chair. She wiped her brow, glad to be in from the freezing cold. She sat for a few minutes to thaw, then heard a knock on the door. Babu was not near and she fought to get up and answer the door.

She opened the door and Ivan pushed himself in.

"Lanya, can I come in? I need to come in." He barged in and closed the door with a quick thump. He leaned against it.

"Ivan, what is going on? You look awful." She slumped into a chair. He did not comment on her frail state.

"I need to stay here tonight." He looked left and right, trying to see if anyone was around. Lanya had a million thoughts.

"Why?" *Why on earth does Ivan want to be here tonight?* Babu would certainly say no, after looking at that notebook. "Why were you not at rehearsal?" Babu tottered into the room after hearing the door slam. She looked surprised to see Ivan. Lanya was too. She looked at Babu and took her arm. "One minute Ivan." She turned Babu towards the bedroom. She stopped hoping he was not in trouble. It was too late for that.

Babu waited for Lanya to speak when they got into the bedroom. "Babu, I do not know why he is here. He says he needs to stay here tonight. I am worried." Lanya paused trying to gather her thoughts.

"He cannot stay." Babu spoke slowly, deliberately. "He is in trouble. I know you have..." Babu paused looking for the right word, then skipped ahead. "If he is in trouble, then we will be in trouble also. He cannot stay here." Lanya nodded.

"Can you tell him?" She looked at her grandmother weakly, hoping she would understand. She did.

"I will tell him." Babu turned to leave the room and Lanya followed. They reached the front room where Ivan was slouched in the chair, looking as if his world was ending.

"Young man," Babu began and waited until Ivan looked at her before she continued, "we cannot have you stay with us. It would put us in danger. You must go, now." Babu walked the steps to the door and opened it. Ivan opened his mouth and looked at Lanya. She did not want to look at him but finally took her eyes off the carpet and glanced at him. She shrugged her shoulders. Lanya would have to apologize to him tomorrow. Ivan got out of the chair, with his shoulders still slumped and headed for the door.

"I am sorry" he mumbled as he went through the door. He walked away slowly but did not look back.

Lanya collapsed into the chair he just got out of. "Babu, you did the right thing. If he is in trouble, we would be too. And the Party would not give us a chance to defend ourselves."

"I think he is in more trouble than we know. He cannot be around us. I wish he was not in charge of your show. You have to work with him but you cannot see him outside the theater. Do not go with him anywhere. They may be watching him now. I do not know what he is doing, but I do not want us to be any part of it." Lanya heard the finality in Babu's voice and knew she was right. Whatever she had with Ivan was completely over. If he came to the factory, she would not talk to him. If he asked to see her she would pretend she was sick. She could not spend another moment with him outside of rehearsal.

Lanya was weak. She had been weak before this day started, after losing the blood, and then she walked to the theater and back in the cold and dark. Now she had this trauma. *What is Ivan doing? Does he even care if we get caught up in it? No, he is selfish and looking out for himself.* Lanya got up from the chair and looked over at Babu, still looking at the door. She patted Babu on the shoulder and went into the kitchen and got the small bottle of vodka. She took it into her bedroom and took a big gulp before she even sat on her bed. She might finish this bottle.

Lanya woke screaming to the pictures of bombs and fires and body parts flying. She woke up with a sweat on her forehead, and Mishka came in to check on her. She saw him and it took a minute for her to realize she was in her own bedroom. She got up and smiled at him so he would not worry. After using the bathroom she joined them in the kitchen to soak up the warmth. She settled into a deep sleep quickly and the nightmares stayed away.

She spent most of the next day in bed, singing in her head and reading. She ate a little and knew she would have to go shopping tomorrow. Rehearsal was after dinner so she dressed and again put on her thickest coat. She was a bit better than yesterday but she did not feel strong. But she wanted this show more than anything in her life, so she trudged through the snow towards the theater. As she walked, she tried to compose a conversation with Ivan. *Should I apologize? Have I done anything wrong? Should I explain how the Party treated my family? Will he understand? Will he be angry?* She tried to predict his reactions, his face and what his expressions would mean. She knew she was not good at reading expressions so she was sure she would have to use words. Explain herself and leave it at that.

She got to the theater and opened the big wooden door. She saw no one. No Ivan, no Andre, no cast members. She opened her eyes large to see in the dark theater and heard something behind the stage. She carefully pulled aside the curtain and there was Andre, sitting on a stack of boxes.

"Andre, I am glad to see you. Where is everybody? Where is the cast? Where is Ivan?" Her questions ran together as she let them jumble out.

Andre looked at her with sad, tired eyes. "There will be no show. Ivan will not be here again and without him we cannot go on." His voice was gritty and his anger was clear.

"Where is he? Is he okay?"

Andre turned to the backstage area with a resigned look. "Ivan was arrested this morning by the Party. Something about being an enemy of the people?" Lanya watched as Andre looked like the life of him drained out.

"What? Arrested?" Lanya sat on another stack of boxes. What about the show? Her lifelong dream? Shattered? "Do you know anything more?"

"I do not know much. I wanted to talk to him this morning so I went to his apartment. Just as I was coming up, I saw them taking him out with his hands tied. They were almost dragging him. And they were yelling at him. Calling him a Nazi and an enemy. I am glad they did not come while I was at his place or else they would have taken me away, too." He turned to look at Lanya, knowing her heart was breaking. "This figures. Try to do a show in a war. I had high hopes for this show and for you in it." Andre got up and walked to the office near the back. Lanya could not move. Her legs were frozen. *My show, my starring role is gone?* She had dreamed of this since she was ten years old. Now gone. Her life was crap. This war, her baby sister gone, her brother damaged beyond all hope and now no show. *Why am I even alive?* Maybe she should not be.

She knew Andre would not come back and tell her more. So she wrapped her scarf around her neck and headed out of the theater, with tears streaming down her face. These tears would freeze before they even met her lips. They would be slivers of ice on her cheeks. She did not care. *Nothing is worth worrying about. Life has no value. Maybe next time they had an air raid I would stay out in the street, hoping to be hit. Maybe I would stop eating altogether, leaving more for Babu and Mishka. Maybe...* she pushed all of this out of her head. Just get home. Nothing else, just get home.

Chapter Twenty-Five

Though there was no life left in her, Lanya went to get ration cards at the Party office. She had done this so many times now, since August that she did not think about it. But she thought about Ivan. *Is he here in this building? The next room over? Is he alive?* Most who were arrested were never seen again. *Will the Party shoot him quickly? What do they think he was doing?* Lanya had no idea.

She got to the counter and the same middle aged woman took her name and handed her the required cards. No greeting, no welcome, no smile. *Perfect,* Lanya thought. The same people were here doing the same menial jobs they always did. Flat. Boring. Like her life now. Worthless. As she turned to go, she saw the same young man with the thick glasses and brown hair. He was watching her she was sure. He got up from his desk and headed towards the door.

"A moment, please." He was at her side as she reached the door. Lanya froze. *Does he know that I know Ivan? Am I in trouble?* Her heart stopped beating and her head was light like she might faint. She stopped and he held the door so she could go outside. "Svetlana, it is good to see you again. I was not sure you would come back. You know." She knew. People were dying every day for lack of food. "Do you need help?" He seemed to struggle with his words. Lanya gave him a weak smile and tried to sound friendly.

"No, thank you. I just came to get our ration cards."

"Of course. We all need them." He paused as if he was struggling to make conversation. "I hope spring gets here quickly."

"Yes, me too." Lanya could think of nothing to say.

"Have a nice day then. See you soon."

Lanya hurried away as quickly as she could. This had nothing to do with Ivan. She was not in any trouble, no one suspected her of anything. This young man was just being nice. As she walked, Lanya wanted to kick herself for not being more friendly. He was just talking like a friend would. Tomorrow, at the factory, Lanya would have a lot to say to Maru. Tell her everything!

At the apartment, Lanya put the ration cards in the drawer. Mishka was in his room. Where was Babu? She was at the kitchen table with her head down. "Babu, Babu, are you okay?" Her head came up and Lanya saw a smile. Not a big smile but at least a smile. "I have a lot to tell you Babu. About Ivan." Babu perked up and she went to make tea. "He was arrested. Andre, the director told me. Andre went to his house yesterday and before he got to Ivan's apartment, they were taking Ivan away with his hands tied. They called him a Nazi. And an enemy of the people. You were right Babu, he was in trouble." Lanya sipped the tea she had.

"I knew it. He was up to something, we do not know."

"And when I was at the Party office to get the ration cards, a young man came up to me. I thought I was in trouble because of Ivan. But he was just being nice. Asked if we needed any help." Babu looked at here and could see there was nothing more. "I was scared but it was nothing."

"I see now why he wanted to stay here. He knew they wanted to get him. They would come here if he was here. We did the right thing, sending him away." Lanya nodded, even though she had some guilt at not taking him in. And now he would probably die.

"I still have that notebook." Lanya spoke quietly, guardedly. Babu looked up sharply.

"You do? I thought you were going to return it to him?"

"I did not see him again."

"We need to take care of that. Go get it." Lanya hurried off to her bedroom where the notebook was on her dresser. She took it to Babu, who looked at it again. "We need to get rid of this. If they come here, this would mean we are with him. Open the stove." Lanya opened the stove wood box and Babu grabbed the notebook and threw it in. Lanya gasped. The book quickly caught flame and the kitchen was bright for a few minutes. Lanya did not question Babu. Lanya paused, and put her hand on Babu's shoulder.

They could have no trace of Ivan in their home. There was a bit of loss though. She had shared intimate moments with Ivan. She did not love him, but he had made her feel good, feel attractive. He loved her voice. And, they had a baby, for a few weeks. Ivan was gone. But no one could prove Lanya and Babu did anything wrong, because they hadn't. They got rid of the notebook. And Ivan. Lanya finished her tea and left the room. As she got to the hall, she looked back at Babu.

"The show I was in, where I had the lead, is gone too. Without Ivan, it collapsed." Tears come to her eyes as she said that. The tears stung. She went to her bedroom. Again, she was despondent. *Why am I even alive? Many died, why not me? Wonderful people were gone, and me, a nobody, was still here. Scientists, artists, mothers were gone. And Lanya, who was only on stage once and has no other skills, is still here. The girl with no true love is here, while others who loved hard are gone.* The tears came. Would she miss Ivan? Maybe.

The air raid was fierce, and Lanya was actually happy with that. She did not have time to think or worry about her own miserable life as she was taking Babu and Mishka to the shelter, making sure they had some food and blankets. Maybe tonight they would get hit. They did not, and after three hours the all clear bell rang. In the apartment, the nightmares started, and Lanya expected them. She knew she would not sleep much.

At breakfast time, Lanya got ready for work. At work, she grabbed Maru as soon as she saw her. "Maru, come over here! I need to tell you stuff." Maru smiled and scurried to the corner where Lanya was leading her. Lanya wanted no one to overhear so they were away from the other workers. "Ivan got arrested! He came to my house two nights ago and banged on the door. Said he needed to stay with us. Babu and I knew it was not good. Because of the notebook. Oh, I did not tell you about that. Ivan had a notebook that was gibberish. Some Russian, some German, all mixed up. Babu thought it was a code. Anyway, we told him he could not stay with us, we did not want to get into trouble. He is bad news. We sent him away. The next day when I went to rehearsal, Andre the director told me he saw Ivan being arrested. And they were yelling at him for being an enemy and Nazi!" She paused for breath. Maru's eyes were wide and her mouth was ajar. "So, Ivan is gone! My show is gone, too. I will not be on stage again."

Lanya could feel the lump in her throat. Maru reached out and took Lanya's hands. She squeezed, waiting for Lanya to finish. Lanya was done, her shoulders slumped.

"Oh no, Ivan was in trouble? Who would have known? Does this mean Leonid is trouble too? I should not see him again then. Maybe he will be arrested too. He had a notebook in code? This sounds like a story! Was he a spy? The Party is always looking for spies!" Maru sounded excited like this was the beginning of a good movie. Lanya did not feel any of the excitement. This was her life, not some story. Maru settled down and said all the right things. Lanya did not know if Maru was going to see Leonid again or not. The whistle blew and Lanya got up from their corner and went to her machine, hoping this day did not last forever.

As she left the factory, Lanya looked to the light post where Ivan liked to greet her. He was not there, of course. Lanya found a lump in her throat remembering his arms around her. *Is he still alive?*

Babu was sitting in a chair when she got home, sleeping. Lanya tried to be quiet. Babu did not normally sleep in a chair and Lanya worried a bit. Hoping her grandmother was not sick, Lanya went into the kitchen to see what she could do for dinner. She put together what she could and went to get Mishka. He was not in his room. Where could he be? She looked in all the other rooms. Mishka was not here. At all. With a feeling of dread, Lanya put her coat on again and went out. As she got to the street, there he was! Mishka rushed to see her. He had a package in his hands. Another fish! Mishka had been ice fishing again! Lanya gave him a hug and went upstairs to make this fresh fish their dinner. Babu was still asleep. When dinner was ready, she went to shake Babu.

"Babu, Babu, it is time for dinner. Can you come to the table please?" Babu woke slowly and rose with a creak.

"I am sorry, 1 don't know what happened. Did you fix this?" She looked at the table with fish and cabbage.

"Yes, I did not want to disturb you. Mishka caught another fish! We will eat like kings tonight!" They ate dinner quietly and Lanya enjoyed the fish.

Sewing group went as normal. One more woman was missing, and the talk was that she starved to death. Lanya knew it could be any of them. How many people would starve? Talk about the Germans was ugly. People were praying for spring to stop this bone wrenching cold. People did that even without a war, as Lanya did every February. There was no new information, even from Lidia, who seemed to know everything. Lanya was grateful when it was time to go.

When she got home, she had a quick cup of weak tea that was mostly colored water and then lay down in the kitchen bed. Babu was next to her and Mishka was nearby. Babu quickly began snoring as she always did. But Lanya could hear the snore was not regular, with stops and starts. *What if we lose Babu? How old is she? Is she ill or just old?* Lanya was lost in the questions as sleep came.

In the morning, Lanya was up first. Babu and Mishka stayed in their beds. Mishka woke and Lanya made breakfast, preparing to go to the factory. Mishka ate but remained quiet.

"Mishka, Babu might be sick. Will you please take care of her today?" Lanya looked at her brother soulfully and he looked back. She hoped he understood. When she left for work, Babu was still in bed.

As she got home, Babu was in a chair in the front room, sleeping. She was sleeping a lot. Lanya did not want to wake her so she did not check for fever. Would she be able to tell if Babu had a fever? Moms knew how to do that but Lanya was not sure she could. She went into the kitchen and started preparing dinner with last night's leftovers. She assembled a decent meal and told Mishka to come to eat. Babu was still asleep. Lanya strained to hear her breathe. She was still breathing. Let her sleep. She set a plate aside for later.

When it was time for bed, Lanya wrapped a blanket around Babu and left her where she was. She went to lie down in the kitchen. After a while, she heard Babu get up and hoped she was okay. Babu came into the kitchen to lie down. Quickly she was snoring. Lanya relaxed. In the morning, Lanya again was first up. No factory today but she needed to go get some food. Babu was snoring. She went out quickly, knowing that any delay would mean most of the food would be gone. It was dark out, but in February it was gray until 9 in the morning. She found what she could and was disheartened by the lack of fresh food. But she stuffed it all in her bag and went home.

Babu was in the chair when she came in.

"Babu, good to see you. Would you like some tea?" Lanya put the water on before Babu could answer. "How do you feel?" Lanya looked at her grandmother and saw that she looked tired. And heavier than normal. Babu did not answer right away. Lanya brought a cup of tea and sat down, her own cup in hand.

"My stomach hurts." Babu croaked.

"I am sorry. Are you hungry?" Lanya had heard that starving hurts.

"No, it is something else. Hurts bad."

"Is there something I can do for you?" Lanya knew there were a few medicines that might help.

"No, tea will do."

"Do you want anything to eat?" Lanya understood that a small amount of bread or a potato might help.

"No, I am fine." Lanya was not sure, but went into the kitchen to put away the groceries. Soon she heard Babu snoring again and felt some relief. Babu stayed in that chair all day, in and out of sleep. At one point, Lanya touched her forehead. A bit warm, but not too bad. Babu got up twice to use the restroom and Lanya guided her. She took some time in the bathroom and Lanya hoped that was good then she was back to the chair. When dinner was ready, Babu was still in the chair. Lanya brought her plate to the table next to her. She and Mishka ate without talking. Lanya wondered if Babu was just going through a tough spot and would be fine in a day or two. An hour after dinner, the air raid sirens went off and Lanya woke Babu to go to the shelter. Babu stumbled and could hardly lift her feet to walk. Lanya and Mishka carried most of her weight. At the shelter, they went to their corner by the file cabinet. Lanya eased Babu to sit and she sat on one side with Mishka on the other. Babu fell asleep almost immediately, even with the sound of bombs going off in the street. When the all clear came out, they were the last ones out and very slowly went back to the apartment. Babu asked for vodka before lying down. Babu did not often drink and Lanya wondered if she was still in pain.

"Babu, do you need anything?" Babu did not answer but gave a short shake of the head. Soon, she was snoring.

In the morning, Babu did not get up. Lanya went to check on her and found her breathing but not snoring. Her breath was labored. Lanya put her fingers on her neck to check her pulse. She did not know much about pulses but knew it should be strong and regular. It was not. It was weak and sporadic. A few pulses then nothing. Then another pulse, then nothing. This is not good. Should she take Babu to the doctor? Could the doctor do anything? Could she even get Babu to the doctor's office? The air raid shelter was two blocks away and that was almost impossible. Lanya had to wait and see what would happen. It did not look like Babu was in pain right now, so waiting was all she could do.

As the day went on, Babu turned in her sleep. Little grunts and yelps came out of her. The fever was a bit higher. No sweat so it seemed not too bad. Should she wake Babu up to eat? Lanya went to make some soup, something Babu could swallow. She got something like broth made from the last bit of fish and crumbled a bit of bread in it. She knelt beside Babu tapping her.

"Babu, I want you to eat. Please sit up and eat this soup." Babu opened her eyes but Lanya could see there was not much there. "Here, take a sip." Lanya put the cup to her lips but Babu's head tipped back, and she did not sip. What was Lanya to do? She eased Babu's shoulders down to rest. She needed to leave the kitchen. She went to the front room and rifled through a magazine that she has seen a million times. Was Babu dying? Was there anything Lanya could do? She knew that the doctor would not do anything. It seemed inevitable.

By dinnertime, Babu's breathing was hard. There were lapses in her breath, with gaps of silence. The fever was rising and Lanya could feel a slight sweat on her brow. It was just a matter of time. Lanya wished to be anywhere else and not see this. When Valentina died, Lanya could not tell there was pain, because she was conked out. At least Babu was not in great pain. Lanya tried to check her feelings. Soldiers saw death every day. Their job was much bigger than keeping a grandmother comfortable as she left this world. *Get over it* she said to herself. When it was time to sleep. Lanya and Mishka lay on their beds in the kitchen. Lanya waited for the snore and it came and went. Finally, Lanya slept. But every time she turned over she listened for the breathing. At one point, she was not sure it was happening and she held her own breath to quiet her own sounds. She heard it and went back to sleep.

In the morning, Lanya got up and as soon as she started the water, she checked Babu's breath. Still there, but it was weak. Her pulse was erratic. The end could happen soon. She needed to go to get ration cards today, and she could not miss that. So she bundled herself up and went out. The storm was mighty, with wind and snow and Lanya put her chin down and cursed the winter. She was sure there were places on earth that were not covered by snow. Kiev, maybe. Istanbul? The Party office was quiet since it was early. She looked at the bland faces again and felt nothing. There was the young man with thick glasses. He smiled at her but did not come over. The lines were still long. Why did this take so long? When her turn came, she went to the counter and showed her identification, got her ration cards and tucked them away. She remembered stories of people who were attacked for their cards and made sure hers were put away before she went out. Good. Back to the snow.

"One moment please." The man with the thick glasses came into Lanya's field of vision. She stopped in her spot on the sidewalk and looked up at him. "Good morning. You like to get here early."

"Good morning. It is best, I think it goes more quickly."

"It does. Svetlana, did you get everything you need?"

"Yes, yes I did, thank you." Lanya wondered why he talked with her.

"I am glad, if not, I might be able to help." Lanya thought that was nice, but since he was Party, she wondered what else was going on. She realized she did not know his name.

"I am sorry, I do not know your name. You know mine." He looked confused, then smiled.

"Josef. Josef Nikolaev, at your service." He made a half-hearted bow but it looked funny to Lanya because the snow was covering them both.

"Thank you. For your concern. I need to go, my grandmother is not well."

"Of course. I wish her well." *Too late for that* Lanya thought as she went into the street towards home. That was nice of him to follow me out. He is a gentle soul. Not her type, but a gentle man.

As she got home, Lanya checked on Babu. Still a fever, still labored breathing. Lanya put the ration cards in the drawer. She wanted to talk to someone, so she went to Mishka's room.

"Mishka, Babu is not well. She may die." Tears filled her eyes. "What will we do without her?" Mishka looked at Lanya and she was not sure how much he understood. It was hard living with him. She never knew what he was thinking. Mishka was drawing on paper with a pencil and Lanya did not stay to see what he drew. She went to her own room and fell onto her bed. Yes, Babu was probably dying. She should get a shroud together, like she did for Valentina. She went into Babu's room and pulled a blanket off the bed. This will do. Anything else? She looked in Babu's drawers for the first time, looking for a memento to put into her hands. She found a crucifix made of wood with small carvings along the edges. This would be good. She set it on her dresser. She folded the blanket and went back to check on Babu.

Babu was not breathing, at all. Lanya checked her pulse. Nothing. She ran to her room to get a mirror like they did with Valentina, and held it under her nose. Nothing. No mist. Babu's skin was not cold, but her forehead was not as hot as it had been moments before. Beloved Babu was dead. Her grandmother had passed from this life. She was now with the rest of the family, far from Leningrad. Lanya held her slack hand and cried, not knowing what to do. She had never had life without Babu. Babu had always been here, in the apartment. Babu had always kissed ouchies, bathed skinned knees, made dinner and snacks. Babu was always here. Now gone.

Lanya was numb. She did not know what to do. No Babu? She hung her head and let feelings come. She had Babu's hand in hers. She sat for a few minutes, then as Babu's hand cooled, Lanya let the hand go. She rested it on Babu's chest. She did not want to hold a cold hand. She remembered the same with Valentina. Should she go tell Mishka? Not yet. How could she explain it? No, she needed to get out. Go outside. See the sky, breathe some fresh air. She pulled on her coat and gloves and placed a woolen hat on her head. A hat that Babu had knitted for her.

Outside, the air was cold but dry. Lanya knew nighttime was close. She started walking. A few minutes later she found herself at Maru's door. She knocked, and Maru's mom opened the door.

"Lanya come on in. Why are you out? It is too cold. Maru is in her room." She waved her arm and Lanya went past. In Maru's room, Maru was at her desk with a book.

"Lanya! What a surprise. Are you okay? You have been crying." Maru wrapped Lanya in a hug and guided her to a chair.

"It's Babu." Lanya blubbered the words. Maru looked at her carefully.

"What happened? Is she okay?"

"No. She is g-g-gone." She stuttered over the last word.

"Gone? Did she starve?" So many people were starving that it was anyone's first thought.

"No. She had some pain and then a fever. And she passed in her sleep today. I needed to get out. I do not know how I came here."

"Of course." Maru embraced Lanya as the tears flowed. Lanya was gulping sobs now. The calm of their apartment was gone. Lanya knew she would always feel the empty space of her grandmother. Always.

"Let me come to the house with you. I will help you prepare her." Maru moved to get her coat and Lanya followed her to the front room. Maru spoke to her mother and explained why she had to go out. Her mother's words to be careful echoed as the women closed the door.

They walked almost silently, arm in arm to Lanya's apartment. Inside, in the kitchen, Babu lay on the mattress on the kitchen floor.

"Come on, let's get her into her bedroom." They tried to lift Babu but the two of them could not do it. "Let's get your brother." Lanya walked into Mishka's room and waved her hand for him to follow. He got up and came with her. He greeted Maru, who gave him a hug like she always did.

"Mikhail, can you help us? We need to get Babu into her room." Mishka nodded and went to her side. As he touched her arm, he looked at Lanya, who started crying again. Could he understand? Mishka got one side and Maru got the other and they lifted Babu to her bedroom and laid her on the bed.

"Thank you Mishka." Maru turned to Babu and began to straighten her clothes. Mishka waited to see if he was needed and left. Lanya was not sure what to do but Maru seemed to know.

"Let's prepare her. Does she have anything special you want her in? A favorite sweater or dress?" Lanya had a hard time thinking with her heart in pieces. Lanya went to the dresser and looked. A few sweaters that Babu knitted were there. In the closet was a flowered dress that Babu used to love in the summer time. Lanya pulled that out.

"That is lovely. She would like that. I remember seeing her wear that one. Would you go make tea please? I would like that." Lanya turned to go, glad to have a task to do. When she came back with two teacups, Babu was wearing the dress with a cardigan over it. Her hair was neat and brushed back. "Did she have any jewelry that you think would work?" Lanya went to the jewelry box. She knew Babu had nothing valuable but she did have a small necklace that she often wore. Lanya pulled it out and handed it to Maru. "Good. That will be nice."

The blanket that Lanya had laid on the bed yesterday was under Babu now. Maru went to it and began to fold it around Babu's form. Lanya stopped her.

"Not yet. I need a minute." Maru backed away and took her teacup to the kitchen, to give Lanya some time. Lanya decided she needed to explain to Mishka. She went to his room where he was toying with something.

"Mishka, I need to explain. Our Babu has left us. She is no more." Lanya slumped onto the bed near her brother. She put her face in her hands. He put his hand on her shoulders. He was gentle but Lanya did not know how much he understood. She started again, slowly. "She will not be here. She will not cook for us. I will have to." His hand was warm and strong. "I will need your help again tomorrow. To take her away." He looked in her eyes but Lanya could not see understanding. She got up and went back to Babu's bedroom and Maru followed her in.

"Are you ready?" Maru looked at her with tears forming in her eyes. Lanya nodded silently. They wrapped Babu in the blanket, keeping her face uncovered.

"We will take her to the cemetery tomorrow. Mishka will go with me." They both knew how this worked. With Valentina, they took her to the funeral home but now, so many people died every day no one used the funeral home. There were no funerals in winter anyway. They would take Babu straight to the cemetery like all families did. And the cemetery would deal with it. They left Babu's room. Lanya closed the door with another small sob.

In the kitchen, Maru finished her cold tea. "Do you need anything else Lanya?"

"No, thank you so much. This is so hard."

"Yes. And this war makes it harder."

"I will walk you out." They got up and Maru put her coat on again. In the hallway, they hugged and this hug lingered. These two friends had been through so much together. "Thank you again." Lanya wanted to say more, felt more, but Maru knew how deep it was.

"Of course. You needed a bit of help. You would do it for me."

"Certainly." Maru walked down the hall and onto the stairs. Her boots clicked as she went. Lanya went back into the apartment and straight to the vodka bottle in the kitchen cupboard. She made a mental note to buy more.

When the sun came up the next day, Lanya opened the heavy curtains. The skies were gray but there was no snow falling. That would make their walk easier. She ate a little for breakfast, then went downstairs to make sure the sled was there. This sled was kept in the basement, it was for everyone to use. Yes, it was right there. Lanya took it to the front entry and went to get Mishka. He was dressed and they went into Babu's room, covered her face and lifted her. Mishka did most of it, getting her down the stairs. They placed her gently on the sled and Mishka grabbed the rope at the front. Lanya followed as Mishka led them through the streets as Lanya guided, towards the cemetery. It was over a mile away and Lanya was again glad it was not snowing. There was plenty of snow and ice on the streets though, so the sled moved along well. At the cemetery, there was no one to greet them. Lanya was not sure quite what to do, but at the perimeter, she saw stacks of bundles. She stopped Mishka and went to go look more closely. Yes, it looked like those were bodies wrapped in blankets. They were not buried, there were never burials in Leningrad in the winter months. Funerals were for when the ground was not frozen. With regret, Lanya grabbed the rope handle and dragged the sled to the stack of bodies. It was wrong to just leave her grandmother here in a nameless stack. But what else could she do? Mishka lifted her and put her next to the other bundles. Lanya squeezed her eyes to stop the tears but it did no good. She grabbed her brother's arm and his other arm wrapped around her. He seemed to understand. They walked back without speaking. Lanya's heart was so heavy. Mishka took her hand and that warmth helped. They put the sled back in the basement and slowly climbed the stairs.

Chapter Twenty-Six

Lanya was back at the factory the next day. Her heart was empty and working might be the best way to avoid that hole. The February gray was weakened and there was a bit of sunshine through the window which helped a bit. Maru came at lunch and sat together with her, as support. As she walked home in the near dark, Lanya tried to detach from her life and look at it like an observer. She was 20 years old. Her parents were gone, her little sister was gone and her steadfast grandmother was gone. Her brother was here, but he was like a child. Lanya knew she would have Mishka with her for the rest of her life. She accepted that with sadness. She had no education and no real skills but she did have a great strong voice. Her dream was to sing on stage and she did that, once. That brought a warm spot to her mind as she walked. Could she do it again, after this war was over? Then she wondered if she would survive this war. Could she stay alive with so little food? With this cold? Well, the cold was bad but nothing new. Could she keep herself and her brother alive? She had no answers. She knew she had to go to the Party office and turn in Babu's ration card. If she didn't the Party would arrest her. So she made a note to do it soon, but waiting until the last day of the month. No point in turning it back in before using it, that is what everyone did. As long as she got it together.

She thought about Ivan. Was he still alive? The Party would not move slowly on this. If he was alive he would be in Siberia. It had been two weeks. She was glad that she and Babu had burned that notebook. No one could find her guilty of anything. But, she admitted, she missed his arms around her and the good times they had at his apartment. Maybe she should go check on him.

The next morning, Lanya bundled up and walked the distance to Ivan's apartment. She was not sure what she would find. She let herself in the entry and went up the stairs. The door was open and Lanya felt her heart jump a bit. She peeked into the front room and saw a small woman with a bucket.

"Do you need something?" The woman asked. Her hair was wrapped with a knotted scarf and she looked like she was hoping for a cigarette, though there were no cigarettes in Leningrad now.

"Um... I just came by to see..." Lanya could not complete a sentence. The place was so empty without Ivan.

"He is not here. Got rounded up by the Party. Something about Nazi spy. That's what I heard. Did you know him?"

"Um, yes. He ran a theater show I was in in December." That was all true. She did not have to tell this cleaning woman everything.

"He will not be back. They have no use for spies. None of us do." She made a fake spit onto the floor.

"We all hate the Nazis."

"Well, it looks like he didn't." Lanya wondered why she was here. "I need to clean this place out."

"Could I look around for a moment?" The cleaning lady looked at her hard and raised her eyebrows.

"Go ahead. Nothing in there, they cleaned it out." Lanya paused inside, then walked to the bedroom and was glad the woman was not staring at her. She breathed a shallow breath and looked around. This place was a mess. Things were thrown everywhere, There were no notebooks, they all got picked up. The dresser was empty with clothes all over the floor and the bed. Lanya looked at the bed. The mattress was upturned and the sheets and blankets were in the corner. The closet looked like a storm had ripped through it. Lanya was sad after her times with Ivan, in this room. But if he was helping the Germans kill her people, he deserved to be gone. She remembered her sister and tightened her heart. What she came for, she decided was a memento. Just a little something of his to remind her. She looked around and moved some stuff aside. A shirt. She found a long sleeve buttoned shirt that she had seen him wear at the theater and at dinner. She picked it up. It smelled like him. She stuffed it into her bag, hoping the cleaning lady would not notice. With one last look, when left the bedroom.

The cleaning lady was in the kitchen, going through things. Lanya wondered if there was any food left. If there were any ration cards, the cleaning lady would deserve to have them. She got to the door and said, "I am all done here. Thanks for letting me in." She let herself out and closed the door.

Goodbye Ivan, you are no longer part of my life. She pulled the shirt out and took a look at it. *Why do I want this?* In the cold of the sidewalk, it looked different. *What will it remind mer of? That I spent time with a Nazi spy? A man who helped to ruin my family?* She got a sour taste in her mouth and knotted the shirt up into a bundle and tossed it into a bombed out building as she walked by. *He is the past, not the future.*

Life got back to some sort of normal. There was no true normal without Babu. There was a huge hole in Lanya. Especially in the kitchen. So many memories in the kitchen. She looked at Babu's bedroll on the kitchen floor. Maybe she should take it back to her room, but not yet. What would normal even look like? Lanya went to work, picked up ration cards, found groceries when she could, trudged through frozen snow and looked after Mikhail. Air raids happened every few days. Not a thought about being on stage. She heard there was one theater still performing but she did not have the energy to even try out. At the end of the first month, she returned Babu's ration card. People would know somehow if she didn't and she certainly did not want any trouble with the Party. Sewing group went well; it was nice to have people to talk to.

At the grocery spot the next morning, Lanya waited in line, singing in her head. She was not paying attention until the shouting started.

"Hey, get back here!"

"What is going on?"

"Hey- you!"

Lanya turned and saw a small crowd gathering. There was someone on the ground beginning to move. She could see in the distance some teenagers running away, looking back. The figure on the ground stood but she was not strong. Her coat was open and her bag was on the ground spilled. She was not old. She had brown hair, pulled tight into a bun. Her coat had a few patches on it. Her shoes were too big and worn. Her stockings were down and she grabbed them to stay warm.

"They stole my bag, my bread! And my ration card!" The woman was crying as she stumbled. She saw her bag and picked it up but shook her head knowing it was empty. Someone went to hold her arm to steady her. These thugs stole her bread? And her ration card? Lanya could not look at her. It was too much. No one had bread to spare. And without a ration card, she was dead. She could go to the Party office and ask for another one but she was not likely to get one. Because the Party did not trust people or believe their stories. Unless someone helped this woman, she would be dead in a few days. Lanya looked at the brittle bare trees and tried to think of anything but this scene. She could not offer to help this woman or her own family would die. The crowd dispersed and the scene passed. Lanya took one more look at this woman who was hobbling along the sidewalk and was full of pity. for the woman and for all of Leningrad. Missing Babu was tough. After dinner, Lanya remembered sitting quietly with her grandmother in the kitchen, talking or just sitting, sharing warm silence. The apartment was too quiet. Without Babu's voice, only Lanya's voice was in the apartment. Lanya decided that she should sing more, to fill the emptiness. If she had a good voice, she should use it to fill the hole of quiet.

One air raid at the end of February shook their building, and when she came back to it she saw things on the shelves had moved and the pictures on the wall were tilted. But the house was still standing and the windows were still in place. Lanya looked for the beginning of spring on the trees. Once in a while a squirrel would pop up but the birds were still far south and the sun did not give much warmth yet. Lanya knew that it would come. She just wondered if she would be alive.

At work the next day, Lanya found Maru at lunchtime.

"Maru, if I get killed somehow, will you take care of Mishka?" Her tone was expectant and she could see that Maru was taken aback.

"Don't be silly. They won't get us. We have lived this far!"

"Well, with Babu gone, I have no one else. And Mishka cannot take care of himself."

"I can see that. Well, of course I will take care of him. He needs you now. But if something happens, you can count on me." Lanya nodded and remembered the days a year ago when their talk was not about death and starvation but about clothes and men and going out. This was so ugly. Lanya wanted this to be all over. Today.

In line, waiting to get her groceries, Lanya faced her bitter thoughts. *What is the purpose? Why bother trying? Will making food out of bird seed like millet make a difference? What if we were all going to die anyway? What will Germany do with an empty city? Is death something to be scared of? Does it hurt? Does starving hurt? Or does your body just slowly, painlessly shut down? At the front, sure there was pain with a bullet or a bomb. But starving? And what if we are all killed in an air raid? Who will sort out the bodies? Will death be better than this life?* That thought created a small bright space in Lanya's mind. *Yes, death will be easier. No cold, no hunger, no nightmares, no worries. Should we just die? Would it be wrong to kill yourself in this situation?* Lanya got her meager bits of food and filled her bag. She headed out into the cold and tried to push these thoughts away. But the 'why bother' question never went far.

At the sewing group that night, they were working on sandbags. The rain would come soon and the sandbags would be needed for their defense at the edge of the city. One of the older woman got their attention:

"I heard this yesterday. This family over in the old section killed themselves. They had no food in the house and the father was already gone, killed at the front. The mother and her sister with their three children, slit their wrists. They left a note saying it was too hard." Lanya was struck dumb by this, after what she internalized today. It was creepy.

"They did what? That is wrong!"

"That is so sad. We do not know who will die."

"Those poor children. If you kill yourself that is one thing, but to kill your children?"

"They all went together."

"I am not sure it is wrong." Everyone stopped and looked at the tired looking middle aged woman who spoke. "I mean, this is hell. The anxiety every day wondering if you are next. They are at peace anyway." It took a few moments for anyone to speak as everyone processed their dark thoughts, and Lanya could understand the concept.

"I am not sure. This is tough, but doesn't God decide when we go?" This was the oldest woman there, who remembered going to church, like Babu had.

"Well, if I could choose, I can see why they did this."

"I would rather choose than the Germans choose!" Everyone chuckled at that. No one wanted the Germans to be in charge of their death. Lanya still thought about it. Would she, could she ever? No, Lanya was sure she could never run a knife into her own skin. Sometimes she hated herself and she often hated her life, but she was not brave enough to cut herself and bleed. She was trapped. She looked around. They were all trapped.

In her bed in the kitchen, Lanya snuggled in and tried to clear her brain. No, there was no empty space. The pictures of a dead family and a shining knife refused to leave. She slept, but the nightmares came quickly. Bombs, running and now blood. After a few attempts, Lanya decided to not try to sleep. She got up and made some hot water to sip since the tea was all gone. She sat in a chair in the front room with a blanket and a book. No sleep tonight.

March came in like a lion, but more sunshine helped. Lanya was irritated with the sunshine. *How dare it be so bright and sunny but so cold?* The sun made you want to get out but the cold kept you in. There was nothing to do outside anyway. No energy for walking or skating. So staying in was best, even with the cruel sun.

Life without Babu was hard, not physically but emotionally. Empty. Lanya admitted she even missed the snoring. During air raids, Lanya and Mikhail went to the shelter but it always seemed wrong. Lanya remembered holding Babu's hands the first few times when she was so scared. Now she hardly worried about the bombings. Living just did not matter much. Her nightmares came and went. Mishka stayed the same innocent child he had been for months now.

Chapter
Twenty-Seven

Lanya sat at her machine with the hand crank going. She was not mad at the old machines anymore, it was just the way it had to be. When the war was over, if she was still here, she would be more grateful for the electric machines. Ivan had been gone for three weeks, and Lanya felt guilty. Guilty that she missed him and guilty that she was glad he was gone. He was probably dead, the Party would not keep a spy alive. Yes, he was a spy. The notebook she burned confirmed that, she was sure.

As she sat there, she saw people who were outsiders enter. Usually, no one came to the factory unless they were employees or managers. These people did not fit in, they were wearing brown Party sweaters. Her heart sank. Lanya tried to see what was going on without looking like she was watching. She knew everyone was doing the same. One eye on the fabric, one eye on the visitors. Then they started walking up the rows. To her area. They stopped at her machine!

"Svetlana Zhukanov?" Lanya froze. Who were these people and how did they know her name?

"Yes." She was shaking. Were these Party leaders? What did they want?

"Come with us." All eyes were on Lanya as she got up from her machine, grabbed her bag and followed the two men and a woman out the aisles. The factory grew quiet, all eyes were on her. One man was behind her, to keep her from running maybe? Lanya was cold like ice and focused on her feet. She did not want to trip and make it all worse. Her stomach was not just a knot but a chunk of granite. She had no color in her face. Was she in trouble? She did nothing wrong. Her brain was racing with thoughts of Ivan. She might put him behind her but the Party might not. Petrified, she had seen people taken like this and usually they were never seen again. What was going on?

At the manager's office, they pulled Lanya in. They put a hand on her shoulder and pushed her into a chair. She hit the seat hard and winced.

"Do you know Ivan Sivkov?" Three pairs of eyes were boring into her. She looked from one to another. Her hands were in a tight grip. Fear was choking her and she hoped the words would come.

"Yes, he was the producer of a show I was in in November." That was true. Not the whole truth, but true. They studied her and she felt naked the way they went over her inch by inch. She looked at her shoes because it was easier than looking at them.

"We think there is more than that." She gulped. What did they think? Should she talk or not? She was not sure what the right thing to say would be. The thought of her parents, in this very same spot, thinking the very same thing, paralyzed her.

"We think you knew what he was doing." Lanya rolled her eyes up from her feet. She did not know anything.

"I.... I...." She looked from face to face, trying to see where they were going. She could read nothing in their expressions, since these were not amateurs.

"We think you knew about his illegal anti-Soviet activities. Come with us." She did not get a chance to argue back before one man grabbed Lanya's arm and pulled her out of the chair, propelling her to the door. As she left the manager's office, Lanya could feel all eyes on her as she was pushed out the front door of the factory. Did Maru see, even though she worked in the back? Would they tell her? They trudged through the snow and slush to the Party office, the same place where she got her ration cards every ten days. They went to the back of the building and went through a different door, to a small room with nothing but a dry metal table and three chairs. Again, Lanya was pushed into a chair. Her mind was a whir- *what is going on? Do they think I am a spy? Do they think I knew something? Do they think I wanted to hurt Leningrad? That I love Germany?* Her back straightened at that thought. She hated Germany as much as anyone in Leningrad. She wanted them all to die like her sister did.

A stack of papers was thrown onto the table and one man, the older of the two, opened a folder and read her name and address. Yes, yes, that was her. And that she worked at the factory, yes. And that her brother was injured at the front. Yes. Did they know about Valentina too?

"Ivan Sivkov was an enemy of the Soviet Union. Tell us what you know about him." Maybe this wasn't about her? Maybe they were making a case against Ivan? Lanya decided that honesty would be best here. Maybe not total honesty, but largely.

"I, um, met him months ago at a show at the Mariinsky theater." Lanya paused because her throat was as dry as a desert. Her fingers were fidgeting non-stop.

"When!" The demand was a bark and Lanya shrunk back.

"August, the show was, um," Lanya paused and struggled to remember the show.

"Was he alone? Were you alone?"

"I was with my friend Maru, from the factory. He was with his friend named Leonid." They looked at each other and one made notes. She did not remember Leonid's last name.

"Tell us more."

"We had coffee after and Ivan, Mr. Sivkov, told us he wanted to produce a show. I was interested because I always wanted to be in a show. He told me we would talk about it more."

"What kind of show?"

"A musical, like the one we were at."

"And you saw him again?"

"Yes, he met me after work and we talked."

"What did you talk about?"

"Mostly the show that he was going to produce. He wanted to be sure it was one the Party would approve of." The other man snorted when she said that but it was true.

"What else do you know about him?"

"He told me he was from Minsk, but that he had seen shows all over Europe."

"Did he say where?"

"Many cities."

"Like Berlin? Munich? Hanover?"

"He might have said that. He named many cities. He traveled a lot." Another snort.

"Did he ever speak about Germany or the war?" Lanya thought for a moment. No, he had never spoken of the war.

"No, he never spoke of the war. Never talked about Germany. But he did have a bit of an accent. I thought it was from Minsk." The other man rolled his eyes instead of snorting. Lanya was sure this small room was getting smaller and she was feeling cramped.

"Tell us more."

"I tried out for the show in September and got a part. We began rehearsals in October and the show started in November, until the beginning of December."

"Did he do anything unusual at that time?" Unusual? Lanya's fingers were fidgeting all over her leg. Lanya did not know what unusual meant since she had never been in a theater production before.

"I do not think so. Except one time he did not show up the night of a show and we had to go on without him." The man was scribbling on a note pad. *Is Ivan still alive? Are they looking for reasons to kill him?* Guilt swept through Lanya but she pulled herself back. She needed to save herself. Ivan was probably not even alive. Her fingers stilled for a moment.

"Did he do anything else that was underhanded?"

"No, I never saw anything." Lanya was being honest here. She never saw Ivan do anything obvious or sneaky. He had more food at his apartment than she did and those notebooks but nothing else. And she was not going to offer information.

All three interrogators stood up and the older man nodded his head and then they left the room. Lanya sat there in the quiet room, trying to hear what they were saying. But they were too good. She did not hear anything. She squeezed her fingers together. So she did what she always did, she imagined their conversation. '*Guilty. Obvious. As bad as he was. We should lock her up. Do we know anything about her family? Maybe we should look. Let's go get Leonid and Maru, they will know something.*' Lanya was wringing her hands so much they were red and swollen. She kept twisting her fingers and could not stop. It seemed like they were out there forever, plotting against her. But when they returned, Lanya sensed that things had changed.

"Get up. We are going downstairs." Lanya looked from one man to the other, trying to understand what this meant. She looked at the woman, hoping for some warmth too, but it was clear she was an ice maiden with no compassion. She did not even look at Lanya, and Lanya felt ill. One led the way, and Lanya and the others followed. She was too scared to ask any questions.

Downstairs it was colder and they took her through hallways to a cell. A cell? Lanya froze. Terrified. Anyone who goes into a cell never comes out into daylight again, unless the daylight is in Siberia. Lanya froze and stopped; she could not enter.

"But wait! I never, I didn't..." Lanya was cut off when the older man behind her pushed her into the cell. They backed out and the door clanked shut. They turned the big metal key, and that sound was a death bell for Lanya. The metal bars might as well have been concrete.

"We will let you know what is next. If you will be arrested and put on trial." Lanya did not answer. She knew that she did nothing wrong. Except sleep with a spy. She hated Germans as much as anyone in Leningrad. She stood at the rails, watching their silent retreat. Her eyes pleaded but her voice stayed silent.

When she could move, Lanya inspected the room. There was no doubt this was a prison. Besides the metal barred door, there was a bed and a box near it. The bed had a wool blanket on it and a flat, tired pillow. There was no window, no light, no heater, nothing to look at. And silence. There was no noise at all. Lanya was used to noise from the factory or a theater and this silence swallowed her up. She sat carefully on the bed. Hard and cold. She threw herself onto the pillow and the tears started. *What am I going to do? What can I do?* Her eyes searched the ceiling. *How many people have been in this room? Was Ivan here? Were my parents in this very same room?* The tears did not stop and neither did the questions. *Can I do anything? Will anyone from the Party listen to me? Why does everything in my life end up so bad? What did I do wrong to deserve this?*

Exhaustion overtook her and she slept. When she woke, she had no idea what time it was. She did not know if it was day or night. She heard a noise and looked through the rails and saw someone coming. It was a young man with a cart on wheels. She smelled something. Was he bringing food?

The young man stopped outside her cell and she realized she was starved for personal contact. Less than one day had passed and she was a mess already.

"Hello? Why am I here? When will I get out? Why don't they listen? I did nothing wrong!" His face was blank and passive. Lanya wanted to scream.

"I have your dinner. I will pick it up again in forty minutes." He was young, close to her own age she guessed. He was taller than she was by about four inches, and very thin. She could see his belt had a few new holes in it, clinched to keep his pants up. Lanya took the covered plate and set it on the box near the bed. As she turned away he was gone already. She heard him deliver food to two other cells nearby. There were other people here? Could she talk to them?

She sat back on the bed and uncovered the plate. It had some herring in a paste-like clump and a half a roll. Not enough food. Of course. She stopped and a horrible thought went through her head. *What will Mishka do? Will he eat? If no one prepares food? Will he starve? Will he go to the kitchen and find something to eat?* Lanya pushed the food around but her stomach was too tight to put anything in it. Her brother, who she promised she would take care of, could die without her. She wanted to die.

Somehow Lanya slept. Exhausted from crying she suspected. If her life went on like this she would sleep whenever it hit. Maybe that was better than not sleeping. Lanya's thoughts went to Mikhail. He was alone in the apartment. No one knew she was here except the people at the factory who saw her get taken. How would Mikhail live? She heard a sound outside her cell and jumped up. Was it the young man again? She craned her neck trying to see. She saw an older woman with an angry face coming with a tray and covered plates. Was it time to eat again? As she approached Lanya backed off and studied her. Middle aged with graying hair. She would have been chunky if they were not all starving. Her hair was pulled back in a severe braid and Lanya worried that she might not be human inside.

"I need help please." Lanya reached out as if to take her arm and the woman jerked away. "My brother is at home alone." The woman did not meet her eyes. "He cannot be alone." Lanya could feel the tears coming again. "He was injured in the war and he is like a child. An idiot. I need to find some way to help him or he will starve." The ice woman did not look at Lanya as she backed out of the cell. She clanged the door loudly to make a point and deliberately made extra noise with the key. She was obviously not going to listen or to help. Lanya flung herself onto the bed again. What would she do?

Lanya got up and looked at the tray. Cereal, cold now. Was it porridge? She tasted it. It reminded her of the wallpaper pancakes Babu had made. Tasteless. Bland, washed out and without any zing. She forced herself to swallow the cold mush in the bowl. No point in starving if they were going to feed her. It was not much but it was here. *Will I get this same mush every day?* She assumed it was morning, from the cereal though she had no way to be sure.

Lanya flopped back on the bed and a bit later the same woman came to pick up the tray. Lanya did not get up and did not say anything. It was like talking to a rock. She peered at her hands. They were red from all the wringing she had done in the hours she had been here. She ran her fingers through her hair and some came out in her fingers. Was this from stress or from malnutrition? She wondered what was next. *Will there be a trial? Like in court with witnesses and testimonies?* She doubted that. The Party did not have to prove anything, they just had to have suspicions. No defense, no testimony. She was sure that if she got a chance to speak she would say the wrong thing anyway. *Why bother. I will probably be taken in front of a firing squad next week. Or put on a train north to Siberia. Are my parents still alive? If I get sent to Siberia can I find them?* They probably had plenty of prisons up there in the snowpack. She would never find them.

Lanya wondered about God. She had only prayed when her sister was dying, but she thought maybe this would be time to start. She knew many people prayed to God every day. She did not know the rules, the expectations. But, she had nothing to lose. She did not want to get down on her knees because she worried someone would see and say something. So she sank onto the bed on her back and looked at the dirty ceiling.

"God, I do not know you. You do not know me. But I need help and I have no one else to ask. If you have been watching me, like some people say, you know I am not a spy. I hate the Germans and I would never in a million years help them destroy my city, my country, my family. They killed my sister and ruined my brother. Ivan may have been helping the Germans but I did not. God, if you care for people like I heard from Babu, can you please help me get out of here? I did nothing wrong." The tears choked her at every breath and she stopped. She did not know what else to say to God. *Am I asking right? Is there some special password that only people who went to church knew?* She did not know anyone who went to church since they were all closed. But she spent a moment reviewing her request to God, and then silently said "Amen" and closed her eyes again.

The days in the cell were frightfully long. Nothing to read, no one to talk to, her hands were still red from the constant wringing. Her hair was coming out because she was grabbing it constantly. She tried to stop, but it was hard. She had no fingernails left. And there was nothing to do but worry. She could worry. She could spend all day worrying, she had done it before.

When the cart came by with her meal, she was happy. *Pitiful,* she said to herself, *that a plate full of a few spoonsful of food glob could make her happy.* It wasn't the food, she realized. It was the contact. This was the young man who came by yesterday. He came to the door and she tried again.

"Please, please, listen. My brother Mikhail is at home in our apartment. He was injured in the war and is an idiot. A bomb went off near him and ruined his brain." The young man looked at her and she thought she saw some pity in his pale eyes. "He cannot cook or feed himself. Shouldn't we help him?" He guardedly glanced at her and she felt that was a win. "My friend will care for him if I can get a note to her." She stopped there. She knew he would get in trouble if he sent a note to Maru. Her eyes begged him to see her. He had already placed the tray on the small table and turned to go.

"I am sorry." He left without another word. Lanya fought back the tears. Now she was angry. She did nothing wrong and Mishka did nothing wrong and he would die in that apartment alone! This was not right! She wished she had a pad of paper to write Comrade Stalin a letter and tell him that his brave soldier would die because the rules would not allow help. She smashed her hand onto the pillow again and again. There was nothing she could do. Her feelings of being powerless were the strongest ever. Maybe next time he came she would scream, so everyone in the wing would know what the problem was.

When the matron came in with her morning meal the next day, Lanya said nothing. She did not even get off the bed. She knew the meal was unappealing and she lifted the lid. She forced herself to eat the small blob on her plate. Maybe she would starve to death in here before they put her on trial.

She spent hours planning how to address the young man. *Can I appeal to his patriotism? His emotions? What questions is he likely to answer? Is he married? Should I flirt?* She knew the matron would never bend the slightest so she decided to focus on the young man.

He came back in the evening. She was strong enough for a new battle. When he came in, she could see that he had a limp, something about his left leg. That would explain why he was not at the front. She thought maybe she could work with that.

"I want to thank you for bringing my food. Can you tell me your name please?" She was sure that names were allowed for communication. He looked at her carefully.

"Sergei", his name was Sergei. A start.

"I see that you have trouble walking sometimes, Sergei. Is that from the war?" He was backing away and did not seem to want to talk. He nodded and got to the door. "I am sorry you were injured. Did you lose friends too?" Again, he nodded and went out. Lanya left it at that. It would not happen in one day. She would need to work on him slowly.

The next day, Sergei came back with dinner again.

"Have you lost any family in this war, Sergei? The Germans killed my little sister. Just a kid, she was killed in a bombing. I miss her every day." Sergei placed her tray on the table and paused, as if he would talk. Lanya tried to think quickly. "Your father?" He stopped as if he was startled and quickly moved to the door. "I am sorry. We have all lost someone. Damn Germans." Sergei seemed to want to run away from her.

Lanya was hopeful things were a bit better, like she was getting through to Sergei. He seemed to have a heart, so Lanya decided to focus on things in common. When he came next, she continued with the relationship building.

"My name is Svetlana, you may know that. I work at the boot factory sewing boots. I am not a spy. I hate Germans. I would shoot them myself if I could. Did it feel good to shoot Germans Sergei?" He stopped and looked at her with a sad half smile.

"I did not shoot. I drove an ambulance until my accident." Lanya thought quickly.

"But if you had a gun, I'll bet you would shoot them." He nodded and hurried out.

The next day, she needed to be direct.

"Sergei, I only need one small thing. My brother is going to die if I cannot get my friend to care for him. Can I please have you send her a note? I need paper and a pen, and I will tell you where to find her. Just one thing, Sergei. You would be my hero." Sergei did not say a word.

But the next day, Sergei had a small sheet of paper and a pen. He handed it to Lanya and waited a moment while she scribbled a note to Maru asking her to take care of Mishka. She put Maru's address on the outside and shoved it to Sergei.

"My hero." He quickly got out, and Lanya watched as he delivered the other trays and left the cell area.

The next day, Sergei did not come in. Lanya panicked, hoping that he did not get caught with her note. She would hate to be the cause of his death. She could hardly eat and hoped that maybe it was just some other issue. When the matron came in, Lanya had to ask, "Do you know where the evening man was? Someone else came in today." The matron looked at her like she was speaking another language.

"My son will be back tomorrow. It is his day off. Even in this war, we get days off." Lanya wanted to rush and hug her, but she was sure she would get smacked hard. She tried to appear aloof.

"Thank you. I am glad he gets time off. I hope you do, too." The matron bustled out without another word. Lanya slumped in relief. His day off. Maybe he was taking the note to Maru today? While his mother worked would be a good time. For the first time in days, Lanya's spirits lifted. Even her dinner was almost tasty.

The next morning, Lanya woke early to wait for Sergei though she knew it would be hours. When she finally heard his cart come squeaking in, she rushed to the door. She waited until he turned to her. He did not have a note but he came a bit closer and whispered in her ear. "I delivered the note to your friend. She said she already has been taking care of your brother for the last week and will until you come home. She says he is okay." Lanya collapsed on the cold floor of the cell. The tears that came were relief instead of fear this time.

"Thank you so much. You really are my hero." She got up and reached out to him as he was retreating. She stood on her tiptoes and gave him a quick kiss on his cheek. His cheek turned bright red and he almost ran out of the cell. Lanya let the tears come, happy that something went right in her life. She was sure this was a miracle, since so few things in her life went right . A miracle in war time.

Nighttime in this dank cell was endless. She could not tell what time it was or what day it was. Without people bringing food she would go stark raving mad. Maybe she was already close. As she lay down after dinner, she heard the air raid sirens. New fears jumped all through her. *Will we go to a shelter? Do they even have a shelter here? Will the guards go? Or would I sit right where I am, with no protection from German bombs?* She jumped off the bed and wished she had a window to see what was going on. The siren was still going. On and on. She heard noises down the hall but could not see anything. Her light was still on, which was good. What would happen if it went out? She paced, back and forth. She knew the number of steps each way and the number in a lap. She walked as the night screeched and she wondered if she would die here. *Not in front of a firing squad or in the forests of Siberia, but here in my town, because they did not protect me from bombs.* She hated Germans. Every last one of them. She could hear the bombs as they struck the ground. Boom, boom, clatter. She heard walls collapse, she knew that sound all too well now. She heard some squeals then nothing. The siren went off. Would she hear the release too? Or was she going to be on edge all night, pacing inside this box tomb?

She tried to clear her mind and think of nothing. Just breathe. No words, no pictures. It was impossible. *How can I clear my brain when the world is being bombed! When streets are turned into jigsaw puzzles and people are turned into piles of bloody death like Valentina?* She could not clear her brain. So she walked.

After some time, she had no idea how long, the release bell went off. The tears sprang up and poured out. *I will not die tonight.* She flopped onto the bed and drenched her pillow in tears. Somehow, she fell asleep, probably from too much stress on her weak body. But the nightmares started early. She woke up screaming. She tried to go back to sleep and almost did, but started screaming again. More bombs, fire and running around. No one she recognized this time. As she screamed again, a light went on in the hall. Footsteps. Someone was coming to check on her. A man she did not know looked into her room and gave her a questioning look with his eyebrows up.

Lanya rolled over and saw his face, looking like he expected an explanation. "Nightmares. Every time we have an air raid, I have them. I cannot sleep." He looked at her, not unkindly. Maybe nightmares in this place were expected. He turned and left, and Lanya wondered what all that was about. *Do they check on me because they care? Is it a requirement? Check on any screams? What if I scream another time? Will they come back?* His footsteps diminished as he went back to what he was doing earlier. They did not care. No one did. The Party did not care for anything except itself.

Chapter
Twenty-Eight

The days were endless but Lanya felt better knowing that Maru was taking care of Mishka. She started to sing, first in her head. She wanted to fight the quiet, just like she did in the apartment. She chose the songs that would uplift her. From the show she had been in, from her favorite movies, and even some that she was composing herself. She was not happy, How could she be,, in jail, but singing made it a bit better. The words came out and soon she was singing out loud. Not projecting, like on stage, but softly. She sang when Sergei came by and told him she wanted to be on stage again. He gaped at her when he heard her voice for the first time. He almost spoke to her but quickly hurried out. She was hesitant to sing in front of the matron unsure what the ice maiden would do. So she waited.

Lanya tried to remember how long she had been in here. She remembered reading a story as a child about someone trapped on a deserted island waiting for rescue and how he had cut marks on a tree for each day. She had no way to make any sort of mark on anything, this place had nothing sharp of course. She tried to remember how many times she had seen Sergei. She came up with close to ten, but he had missed a few days. *Had she been here more than ten days?* It hurt to think about it.

The next day Lanya was singing quietly and a sound behind her near the door surprised her. It was the matron without a food tray.

"You have a visitor. Do not get loud or excited, or they will be taken away." She left and Lanya looked down the hallway wondering who was here? Maru maybe? No one else would come see her. She peered down the hall and strained her eyes. She tried to hear footsteps, expecting Maru's quick delicate steps. Nothing. Then, a shape, a man. What man? Lanya looked carefully at him. He seemed familiar. Thick hair with a wave- the man from the Party office! He had been nice to her. What was his name? Lanya backed away from the door. Was he here to cause more trouble? A Party man coming to see her?

He approached her door and she could see him well. Yes, the kind young man with the thick glasses from the Party office. He stayed on the other side of the barred door.

"Svetlana, I heard you were here. They will not let me in so we can't talk more quietly. Sorry about that. I, um..." he paused. He was tense, as Lanya was. Her fingers kept drumming. What could he say to help her? Lanya had a hundred thoughts in her head but did not know him well enough to ask anything.

"Josef, it is good to see you. To see anybody." She gave him a genuine smile and he smiled back. She was glad she remembered his name at the last minute. He looked her up and down as he searched for words.

"Svetlana, I am going to see what can be done. I believe there has been some false information in your case." She could tell his words were guarded. He had to protect himself. His words were barely a whisper even at that.

"Thank you Josef. I am not a spy. I hate the Germans as much as any Leningrader. I knew a man called Ivan, he produced that show I was in." Josef showed half a smile. "He was arrested for being a spy. I did not know anything he did. I swear on my life." She paused, wondering if this was enough. "I am sure this is some mistake that can be rectified with some digging." Her words were careful also but she could speak at a normal level. She was already in jail. He quickly looked at her face then his eyes went to the floor.

"Not much comfort in here, is there?"

"Not much but I get two meals a day. More than some I think." She did not want to complain and be viewed as a whiner. She did not take her eyes off him. He had trouble looking at her.

"I will see what I can do. I will talk to my supervisor."

"Thank you very much." She wanted to reach out and grasp his hand but he had already started backing away. "I hope I see you again soon Josef." He walked away and Lanya watched him with sad but grateful eyes.

He came to see her. He wanted to get her out. He was thoughtful and kind. She did not know him and now she was angry with herself for not being nicer to him when she saw him at the Party office. She had treated him like all the other officials, and now he was trying to get her out of this hole. Why was she such an idiot? Lanya walked the cell perimeter first for an hour then back and forth down the middle for an hour. She had lots of things in her head. *This good man, Josef, is looking out for me. But who do I choose? A beautiful man who cared more for himself and his skewed morals than for me. Ivan would sleep with me but never protected me from anything. And here I am in jail, and who knows if I will ever get out? Why couldn't I fall for a man like Josef?* This whole thing was out of her hands. People disappeared every day in Leningrad and sometimes they were never seen again. She hoped she was not one.

Sergei did not bring dinner; it was another woman she did not know. This woman was small and so thin it looked like she could break herself with a strong sneeze. How was she alive with zero fat? Most Leningraders had lost their fat in the last eight months but this woman had none to start with. She brought the tray and did not smile or speak with her quick stop. *No personality,* Lanya thought. *No shape, no smile, no personality. Does the Party make them this way?* She remembered the people at the Party office and they all seemed like cardboard. *No personality in the whole building. Maybe those cardboard people do better working for the Party than any other work. Follow rules, do not question, do what is expected. Is Josef carboard, too? Are they all scared of the Party, like I am? How many people here in Leningrad smile and cheer and follow the Party line, but are too scared to say anything against the Party? Like I am?* Lanya wondered if anyone saw her as cardboard. She hoped not.

The next two days went slowly as only time in jail can. When Sergei came next, Lanya approached him.

"Sergei, you heard me singing the other day." He looked at her with expectant eyes. "Did you know I was in a show, in November?" He did not talk so she kept going. "Tell you what, when I get out of here, if I do," she paused, hoping he might offer something but he was still silent; "If I get into another show, I will send you tickets. So you can see me on stage. Would you like that?" His eyes lit up and his smile was huge.

"You would do that? For me?"

Lanya nodded, "Yes, since you were good to me in here. No one else says anything and I hate silence. But you have been kind, so next time I am on stage, you can come see me. And when you come to the show, I would like for you to come backstage and say hello. Will you do that?" His eyes were so big Lanya worried they would pop out of his head. He nodded. He uncovered the plate and hurried to the door. As he left the cell, Lanya could see he was light on his feet even with a bad leg, like he was flying. She wondered if he had ever seen a theater show. But she could promise this. If she ever got on stage again, she would be as kind to him as he was to her.

The next morning, Lanya heard footsteps after breakfast was cleared and wondered who was coming. Josef arrived, bringing another man with a stern face.

"Svetlana, good morning. I wanted to see you if I may?" The other man used a key to unlock the door and came in. There was nowhere to sit so they all stood. "This is Gregori Tuchkov, with the Party, and he had a few questions for you." Josef said, Gregori nodded and pulled out a small notebook.

Gregori went through the usual name, address, and birthday norms and then his face got even more stern.

"Did you know Ivan Sivkov?" Lanya noticed the past tense but put it aside for now.

"Yes I did. He produced a theater show I was in during the fall." Past tense.

"I understand. Was there more?" He waited for her answer but Lanya could feel the tension and chill between them.

"What do you mean? There was only one show." Stupid might work.

"Where did you meet him?"

"I met him at a show I went to with my friend in August and we talked then about a show he would produce. I wanted to be in the show."

Gregori nodded. "Did he talk about his life before Leningrad?"

"He said he had seen shows in many cities and that he was from Minsk."

"Minsk? Ha!" Gregori wrote a few notes. "Did he ever mention Germany?"

"I think he said he saw show in Berlin. That is all. Nothing else." More notes. Lanya waited. Why was Josef here? She had answered these questions earlier. She added more. "I saw him after the show ended in late November. He came by in December with an idea for another show and asked me to try out. So I met him at a theater and tried out. In the new show, I earned the lead part and was excited to be in it, but he was arrested before we had any rehearsals. I did not see him again." Not exactly true, since he did come to their house and asked to stay. Unless they followed him they would not know that. What if they did follow him? Was she in trouble for that?

"Another question. Did he come by your house just before he was arrested, in the evening?" Lanya froze but tried hard to hide it.

"I, I, I am not sure. My grandmother said someone came by but did not say who and she did not know him. I do not know what day he was arrested so I am not sure. Some nights I go to sewing group to help make things for the troops. Maybe that is where I was."

"So you did not see him?"

"No, the last time I saw him was at the theater."

"I understand. Did he seem in any way underhanded, secretive?"

"I am not sure. We did not talk much, in the theater. I never saw anything that I thought was secretive." Lanya bit her lip. She was lying through her teeth, but no one would know.

"Is there anything else we should know?" He looked at Lanya with an icy stare and her stomach was in such knots she was not sure she could ever eat again. This man was not cardboard, he was steel.

"Um, nothing comes to mind. He seemed quiet, to me."

"Thank you." Gregori turned to leave. Josef had said nothing else but gave Lanya a warm smile as he turned to go. As they walked out, in the hall, Lanya heard him talk to Gregori.

"I told you. She knows nothing. She does not belong here."

"Hush Josef. I will decide that. Be quiet!" Gregori tried to whisper but in this tiled hallway nothing could be kept quiet. They walked quickly.

So Josef had come and brought some Party big wig to interrogate her, trying to get her out. *Why does he care? Does he think he knows me? He never told me he had any feelings. He never touched me or shared more than a few words with a smile. What was going on?* Lanya walked the small room trying to sort it all out hoping that her stomach would settle down and relax as she walked.

Chapter Twenty-Nine

The waiting was interminable. There was nothing to do, except worry. She wondered if her parents had the same concerns. Maybe they did whatever crime they were brought here for. *Were my parents in this same room? Can I ever know? Do she want to know?* Sounded awfully morbid. She tried to get back to singing, but the melody was frozen. Like her heart.

A sound down the hallway perked her ears. It was too early for breakfast. No one was talking, but she could hear the footsteps. A man. She craned her neck, looking out but saw nothing yet. Maybe they were going to someone else. She never heard others, but she never spoke to anyone either. She had heard people coming and going at different times, so she knew she was not alone. A man showed up and opened her door. Not a man she had seen before. *Is this the end? Am I going to be taken out and shot? Like Ivan?* Her feet seemed glued to the floor.

"Svetlana Zhudanov? Come with me." He followed her out though she was not sure she could walk. Each step was torture. She would not be able to say goodbye to her brother or Maru. Babu was already gone. Would she meet them on the other side? Her parents, her sister, Babu? Would she know them? Would they know her? Her own footsteps echoed in the tiled hall and they came to the room where they had questioned her. In this room, the man who came yesterday was waiting with a folder. He gestured for her to sit.

"Svetlana Zhudanov, we have chosen to release you today. We did not find evidence of spying. For Ivan Sivkov, we had evidence, but you we do not. But we will be watching you. Every minute." As if he needed to say that last bit. He opened the door and led the way out. Leaving? Release? She did not know the Party ever did that. He went through hallways and she saw herself at the door they brought her in through, at the back of the building. He opened the door and stood aside. Lanya got out as quickly as she could. The air was cold but it was fresh air. He closed the door behind her and Lanya stopped and took a huge breath of fresh air. She had not had fresh air in forever! She looked up, the sky was a pale blue. But it was wide open! Lanya tried to run, but could not. Her muscles were weak from lack of use. So, she slowly began the walk home.

Lanya opened the apartment door slowly, not wanting to upset Mishka. She heard nothing but the familiar smell of fish was so comfortable she started crying immediately.

"Mishka?" She started into the hall, looking for her brother. There he was. He jumped up as he saw her and leaped across the room to give her a hug. "I have missed you! I am so glad to be home!" The tears clouded her eyes. He studied her. She backed away to look at his face. He looked okay, he had not lost any more weight. "I am so glad to see you." She gave him a tighter squeeze and backed out of the room. How was the rest of the house? The kitchen was fine, she could see evidence of breakfast in the sink. The stove was still burning and there was a small pile of wood in the corner. Not much food, but that is just how it was. Ration cards in the drawer. All good. Her bedroom was unchanged, no one had even come in. The door to Babu's room was closed and she did not bother going in. Time for a bath, after almost two weeks without one.

The water took a long time to heat, but the bath was heavenly. She pulled out the gift soaps that had been in the back of the cabinet for a long time, saved for a special day. This day was special. She soaked until the water cooled and slowly got herself dressed. She found a box of tea in the kitchen then made a cup and found some bread for a snack. Back to household duties, but she was happy to do it. She would go tell Maru that she was home, after she got some energy back.

She walked to the factory and caught Maru as she was leaving. She stood almost where Ivan stood, months ago, when he came to pick her up. Her stomach dropped a bit with that memory. What a fool she had been.

"Maru! Maru!" Lanya rushed over and wrapped Maru in a bear hug like never before.

"Lanya! How did you? When did you..."

"I got out this morning, I went home and I had to come tell you." Both women let the tears come and did nothing to try to stop them.

"I thought I would never see you again! Tell me all about it. Come to my house, my mom just made some biscuits I think." They walked the twenty minute walk to Maru's apartment. The familiarity again made Lanya choke up. She pushed the tears away. While nibbling the biscuits, they sat at the kitchen table and Lanya told the story about the arrest, which Maru had heard from others at the factory. About the questioning, about the cell, about her fears for Mishka. Lanya told about her Sergei and the matron, the cold food and the worry that she would never see daylight again.

"I only got out because of Josef. Remember, I told you about the man with the thick glasses from the Party office who spoke to me a few times when I was picking up ration cards? With the thick glasses? He came to visit me with some investigator a few days ago. The investigator was a cold, harsh man, who asked me all the same questions I had already answered. But as they left, I heard Josef say to him that I did not belong there. And today, they let me out. They said they did not have enough evidence to prove I was a spy. I would never spy for the Germans- I hate Germans! I did not know the Party ever released people! But here I am." Maru was listening carefully, soaking in every word.

"I did not know they released people either." She was almost dumbfounded with that idea.

"And I owe you so much, for taking care of my brother." Lanya took Maru's hand in hers and gave it a squeeze.

"No, knock it off. I promised you I would take care of him, so I did." The biscuit was gone and Lanya was tired, so she left early.

"I will be at the factory tomorrow, so I will see you there."

"Good." Lanya walked home with a lighter step than before. It was so good to have Maru in her corner.

She flopped down on her bed in her bedroom. It was not as cold so they did not need to sleep next to the stove anymore. Her bed was like heaven after the flat, thin mattress in the cell. Sleep came easily.

At the factory, people were shocked to see her. She got to her machine and saw a few dried flowers on it. They thought she was not coming back. Her heart swelled, grateful for these good people. Her day was a normal day, except for the smiles and pats on her shoulder as she sewed. She made a point to go to the foreman and explain why she was gone, and she also made a point to go see the biggest gossip at the plant, to tell the truth and dispel all the rumors. Yes, she was arrested and accused of spying. They did not find evidence so they let her go. Her brother was fine, Maru had taken care of him. The Party was good, looking out for the people of Leningrad, and taking care of them all. She almost choked saying that, but she wanted people to know that she was loyal to the Party, even though her heart was not.

She was tired and went home dragging. She had been in jail two weeks and it felt like years. She rummaged around the kitchen looking for food, found some and made some weak soup for herself and her brother. The frozen Road of Life across Lake Ladoga would break up any time and things would get tight again. When would this war end? This was the longest nine months ever.

Her next day off, she went by the Party office to renew her ration cards. She was glad the cards were unused when she went into jail, so they had enough to get through the two weeks. She stood in line at the door in the cold March air with coldness coming from inside, not just outside. She did not want to go into this building. She had fear all over her. She had spent enough time in this building before she went to jail and too much in jail. She peeked around the corner and saw the door that she had gone in and come out. When it was time to move up in line, she had to put her hands on her legs and force them to move. This was harder than being onstage!

Inside, the air was a bit warmer but the cardboard people were doing their mindless routine. She looked for Josef but did not see him. He was never at the counter, so maybe he was a manager of some sort. She waited patiently, telling her stomach to relax and breathing slowly. Her stomach did not often listen to her brain. Josef came out and did not look for her but she saw him. Her stomach relaxed on its own. He was busy. How could she get his attention? She took a moment and looked for the ice man interrogator, he was not in the main room. Was he in the far back? Or the investigator rooms at the back near the jail? She did not want to see him again.

Lanya was called to the counter, showed her papers, and without question was handed the new ration cards. Crisp and clean. She turned to go, looking one more time for Josef. He was not nearby so she gathered her ration cards into her bag, pulled it into her coat and opened the door to leave. The air was fresh and she wondered why the air just outside the Party office always smelled so fresh.

"Svetlana." She turned as soon as she heard her name, knowing it was Josef.

"Josef, I saw you inside but did not want to draw attention." She turned to face him and wondered if she should reach for him. "Josef, you saved my life. I owe you so much. Thank you a million times." Josef faced her and he did not look as timid as before.

"Svetlana, it was the right thing to do. I knew you were not what they said you were. You told me before about your little sister and your brother, so I knew you would not work for the damn Germans." Lanya nodded, holding back tears.

"You are right. I hate Germans. I hate this war. Thank you again. I cannot thank you enough."

"It was the right thing." The shyness came back. "I hope I see you again in a few days when you come back."

"I will look for you, of course."

"I will look for you, but you were right not to draw attention. In ten days I will look for you at this time."

"That would be great. I owe you." The tears were making it hard to talk, so Lanya added nothing more. Her hands were clenched in front of her.

"See you then."

"Yes, see you." Josef went back into the office and Lanya again wondered why she was such an idiot. This man had put his neck on the line for her and she did not even touch him? She had done everything with Ivan and Josef was twice the man Ivan was! She walked home with her brain a mess, asking herself how to repay Josef. He never asked for anything.

The women of the Wednesday night sewing group were shocked to see her. They had heard she was arrested and like most arrests, thought they would never see her again. She settled in and explained her story, just as she did to the factory gossip, why she was arrested, why she was released, and how grateful she was for the Party looking out for all of Leningrad. It almost did not hurt to say it anymore, she had said it so many times. Almost like playing a part, she thought, saying the given lines each time. Say them convincingly enough, and you can earn another part next time. The women were warm and friendly and Lanya was glad of their comfort.

One of the women was so excited. The Party had decided that this year, the city would not have grass in the parks, but allow residents to garden and farm in the parks. Leningrad had plenty of parks. Cabbages, onions and potatoes were quick to be offered to plant. Even women who had no planting skills, like Lanya, decided to give it a try. How hard could it be? March was too soon to plant, this far north, June would be better. They were still having occasional snowstorms and the ground was partly frozen. Would they be able to get seeds? Start them indoors? Lanya listened hoping to glean information. She had never put her hands in the earth, but if she could get some to work with, it would not hurt. It would be good to eat something she planted when winter came again.

Lanya did not see Josef the next time she went to get ration cards and she was disappointed. She wanted to again show her gratitude. The days ran into each other, and Lanya was numb. Nothing new, nothing exciting. Life could not get any worse, she was sure. Except the bombs. Every week, a shower of bombs that killed innocent people, destroyed homes and ruined families. The power was still out and gasoline was impossible to get, so the trams were still not running. But if the army needed gasoline they should have it. So Lanya walked and was glad that winter was gone so she could go out without wearing four layers of coats.

Chapter Thirty

Towards the end of March, the Party had made the official announcements about using city parks and land outside of offices for people to use as gardens. The snow was melting and by June, the city would be green and vibrant. People had to sign up at the Party office if they wanted a plot. Plots were small, but anything would help. Lanya had never gardened, had never planted anything but she figured she could learn. Her grandparents had been farmers, so maybe it was in her blood. She signed up for a plot, gave her address so it would be close, and waited. She knew that nothing would grow until it warmed, so she was not worried.

It was April before the plots were assigned. Lanya was not sure where hers was and decided to ask the sewing group ladies about the plot and what she would do.

"You got a plot? Good for you! I am too old for gardening anymore."

"Where is your plot? I know that area, it's near St. Isaac's."

"Make sure you start them in the house for a month. Don't put anything out until the end of May or it will be too cold."

"I got one too, I think I will plant lots of cabbage." Lanya listened to the suggestions about what to plant and when to start. She was scared. What if she failed? What if she grew nothing but weeds? What if she thought her cabbage was weeds and pulled them out?

Lanya decided to walk to her garden plot and see what it looked like. St. Isaac's was a few blocks away and there used to be flowers and shrubs here. She had some guilt, ruining a flower garden, but not for long. They couldn't eat daffodils. The plot was small, but she did not want big. She had to work it herself, with Mishka's occasional help. She could have gotten two plots but this year she decided one was enough. She saw the posts and string with labels separating the lots. She found the number she was assigned and walked to the middle. She walked around, touching each corner. It took about 20 steps to get to the corner and 20 more to the next corner. Corner to corner it looked huge! *How am I going to fill this with plants?* Ideas and questions ran through her head. She was sure that Babu would have made it work. Maybe Maru and her mother would have ideas?

Lanya used ration cards to get seeds and went back to her plot to gather some dirt to take home. She put the dirt in several bowls and dropped seeds in each. A little water, then wait. She planted cabbage, onions and carrots. Potatoes would be next. Lanya checked her bowls every day. She remembered an old saying about a watched pot never boiling and wondered if it was true for seedlings too.

An air raid the next night sent Lanya into a new set of fears. What if they ruined her plants? What if her house was bombed and her new seeds were hit? What if her garden was hit? Would the Party give her more seeds? She doubted they would, but she went to the air raid shelter with Mishka, and her brain was not worried about her own safety, just the safety of tiny little dots in bowls on the kitchen counter.

Lanya watched the little bowls and worried about them. The apartment was warm and she showered the seeds with a few drops each day. She had no idea if they needed more or less, she knew they did not want to be swimming in it but she also did not want them too dry. *How do people do this? How do they know?* After four days, she saw a tiny speck of green and was so excited she jumped up and shouted! She knew better than to touch it. She would show Mishka tomorrow but today this was her little victory. She checked it when she got home from work and there was another three green dots in the bowls! She was gardening!

Over the next week, there were many sprouts. Lanya hoped they were not too crowded. If they got crowded, should she transfer some to bigger bowls? When the next air raid came, she quickly put these valuable bowls under the kitchen sink to protect them from any debris or dust. She treated them like children!

At the end of May, after many worried nights in the air raid shelter, Lanya was ready to put her sprouts in the ground. Some were getting tall with leaves budding out and Lanya was proud. She laughed at herself. *I used to be proud that I could sing, now I am proud of three inches of green in a bowl!*

She borrowed a shovel from a neighbor and asked Mishka to help, not because it was strenuous, but because she wanted him to be a part of it. They got plenty of rain, so she did not have to worry about irrigation. She had dreams about an apple tree, but the plot was too small and would not remain hers when this war was over. Mishka was much better with the shovel than she was. She could not do too much, since she was weak from too little food. But they made some rows and planted some of their sprouts of cabbage, potatoes, onions and carrots. The ground was no longer frozen, so the plants would do fine. Every three days, she and her brother went to check on her plot and check for weeds. The bugs might eat the sprouts so Lanya checked every leaf each time she visited. She had a real garden! She dreamed of a table full of vegetables and her stomach rumbled in anticipation.

May turned into June and soon, the one year anniversary of the war came. It was mostly quiet, since no one was proud of what was going on. There were speeches made about the courage of the soldiers and the strength of the leadership, and a band played a few tunes outside the Party office. But no one knew what was next. Any day the German army could do more than nighttime raids. Any day, there could be tanks in the streets. So the anniversary was not a celebration, unless resilience was worth celebrating.

Summer in Leningrad was always a time for festivities, but not this year. The daylight lasted well into the night and the hours of darkness were short. Vegetables and grains were sneaking into the city across Lake Ladoga, just like the frozen "Road of Life" over the winter, brave boat owners willing to smuggle in food. Rationing had eased a bit, considering so many people had died over the winter, fewer people needed food so they relaxed a bit. Lanya saw the cabbages and produce at the grocers and wished she knew how to can the food. Babu could, but Lanya had no idea. But she decided to do what she and Babu had done a year ago- make rusks. Make more bland, boxy bread chunks that would help when winter came. So she bought all the flour she could and spent afternoons mixing and baking. She remembered doing this with Babu and missed her grandmother intensely.

One warm summer afternoon she was especially brave and opened up Babu's room. She had not been inside since Babu had died; it was too much for her. But here, in Babu's room, she could smell the hint of cologne and soap that Babu used. She could almost feel Babu with her. She opened drawers and looked into the closet. Would she ever wear any of these old things? She hoped not! Maybe she should box them up and give them away. But these were Babu, how could she? Maybe she could find another use for some things.

In the closet,, she found a box with old photos. Just a few since photos were so expensive. She recognized Babu as a younger woman and her mother as a child. In the same box she found a few journals. A journal? She did not know that Babu kept a journal, she had never mentioned it. She checked the dates. She opened the most worn one and saw an opening date of 1925. A quick story about moving to this apartment with Lanya's parents and Mishka and Lanya as tiny children. How Babu was happy to help out the young parents and cook and clean while they worked.

Lanya sat on the bed and folded her legs under her. She would see Babu in a new light. This journal had stories of Lanya losing her front teeth, of the birth of Valentina, of Mishka getting into a fight with another boy at school over a slingshot one made. Family stories. Lanya did not feel like she was invading Babu's privacy. Babu had been gone six months now. Lanya was sure that Babu would have shared these if asked. Notes about Lanya's father and the pressure he was under at the shipbuilding factory where he worked were included in this journal. The quotas made him uptight, so he drank a lot. Lanya remembered her dad always having a small glass of vodka near him in the evenings.

Lanya put the journals down and went to the kitchen. She could come back to these tomorrow. Lanya was relieved to have more food in the house. Her skirts were not as loose and Mishka had filled out a bit, his cheeks were not as gaunt. As they ate dinner, Lanya looked at him. He had not spoken since he came home in September. *Will he always be this way? Can I do anything to help him? Will I always have to look out for him? I could never put him in a home or a hospital, but I cannot see myself at sixty years old caring for my older brother who is still like a child.* Too much, she said to herself. I do not want to think about all this now.

The air raid that night was rather short and she was happy to get back to her own bed. The longer days meant less dark time for the raids, so Lanya understood that meant raids that were less than three hours. The nightmares came as they always did, but she did not scream out. *Am I getting used to these? Will I always have nightmares? Or will they end when the war ends?* Tonight's nightmare was quick and over without much screaming. She did not have many nightmares before the war, so she hoped this was only because of the war. The nightmares were always vivid war scenes, not family trauma.

The next afternoon, Lanya went into Babu's room and pulled the box out again. One journal with dark red leather covering it seemed to be the earliest. Lanya wanted to read it fully, not just skim like she did yesterday. She took it back to her room, she could not see herself lying on Babu's bed to do this. In her room, she lay back and opened the journal. It started when Lanya was a child but gave no exact date or explanation of why Babu started to keep a journal. What she read were family stories, back to the missing front teeth, and Mishka being a typical boy. Happy notes with nothing underneath. Then there was a note about Lanya's grandparents, her father's parents. Lanya had met them once when she was small and Valentina was just a baby. The family had taken a trip to the Ukraine region where her grandparents were farmers. Lanya remembered the trip and the cows she got to pet and milk. Lanya remembered it fondly. But in the journal it talked about Lanya's father being upset with the Party's plan to socialize the farmland. Doing this meant farmers would not be able to keep the farm produce they grew and that could cause trouble. Back in Leningrad, Lanya's father was angry with the Party and one night was screaming and drinking and making a scene. Babu recorded it factually. Then, the note came that Lanya's grandparents had died. From starvation. Babu mentioned a telegram that came to the apartment. *How does a farmer die of starvation? What kind of system makes this happen? Farmers are the last to starve to death!* When everything they worked for was taken away, and they were not able to get more food. This had taken months to happen and Lanya remembered her father getting letters from her grandparents and him drinking more each night. Then they died. Lanya got a tear in her eye remembering. She did not remember when they died but she did remember the times when her father drank often and became argumentative. How had they coped with this?

On a fresh page, Lanya saw a note that made her pause. It was an old phrase that Lanya had heard before but wondered if it meant anything now. In clear letters, larger than the other notes, was this note "There is no misfortune without a blessing in it." Why this note, now? Lanya folded the journal closed and let her mind wander. *What blessing would come from this time when farmers starved. And what blessings can come from this war, now, when so many were dying? How can there be a blessing from this?*

Babu noted a few pages later that Lanya's father had a really bad night and left the house screaming and punching walls. Lanya must have been asleep. She had no memory of waking up the next day, but she had a clear memory as she was getting ready for school, the pounding on the door and the men in suits. They demanded her father come to the door. Her dad was still in bed and she could hear his angry words as her mom went to get him. He came out in his pajamas and froze as he saw the men. Lanya's heart sank. No one said anything and all eyes were on the men in suits. She did not quite understand what was going on but she knew it was not good. Her father asked if he could change and they nodded. "Be quick!" They demanded. He turned to go without looking at anyone. He came back dressed just a moment later and Lanya's mom started to wail, a piercing scream like a child had died. Her father paused at the door and nodded to the family and without a word, walked out. The children watched silently as did Babu. Her mother fell into a chair. The men in suits followed him out and shut the door with a firm clank.

Reading this, Lanya was overcome with emotion. Babu's notes had some details but Lanya's teenaged brain remembered it clearly. The last time she ever saw her father. She later learned that he was taken away by the Party for "anti-Soviet activities," whatever that meant. Her lip curled up and the tears crept up on her. She had not thought of this in a long time. It hurt too much. She took a few minutes on her bed to remember her dad. Hugs and laughs, jokes and pokes. He drank and he was angry but she still loved him with all a girl could.

After a few minutes, she picked up the journal again, hesitant to see what was next. Babu came back in the next few days and explained what happened. Her dad had been on a drunken rampage that night, went to the Party office and threw a Molotov cocktail through the window. The office went up in flames and her dad was glad of it. He was mad at the Party for what they did to his parents in the Ukraine, dying because they had no food even though they were farmers. But to attack a Party office? And someone turned him in? Her dad must have known what was happening that morning. He knew he would be gone forever. But he never said goodbye. The tears came full force now and Lanya remembered the hurt and feeling of loss like it was yesterday. Why would he do that? Why would he stir up trouble, knowing the Party had no forgiveness? It's not like passing out flyers or saying things about the Party. A Molotov cocktail? No way to hide that! Lanya felt anger well up. Anger with the Party and anger at her father! *What was wrong with him? Why would he do this when he had a family that needed him? Was his own anger so strong nothing else mattered?* Lanya wanted to punch walls herself. She decided it was time to go outside for a walk.

Chapter Thirty-One

It took a few days before Lanya was ready to go back into her room and look at the journal again. But she was sure she had to, to unlock family secrets, to know her parents in a different way. Her anger had dimmed but was not completely gone. With feelings of betrayal, she picked up the journal and settled down on her bed.

After her father was gone, Lanya remembered how quiet the house was and how it seemed like a ghost was present. She remembered her mother struggling and drinking and Babu working hard to maintain some sense of normalcy. The journal went on, explaining how things changed after Lanya's dad left. There was nothing more about what happened to him. Because the Party never explained. All Lanya knew was that he was gone and she would not see him again. She had not questioned it as a teen, it was just the way life was. More in the journal about Lanya, Valentina and Mikhail growing up, school and clubs. About life in Leningrad. Nothing more about the Party. No one would put that it writing, Lanya knew. There was some mention of her mother being in despair and crying often and drinking daily. Lanya had some memory of it. Finally, Lanya got to the section on her mother. It was clear this was painful for Babu to write. She could almost see the old woman's eyes tear up as she read the next bit.

Her mother had been too distraught over the loss of her husband to work for months and Lanya had some memory of her mother lying on the chair many mornings. Babu wrote that more than a year later, after a very distraught night, her mother got up and dressed herself and left the house without eating one morning and Lanya never saw her again. Babu writes that they came and knocked on the door later that day saying they had her mother in custody and a trial would be coming. Lanya read that her mother had gone down to the same Party office where her father had thrown the Molotov cocktail through the window, and screamed and wailed for over an hour. Said some harsh things about the Party and how they wrecked her home and her life. No one criticized the Party in public, everyone knew that. Her mother had been dead drunk and screamed and wailed for over an hour. Babu wrote that they allowed her to go on for a while since they figured it was the alcohol, but mother did not stop. So they took her in. Lanya could feel her own tears. *My mother did exactly what my father had done, put her own concerns above being a parent! Dad was violent, but my mother was out of control!* Lanya's heart sank, knowing that her parents were not what she had thought they were. Both her parents were taken by the Party; Lanya always thought of that as sad but somewhat romantic, and that they were tragic heroes. But now, Lanya saw for the first time that they deserved their fate. They deserved to be arrested and taken away. Maybe not for as long as they were taken, but they deserved some punishment for what they did to the Party. Lanya felt like her life was built on falsehoods and her sobbing wracked her body for a long while.

Lanya wanted to talk about this to someone, anyone! Babu understood, but she was dead, Mishka would not be able to have a conversation and Valentina was long gone. She had no one to share these lessons with. That brought her heart down even more. Maru would not understand, so Lanya decided not to share with her. Lanya wondered what her life would be like if she had Maru's parents It would be much more stable for sure.

Lanya went outside for another walk, hoping to clear her head. She walked without a plan and just kept walking. She went to the edges of the city, knowing the army was only a mile away. The army was better at protecting her than her own parents had been. Lanya walked and walked. As she walked she made a plan- *if I ever have children I will put my own needs second and theirs first. I will never let some inner conflict spill over onto my children or take me away from them. I will put up with anything as long as they know they are my first priority.*

Lanya was grateful there was no air raid tonight; she was not sure she could handle anything else. Times like these were when her stomach knotted and her breathing was shallow. She made a simple dinner and shared it with her brother. She went back to her room but did not pick up Babu's journal. Not today. She had a bottle of vodka nearby. Drinking was easier than thinking or feeling. This was going to be a very long night. Nightmares came, but instead of explosions and shrapnel, it was monsters tugging and twisting her. She did not scream, but woke up crying.

It was now the middle of the summer and Leningrad was daylight well into the night. Lanya was glad of the dark curtains so she could sleep. Leningrad was not a fun city this year. Lanya sadly remembered the late night walks and adventures in earlier days. But now, summer was as dull as winter since there was nothing to do.

One day, she walked past the Mariinsky theater where she and Maru saw the show and she first met Ivan. She paused and looked at the locked doors. She remembered Maru being boy crazy and Lanya tagging along. She remembered the show she did here and the one night she got to play the lead. The theater was sad looking now, all closed and dark. *Will Leningrad ever recover from this war? Will it be bombed to oblivion and none of the grand old homes still stand? Will the factories be blown to bits and St. Isaac's be just a memory? What will make the Germans lose this war? Anything?* Lanya did not understand all of it for sure. And she did not believe all the Party said about the progress. The German army had been outside the gates for almost a year and there was no change she could tell. Maybe they were just waiting until other fighting was over? And Leningrad would be the last to go?

Lanya's small garden was doing well and she was surprised, that she could make things grow! Nothing to harvest yet, but Lanya could see the leaves and checked every time she was there for pests and weeds. And every time there was an air raid, she worried over losing her little patch.

After she got home, a knock on the door made Lanya jump. She was sitting, still, in her own thoughts about family, war and her time on stage. She crossed to the door and opened it. This was Boris, Mikhail's other friend.

"Boris, nice to see you. Would you like to come in?" He did not smile and had an impatient look on his face.

"No, I am not here on a social call. Aleksander is in the hospital and asked me to come tell you. He got hurt in the fighting. He will be okay, but he wanted you to come visit." He turned to leave and Lanya touched his shoulder.

"He sent you? He is in the hospital? Which one? Thank you. So much." Boris muttered the answers, nodded and almost stormed off. *Not a friendly man,* Lanya observed. She went back inside. Aleksander was in the hospital? She should go see him. Right now. Lanya gathered her things and looked around to see if she had some sort of gift. Maybe she would stop at a little shop in town as she went across town to visit. Could she get flowers now? She did not remember seeing any in any of the shops. But she was not in a hurry so she went into two shops. No flowers but she got a book about horses. That was all they had. She hoped he would like it.

The hospital was quite a walk, and Lanya let her thoughts run. *Why does Aleksander want me to know he is in the hospital? Does he like me? Do I like him? Why is Boris so unfriendly? Did I do anything to him? What is his problem?* She could not remember being harsh to him. She walked quickly and was a bit winded when she got there. She hated hospitals and wondered if there was anyone on earth who didn't. The smell alone was bad enough. Hospitals always smelled like antiseptic and vomit. Her stomach wretched as she went to the front desk and asked for Aleksander. It was a large hospital and she got turned around but within a few minutes she found his room. The door was open and she saw him lying on the bed. She thought it was him. On his stomach. Most people laid on their backs. Why was he on his stomach?

"Aleksander?" Lanya asked, hoping she would not wake him up. His head jerked to the side and she saw his face. He broke out in a big smile.

"Svetlana! I hoped you would come!

"Boris came by and told me you got hurt. I brought you a book." She held the book to him and he thanked her. He nodded to a table and she set the book there.

"Sorry I cannot sit up. I got hit by a mortar on my behind. Metal flew everywhere. Two of our men were killed. I got hit, but this is rather small. It will heal quickly. But it does hurt! So I have to be on my stomach." With that, Lanya pushed the chair back and sat on the cold tile floor. She could see him a bit better.

"How long will you be in here?"

"Two weeks, maybe three. They hope they have the right medications. Many things are not available, so the doctor is hoping it will not get infected."

"Oh yes." Lanya was not sure what else to say.

"So Boris did come by? He was in another trench when this happened but came to check on me. I asked him to go tell you and he did not want to. I had to pay him money to come to you!" They both chuckled but Lanya knew that Boris did not come by because he wanted to. "I did not get a chance to come by again. They have us on some new maneuvers and I could not get away. I am sorry."

"Oh, do not worry. I was not expecting anything." They spoke of things for a few minutes more until a nurse came in and shooed Lanya out so she could clean the injury. Lanya wanted no part of that, so she quickly said goodbye and promised to come back soon. She left the room and hurried out of the hospital.

As she walked home, she thought about her few short visits with Aleksander. *He seems like a good guy. Certainly not a spy, like Ivan. He might care for me.* Lanya decided she should see him again in a few days.

On her next day off, Lanya went again to the hospital to see Aleksander. She brought him some candy this time. She checked at the front desk and the nurse there looked through some folders and checked another stack.

"He is not here. He was sent back to the military hospital because he was healing so fast." Lanya was crestfallen. She had waited for days to come see him and now he wasn't here. But he was healing so that was good. But she wanted to see his smile! She walked home again with mixed feelings. She did not see him but he was back among his own people. Maybe he would come by the apartment soon.

Chapter Thirty-Two

August started with rain and fog, but the fog did not stay long. Lanya's little garden patch showed promise, she could see the start of little cabbages and the carrot tops were getting tall. She had a thousand questions and decided to wait for sewing group to ask. There was an older woman at a patch near hers and maybe she had answers. The air raids were less than once a week, but with skies light so late they seemed less threatening. Not so scary if you could almost see the planes. Mishka was the same, playing with toys and not talking. Lanya often wondered if a doctor could think of some therapy that would help. But she was afraid for anyone to know, afraid they would send him back.

One evening after dinner, Lanya heard a knock on the door. Almost a pounding, not a gentle knock. She went to the door and opened it, surprised to see Mikhail's friend Boris standing there again.

"Boris, how nice to see you. Will you come in?" Lanya looked around to see if Aleksander was behind him. Boris barged in and turned to look at her.

"He is not here. He will not be back. He was blown to bits by a German bomb two days ago. The bomb went off and there was nothing left. We never found his body; it was in pieces. He told me he wanted to come back and see you again." Boris crossed the rug and stood right in front of Lanya. She could smell the alcohol on him. "But he is not what you want. He was weak. I am strong. I am what you need!" He grabbed Lanya by the shoulders and brought his lips onto hers with a kiss that was like a punch. Lanya almost fell over. If Boris had not been holding her up, she would have. She tried to speak but he kissed her again. "You need a real man," he said when he caught his breath. Lanya tried to wriggle out of his grip but couldn't.

"Boris!" Lanya wheezed his name as she tried to catch her breath.

"Yes, you need a real man!" Boris grabbed at Lanya again and put one arm around her back and his other hand came to her front. He grabbed at her blouse and tore off a button as he tried to rip her shirt off her.

"No!" Lanya had her breath back and was trying to get some control. The arm on her back pulled her in close and one large hand went over her breast. *What is going on? What is this man doing?* Lanya tried to squirm her way out and Boris turned her around so her back was to him. One of his hands was groping all over her breast, trying to get under her shirt. She felt her bra being grabbed. His other big hand was covering her mouth so she could not call out. Lanya tried to scream. No sound. She racked her brain. Elbows. She took one elbow and jammed it into his ribs, hoping that would slow him down. He caught his breath and moved his hand from her mouth.

"Stop!" She yelled with all she had. *What if he doesn't? What will he do?* The hand that had been at her breast now moved lower. He grabbed her skirt and bunched it up in his hand. He pulled at her skirt and Lanya heard it rip. His calloused hand was on her legs and she could feel it through her underwear. Was he going to touch her there? She tried her other elbow when all of a sudden Boris was yanked off her. She turned and saw her brother standing there like a bear. Mishka was breathing hard and Boris was trying to stand upright. Boris came after Mishka and swung his arm. Mishka moved and the swing missed. Mishka swung and hit Boris right on the chin. His head rolled back, but he did not fall. He came in towards Mishka with his head down, like a ram in a fight. His head hit Mishka in the stomach and Mishka fell. Lanya had to watch. *What can I do? Can I hit Boris?* Boris looked around for a weapon and did not see Mishka get up and grab a wooden chair. The chair hit Boris hard and he stumbled. He fell and Mishka got closer and hit a few punches. Boris had blood coming from his nose. Mishka was getting ready to swing again but Boris moved away, heading for the door. Mishka followed and swung as he got close. Boris ducked but opened the door and hurried out. Mishka followed him. Lanya followed too. What would happen? Boris was running for the stairs down the hall. Mishka was fast, and as Boris got to the tops of the stairs Mishka hit him with another punch. Boris let out a loud groan and stumbled down the steps. They launched down the stairs and into the street; Mishka was close as Boris got out and Mishka threw another punch. Boris was trying to run. Lanya watched as they went at it, one would punch and the other would hit back. Boris knocked Mishka down and Lanya could see the Mishka's nose was smashed and bleeding. She shrieked, hoping that Boris would run away. She was not big enough to pull them apart. Other people on the street came close to watch. Punches and kicks went on and on, but it probably was not as long as it felt. Boris was cursing, but Mishka only grunted. After what seemed like forever, two older men came up and pulled them apart. City police, it looked like. Lanya was relieved that it was over. The men were separated and led away. Lanya had to go with them. Who would explain for Mikhail? She followed the group down the road, trying to speak with the man who was holding her brother.

"This is my brother. Boris was attacking me. My brother tried to protect me." The man kept walking quickly, and Lanya knew they were headed a few blocks over, to the police station. She gave up on trying to talk to him and worked on just staying close. What would happen? Would Mishka be put in jail? How could he defend himself if he could not speak? The police station ahead was foreboding, even in full evening sun. They did not go to the front door but went off into an alley on the side. A smaller door was opened and both men were herded in. Boris went one way, and Mishka was pushed another.

"You have to stay out. You can wait up front. Go now." One of the officers faced Lanya as soon as Mikhail was seated in a small room. He put his hands out to shoo her away.

"You do not understand. That is my brother. He was protecting me. He does not talk. He was hurt in the war." The man lowered his arms and gave Lanya a firm look.

"Explain yourself. Who are you?"

"Svetlana Zhudanov, I work at the boot factory. This is my older brother Mikhail. I am glad you came along when you did. Boris, the other man, came to our apartment and was grabbing me and kissing me and," Lanya paused with sickness remembering Boris' hands on her. "My brother heard me trying to get away from him and came out, they started fighting. It spilled into the street." The officer looked away from Lanya to Mishka, who was sitting there looking at his hands that had blood on them. When he looked back at Lanya, she continued. "He went off to the war, but in September, they brought him back home. An explosion went off near him and he is like an idiot. Like a small child. He does not talk." The officer looked back at Mishka and turned.

"I need the captain. Do not move." He left the room and the door closing sounded like a slam. Lanya went to Mishka and covered his hands with hers. He did not look at her, so she took his jaw and turned his head.

"Brother, I am going to do everything I can. I do not know what they will do but I will explain everything. You can count on me." He gave no acknowledgment that he heard her, and Lanya was disappointed.

The officer came back and was followed by a squat man with a wide moustache. This man looked like he had never once smiled. He sat down at the table across from Mikhail while the other man stood near the door.

"Tell me your name and why you are here." His voice was not deep, but you could not hide from it. Mikhail said nothing and was looking at his hands again.

"He is" Lanya tried to explain, but the officer at the door stepped in front of her with his hand up to stop her. She froze.

"Tell me your name." The other man repeated a bit slower. Again, Mishka acted as if he was not even there. "Your name!" With this he pounded his hand on the table, which startled Mishka. He looked up. The captain was standing and put his face close to Mishka. "Your name!" Mishka did not say anything and Lanya could see the captain becoming irritated. The captain looked at Lanya and said "Why are you here?" Lanya paused and looked at the man by the door who gave a slight nod.

"He is my brother. He cannot talk. He is like a young child. A bomb went off near him in the war and it made him like this. He has not spoken since September." The captain sat back down and Lanya could see he was thinking.

"He does not talk? Does he understand?"

"Not much. Some simple things." The captain fiddled his pencil as he thought what he should do. This was new for him.

"Let me see". The captain got up and circled the room. He opened his mouth and paused again. "I hear the Germans are going to break through. Come right into the city and kill us all." Lanya gasped thinking about Germans in Leningrad. Was this true? The captain eyed Mishka. Mishka did nothing. Lanya looked again at the captain and realized he was trying to bait Mishka, like the man at the Party office did. Mishka did not say anything or look around. The captain circled again. "Well then, you will have to talk for him. What happened?" Lanya relaxed. If she could explain what Boris did, this would all be over soon. She slumped into the other chair and hoped it would work.

"We were at home and Boris came by. He knew Mikhail at the front, so I let him in. Mishka was in his bedroom. Boris acted all nice. But then he started grabbing me and kissing me and he ripped my clothes." Lanya pointed to the blouse that was still open and showing skin. "He put his hands everywhere." Lanya wondered if she should point, but she just fingered her torn skirt so he would look at it.

"And?" The captain was not patient.

"I tried to get away but he grabbed me. I screamed, and that is when my brother came out. I did not talk to him, but he came out and must have hit Boris in the face." Lanya paused, trying to make sure she was telling what happened accurately. She looked at the captain but his face was passive, listening. "They punched each other and Boris got out of the apartment and Mishka followed, down into the street. I went after them. In the street they hit each other again. People came out. Then you police came and separated them." Lanya stopped, hoping that was enough.

"Alright. Let me check the other man's story." He and the other policeman went out, and Lanya laid a hand on her brother's arm and he looked at her with a small smile. He had no idea what was going on. She could see a smear of blood on his face and a kink in his nose, and could see that bruises along his cheek and jaw would come soon. Not too bad. What if Mishka had not come out? Would Boris have raped her? He was drunk and strong. Lanya shuddered to think about what could have happened.

After a few minutes that seemed like hours, the two men came back in. Lanya was worried because there was no smile. "The other man says it was different. He says you had a date and you called your brother to come out and he" pointing at Mishka, "started the fight." Lanya looked at him and her jaw dropped. Boris said Mishka started it? How could he say that? The captain went on "But I am not sure he is telling the whole truth. He has been drinking, that is obvious. What soldier has a date in the middle of a war? I see your blouse is ripped and missing buttons. You would not do that. And I am not sure that your brother knows enough to start a fight." The captain fidgeted with his pencil as he talked. "So this is what will happen now. You two go home. If we have any questions we will come see you at home. We are going to watch Boris and see if his story changes. I do not want to see either of you again!" The captain opened the door. Lanya got up and lifted Mishka's arm, so he got up, too.

"I hope Boris pays for what he tried to do. If my brother had not come out..." Lanya did not finish, knowing that police knew what she meant. She held Mishka's hand as they left the small office and went out the main door.

Outside, she breathed easier. She kept hold of Mishka's hand. *What is wrong with Boris! And what did he say about Aleksander? He was dead? He got blown up?* Lanya tightened hold of Mishka as the tears started. She was not in love with Aleksander, but she had hoped they could meet each other and see what developed. She remembered his smile and his gentle way. The Germans killed another good Russian. *Damn Germans.* Vodka would be the dessert again for tonight.

Chapter Thirty-Three

The night passed slowly and Lanya almost wished for an air raid. That would take her mind off this awful day. Boris grabbing and ripping her clothes, Mikhail being hauled to the police station, having to explain while she was in knots hoping the police understood that Mishka was not at fault that he was just trying to protect his sister. Boris was drunk, that was for sure. She was pretty drunk now, too. And Aleksander? Did he really get killed? The tears had been on and off and now were on again. She remembered his sweet smile and how he wanted to take care of her. Her brain went to Ivan and what that had been. That started off exciting but quickly dimmed. Sometimes she wished she had a crystal ball. Oh, well. Another sip.

It had been a year since beautiful Valentina was killed. Lanya remembered the fight at the train station, then hearing the Germans were coming right through that area. They had worked through that. Then Valentina went to spend the night with her friend and Lanya brought her home after the bombing, and she thought of how Valentina had slipped away, right here on the couch. Lanya felt the tears but was not ashamed of them. Her little sister was killed by evil Germans. Then she and Babu prepared Valentina with sentimental choices for clothing and jewelry, then the burial. And the emptiness of the house then. The house still was so very empty. There were days when she wished she was in the army to kill a few Germans herself.

Lanya thought about Mikhail. He came to save her from Boris, but did he understand what was happening? Somehow he knew she was in trouble and came out to fix it. But he had not improved. Though he could gather wood and catch fish. How could she find out more? She wondered if the library would have a book about injuries like his. Was the city library even open? Maybe she should go ask a doctor at the hospital. They were so busy with all the soldiers that she hated to interfere, but just a moment for a question wouldn't hurt.

After work the next day she decided to go ask. She walked to the hospital where she had gone to see Aleksander. It took a while to get there and as she walked she saw squirrels rushing to hide the acorns they would need in the winter. There were some trees still standing, though many had been bombed. The hospital was busy, as it had been last time. People were coming and going. At the front desk, a tired looking nurse was checking folders. Lanya walked up and began.

"Hello, I have a question for a doctor. Is there one near? I will only take a moment." The nurse looked up and Lanya did not see any warmth in her eyes.

"If you want to see a doctor you need an appointment."

"But I only need one minute. About my brother and a brain injury." The nurse shuffled folders and turned her back. "Please, just one minute." The nurse turned around again and nodded out as a small man came up.

"Here you go, ask him." The nurse walked away without a smile.

"Hello, I have a quick question." The doctor looked at her and Lanya saw a faint smile. "About my brother. Um, he was injured at the front last year. A bomb went off next to him. He is okay but he is an idiot. Like a child. He does not talk. What can be done?" The doctor raised his eyebrows as Lanya talked and gave a slight nod.

"He does not talk? Does he understand things?"

Lanya got all excited and stumbled on her words as she replied. "Some things. He will come if I gesture but not if I just say it." The doctor's face got grim.

"This is very serious and it is a miracle that he was not killed. This kind of thing cannot be cured. Medicine can do nothing. Time is the only thing. Though I did hear once that a man recovered after being kicked in the head by a mule. Another injury cured him. How is that?" The doctor grabbed a folder and moved to leave.

"Thank you so much. Sorry to take your time."

He paused. "Always happy to talk to a pretty girl." Lanya almost kissed him! She walked out of the hospital feeling much lighter than she went in. It wasn't the diagnosis but the kind words. Lanya realized that few people during this war had been kind. Herself included. She would work on that.

Medicine could not help. Time was the only thing. Lanya was pretty sure that he could not learn how to read since he had such trouble understanding. But could he learn how to cook? Or knit? What could he learn?

September came in with rain. A gentle rain, but the skies were gray. That wasn't so bad because Lanya knew there were fewer air raids on cloudy days. If the pilots could not see, they would not drop bombs. So rain brought some peace. Peace. During wartime. Lanya had not been alive during the Great War before the Revolution, but she was sure it was not like this. She never heard Babu talk about that war. She remembered that the Soviet military had few planes and nothing like the bombs they had now. Just men on the ground.

Rain would be good for her garden, and Lanya reminded herself to go check after work. She had harvested a few things but she knew more would be ready. After work, she walked over to her plot, remembering her first visit here. Then, it had been just patches of brown all turned up. No green. Now, it was lush with green every-where. Every plot had things ready to harvest. In her small segment, she had a few potatoes that were leafy. When was the right time to harvest? She could not see the buried potatoes. Would they be good? Her onions were looking good; she could take one and leave a few for later. Her cabbages, what she was most proud of, were nothing special. They were small, not much bigger than her hand. How did they get those big ones that would cover a plate? *They are professionals with tractors and fertilizers. Just be glad I got these.* Lanya cut one to take home. These would last or she would find a way to preserve them. She would be glad for these in January.

Next week would be a year since Mikhail came home. Lanya was glad to have her brother safe, or at least as safe as anyone in town. But she missed the man who had gone off to war, with the big smile and the hearty laugh. The man who would tweak her nose as he left the apartment. She missed that man. The man she had here now was so different. She never had a little brother, but she did now. The doctor said time was all she could hope for. She had plenty of time.

The first frost came the middle of October. Lanya was glad of it. She knew what was coming and she wanted to be ready. She cleared out the garden of all she grew and stored things in a dark cupboard. She made rusks till her arms were tired and put those away too. She racked her brain trying to think of ways to make it through this winter. She and Mishka would go and gather wood from bombed out buildings. She wanted a good pile in the bedroom to keep them warm. She had enough blankets and coats. A wave of being alone swept over her. She always had Babu to think about these things before, but now it was all on her.

Chapter Thirty-Four

October was not unpleasant; the days were cool and they had snow now and then. Lanya moved them both to the kitchen to sleep, to keep warm by the oven, like last year. November came in with a fierce storm and Lanya was glad she still had her good coat for the walk to and from the factory. Her job would never go away as long as this war kept on.

No one talked about the front. People were scared to question how the Party was running the show, and no one wanted to appear unsupportive. Any questions could lead to a knock on your door. And jail. Lanya knew that one too well. The women in the Wednesday night sewing group would throw ideas around. Lanya listened but did not say much. She already had problems with the Party and would not make it worse. The women talked about the Battle for Moscow, which had been going on for over a year. The Soviets fought back with everything they had and stopped the Germans. The Germans never conquered Moscow. The Soviet army was beginning to push back. Relief flooded through her. The women asked why they did not fight so well to protect Leningrad and Lanya knew it was because Stalin lived in Moscow. If he lived in Leningrad it would be different. But knowing that the Germans did not get everything they wanted was a relief to Lanya. They could not run the world, as they wanted everyone to believe.

What would happen now that the army was not focused on Moscow? *Will they send the Germans back to Germany? Will the Red Army gain ground?* Lanya wondered what was next. Life in war-torn Leningrad had become somehow livable. Would it ever, in her life, go back to what it was before this war? As these thoughts went through Lanya's head, she could feel her stomach tighten. Life before the war had been good, but without Babu, Valentina and Mikhail, her life would never be good again. *How do people survive?*

At the Wednesday night sewing group, the women were quick to ask questions.

"Will this open up the railroad? So we can get food? From Moscow?"

"And shoes? Mine are like paper!"

"Will the soldiers get a break, maybe come home for a week?" Women were shaking their heads; no one expected a vacation from this war.

"I heard that Stalin was praising the United States!"

"What? That is not likely!"

"I would want to see that myself. What have they ever done for us?"

"Stalin would not say it unless he meant it. What did you hear?" Everyone turned to look at the woman who first spoke about it.

"You know my sister works in the Party office." Lanya remembered that with a dark memory. "She said that Stalin made a toast to the United States! They are shipping us Jeeps and steel and fuel and food. A lot of things that will help our boys. And us, I hope."

"Hold it- they are not in the war but they are sending us things? What do they want?"

"They will send us Jeeps? And food! If they do that, I do not care where it comes from!" A round of tired laughter went through.

"Why don't they just join the war?"

This was all coming so fast that Lanya had trouble keeping it straight. The United States, a country that she had never heard one good thing about, was helping the USSR during wartime? Didn't they hate them? The USSR hated them. But what was going on?

"My sister said that food will be coming. They are flying it in to Moscow and will send some to us soon." Lanya felt a wave of relief, fresh food was always good.

Another battle that the women talked about was Stalingrad. With the Germans unable to conquer Moscow they turned to the next industrial city, Stalingrad. Like Moscow, Stalingrad fought back with everything they had. Details were sketchy but the women knew that certain troops were sent there from Moscow, since Moscow was mostly secure. Every woman in the sewing group was hoping that Stalingrad was another victory, even if it was hard won. They all promised to share if they heard anything new and Lanya wanted to hear it too. Lanya took a moment and was glad her brother was home and safe. Too many men would never come home. *Damned Germans.*

Snow came often in November, as was normal. Lanya welcomed it. She did not know how people could live where it did not snow. Snow was cleansing, at least early in the winter. The fresh snow was so bright, so clean, it was almost like there was no war going on. Fresh snow covered the debris and dust of the bombings. It did not stay long since the ground was not frozen yet, but Lanya knew that would change. But as she walked to work, she was grateful for the bright pale sun and the white snow.

The anniversary of the 1917 Revolution always had a parade with fireworks and parties. Last year, there was a small ceremony at the town hall. This year, they could not do speeches and celebrations without electricity. Red posters with the Soviet flag showing brawny workers were hung at intersections, but there were no bands, no parade and no celebrations. The factory had a few extra flags and a bit of cake. It was not what was normal, especially in the city where the Revolution started. Lanya wondered if the Winter Palace on the Neva would celebrate more, since that is where the workers seized power. Valentina used to like to walk through the historic sites and Lanya felt empty remembering those times.

Work was the same and Maru was chatty at lunchtime. Work never changed. That was comforting to Lanya who felt like her world was always changing. As she worked the old machines with her arms, she knew there was more shape in her arms than there used to be. *How ugly* she thought, *who will want to see a woman have bulging muscles? What will be next, pants on women?* Lanya shuddered, but smiled a bit. Things change, especially fashion. As she sat at her machine, she thought about Josef. He had been so good to her while she was in jail but she had not seen him for months. Did she dare ask for him at the Party office? Maybe he was sent to another city. She hoped he was not dead but with weekly bombings people died all the time.

As Lanya walked to work in the November morning she covered her face with her scarf. The snow was gone now and the air was thick with dust from the bombing last night. It hung in the air and had a nasty smell. This neighborhood, that Lanya walked through every day, had been hit bad. The buildings looked almost like honeycombs, with walls and roofs gone. Lanya wondered how any buildings in town had windows at all. *It is just a matter of time before they were all gone and we are living a life without walls and roofs,* she grumbled. She hoped for rain, or snow, to settle the dust. *When will this war be over?*

In line for groceries, Lanya heard a rumor. She listened carefully.

"Eggs! I hear we get eggs!"

"No way, quit lying!"

"Eggs, but powdered. But still eggs!"

"And lard! We have not had lard for so long!" Lanya heard this with an excited ear! She was salivating! As she got into the shop, she went first to the line for the lard, and there were three boxes left. Her ration ticket would only allow one so she snatched one and hugged it to her chest. *I am being silly* she thought. She moved along and saw bacon. *Real bacon?* She grabbed one of those also. She had never eaten American bacon, but she would now. She found a can of powdered eggs and was happy to have her bag full. Outside, she wrapped both arms around her bag and held her food close to her chest. *If the United States is going to send food, I am going to eat it! Maybe Americans are not as bad as I have been told.*

December came in quietly with a gentle snow but ice everywhere. Normal. Days were dark and Lanya walked to work and home in the dark. Before the war, there were streetlights and house lights but now because of the blackout, these walks were completely dark. Lanya was glad for the sun as it gave pale light in the morning. December used to be her favorite time of year. Cold, but it was all about family and holidays. Not this year. The Road of Life across frozen Lake Ladoga was running again so there were some fresh vegetables coming in and Lanya bought a potato and a cabbage. She had a bit in her cupboard from her garden and plenty of the dreaded rusks. She remembered last December when so many people died. She had not heard of starvation yet this year, so maybe the Party had taken care of that.

Christmas came and went, and the Party gave out a bit more in food rations as a goodwill gesture. Lanya appreciated it and made some simple cookies with the extra. Mishka wolfed them down with a smile. Lanya tried to get her brain ready for 1943. She usually enjoyed the new year with fresh hope. But this past year was a drudge and there was no hope. On the eve of the new year, when there used to be parties, the Germans dropped extra bombs, so everyone in town celebrated the new year in a bomb shelter, huddled for warmth. Yes, there was vodka and some singing. Lanya joined the singing because she loved it and people liked when she sang. She wondered if she would ever be on stage again.

Two weeks later, the "Old New Year" came about and Lanya wondered why this was even a celebration. No one used the old calendar anymore, but she remembered Babu always had something special planned for this day. Lanya felt guilty dismissing it. Every day, she remembered a year without her grandmother, and she felt such emptiness.

Chapter Thirty-Five

Lanya was often grateful for big storms, because they usually kept the Germans out of the air, so the nighttime raids were smaller and sometimes did not happen. But in the middle of January during a huge ice storm, the raid came. People were slow to get to the shelter and Lanya and Mikhail did not even get out of the apartment when it hit. Lanya knew it was her job to protect him but she could not get moving. The bombs hit close so Lanya and Mishka hunkered down in the kitchen, hoping the bombs would miss them. *We might die today*, Lanya thought as she wrapped her hands around her scarf. She wished she was underground in the bunker with the regular crowd. *Isn't that ridiculous*, she thought. *To wish to be in an air raid shelter.* But she would even be singing and drinking along with them. Bombs hit the apartment. Lanya could hear the windows shatter in the bedrooms. Mishka grabbed her hand and gave her a weak smile. He was being so very brave. She was glad of that since she could not explain things. The building shook. She could hear nearby walls crumbling and bricks hitting the ground. This was the closest she had ever been to being hit. The building shook again. Lanya was glad her brother was with her. She hoped they would go together. Maybe tonight.

The windows in the front room exploded and Lanya felt the icy night come into the kitchen. That would be tough to repair. Then a massive hit. Right on top of her. Lanya was thrown across the room. She opened her eyes. She hurt. Another bomb. She looked around. She tried to move her head but it hurt. She brought her hand up to her head to see if there was an injury. She touched her scalp. No blood. It hurt to move so she moved very slowly. She touched her face. No blood. Another bomb. Her hand was covered in dust and chalk from broken mortar, but she could not feel any blood. She rested, unable to know what happened. She moved her legs, rolling them sideways then pulling up her knees. She hurt. She relaxed. She would move later. Mikhail! Where was he? Was he hurt? Lanya knew she needed to check on him. She turned her head, looking around the room. Her head hurt but she needed to find him. She paused and listened carefully. All she could hear were more distant bombs and falling debris.

"Mishka?" She called out, knowing he would not answer. But if he heard her voice it might help. "Mishka?"

She heard a growl from across the room. She pushed her chest off the floor to see where he was. Across the room, half under the broken table, was her brother. Maybe he was still alive. She wanted to use her arms to pull herself to him, but it was impossible. She flopped back down and covered herself against the cold. She could not move. She would wait.

Lanya woke up later, unsure of the time. It was dark still and the kitchen was freezing cold. The window, yes the window was completely gone. The heavy curtains were there but they did little for the cold. They could freeze to death if she did not get them covered. She pushed herself up with her arms. Her arms were tight and she could feel her fingers going numb from cold. She needed to move. The bombing had stopped. It was quiet. Eerily quiet. How many people in the building would not see daylight? The walls and ceiling were still up. Lanya rolled over onto her knees. She would crawl to Mishka. She could hear him breathing. The fire in the stove had a small glow, so she could see outlines. She moved her legs and shuffled on her knees to her brother. She put a hand on his chest. He was breathing. She found his hands. Cold, like hers. She breathed a sigh of relief. She tried to stand. It took two tries and she leaned on the rickety table. Standing she looked around the dark room. She could see shards of glass sticking up where the window had been. The furniture was a shambles, in pieces and thrown about. The walls were standing but the whole place was covered in dust. She stepped towards the wall and put her hand on it. She leaned her weight on it. It stayed. The walls were okay. Good. They would not have to move to another place.

Mishka groaned. Lanya turned to him. Let him sleep. He groaned again.

"Wha...?" he said. Lanya dropped to the floor. Mishka said a word? He had not said a word in over a year!

"Mishka! Mishka!" She shook his arm. He could sleep later. He groaned again.

"Mishka! Wake up! Talk to me!" Lanya was scared, not knowing if he was hurt or exhausted. Mishka rolled over and Lanya saw him open his eyes. She smiled. "There you are. Glad to see you." She waited for his response. He blinked and cleared his throat. Mishka raised his head but quickly laid it back down. He moved his arms and tried to disentangle from the table.

"Mishka!" He shook his head. Lanya put her hands on him, and could feel tears running down her dry, dust covered cheeks. He said a word. What was going on? Was he cured? Would it happen again? What could she do? A rough growl came from his throat. Lanya almost smiled, any noise was better than the last year! "Mishka, are you hurt?" His head rose up and he looked at her. He groaned again. With the cold and the pain, she smiled. Mishka knew what was going on. Lanya stayed next to him on the floor and her heart felt warm like it had not in a very long time. Her brother was Mishka again. Or would be. With that, she covered them as best she could and fell asleep.

When she opened her eyes again she could see the beginning of the day. A gray light was coming in and she tried to sit up. Slowly, her head came up. She had a headache, and she was sure she would have bruises. Good enough. She looked for Mishka. He was right next to her, breathing quietly. Should she wake him? No, let him sleep. She pushed up from the floor to crouch, then slowly drew to standing. Yes, she was sore. Her back, her legs. She tried to step and was happy that her legs moved. Gingerly she moved to the kitchen. The counters were there and the stove was still hot so that was good. She put on the kettle for tea. She looked to the window, and saw what was left of it. Not much. If the heavy curtains had not been there, she was sure they would have been killed by flying glass. The glass was all over. Easy enough to clean. But to cover the window? She knew there were a few more blankets in the bedrooms and could cover.

She heard her brother groan. She limped over to see it he was awake yet. His eyes opened and he turned his head. "Mishka" she said, hoping that he would be clear headed like last night. "Would you like some tea? Almost ready." She slowly moved back to the stove and heard another groan. She saw him sitting up and could feel his discomfort. She prepared the simple tea and brought the cups to the table. Mishka held his head in his hands, and groaned again. "How do you feel?" She knew what she wanted to hear and worked hard not to rush him. She watched his face to see if he understood her.

"Wha..." He did not finish the word but he did not need to. Lanya almost jumped out of her chair.

"Mishka! You talked!" He looked at her while he shook his head. She very carefully crossed to him and touched his head. "You talked. You have not done that in so long." He looked at her like she was crazy.

"What..." He stopped. He looked around the room and his jaw dropped. She followed his gaze.

"We got hit hard last night. We didn't make it to the bomb shelter. I thought we were dead at first." He tried to rise but could not make it.

"I....I.... hurt." Lanya searched his eyes to see if there was clarity. It looked like he understood her. She smiled again. Lanya went to go get some aspirin, walking carefully, avoiding debris all over the floor. She brought the aspirin to Mishka and he looked at her. Lanya jumped at the chance to explain.

"Mishka, I hope you are okay." She paused, waiting to see what he might say. He said nothing so she went on. She wished she knew more about the brain and injuries and thought carefully before she went on. She put his hand on top of hers and he looked at her. "Mishka, if you can understand what I say, squeeze my hand." He looked at her like she had lost her mind. What did that mean? "Please try." She could feel a tiny squeeze. She squeezed back. "Now, I am going to show you fingers, and you show me back." She held up her hand with four fingers up and he looked at her like she was crazy again and held up four fingers. Lanya wanted to dance! His brain was working! She never tested him like before, this but she was sure that if she asked him to do this last week, it would not have worked.

She worked to pull him into the kitchen chair. Sitting in the chair, Mishka tried to stand. Lanya put her hand on his arm, "No need to move yet. We made it through though." He remained sitting. "Let me make something to eat; you are usually hungry early in the morning." He said nothing and Lanya carefully got up and turned to the kitchen.

The sun was beginning to allow some gray to come through the curtains so Lanya could see the kitchen. Mishka had his head in his arms on the table. Let him rest, she thought. He needs it. Her brain was running. He'd squeezed her hand, held up fingers and said a word. What did it all mean? She assembled some breakfast then put it on plates and brought them to the table. "How do you feel?" she asked as she started to eat. She was not sure she would get an answer. He raised his head and saw breakfast and almost smiled. He loved food. He took a few bites and seemed okay. Should she update him on what was going on? Was this the right time for news? Or did he need to come back more? Would he understand her words?

"Lany..." He spoke. She turned and sat down, searching his eyes. "Lanya, what is going on?" His voice was rough but Lanya swore it was the best thing she had ever heard! The words came out broken, but Lanya understood what he meant. He spoke!

"Brother, we are at war. You know that. The damned Germans attacked us. You went to fight. They have surrounded our city but have not sent troops in. Yet." She looked to see if he understood. He was eating, slowly. She could see where bruises were beginning on his head and was sure she looked the same. Should she go on? She waited while she took a bite, wondering if he would ask more questions. He did not. "You were hurt in the first few months. Your sergeant brought you home." He looked at his arms wondering how he was hurt. "It was your head, your brain. It did not work." He looked confused and Lanya was glad to see the comprehension. He was following her words. "The Germans bombers come into town every few days. We got hit hard last night." His eyebrows went up in surprise. He had no memory of what a bombing was like. "Usually we go to the bomb shelter two blocks away but last night we did not make it." She needed a minute so she picked up their empty plates and took them to the sink.

"Lany...", Mishka said and pointed to her chair. He wanted her to sit, so she came back to the chair. He rotated his hands, gesturing that he wanted more information. The words were not coming quickly. But they were starting.

"It is January, 1943." His eyes grew wide. "We have been at war for more than two years. Our army is fighting Germans at the outside of the city near the river." He was listening but not reacting. "The Germans are trying to take over all of Russia, fighting in Moscow, the

Ukraine, Crimea and Stalingrad. We are doing everything we can to stop them." He shivered and she grabbed a blanket from the floor and draped it over his shoulders.

"Bab...?" He was asking where Babu was. Lanya felt her loss like the first time. She grabbed his hands.

"Mishka, our Babu is gone. She died last year. I miss her every day." His eyes had a faraway look and he was remembering her. Lanya was sure he was understanding. "She cared for you as well as she could, here at the apartment." His face softened, probably remembering how their grandmother handled things here. "She got sick and passed in her sleep. Not in a bombing." She looked around the shattered home and was glad that Babu could not see it now. Mishka squeezed her hand.

"Val...?" He wanted to know where Valentina was. What could she say? Could she tell him? She looked around the room and saw the couch that she died on, shredded into small pieces. She hated that couch and had not sat on it since the day Valentina died.

"Our sister is gone, too. She was killed in a bomb blast in August two years ago." She looked at him and he looked like he was shocked. "She went to stay the night with her friend and their house was hit in one of the first bombings. I got her home and she died quickly." Lanya felt her throat close up and tried hard not to cry, though every time she thought of her sister she choked up. "It was very hard."

Lanya felt a breeze come through the broken window. She wanted a break. "Can you help me cover these windows? Or we will freeze to death." She got up and went to get blankets out of a back room, and found nails and a small hammer in a drawer. She helped her brother get up and led him to the window where he held that blanket while she nailed the edges. She put up two blankets at a time, as one would be too thin. As she did she broke off pieces of glass and dropped them to the floor. Mishka helped with that. After a few nails, he grabbed the hammer and she held the blankets. He would be better at nailing. She felt good that her take charge brother was coming back. When the windows were covered, he went back to the table and Lanya went to make more tea.

"It is just us now?" Mishka asked slowly, faltering with each word. She looked at him with great sadness.

"Yes, just us."

Chapter Thirty-Six

Lanya and Mishka got into a new routine. Having her brother back was such a blessing. She hoped it was permanent. His words came more freely but she could see there was a struggle now and then. After a few days, Lanya said to him, "We cannot let the world know you are back. They will send you to the front lines again." Mishka nodded and was deep in thought.

"Shouldn't I be at the front lines? Like all patriotic Soviets?" He said the words but Lanya was not sure how much he believed them. Those words, which Lanya had dreaded, filled her stomach with knots.

"You can't go. You aren't one hundred percent yet. You aren't ready." Lanya knew that if he left, she would die. "Let's give it some time. But for now, no change. Okay?" Mishka looked at her hard and he could see the strain on her face and understand the loss. He lost his family too. So, for now, no change.

"I am not sure what I can do every day though. I can't go back to work."

"No, you can't go back to work. But, even when you were hurt, you did some ice fishing and collected wood to burn."

"Wood? Where did I get wood?"

"Broken furniture from bombed homes. There is so much of it, and no one wants it. That is how we heated the apartment last winter, by collecting broken wood."

"That seems simple, and even a child could do it. I will get to it. And I caught some fish?"

"You saved us, more than once."

"Well, you saved me for more than a year." She needed to go out in the cold for ration cards today. But this was nothing new. As she put her coat on she saw Mishka getting his fishing gear together. Maybe they would not be so hungry this winter.

At the Party office, the line wound around the outside of the building, as it always did. People stood there, quietly, waiting for their turn to get inside, where they would wait even more until they got their ration cards. Lanya saw some familiar faces, the same people who get their cards every ten days. She knew a name or two, but no one she was close to. When she got into the office, she saw the same faces that had been handing out ration cards for over a year and a half. Machines, almost. Not a smile or a friendly word in the building. She no longer expected that. She looked for Josef, as she did every time. She knew he would smile and be friendly. He was not here. Where did he go? Did he get killed in an air raid, like so many people? Did he get sick and they could not get medicine, like so many people? She knew not to ask but her heart was dampened by the loss of this man who had been good to her.

When she got home from work, she could smell the fish cooking. It was so good to have Mishka back, maybe he could help with food. As they ate dinner, Lanya decided to ask him about his time at the front. "Do you remember Boris and Aleksander from your army group?" His eyes lit up and he had a quick smile.

"Yes, I remember them, Boris always cheated at cards. Why?"

"They came to see you, after your sergeant brought you home. They wanted to see how you were." Mishka nodded and Lanya could see a small smile at the edges of his mouth. "They were concerned, because they were with you when you were hurt."

"What did they say?"

"They said you were out in the trenches doing normal things. Then the bombing started and a big one blew up right in their trench. A few men died, but you were blown a few feet away. You were not hurt physically, but something was not right. You could not talk, but you could walk and see fine. You could not follow orders. After a few days, the sergeant decided that you needed to come home. He brought you and a month later, Boris and Aleksander came by."

"Did I recognize them? This is so bizarre."

Lanya wanted to tread carefully here. She was not sure what was best for him. "You did not recognize them. They were excited to see you as you came in the room and they jumped up and made noise and you swung at them. You were frightened. We got them out and you calmed down." She paused. "You did not know them."

"Oh, I would know them anywhere! Do you know who was killed in the blast?"

"They never gave me names. No, I do not."

"Too bad."

"Aleksander came by again. Just to check on you again. He stayed quiet and watched you from a distance. You saw him but did not recognize him.

"I do not remember."

"Of course you don't. He was later hurt and Boris came by to tell me he was in the hospital. Some shrapnel in his behind. I went to see him."

"That was good. I'll bet he liked that." They both smiled and Lanya had a brief warm feeling.

"He did. I went to see him a few days later and he was already gone."

"Oh."

"Boris came by again." Lanya moved her fish around on her plate. Should she tell him? Her brother had saved her from Boris' attack, so she decided he should know. He looked at her to see what she wasn't saying.

"And?"

"It got ugly. Boris was drunk, and he attacked me. Told me I needed a man like him, not Aleksander." She paused, judging his reaction. His eyes were wide but he was silent. She went on. "He tried to kiss me. He grabbed at me and ripped my shirt. He tried to do more, but you heard me scream, and you came rushing out. I was so glad. You fought him. You punched him and he punched back. You pushed him out the door. He fought with you, but he eventually went out. You followed him down the stairs into the street." She paused again. Mishka waited for the end of the story. "The two of you fought in the street. You did not say anything but he was cursing and swearing at both of us. Neighbors came out and broke it up and the police hauled you both in."

"I got taken to the police?"

"Yes, and I went along. You could not explain." His look softened. "They took you into a room and tried to keep me out. The officer did not believe that you could not communicate. He tested you. I explained what happened and what Boris did and tried to do to me. And how you protected me. They saw my ripped shirt and how upset I was. They questioned Boris, too, in another room." She looked again at him. He had no expression so she finished. "After my explanation and what they asked of Boris, they let us go. I did not see Boris again. He has not been back." She reached and put her hand on him. "You saved me. Boris would have raped me but you saved me. I love you brother."

"You were pretty good to me, too. Keeping me out of trouble."

"I just explained what happened. And they saw my clothes."

"If he ever comes back, I will handle him." Mishka got up and took his plate to the sink.

"If he ever comes back, I never want to see him again."

"You won't."

"Boris told me that Aleksander was killed." Mishka looked down and his face was sad.

"I am sorry about that. I liked him. He was a good guy. And he never cheated."

"That is too bad. He was good."

The conversation was over and Lanya took her plate to the sink too. Memories of that day still brought a touch of fear to her when she remembered Boris, his groping hands and the police station. She pushed those thoughts away as she cleaned up. It was a bit harder to push thoughts of Aleksander out of her head and sadness lingered.

There was another air raid that night. Not as close as the last. Lanya and Mishka scooted down to the shelter. As they walked, Lanya quietly said to him, "We know these people, we have been together in this shelter over a year. They know that you are broken so they will not talk to you, but they may talk to me. Just be quiet and it will soon be over." The bombing lasted an hour and the raid was silenced after two. Mishka was quiet until they got home.

"Is it always like that? That was terror! How do people live through this?" Lanya could see her brother was shaken though to her it was no big deal, now.

"I hate to say it but that was not too bad. We have seen worse. People go down and wrap up in blankets, eat, smoke, and drink. It is not so frightening any more, but the first few times it was. Now it is just part of the day." Lanya was blasé about it because it was almost normal for her. But Mishka had never experienced that like she had.

"How often does this happen?" His eyes were still big.

"About once a week. When it is stormy, less. When the skies are clear, sometimes more."

"And the whole town lives with this?" Lanya nodded, not feeling any need to explain more. *"Damn Germans!"* Mishka left the room.

Chapter Thirty-Seven

Lanya remembered to pick up more vodka when she got groceries. The vodka was for her brother, though she knew she would share it. And the ration allotment was a bit larger than last winter. Probably because so many had died in the last year. She heard that the frozen Road of Life was doing well. The Germans bombed the frozen lake, but it froze over again so quickly that there was not much interruption.

Should Lanya tell Maru that Mishka was back? She went over this in her head many times. She decided not to say anything just yet. Some secrets needed to stay secrets. But Lanya noticed that her walk was a bit peppier and her smile was a bit quicker, knowing that her brother was doing fine. And she liked that the house was not so silent.

Even with Mishka back, Lanya knew her days were still a drudge. Dark long nights and gray stormy days. The walk to the factory three days a week, using the old machines to make bags and boots and whatever the soldiers needed was bleak. She tried not to think about the soldiers as she sewed; it was too much. The lines to get ration cards, standing in the snow. The lines for groceries, standing in the dark. Even without the war, there were lines, but never this long. Lanya tried to think only about the present as she was in line; to think back to better times brought heartache and to think of what might come was impossible.

So, she stood in line and songs would come in her head on good days. She sang in her head like she was on stage again, and she pictured the spotlights and the applause. Sometimes she hummed. When she hummed, people looked around trying to see who was doing it. When she caught their eyes, she did the same, trying not to be discovered. Humming was not as good as singing, but it was better than nothing.

Wednesday night sewing group went on like always. Sometimes a woman was gone, and if she was gone for a few weeks often someone heard what happened. Usually, it was because of a bombing. There was usually news, about the war or the government, too.

"The battle is still going on at Stalingrad. Who knows how many boys have been killed."

"My oldest is gone. I got the notice last week." The woman spoke slowly and her eyes filled with tears. He neighbor reached out and gave her a strong hug. "My youngest, I do not know. Maybe no news is good news?" Every head nodded at that. Things were quiet for a moment.

"My son is here, outside of the city. He came home for a night a few days ago and he told me something funny." Every eye looked up, hoping for a break in the sadness. "They are getting canned meat from the Americans. Kind of like what we have seen at the grocery store. This one with pork packed in lard is called tushonka, and they eat it cold!" They all smiled. Every one of them knew they would eat it cold if that was all they had. "But they have a nickname for this meat, they call it "second front." She paused and looked to see who understood. No one nodded, they were all trying to understand what "second front" meant. "I had to have him explain, like you. A second front in war is when the attackers hit in another spot, so it is good for you." A few heads nodded. "America is not sending soldiers, but the canned meat is almost as good as having more soldiers!" She smiled to see who understood the name. Most women were smiling a little. Lanya was trying to figure it all out. But she was glad the Americans were helping in some way.

On her next trip to get groceries, Lanya was thrilled to see flour. Plain old wheat flour. Did this come from the Americans too? Or did this come from Soviet farms, brought in since Moscow was safe? She did not ask but picked some up. Maybe she could make bread? Wouldn't a hot loaf of bread be nice? It would take all her flour, but it would be worth it. And it would be so much better than what they had been using. She remembered the small tin of yeast that was unused in the last 18 months. Did she have Babu's old recipe? She had seen her make it so many times she was confident she could make it from memory.

February dragged on. How could the shortest month take so long? It was dark well into the morning this far north, and would be for a while. The cold was not as bad as last year, and that was always welcome.

At the factory there was quite a buzz. Stalingrad? Over? Lanya listened to the questions and answers though many people were spewing information.

"Starving! The Germans were starving!"

"I heard they ate their horses!"

"And they can't handle our winter! General Winter always wins here!"

"Hope they like to starve! They forced us to starve!"

"They lost so many men! Sounds right to me!"

"We lost so many too- my own son!"

"Of course we had to win Stalingrad! The Germans would never surrender a city named after Hitler!"

"They should have given us here that kind of support!"

"We did not get hit like they did- I hear not many buildings are still up. We still have buildings." This went on and on. Lanya listened and went to her machine. She wanted to think this through. The Red Army had beat the Germans again. Two major cities, Moscow and Stalingrad. *Does this mean the Soviets are winning? What does winning feel like? Will the grain from Kiev be coming back? Will they push the Germans back to Germany? Or will the Germans come back to Leningrad for another push?* Lanya did not understand war or the thinking that went into it. And why countries had to push and take. She sensed a headache coming on and wished she had some coffee.

Winter dragged on. The ice was thick and the Neva was completely frozen. Lanya looked at it longingly. She used to love to go ice skating across the river. Last year, no one did because there was no food and everyone was too hungry. This year, maybe she would have the energy to go. Mishka would like it too. He was living mostly in the apartment, only leaving to gather firewood or fish. He had no friends around, since they were all fighting. Lanya smiled and thought that they were both living like they were seventy already.

After dinner one night, Mishka put his fork down and turned to Lanya.

"Tell me more about Babu dying. I miss her every day, and I am sure you do, too." Lanya paused. There was no mystery here so she gave him a complete answer.

"I do not know how old she was. She stopped going out for groceries not long after the war started. Going up and down the steps was too much for her. She stayed here in the apartment. She slowed down quite a bit, spent lots of time in her chair over there." Lanya nodded to the armchair in the corner with a blanket on it. "One morning last February, she did not get up to make breakfast, which was not like her. So I checked and she had a fever. I stayed home with her and she just faded. She was not in any pain that I could see, and her fever did not get too high. She just did not move for the rest of the day and the next day she was gone." Lanya looked at him. "Nothing to do with Germans."

Mishka nodded and said "She did not go to the doctor?"

"I asked and she said she could not get out and across town. The trams were all turned off and she could not walk across town to the hospital."

"Is she buried at the cemetery?"

"Yes, just like Valentina. But I do not know where Babu is buried. The ground was frozen, of course so we did like everybody did. You helped me, we put her on a sled and took her to the cemetery where there were stacks of bodies" Lanya paused again and choked on tears. It sounded horrible, to just dump her grandmother off in a stack of bodies. But there was nothing else to do.

"You had to leave her there in a stack?" Mishka sounded angry with that. But he traced the edge of his plate with his finger and looked at Lanya. "I guess there was nothing else you could do in February. No way to bury anyone."

"And there were so many people dying every day. Even in summer they could not keep up with that. The stacks were all over." After a few moments she went on, "I have not been back. It is too much." Mishka put his hand over hers to comfort her. He could see her eyes glistening. Lanya knew it was silly, an overreaction, and that it had been more than a year ago, but she still cried over Valentina. At least she knew where Valentina was buried.

"Maybe when things warm up we will go over. Just to see. Take some flowers if we can." Lanya nodded, not sure she wanted to even go close.

"Mishka, there is something else." He looked up with wonder on his face.

"What?"

"I was looking in Babu's stuff and found an old journal." She thought quickly about how to share this. The journals had shocking information. "She kept notes about our family and about our parents." With that, he looked up and his eyebrows went up. "Let me go get them." Lanya got up from the table and went down the hall into Babu's room. It was almost untouched. She went into the closet and got out the box that had the journals and brought it back to the kitchen. "Do you want to read them?"

"Not right now. What do they say? About our dad? And mom?"

Lanya thumbed the journals and gently put them on the table. "She talked about what they liked and who they were. And why they were taken." Mishka said nothing, wanting Lanya to go on. She swallowed and started again. "Our dad did something stupid and was caught. Do you remember when we were children going to the farm in the Ukraine to see our grandparents? Our dad's folks?" He nodded. "Well, the Party killed them, our dad thought. When the collectivization was done with the farms, many farmers were unable to feed their families. Some starved. Our grandparents starved that first year. It took a while for dad to find out the truth. When he did, he got very angry with the Party. He went down to the Party office and yelled and screamed and threw a Molotov cocktail through the window and the office burned. Almost to the ground." She swallowed again, her mouth as dry as dust. "They came to get him. Do you remember that morning? I do. He did not even say good bye. Just looked at us and left." She had fresh tears, but these had some anger in them. She was angry that he would let his own feelings take over and remove him from his family. What kind of a dad would do that?

"I remember that day. I was not sure what was going on. But he gave us the look so we could not say anything. I remember mom being a mess for weeks."

"So he was taken and charged with 'Anti-Soviet activities', whatever that means, and we never saw him again. We do not know what happened to him." She wiped her eyes.

"Well, that is a lot to handle. Our grandparents were killed by the Party plan to take over the farms. People who had their hands in the dirt every day starved. That is plenty to be angry about."

"But couldn't he have handled it differently?" Her voice rose as she asked the question that bothered her the most. "Shouldn't he have thought of us? All he thought about was himself and how angry he was. What a mess."

"How could they? Why didn't they think about us?" Mishka seemed angry, like Lanya. She shook her head with angry vigor.

"I don't know. Seems like they should have. I have always thought they were good parents, but now, I am not sure." He picked up the journals and walked out of the kitchen. Lanya stayed, with her head in her hands. Not good parents for sure. Selfish. Short sighted. No role model here.

Mishka stopped as he left the kitchen. "I will read these later. Was he drunk when he did it? I'll bet he was. He drank so much, I remember that." He looked up and asked Lanya "What about Mom? Does Babu say anything about her?"

She nodded. "Babu explains that one, too. She says our mom was in such despair after Dad leaving, she hardly got out of bed and drank all day. So after a year or so, she went out, again not saying goodbye, went to the same Party office he burned down, and was screaming and ranting, as drunk as ever, for hours. Not sure what she said but it must have been bad. They tried to stop her but she went on and on. So she was arrested too. Same charge, same result." Lanya took a deep breath. "Babu had one thing in there that I think about now and then. I am not sure it makes sense." He raised his eyebrows waiting. "She wrote "There is no misfortune without a blessing in it. Can you believe that? I do not see any blessings!" Mishka did not say anything, he could not see any blessings either.

Lanya told the story and the hurt was there. But she was getting used to it.

Chapter Thirty-Eight

The talk about Stalingrad lasted for weeks. Everyone heard something, but no one knew anything. It was all rumor, and no one who was there had come to Leningrad. No one knew how many Russians died or how many Germans. No one knew what was next. But everyone wanted to share what they heard. So Lanya listened, hoping for something real. The Party had put some posters up on lampposts, about how strong the Red Army was, about how Soviets never surrender. Everyone saw them but no one believed them. No one knew if the Soviets were going to win this war or not. It was too soon to tell.

The sewing group was the same. Everyone had something to contribute but no one knew enough. This week though, there were some cookies made. Flour was available in the grocery store, real flour, not cut with sawdust or millet. Real, genuine flour from wheat. Might be from the Americans, might be with opening train lines from the Ukraine, but the cookies were light and crisp and heavenly. Lanya ate two and wanted to take some to her brother but decided she could make some if she could get more flour soon.

At the factory, new leather came in, much more supple than what they had been using. Lanya was glad to have it in her hands; this would make nice boots. For a moment she hoped to have new boots herself since hers were worn and thin. Fresh boots in winter were a joy.

Lanya could feel the tension in the city. Faces were not relaxed and bodies were stiff. Even as a bit more food and supplies came in, it seemed that everyone expected the Germans to take their losses out on Leningrad. The birthplace of the Soviet world was just sitting here, like a ripe plum to be pillaged. Maybe not a ripe plum, since war had ravaged the city, but it would strike a blow to Stalin to deface where Lenin lived and Marxism thrived. And everyone was sure that Hitler wanted to disgrace Stalin, especially after losing Moscow and the difficulties in Stalingrad. When would it happen? Lanya knew it in herself too. With each air raid, she wondered if this was the one. There was nothing she could do to protect herself. Nothing she could do to protect her brother. None of them could get protection. They were all sitting there, waiting for the Germans to wreak havoc. It was just a matter of time. This was how the whole city felt. A resignation to an doomed fate.

Lanya could see this in faces. No one looked you in the eye, no one smiled. Just a quiet trudging along, waiting for the inevitable. Again, *Lanya wondered what it could be like if the Germans take over the city. Are the Germans strong enough now, after Moscow? Or will they just unload all the planes and destroy the city from the air? Is the Red Army chasing them from Russia? Or are they fighting back?* Lanya felt this in her stomach every day. When she ate her stomach was often twisted and she had trouble keeping food down. She was drinking vodka every day to help her sleep. The air raids, which she had become used to, were still the worst. They seemed to last forever, though usually they were only a few hours long.

The second anniversary of the start of the war was dismal. The mayor had a ceremony that few attended. Lanya walked by it but did not stop. The city hall had been hit more than once and there was no grandeur left. The day was warm and the nights were short, but Lanya knew the sunshine was false. There was no recovery in the air.

The electricity came back in October. The lights in the house were bright! The street lights were bright, though they were kept off because of the air raids. The trams were working, during daylight. They could not work at night because of the nighttime blackout. If there was no rationing and no air raids, things might return to "normal".

The air raids slowed down. They were every two weeks, then every three. Were the Germans giving up? Lanya noticed the change, the tension that had been overriding the city lessened a bit. People were not as worried about the Germans coming into Leningrad as they had been.

"They are losing. They know it." Lidia at the sewing group was sure of it.

"You don't think they are trying to give us a false sense of security? That is what I worry about."

"It sure is nice to sleep through the night!"

"And I haven't had to buy lamp oil in a week!"

"When will this hell be over?" This woman had tears in her eyes and wrinkles that were not there two years ago. Lanya knew she had lost her son and her husband. Her grief was all over her. The talk went on, and Lanya wondered if the Germans were losing, and if the Soviets were winning. *How can the almighty German army, that has made their life hell for over two years, be weakened? What will victory feel like?* Or, as the one woman said, what if they were just giving a false sense of security and would be bombing more any time? Lanya had another headache, almost every day now. All these questions made her head swim.

At the factory, Maru was chatty, as usual. Lanya wondered again if she should tell her about Mishka, but decided to wait. Unless Mishka said go ahead, she would wait. At lunch, Maru grabbed her arm and guided her to a table away from the crowd.

"Lanya, have you heard? The Mariinsky theater, where we went and met the men, is opening! They have a show coming! Now that we have some food, we can go see a show!" Lanya opened her eyes wide. A show! She had butterflies in her stomach! They had not been to a show in a long time and that was one of Lanya's favorite things to do!

"What show? We have to go!"

"I don't know what show. I will go by today and take a look."

"Yes, that will be good." Lanya wondered if there would be any musical shows coming, that she could be in. The butterflies in her stomach were buzzing now. She wanted to be singing and on stage again.

Lanya did not wait for Maru to go by the theater; she went herself. She saw the poster out front with the name of the show. Not a musical. She recognized only two of the actor names, and was sure that some might not have made it. The play was a typical Party show about hard work and loyalty, but still, it was a show. She saw the director's name and knew him, it was Andre, who had directed her in the show Ivan produced two years ago.

The next time she went to the Party office for ration cards, she looked around, hoping to see Josef's face. When she got to the front of the line, instead of just grabbing her cards, she paused and waited for the clerk.

"I am looking for Josef who used to work here." She paused, wondering if this was going to cause trouble, either for her or him. The clerk looked at her for the first time.

"Josef?" She looked around the small office. "He is not here."

I can see that, Lanya thought. "Do you know where he is?"

The clerk looked around again, then looked over Lanya's shoulder to the people behind, indicating that she was tired of this and that Lanya was taking too long. "I don't know. Go ask Pieter." She nodded to a man in the corner. Lanya picked up her ration cards and turned to go see Pieter. He was sitting in a corner at a desk and Lanya made sure she did not bump his cane that was leaning nearby. He looked up and Lanya saw his eyes were bloodshot and weepy. Lanya sensed it was from too much vodka. His red nose confirmed it. He looked up at her.

"What do you need?" He did not smile.

"Um, I was asking where Josef is. He was very kind to me." Lanya did not want to explain.

"He is not here."

I can see that, Lanya thought again. "Can you tell me if he will be back? I would like to thank him."

"He went to see his family near Moscow. He should be back soon, now that the battle is over, there." The man went back to the papers on his desk, telling Lanya that the conversation was over. She meekly walked out the door of the office. Outside the office, she breathed more deeply. She always felt like there was something tied around her neck in that office. Relieved to hear that Josef was not dead like so many, she had a lighter heart leaving than when she went in. She hoped her inquiry would not cause any problems when he came back.

So, Josef would be back. The electricity was on, there was food available, still rationed but no one was starving this year. Her brother was almost back to normal and as bored as he could be. And the local theater was up and running! If it wasn't for the damn Germans this would not be too bad.

The first snow came the second day of November. Lanya always loved the first snow. And this year, even more so, because it again covered up remains of war. the debris and dust. Walking in the streets was an exercise in object avoidance. More than once she had tripped on something or landed on something. And the dust after every raid was enough to choke you. But with snow, it was all clean. And the white blanket meant you could not see the war every time you walked out. So Lanya enjoyed this day.

The show at the Mariinsky was good. Not superb, but good. Lanya loved the theater, whether she was on the stage or in the audience. The smell of it, the feel of it. She knew that this was where she wanted to be. She wanted to bring her brother, but knew that if she did, people would question his disability, so he had to stay home. Maru had not seen him since his recovery and Lanya was being very careful. The actors did not seem relaxed on stage. Maybe they are rusty from not performing in two years, Lanya hypothesized. She wanted to stay after and see if she could catch Andre the director. She asked Maru to wait in the lobby and snuck behind after the show. She looked around and did not see him. She touched an actor on his arm as he hurried by where Andre might be.

"He is in the office, I just saw him." Lanya thanked him and hurried to the office, a place she had been many times.

As she walked, her memories of being here with Ivan came back. She noticed the tension and stuffed it down. That was all over a long time ago and she did not need that now. Andre was sitting at his desk, looking frazzled.

"Andre, how are you? Good to see you." He looked up and a huge grin came to his face. He rushed over and enveloped Lanya in a hug.

"Lanya! My sweet. How are you?"

"Andre, I am good. I saw your name on the poster and knew I had to see you. You look good." He didn't but he was not as skinny as he had been that first winter two years ago when there was no food. He just looked tired.

"I am glad you came by. You saw the show?" She nodded but he kept going. "Not a bad show, and it is good to give people a break. This damn war. I am so ready for it to be over." He looked her up and down and his eyes showed he like what he saw. "I am glad you are here.

I heard there was some trouble, after Ivan." She nodded, not wanting to say much.

"That is all over. Things are quiet now. Andre," she paused, wanting to word this carefully, "do you have any musicals coming up? I want to be back on stage so bad!" Her eyes sparked as she said it and he could see her anticipation.

"We have two more weeks of this show. Then the holidays are coming. I may have something after the New Year. Should I let you know?" Lanya nodded again, eager to be on the boards.

"Let me give you my address so you can send me a note. We do not have a telephone."

"That is great. The telephones in town have not worked for years, anyway." She wrote her address on a slip of paper and handed it to him. He put it in the top drawer and gave her a light hug. "I need to get going. It really is good to see you. I would like to work with you again."

"Me, too Andre. Please let me know. Thanks so much." She hugged him back and then left the office. Her heart was singing. He would tell her when the new show came; he had always been good to her. She was smiling as she came back to Maru.

"I found him. He will mail me in January if he has another show coming up. I sure hope so!"

"That would be so good, you are such a star when you sing!" As they walked back out and headed for the tram, Lanya sang some of the songs from the first show and Maru sang along.

Chapter Thirty-Nine

December came in with an icy blast. Lanya wrapped her scarf around her neck and face as she waited for the tram to get to work. She was glad the trams were running, or she would have walked for thirty five minutes to get to the factory. They had power again so the electric machines were back which made sewing much easier. And they could all get more done. Her arms would lose that muscled look they had and she would be glad when they looked like they used to.

There had not been an air raid for three weeks and life seemed almost normal. Soldiers were coming into town now and then from the front outside the city so they must not be on high alert. Lanya watched carefully to see if Boris would come back. If the men were in groups she did not notice but if she saw a soldier alone she was on alert. Boris was the last person she wanted to see after what he had done to her.

As she prepared for bed, Lanya heard the storm thrashing outside the window. She knew that if the clouds left, tomorrow would be frozen and icy. But, this was normal. She lay in the kitchen next to the stove and was glad that Mishka had brought in plenty of firewood for them. A stormy night meant an air raid was not likely. Sleep came quickly.

Lanya was woken up by a huge blast! She opened her eyes and the kitchen was wide open to the outside. The noise was a loud as anything she had ever heard and her ears were ringing. What happened? Snow was coming in! She looked for Mishka and he was nearby, starting to get up. Lanya moved her legs but they did not want to move. The cold was intense but Lanya was more worried about moving. Was there an air raid? She did not hear the alarm. She rolled over and felt the warm floor underneath her. She pushed with her arms, trying to raise herself.

"Mishka? Mishka?" Her voice was weak, and she was not sure she could be louder. Her throat was tight. What happened? She pushed herself to sit and saw her brother was doing the same. He turned his head but fell back. Oh no he was hurt. She was hurt, too. Her back was in pain as she sat there on the kitchen floor. She rolled her legs, hoping they would work. Her neck was giving her jolt of pain so she did not move. she knew she could not stay there with snow coming in on her. She needed to get out of the kitchen. She pushed herself back up, breathing carefully through the pain. Could she stand? She grabbed an open drawer in front of her and took a few minutes to move her legs and rise to standing. Her legs were shaking. She looked around the apartment. The kitchen was completely blown away, the roof and the walls were gone. The living room had one wall but the back of the apartment was not too bad.

Mishka was on his knees, shaking his head. "Mishka, Mishka, are you okay?" He turned and looked at her and gave a slight nod. Lanya took a step and almost fell. She held on to the cabinet and waited.

"What happened?" Mishka asked with a gravelly voice.

"I don't... I don't know." Lanya replied. Mishka stood but leaned as he stood.

"It wasn't an air raid, there was no alarm."

"No alarm." He turned and Lanya saw the look on him. *Is this is how he felt when he got hurt at the front and was so badly injured?* She took a step and felt a bit better.

"We have a problem here," he said, looking around. Lanya might have laughed at the snowflakes in his hair but she knew she had some too. "Is the whole building blown up? If we have no roof, the floors above us are gone." He stepped to the side and Lanya saw that he took careful steps. "I wonder if others are hurt or worse. Are you okay?"

Lanya nodded but added "I have some pain in my neck and my back. But nothing is broken." She took a few steps out of the blown apart kitchen and got to Mishka. He wrapped his arms around her and held her for a moment. She was glad for his strength and his warmth.

"I am glad" he said. "We need to see what is going on. Get your coat." *He wants to go outside? In this storm?* Outside was no worse than inside right now, Lanya thought. She moved carefully and went towards where the door used to be and rummaged through debris to find her coat. She pulled his out, too.

"Here you go." She slid her feet into her heavy boots nearby and waited for him to be ready. They moved through the hole that was the front wall and heard voices. The others in the apartment must be going out also. The steps were broken but they could walk down if they held the rail and watched their steps. Outside, there was a small crowd from the building all looking at the shattered shell that was left. As she approached them, she looked at Mishka and bit her lip, to remind him to say nothing. No one knew he was recovered and they could not let that secret out.

"What happened?"

"Wasn't an air raid."

"My apartment is blown apart."

"Where are the Gotskys from the top floor?"

"I see Dmitri and his family, right over there." Lanya looked. Her neighbors were here, mostly. She did not really know them but she recognized their faces.

"Is anyone hurt?" Lanya asked. She was given an assortment of answers but everyone she saw was mobile and had no great damage. No one was lying on the ground or bleeding.

"What was this?" The man who lived right under Lanya was asking the question that everyone wanted answered. The air was cold and Lanya wondered where they would spend the rest of this night. Could they go back into the building? Or would it fall down as the bricks shuddered with the change in weight. The group huddled together. Mishka came up to Lanya and looked at her, turning his eyes to the side. A message. She grabbed his hand and they walked away from the group.

"Let's walk around. Maybe we can figure this out." Lanya heard the rescue team truck coming close. She and Mishka walked to the edge of the apartment. Usually their apartment was connected to the next building but now, there was a gaping hole between the buildings with bricks thrown here and there. Lanya looked up as she walked and even in the dark could see curtains blowing in the icy wind. "Let's go around back."

They carefully walked through ice and snow and debris to the edge of the wall and picked their way through rubble. The back of the apartment was an alleyway used for deliveries and Lanya had been there a few times just never from the front. The back was a jumble of bricks and wood and stones that had been thrown here and there with the blast. Lanya stopped but Mishka kept going. Then they heard a sound. They both stopped. A groan. They looked at each other.

"Someone is back here. Let's help." They walked into the mess and skirted the jumble of building rubble. The groan happened again.

"Over there." Mishka pointed to the other edge of the building where nothing was left standing. They hurried over to the corner and heard another groan. They saw a body and moved closer and could see it was a man.

"He is injured. Can we help him?" Lanya felt bad that he was hurt and out here in the freezing cold. Mishka looked and saw that a beam from the building was lodged on his legs and he tried to move it. The beam did not budge. Mishka was pushing with everything he had. The groaning got louder. Lanya leaned down to speak to him.

"We will try to get you free. Are you hurt?" She was not sure he could answer. She looked and saw a man, with short hair wrapped in a good coat in gloves and boots. She looked closer and recognized him. It was Boris! The man she never wanted to see again! The one who had almost raped her! She stood up and backed off. Mishka saw the fear on her face and came to her.

"What?" he said when he saw the revulsion. She did not speak but pointed to Boris. He looked and crouched down. "Oh! Boris! What is he doing here!" Mishka's voice sounded light, like he was happy to see Boris in the debris unable to move.

"Why ...are you here? Boris said with more groans. "Why are you alive?"

Mishka moved closer. "Why do you care? Why are you here?"

"You ruined my life." Boris's breath was labored.

"I ruined your life?"

"Yes, you did." His voice was a bit stronger. Lanya stood to the side and was sick from being near him. "You got me in trouble and I got sent back to the front. But they put me in a different division. More dangerous. I almost died twice. Then I was sent to learn explosives." His breathing was hard and Lanya hated to hear him speak. She thought maybe he should have been killed.

"But you made it. And you are here."

"I wanted to make you pay for what you did to me."

"What?" Even Lanya said that in her head as Mishka said it aloud.

"I knew you were faking that injury. You understood everything at the police station. Your sister covered for you, but I knew you were faking it. You should both be dead. For what you did to me."

"I don't know what you are talking about with police station. My sister told me what you did. You should be dead for what you almost did to my sister!" Mishka kicked his ribs and he moaned, in great pain.

"You ruined my life." Lanya could not believe this man. He had come to the apartment, almost raped her, and fought with her brother, but they ruined his life? She kicked him too and was glad to hear another moan.

"You are a worthless person!" Lanya did not usually talk, like that but he deserved worse.

"Are you going to get me out of here?" His breathing was heavy and it sounded like he was struggling.

"Why should we get you out of here? You came here to kill us? And you want help?" Mishka was angry now.

"You should help me. We fought together." Mishka looked at him, unable to believe his twisted mind.

"Yes, we fought a common enemy. Now you say I am the enemy?"

"You and your precious sister deserve to die. This bomb was supposed to take care of it. But somehow you are alive."

"I would not save you even if I could. You are worthless." Mishka kicked him again, this time with gusto. He smiled when Boris whimpered, too weak to speak.

Mishka picked up a concrete rock that looked very heavy. He held it against his stomach, and moved closer to where Boris lay pinned down. Lanya moved over to be near.

"The Germans won't get a chance to kill you. And the police won't ever know." He raised the big rock to his shoulders ready to throw it. Lanya saw what he had in mind. She put her hand on his arm and shook her head.

"No, Mishka, let winter do it. He will be gone in a few hours from the cold and we will have nothing to do with it." He dropped his arms and threw the rock on Boris's arm. They heard the bones crunch.

Mishka put his arm around his sister and they turned away. From some dark corner, Lanya remembered her grandmothers words about every misfortune having a blessing. Boris is truly gone.

"Hey, you can't leave me here!" Sobbing and grunts were heard as Lanya and Mishka walked back through the broken wall to the front of the building. The rescue team was here and helping people with first aid. One of the men saw them and came up to them.

"Anything back there?"

Lanya had her hand on Mishka's arm, to make it look like he was feeble. She shook her head. "We were looking to see if anyone was back there but it was too dark. We did not see anything." She tugged his sleeve to lead him away.

One of the rescue team women came to them and gave them an address where they could go for the night. Lanya looked at it, it was a few blocks away. "Thank you" she said as she took the slip of paper. They had coffee Lanya almost cried when she saw it. They tried to get away quietly and walked to the rescue place.

Chapter Forty

Lanya and Mikhail found the small apartment that was the safety center and went in, happy to have a safe place. A few of their neighbors were already there, spread out on the floor. They were offered snacks, aspirin and more coffee, but Lanya was ready to lie down. They went to a corner and laid out the blankets and pillows they were given.

"Goodnight brother" Lanya said quietly. Mishka squeezed her hand and she squeezed back.

When Lanya woke up, she could not move. Her body was stiff and sore. Mishka was next to her, asleep. She nudged him, hoping to wake him gently. His eyes opened. "We made it through the night." A small smile crossed her face. "We are alive." She sat up and hated herself for it. Her head was pounding and she rested her face in her hands. "We should go see the apartment" she said in a whisper. There were people around and most of them were asleep.

They quietly left the safety house but knew they would have to go back. Getting to their own home was tough; the streets were iced over and snow and sleet kept coming. Lanya missed her heavy coat but remembered that she grabbed whatever she could.

"Will we be able to go into the apartment? We need to get our things."

Before he answered, Mishka looked around to make sure that no one they knew would see him talk. His recovery was still a secret. "We will see. If we made it down the stairs we can probably go back up. But let's see what is going on. They might not let us inside."

They approached the building and Lanya stopped dead. The whole front of the building was torn away. She could see right into every home. The side wall was leaning dangerously and Lanya could see the staircase they had come down. It was missing steps. How did they get out of there alive? The rescue crew was finishing and packing their things. Lanya walked up.

"We live here. Do you know what happened?"

The woman who answered her looked tired and frozen. "We have been out here all night. We are not sure. It wasn't the Germans, we know that. Some explosion but we are not sure what caused it."

"Oh. We live here, or we did. Did people get killed?"

"Well, we found two bodies upstairs but they just could not get out in time. And there was a man at the back who was pinned under a beam. Not sure how he got into that. They have all been taken away now." Lanya breathed a sigh of relief. Boris was gone, in every way. Two other people died. Lanya was glad that she and Mikhail had made it out when they were the intended targets. Her warm breath created a cloud around her face.

"We need to get some things. Can we go in?"

"The woman stopped folding towels and looked at her. "You want to go in there? It could go down any minute. If you pushed on that wall, the whole thing might go." She put something in a sack. "I wouldn't go in. You do what you think, but I do not want to come back here and rescue you again." She turned to join her crew and did not look back.

Lanya turned to Mishka. "We need to get our clothes." He nodded. He looked around again.

"You stay here. I will go. It is not safe."

"If you go, I go too."

"You are as stubborn as Valentina!" Lanya did not cry when he said that but remembered her sister with a small smile.

"Maybe I am."

They walked very slowly into the building and were careful not to touch the leaning wall. Lanya put her foot down in Mishka's footsteps so she did not weigh down on anything new. It took quite a while to get to their level and find their apartment. The door had been blown off and the wall was gone. Lanya had never seen so much light in their living room. She sat in the broken chair where she had spent many hours of her life. Tears came quickly and she did not try to stop them. This was where her parents lived, where Valentina had died, where Mikhail had come home so broken. She looked at the chair where Babu breathed her last and the kitchen where so many meals were shared. Letting go of this place would create a hole in her heart. This apartment had been her home since she was six years old. There were so many memories.

"We will find another place. Do not cry. Maybe closer to the factory so you do not have to travel so far every day. Maybe closer to Maru. You would like that, wouldn't you?"

"You would have killed him, last night. I stopped you."

"Yes, I would have. I have killed many men. Most did not deserve it like he did. I wanted him to suffer for what he did to us. And he said we ruined his life? The world is better without him." Lanya nodded. What he said about killing men left her feeling empty and hurt. "Let's get our stuff and get out of here. We need to find another apartment before it gets dark this afternoon. We only have a few hours of daylight."

Lanya got up and wiped her eyes as best she could with the ice on her gloves. She went carefully into the bedroom and got a few bags, filling them with some clothing. She thought she could come back tomorrow if she needed to. In the kitchen she got what food she could and the precious ration cards. She went into Babu's room and gathered her journals and a few mementos. As she was in Babu's room, another deep sense of loss flooded over her. Her grandmother had been such a rock in her life. *What rock do I have now?* A voice in her head came back with "None". She felt so empty. Lanya quickly remembered that her brother was back and living well, and she tried to shut out the feeling of loss. In her parent's room she wondered what was important. She never went into that room, so she just closed the door. If she came back, she would collect sentimental things.

Mishka had three bags and Lanya had two. She wrapped her arm around one and threw the other over her shoulder. "Going down could be tricky. Step very carefully" Mishka said as they went through the doorway. Lanya took one look back into the front room and then focused on her feet and the steps. The bags did make the weight difficult, but they came outdoors in a few minutes and laid the bags down. They looked at the building again and were struck by how they lived through that bomb. They trudged through the snow back to the safety house. People were awake and food was being prepared.

The matron who helped them last night was still there answering questions. After getting food, Lanya asked her where they might find another apartment. Lanya sent Mishka into a corner with their bags so he would not look capable. The matron had a map drawn showing where available homes were. She assured them the Party would help them in their search and approve their new place. Lanya thanked her and went to Mishka.

"She has some apartments open, we should go look. After you eat." Mishka took the food and quickly ate. He always ate more when he was cold. They left the bags in the corner and went out again, remembering where the homes were on the map. They spent most of the day in the snow and found two that looked like they might work. Back at the safety house, Lanya spoke to a new matron and told her what they had seen and she wrote it down, telling Lanya she would take this list to the Party office tomorrow for approval. "The Party will help with your needed supplies, like towels and pans. They have been doing this since the war started." Lanya nodded and went to Mishka and sat down. Her body was so sore after the explosion and being in the snow all day. She flopped back and was asleep immediately.

In the middle of the next day the new matron called their names and Lanya went up.

"You have been approved for the first one you saw. The building supervisor will give you keys when you get there. There are beds and furniture. Take your things and get settled." She smiled and Lanya had the first small glimmer of hope.

Chapter Forty-One

The new apartment was smaller, but there was only two of them. And it had a funny musty smell that made Lanya want to open the windows. No one opened windows in December in Leningrad. The beds and sheets and towels were all right there and Lanya was glad to get set up. She wondered if they would have to sleep near the stove like the old apartment, and decided to try the first night in her bedroom. She put her clothes and the food they had brought away. She made sure the vodka was in the front cupboard.

The next time Lanya went to the Party office, she looked for Josef as soon as she got inside, but he was nowhere to be seen. It had been almost a year since she had seen him. Maybe she should stop looking for him. Maybe he was gone, like so many people she knew. The mouse behind the desk did not look up until Lanya asked for new cards when it was not her normal day. She gave Lanya a look of disbelief when she asked.

"Mine were blown up in my apartment."

"An air raid?"

"No, not an air raid. We do not know what did it." The look of disbelief was stronger than before. Lanya wanted to defend herself from that look. Her stomach was tight. What if they did not give her new cards? Could they know she got a few from the blasted kitchen? Would they make it until next week when she would go in on her normal day? She had grabbed some food at the old apartment but it might not be enough to last the next six days.

"Let me ask." The mouse turned and went to a supervisor in the back, who looked at Lanya and nodded. The mouse came back.

"The director says we can help. He heard about that explosion and says we can give you fresh cards." Lanya released the breath she had been holding.

"Thank you." She grabbed her new cards and escaped as fast as she could from that suffocating room. The air outside was frigid, but fresh. She breathed deeply. She heard steps behind her and turned around. It was Josef!

"Svetlana!" His smile was huge and he was happy to see her.

"Josef, I am so glad to see you. I looked for you but did not see you." She reached out and grabbed his hands, so glad to see him.

"I was in the back for a while."

"I am glad you came back to Leningrad, that you are okay. And Josef, can you call me Lanya? No one calls me Svetlana when they know me."

Josef smiled and his cheeks went a bit pink. But then he remembered what he wanted to say. "Yes, I went to go see family when the battle was over." He looked to the ground, "I lost my cousins in the battle."

"Oh, I am so sorry. So many good people..." Lanya stopped, knowing if she kept going she would lose it over her sister again.

"I am glad you are back. I looked for you and finally someone told me you would be back. I thought maybe you got bombed."

He smiled too but did not let go of her hands. "No bombs for me. But I heard about your building, what happened?" she thought.

"Some explosion- no one knows. A few people died but Mishka and I are fine. We have a new place now."

"I am glad. I have to go back or they will say something. I hope I can see you again in less than ten days."

"I am not sure but that would be nice. Good to see you."

"Good to see you, too." He leaned over as if to kiss her but froze and let go of her fingers. She watched him walk back in and turned to leave. She felt warm inside. He wanted to see her and was safe. The relief she felt was huge.

Christmas was a few days away and Lanya could tell that things were different. The rationing was not so tight as last year, with help from America and some train lines open from Moscow. And the frozen Road of Life across Lake Ladoga was going well due to fewer bombing raids. Wednesday night sewing group had cookies and tea. And opinions, lots of opinions.

"The Germans are running away! They will be gone soon!"

"We will have a new offensive soon."

"I hope the air raids are over, I hate those!.."

"Zhukov will be back. You wait." General Zhukov had been the first to protect Leningrad when the war broke out but was sent to Moscow, then Stalingrad. Quite a hero. If he came back to Leningrad, everyone was sure the Soviets would win.

"My son came in from the trenches the other day and said the Germans are not fighting much. Some of the tanks have even left!

"The trash will take itself out!

As usual, Lanya listened. She was unsure of what to believe. Like most, she believed that General Zhukov was their best hope.

As Lanya walked to her new home in the dark, her heart was lighter. Maybe this would be over soon. As she was halfway home, the air raid siren went off. Lanya was not sure where her new shelter was, but she saw people hurrying into this nearby building so she followed. She hoped her brother was able to find a safe spot. When she got into the underground basement, she looked around. She did not know anyone. Then she heard singing. Like a magnet, she was drawn to the singing. She found the group and saw that most people were clustered together, around a man who was looking the other way. She knew the song so she sang along too. When it was over, the man turned around and Lanya saw her friend Nicholas! She thought she knew that voice! Nicholas was a solid tenor who had been in the show three years ago. He had been lots of fun and kind to her. He saw her as she walked towards him and his face lit up!

"Svetlana! What a wonderful surprise! What are you doing here?"

He gave her a one armed hug and she answered, "I was walking home and the siren went off, so I rushed down. And here you are, singing!"

"That is what we do down here, makes the time go by better. They all like to join in." He stepped back and she wondered why he was here, and not at the front like almost all the men. "Oh, I see, I spent some time in the army," he held up his left arm, which had no hand, "they decided they did not need me anymore! So they sent me home!" Lanya had a weak smile but her stomach was ugly; he had no hand! "So, we sing. You should join us, maybe we could even do our show again!" This was such a warm greeting Lanya was touched. She remembered why she never looked at Nicholas. She had seen him watching Ivan, and the smile on his face. Nicholas was not interested in women. Lanya had seen a few of these men in the theater and it never bothered her. They had always been good to her so she was good to them back.

The release bell went off and Lanya smiled as she always did. Nicholas put his remaining hand on her back and said "If you come back this way again, join us! We would love to hear you again!" He gathered his things and Lanya adjusted her bag, Nicholas walked out to the dark street, and Lanya followed. As she walked home, she felt good.

Christmas at the new apartment felt empty. No memories, no decorations. Lanya bought a few red ornaments to lay on the table. The Christmas dinner she made was better than last year. Not much of a celebration, but better than the last two years.

When Lanya went to get ration cards again, Josef was waiting near the front, knowing she would come. As she left the building, he quickly came out. It was snowing lightly and they stood on the street.

"Lanya!" He smiled as he said that. "Good to see you again. I knew what day you would come, had it marked on my calendar so I would be ready." He held his hand out with a small package. "For you." Lanya took it, with a smile. She was glad she had packed up some of the spice cookies she had made yesterday to share with Josef. She opened the wrapping and saw a small brooch with glass beads. The colors were beautiful in the dreary winter day.

"Josef, how very nice. I did not expect this. You are too kind."

"I saw this the other day and loved the colors. It reminded me of you, since you are such a bright spot for me." She was touched. She took his hand with one of hers and tucked the brooch into her pocket.

"I have something for you." She let go of his hand and opened her market bag and brought out the cookies. "It is not much but it's a favorite of ours." He took the small bag and opened it. He brought it to his nose to take a sniff and a huge smile spread across his face.

"Cookies!" He bit into one. "With spices! Lanya this is heaven! My grandmother used to make these!" He finished the first cookie and started another. Lanya was glad she had brought a few.

"My grandmother did, too. My mother loved these. I have not been able to make them for years because we could not get flour."

"I need to get back." He brushed crumbs off his face. "Can I see you?"

"Yes, would you like to walk me home from work?" Ivan had done that.

"I am not sure my schedule matches yours."

"Can you come to my new place then? For tea?"

"Yes, that would be perfect." Lanya could see his tension growing as he stumbled with his words. She told him her address and set a date for tomorrow after work. He nodded and rushed away. "Thank you Svetlana," he said over his shoulder. Lanya smiled as he left. Talking to him felt good.

The next day, Josef showed up right after work. Lanya opened the door and Mishka got up to leave the room. He could not stay here while Josef visited, though he gave Lanya a funny look as he walked out. Lanya had the tea setup on the table and they sat down. Lanya spoke first, "I am glad you could come. It is hard to say much when you have to rush back to work."

Josef nodded, "Yes, and the supervisors watch us like hawks. They would be gossiping like crazy if they knew I was here. Gossip is like a sport in that office." Lanya understood that from working at the factory. Secrets were not secret for long. The tea was hot and Josef grabbed a spice cookie quickly. "The cookies you gave me did not last long, my mother even complimented you on them." Lanya thanked him. They shared small talk, about the new apartment and about the weather. Nothing about the war or the Party. Once the tea was gone, Josef moved to go, and Lanya was glad of it.

As they moved to the door, Josef asked "Can I see you for New Years's? To walk through town?" This is what Leningraders did on New Year's Eve most years, walk through town sipping vodka and eating snacks like roasted nuts. The last two years there had been none, but this year with the food rations better and the trains running, there might be some life in the city. Lanya was surprised by this. She did not expect timid Josef to ask her out.

"I am not sure. I need to stay with my brother, you know?"

"Could you bring him along?" Lanya did not think that was a good idea. Josef might see too much.

"What if I walk with him and we see you around?" Josef cast his eyes down, his disappointment was clear.

"That will do. Maybe my mother will want to walk." Lanya nodded and Josef stepped out the door.

Lanya questioned herself. *What does Josef want? What do I want? Can I like him?* It seemed like he would be happy to jump into a relationship but she was not sure. *He is a Party man and the Party never set right with me, after what my life had been like. But he is a good man and a gentle man and that warmed Lanya. Too much thinking!* She corrected herself. *Just let it happen!*

New Year's Eve was a clear night without snow. It was as cold as always but the moon was out and the snow sparkled. Mishka was eager to get out of the apartment where he felt cooped up. After dinner they bundled up and headed out. They went towards the center of town where people gathered, and where Lanya had told Josef they would go. Lanya was happy to see a woman selling *sbiten*, the warm honey spice drink that had little alcohol but went down well. With her cup in her hand, she and Mishka walked and talked, nodding at people they recognized. She saw a few of the people from her old apartment and air raid shelter and they smiled and said hello. She looked for Josef as she walked. Mishka saw her looking and knew what she was doing.

"What is going on with that guy, with the thick glasses?" He peered a sideways look at her as if he was her father.

Lanya giggled. "Nothing. He is a man from the Party office that I have spoken to a few times. He helped me when I was in jail. I think he likes me." Lanya smiled and laughed at herself for the giggle. *Am I thirteen still?*

"Well, that is obvious. As long as he is good to you. A Party man?" Lanya had nothing to say. They both knew of the struggle with that. Just as she was trying to find an answer, she saw Josef, across the street, walking with a woman who was probably his mother. He did not see her yet. Lanya grabbed Mishka's hand and pulled him across the frozen street.

"Josef, Josef!" Lanya's voice was muffled through the scarf across her mouth. Josef stopped and smiled. He walked up to her.

"You remember my brother Mikhail. He cannot talk but he sometimes understands me." Josef put his hand out for Mishka to shake. Mishka did shake it and let his hand fall.

"My mother, Marie." Lanya extended her hand and they shook as well.

"This is a nice night. Good to be out." Marie said with a smile. Lanya uncovered her mouth so she could talk freely.

"Yes it is nice, as long as the Germans stay away." Marie nodded and Josef agreed.

"What is in your cup?" Marie asked.

"*Sbitin*, from on the corner over there." Lanya pointed where they had come from.

"Josef, let's go get some. That sounds so good! Warm and tasty!" Marie tugged at Josef's sleeve and pulled at him. Lanya was not sure if Marie really wanted the drink or just to get away from a woman Josef liked. Maybe both.

Lanya and Mikhail walked a bit more, enjoying the freedom to walk and the light feeling of knowing the Germans were on the run. They saw Josef and Marie once more but they were talking with another group and did not stop. She knew she would see him in a few days. When midnight rang, the city speakers played a marching song and one older man had a trumpet out and was blasting songs. Lanya enjoyed the cheer.

New Year's Day was quiet. Lanya still did not have the energy to go ice skating but maybe soon, if they eased the rationing again. Another air raid that night confirmed that this war was not yet over. *Damn Germans.*

Chapter Forty-Two

The start of 1944 was a lot like the start of 1943. Little food, lots of cold, and fear from bombing raids every few nights all were still present. The railway from Moscow had been repaired and food and medicine were coming in. Supplies from the Americans were helping too. There was more food to buy, but rationing still had people wishing for more.

Sewing group had chatter galore.

"My son came in from the front for a visit, and he says the Germans are scared."

"How can he tell?"

"He said some of their stuff is leaving. Trucks are leaving the front."

"In winter?"

"How are they getting their trucks out? In this snow, it is impossible!"

"The Germans can't handle our winter. We showed them that at Stalingrad!" Women agreed and heads nodded.

"A few trucks leaving does not mean anything. When the tanks leave, then we will celebrate."

"As long as they keep bombing, I do not think they are going anywhere." These women had become so jaded by this war, by death and starvation, that they were not going to believe it was over until they saw it with their own eyes. Then one woman said out loud what they all thought:

"Until I can walk out the gates of Leningrad and not see anything German, this war is still going on!" They all nodded. Lanya picked up the cookie she had next to her and nibbled. She was jaded too and did not know when, or if, this liberation would happen.

As she walked home in the arctic night, Lanya wondered about the war. *Is it almost over? Will the Germans leave?* She felt guilty about her thoughts from the early days when she used to wonder if the Germans might be no worse than the Party. She was glad those thoughts were never shared with anyone.

As she entered the apartment, she was glad for the heat and the lights. For almost three years she had neither. Mishka was at the kitchen table. The vodka bottle was empty near his right hand.

"Lanya." His voice was slurred. Lanya could sense the tension. He had been drunk a lot lately. Maybe he was bored.

"Yes" she answered quietly.

"Lanya, I have to get out of here. This is killing me."

"What do you mean brother?" She had a feeling boredom was not the biggest problem. Was vodka the problem? Both their parents spent a lot of time with the bottle. And it caused problems for both of them, for all of them.

"I need to go out with the army. With my brothers. I have been hiding here too long." Lanya felt her heart drop. He could not go! She started to cry and then caught herself. *Listen first,* she thought.

"What do you mean brother?" She asked again.

"Men are dying and I am here hiding behind your skirt. I am healed now. I need to go out there and kill Germans! For what they did to Valentina, to me!" She did not say anything and hoped he would go on. Or, that he would fall asleep now and remember nothing of this. He picked up the bottle again and tried to drain it a bit more but it was completely empty. He banged the bottle on the table and got up. "I would rather die in a battle than die of boredom." He turned to leave the room and stumbled over his own heavy feet. He tromped down the hall to his room. Lanya sat at the table and put her head on her hands. *He wants to leave? He could get killed!* She did not stop the tears as they came. *Valentina is gone, Babu is gone, Mishka was gone and came back, and now he wants to go again?* Lanya got up from the table and went to the cupboard for the second bottle of vodka she kept as backup. She was too tired to think.

She did not see him at breakfast but after work he was at the table. There was a nice stack of wood pieces for the stove so that must have been where he was this morning. He did not say anything right away so Lanya brought it up.

"You said something last night that frightened me. Do you remember?" He looked at her straight on with blank eyes.

"Yes. I know you hate it, but I need to go back to the army. I am not doing any good here, except for you. And the needs of the Soviet Republic are bigger than yours. Svetlana. I need to go back. Maybe I can save a few men, and kill a few Germans. Maybe they need a welder. I will go down tomorrow to talk to the office about this." He did not look ready for a discussion so Lanya said nothing again. Her heart was in pieces and he could see it. He touched her arm. "It is wrong of me to stay here when I am able to fight. Can't you see that?" Lanya looked at him, trying to see his point of view. If it was anyone but her only family, she could understand. But he was all she had left! He waited for an answer and she could not find words. Her throat was choked up. So she nodded and did not stop the tears that dripped down her cheeks. He left the room.

The next morning, Lanya did not work so she waited for Mishka to come out. She had breakfast ready and he sat and quickly ate his porridge and coffee. "I am going to talk to the army office, you know. I may have to leave right away. I will come home tonight though." He left quickly, almost like he was glad to be out. Lanya sat at the table and felt frozen.

That night there was a big bombing raid. It seemed to go on for hours and Lanya sat next to Mishka in the shelter and held his hand. *What if this is their last air raid together? What if he never comes back? What if the rest of my life is lonely and without comfort?* Finally the all clear rang and they slowly emerged from the basement into the icy air. The walk home was silent, and Lanya was sure he was thinking the same things.

He was gone when Lanya got up and she went to work like there was a rock where her heart used to be. The day lasted forever and she hurried home to see what Mishka had done. She opened the door and he was at the table.

"Mishka?" The question in her voice was clear.

"Lanya, I leave tomorrow. They did not want to believe me, that I was hurt. But they found the record of it somehow and they had proof. So I report in tomorrow. Might need to get into shape, but they will not fuss. They need every man they can get." He took her hand and touched her cheek. "I am sorry little Lanya, but I need to. I cannot let the other men do my duty for me. I have to go." He kissed the top of her head and went to his room.

At lunch the next day, Lanya cornered Maru and the tears started as quickly as they were separate. "He left! I am dying! He said he could not have other men do his duty and he left!" Maru was open mouthed.

"He what? Mikhail did what?" They sat down and Lanya put her head on Maru's shoulder.

"Mishka came back to me. We had a big bomb weeks ago, before the one Boris did. Remember? And Mishka came back. It took him a bit but he was talking and almost like the old Mishka." Lanya paused and Maru was staring with her mouth open. "I did not tell you yet, because I wanted to be sure it would last." Almost true. "He has been bored. And drinking. He got angry. He said he needed to go back. Said he was hiding behind my skirt. Said he would rather die in war than of boredom. Wanted to kill Germans for revenge. So he left this morning before I was up. I may never see him again!" Maru was crying too.

"He will be back. He has to. After what he already went through, driving the Germans back will be nothing." Lanya looked at her and saw it was pretend bravery, her tears gave it away. They did not eat much. The rest of their lunch break was quiet.

The apartment was empty, emptier than it had ever been. This new apartment did not have the warmth of many family years and Lanya was as cold as the icicles she saw on the trees outside. Vodka was her dinner.

There was no air raid that night or the next three. Sewing group was all a-chatter and the hostess had cookies again. Lanya did not share about Mishka; she was still stunned that he was gone again. But the ladies had information, so Lanya waited to see what they would share.

"My son said the tanks are leaving!"

"Really?" The tone of disbelief was tangible. "Soldiers? When do they go?"

"We have not had an air raid for almost a week."

"I am afraid to believe this."

"Did the Party say anything yet?"

"There was nothing in the announcements this week."

"I don't know. This is too good to be true."

The comments went on but Lanya was no longer listening, thinking about her brother. *Will this be over soon? Will he come home?* The talk went on, and as Lanya got to the street in the January cold, the air raid sirens went off. She was near home, so she hurried to her new shelter. She snuck into the shelter and saw only a few faces that were familiar. She was alone. This was her first air raid alone. Every other time she was with Babu or Mishka. She bit her cheek to calm herself. This shelter had people who were playing cards and sharing a vodka bottle but Lanya kept to herself. If a song broke out she would join, but she was not strong enough to start one.

The raid lasted about as long as all the others and as Lanya walked into the night she wondered when this would all be over. If it would ever be over. *Will the Germans go back to Germany? Will Leningrad ever again be a bright spot on the Baltic? Will I ever sit and laugh with Mishka or Maru again?* She remembered afternoons with them near the Neva when they had been drinking and singing as they walked. Mishka did not like singing but he would sing along with Lanya and Maru. Lanya tumbled into bed alone in the apartment and the nightmares came as they always did. Again she was being chased and there were bombs going off and explosions everywhere. No one came to check on her when she woke up screaming.

The next few days were a blur. Lanya went to work in the frigid air, came home and ate something then used vodka as a pacifier; it did help her sleep. She lay down on the night of the 26th of January with the same agenda, eat, drink sleep. She woke to explosions and screams. Was it a bombing? There was no air raid? What happened? She scrambled out of bed and remembered her coat, pulled the curtain aside and there were planes in the air and things were flying! This was a close call! Her look out the window made her question leaving. *Will outside be any safer? Why is there no siren?* Lanya went back and forth in her head- should she stay here where she might be okay or go out? She saw a few people in the street. The vodka said stay here. She plopped down into a chair and let her head fall back. She would stay here. She was not sure she wanted to live anyway, all alone. The bombs faded as Lanya sat there feeling like her world had been yanked from her. She did not like this life. She dozed and was grateful to vodka, the "water of life" for her sleep.

Lanya opened her eyes to a bit of sun coming through the dark curtains. She was alive. Oh well. She pulled the curtains aside and there were people everywhere. Trucks, people, and lots of noise. She did not want to open the window in January, but decided she wanted to see what was going on down there on the street, got dressed in a sweater and a long skirt with a scarf. She pulled a beanie on her head as she opened the door. She had her ration cards and would go to the market for something for breakfast.

On the street, people were yelling "They are gone!" Who is gone? "The Germans have left!" What?

Lanya turned and grabbed the arm of a woman walking the other way. "What is going on?" Lanya was afraid of the answer.

"After last night's bombing, the Germans have left. We woke up to the backs of their tanks and trucks. The Germans are leaving Leningrad!" Lanya froze. Leaving? Was the war over? Where was Mishka? She was not sure she believed it. She decided to ask again. She saw a younger man with a cane, probably hurt in the war. She tapped him on the shoulder.

"Is it true?" She was going to say more but her grabbed her by the waist and hugged her, almost knocking her over.

"The filthy Germans are leaving Leningrad. They are limping home to Berlin. We are going to kill them all as they try to sneak out! Damn Germans!" Lanya was limp and had to stabilize herself as he let her go. The Germans really were leaving? This horrible period was over? Lanya looked for a place to sit but did not find one so she leaned against a light pole. The Germans were leaving? Certainly, the war was not over, there was a long way to go to get back to Germany, but Leningrad would be fine! Lanya decided to walk to the market to give her time to understand this whole thing.

The Germans were leaving. They never came into Leningrad, they never destroyed her city. The Nazis were not a match for the Communist Party! Lanya felt good about that and wanted to explore this idea. People she walked by were smiling and laughing and hugging. She was hugged a few times as she went down the road. People were happy. Happy like they had not been for three years. Maybe they would be okay.

At the market, people were still smiling and hugging. One older man brought out his accordion and was playing folk songs. Lanya found herself smiling too. She felt so light she went to the musician and started singing the old songs. His grin covered his face and Lanya smiled with him. A crowd gathered, singing and linking arms. It was good to be Russian today.

Chapter Forty-Three

The feeling of lightness never left Lanya all through the day. She smiled at anyone she saw and she had songs in her head all the time. As she sang, she wondered if songs were the key to her mental health. Maybe she should have used singing in her tough times, instead of vodka to lift her spirits. Why she was thinking about those tough times now was beyond her. *Just enjoy this minute* she said to herself. She saw army men coming through the city, maybe they got a break before they chased the Germans, and she studied each one for her Mikhail. She did not see him. But she was sure he was well. Had to be.

The speakers in the city boomed out marching music during the middle of the day. It was January cold but no one noticed. Lanya was buoyant, like a balloon. The sun was out. As Lanya walked home with groceries she wondered if she would have any trouble sleeping tonight. Would the nightmares continue? She did not have many before the war started, but during the war they had been relentless. *When will they give up?* Not soon, since the army still had to get Germany to surrender. *Will they surrender? How long will it take?* Lanya decided not to worry about that. What else would change? When would rationing end? There was food available, but when the train tracks all got restored there would be more. *Will people who left town come back?*

Sleep came easily for Lanya, without the vodka. She had dreams but not nightmares. She woke rested and prepared for work. At the factory, people were not ready to settle into their machines.

"They are gone, damn Germans!"

"I knew they would leave, like a dog with its tail between its legs."

"You cannot beat Mother Russia. You just can't."

"This war will be over soon. And we will decide the rules. Not like the last war." The mumbling went on and on until a supervisor came out and waved a clipboard and ordered them to their machines. Lanya saw Maru across the room and scurried over.

"Can you believe it? The Germans are gone!"

"I am so glad. I can get some sleep now!" The supervisor was still nearby with a ferocious look, so the women scattered and sat down to work. Lanya made her boots with a smile for most of the day, just a smile. At home, her heart jumped when she had a letter in the mailbox. She did not check it often but for some reason she did today. It was from Mikhail, and it was full of news.

'Little Lanya, we are chasing the Germans and they are running as fast as they can. I cannot tell you where we are, but we are west of you. There is snow but not as much as at home. They feed us pretty good, but I am sick of fish. I do not know any of the men I am with but a few are from our town. I think they might want to pull me into another area so I can weld, I would be happy with that.' The letter was short but Lanya clasped it to her chest. It felt like he was close. Maybe he would come home. Checking her mail every day would be her new plan. She wrote back in a chatty way and made sure to include updates about Maru. She hoped her letter would bring him as much warmth as his brought her.

February came in bright but cold. Lanya could see evidence that the Germans were gone. The statue of Peter the Great that had been covered in mud was being picked clean and the ugly gray cake that was on the dome of St. Isaac's Cathedral was coming down. The anti-airplane guns that were in squares around the city were being towed off. Trains were not yet repaired but there were cars now and they were going through the streets. Lights were on and the trams were running.

Letters from Mishka came every few days, and Lanya's heart was eased. She could see him trekking along, repairing machines, welding when needed. She did not worry every day about his safety, not as much. From what he said, he was not on the front lines and Lanya was glad of that. Some days she felt like he was right there with her.

People who had evacuated Leningrad returned slowly. They brought new clothes and books and ideas. The war trudged on and on though. The Party's daily announcement always claimed the Soviets were winning, and without the German air raids, Lanya believed it.

The days went by in a blur. Spring came and Lanya worked on her garden plot with more success than last year. Letters from Mishka came and were returned. Boots were sewn and sleeping bags repaired. Lanya heard about a show or two but was not ready to try out. She and Maru went to see one and Lanya again yearned for the stage but never pursued it. Railroads were repaired and food and goods came into town. Though there was still rationing but it was enough. The Hermitage opened with all its glory and Maru and Lanya walked the halls amazed that their culture was unbroken and the art was returned. Injured men came home, and injured women as well, pilots and nurses.

Chapter Forty-Four

Lanya's days ran together. Work, sewing group and seeing Maru helped her make it through each day. Letters from Mikhail came about once a week. She did not know where he was, but he seemed chipper and she always wrote back with a smile.

Rationing was still happening, but there was a nice variety of food and supplies. The fresh produce made Lanya smile, remembering years with none. Train lines were repaired and people could come and go from Leningrad with ease. Veterans came, with stories, and Lanya was happy to see them in town. Word was they were through Poland and close to Germany, and Lanya hoped it was over soon.

The Communist Party was still searching for German sympathizers, but Lanya never asked how it went. She knew they would arrest anyone, so no one ever mentioned it. Party officials from Moscow were easy to spot in their brown sweaters and grim faces. After being in jail two years ago, Lanya did not have quite the same fears, since she had lived through what was almost the worst they could dish out. It was resigned acceptance of the power of the Party.

Wednesday night sewing group went on and this was more like a group of women gossiping at the market, instead of angry at the world. Every one of them had lost family, some more than one. But they were comfortable with each other and laughed and snacked and seemed like old friends. *War can do that to you*, Lanya thought. *These women who I would never have known in Leningrad are my friends now and we know what each has been through.* She smiled at the thought. She liked when they asked her to sing for them, and she chose songs they could sing along.

Leningrad was being repaired. Factories were opening slowly, since most men were not back. Buildings were being demolished or rebuilt. Roads were open and flat again. Canals were cleaned and running well. Restaurants had tables on the sidewalks. Windows were replaced and gardens were planted in the summer. Flowers were everywhere in the spring of 1945. Birds that had gone into hiding when the shelling was happening returned, and chirping and hopping, squirrels scampered for food.

One letter from Mikhail was disturbing.

'We came into this area last week that was the ugliest thing I have ever seen. It was a camp of some sort, but the smell was revolting. The first group had already been there two days when my group got there, and I have never seen such death. Bodies were stacked everywhere and we were told to clean it up. Every one of us threw up until our stomachs hurt. We dragged bodies into pits and covered them. My officer later told me this was what the Nazis did to Jewish people- they held them and let them slowly die. I cannot imagine what they would do in Leningrad and am so glad they are gone from our Soviet world. I will never forget this place and hope my dreams let me forget.' Lanya felt sick as she read it. Bodies piled up, the stench, she tried not to picture it and was glad she could not imagine it. She remembered the bodies in the streets the first winter of the war. She did not understand who could do that to anyone. Damn Germans.

Mishka did not say where he was but the speakers in town and the women at sewing group gave her the idea that the Red Army was in Germany and that this would all be over soon. One day in early May as she waited for the tram to take her to work, the announcements came on with a huge blast of sound, then a booming voice announced that the Red Army had captured Berlin! Lanya stopped and looked around, just like she did when they abandoned Leningrad. Everyone on the street stopped and did the same. Then she heard hoops and yells, and people were hugging and crying. Cars honked and guns were shot off. The Germans were defeated? She got caught up in a hug and tried to hug back, then she was passed to another hug. It was fine, she hugged back and she could feel the tears. *No more war? What will that even feel like?*

She got to the factory and her co-workers were milling about, no one was sitting. She found Maru and they crowded around the shift leader who stood on a chair. "No work today. Go home and get drunk. Make love, eat cake, the Red Army has captured Berlin, the war is over! The toothbrush dictator shot himself. Damn Germans deserve to lose. Go on home. Proud to be a Soviet today! Hope our boys are home soon." Lanya knew he had a son in the Red Army and she hoped they would all come home soon. The crowd cheered and Lanya cried with joy. No more Germans, they were done. Mishka would be home and Leningrad could come back, as it had started to already.

The next day was a celebration, the anti aircraft guns were shot off at noon, a parade of tanks and trucks came through the street and every person in town was watching with tears streaming down their faces. The factory was closed again and Lanya wanted to share this moment with Maru. Or Josef. But the streets were a party and she was spinning around, singing and dancing. Musicians were playing and patriotic songs were sung on every corner. Years of death and strain and trauma were forgotten for today.

The next letter from Mishka came a week later, and he said they were singing and dancing in Berlin, he could tell her now. They went into homes and stores and ransacked anything they wanted. They did not care about who owned it. He said the stores were empty, but the homes had nice things. The Red Army was celebrating with gusto because they liberated Berlin, not the British or the Americans. The Soviets captured the capital! The whole army did whatever they wanted to hurt the Germans as much as they could. Mishka told her they would be home in a few months, and Lanya cried again. Her strong, loving brother would be home soon! Life could go on!

Chapter Forty-Five

The letter from the Communist Party came and Lanya with Maru and Mishka went to the ceremony in August. And the conversation with Josef the next day, where he told her of his wish for more, for her to be his girlfriend, to be together years from now, to live in Moscow, that was last week and Lanya was still confused. *Josef is a good man who has helped me get through the worst days of my life. But he works for the Party, and that was not likely to change.* Even as she said that in her head, Lanya's heart choked up. Josef is a Party man and Lanya could never be a Party person. *Will that ruin any chance with Josef? Do I want a chance with Josef? What does marriage take? What makes marriage work? Is he even talking marriage? Or am I just jumping ahead? He says he wants a girlfriend, not a wife. But years from now?* Lanya felt like the kaleidoscope in her head was back. Would Maru have any answers? Maru knew men more than Lanya ever would. Lanya decided that this was a bigger talk than lunchtime at the factory.

The next day, at lunch, Lanya said to Maru, "We have not been out together in such a long time. Can we go out? Get a drink? Enjoy a summer day?" She paused, hoping Maru would respond.

Maru's eyes lit up! "What a great idea! When?"

"Tomorrow. We do not work the next day. Not Mishka, just us?"

"Sure. I will pick you up. Wear your new dress!" The date was set, and Maru seemed excited.

They got to the club the next day and Maru ordered something fruity, so Lanya copied her. Drinks in hand, Lanya found her courage and started. "Maru, I need your advice." Maru put down her drink but said nothing. "You know men. You do not know Josef, but you know how good he has been to me." Maru was silent, waiting for more. "Josef wants to be my boyfriend. He is getting transferred to Moscow with the Party. You know how I feel about the Party. But Maru, so many men are gone!" She looked into Maru's eyes, wishing an answer would appear like a light. "What do I do?"

Maru took a deep breath. "I wondered if there was something when you said let's go out. I am always the one who says we should go out." The club was nearly empty so Maru knew no one would be eavesdropping. "I am glad you asked. You want to make the right choice." She paused for a moment and Lanya clenched. Maru was usually quick to offer advice. "First, I do not know him, and from what you have said he is not like the guys you normally like. These are not normal times. The biggest problem is not him, but his job. You could learn to love anyone, couldn't you?" Lanya did not expect that question. *Can I?* "But you will never learn to love the Party. And from what you said, Josef is not likely to leave the Party." Again she took a deep breath. "And if you leave Leningrad, I will die!" This earned a smile. Maru was trying to keep it light. Lanya did not feel light. This was a life changing decision.

"Josef is a good man, I am sure of that. And there is some chance that I could learn to love him. But, you are right. If he loves that Party and I want him to leave it, that is not fair to him, is it? Maybe like asking me not to sing?" As she said that, it struck her. She could never ask him to leave the Party, it was part of his core. Her decision was made. "Well, that clarifies it. I should go tell him and be completely up front. I might break his heart though."

"Tell him how you feel. You cannot be false with him. That would cause problems. Be honest."

"You are right, as usual! What a great friend you are! I do not deserve you!" Lanya wrapped her arms around Maru and was comforted. So smart.

Chapter Forty-Six

The July day was hot, but Lanya was okay with it. The factory had all the windows open, but there might have been more gossip than work that day. Two trains had pulled in this week bringing men home from Germany. Lanya was not at the train station but her friends had been. The celebrations were loud and full of smiles and tears. No one was stoic about this; their men were coming home!

Lanya did not know when Mishka would be home. Her last letter from him was two weeks ago and he said they were doing clean up in Berlin and he did not know where the next orders would send him. Lanya wondered if that was true or if that was what he was supposed to say.

As Lanya got off the tram near the factory, she saw the groups at the train station, ready for their men. She was not sure if they knew their men were coming or if they were welcoming any men home. She decided she would talk with Maru, both of them could come to the station, to welcome random men, who might not have anyone. She was sure that plenty of soldiers had no one to meet them, since so many Leningraders had died. Parents, sisters and wives were gone. Maru would like this idea to bring flowers or candy for these heroes. A real welcome. Even if it was not her brother.

Maru loved the idea and they decided to check with the station to see when would be a good time. After work for the next day would fit their schedule. So Lanya and Maru gathered some small candies and flowers they bought, and made their way to the station. The platform where the men were coming in had a few grandmothers and young women on it, along with a few small children.

Lanya and Maru sat on a bench and heard the squeak of the train wheels. They got up but stayed behind the other women, since they were just welcoming random soldiers. As the train stopped, the men on board jumped off and let out a whoop, happy to be back in Leningrad! Lanya could understand that. Men were hugged and tears flowed on every face. Lanya cried too; it was so good to have won this war that killed so many. The family groups began to lead away and other men gathered their rucksacks. Lanya and Maru walked up with candies in hand.

"Welcome home, brave heroes." Maru said it first and Lanya echoed it. They held out the candies. Lanya looked for Mishka but he was not here. Yet. He would come. The soldiers smiled and hugged Lanya and Maru. Lanya got a kiss on the mouth too, which surprised her! She smiled, they smiled, and her heart was flying. The train was full, so the men moved on and they offered candy to new men as they exited the train. Maru was laughing, she remembered one of the men, he used to work at the factory. Lanya did not recognize him and figured that after a war, a man might look different. The train emptied and the men smiled and cried, Lanya smiled and cried and felt like this was one of the best days of her life. When she and Maru were alone, they hugged each other.

"Let's do this again, as soon as we can!" Lanya was beaming.

"Yes, this feels so good!" Maru could not stop the smiles and Lanya could see the tracks of the tears that had run down her cheeks. They left the station holding hands, feeling like heroes themselves.

It took two more days to get back, but Lanya and Maru were there at the same time and gate. Again, the families were crowded and Lanya and Maru stayed behind. The families moved away and Lanya and Maru moved up, candies in hand. The later soldiers came out, smiling and grateful to be home. Again, hugs and tears and kisses were everywhere. Lanya laughed to herself and wondered what Maru was thinking. Was she shopping, looking for a potential husband? Maru did that every day, and the last four years had been like starvation for her. As they left, they decided to do this more. The men appreciated it that was certain. And Maru felt like she was at a buffet, of men! Three times this day, men had asked about her, but she only gave her name and the name of the shoe factory. If they really wanted to meet with her they could find her there. Lanya felt like she was saving the world. That felt so good after the war years. Worth doing again.

Two weeks later, after coming to the station many times to welcome men home, Lanya was still feeling good. How long would they be coming home? When would her brother be back? Maybe they kept him, needed some welding? She wondered as she greeted these heroes and gave hugs. He would get home when he got home, she tried to tell herself. The train emptied, and Lanya could see two more men coming and got herself ready. Maru moved forward and Lanya hung back a bit. Maru screamed and Lanya jerked her head up. "Mikhail, it is you!" Lanya wished she had seen him first, but Maru was wrapped in Mishka's arms as tight as a bear. He saw Lanya just a foot away and wrapped her in his arms too. The tears erupted for all of them.

"I could not tell you when I was coming, I only found out two days ago and had to get right on the train, I am so glad to be here! You met me!" Mishka was exuberant and his rucksack fell as his arms were around the women. He released them and they started towards the exit, but walking was hard because they were so wrapped around each other. Finally, Maru let go so Lanya could walk with her brother. One arm around Lanya one around his pack and they made it to the tram. Maru went home with them and it was perfect.

At the apartment, Lanya got out the vodka and a small cake she had made two days before. Mishka threw his bag into his room and plopped at the kitchen table.

"Everything looks the same here, good to see."

"I did not change anything." Lanya was glad she did not change the apartment. She chose to leave everything as it was, not knowing if her brother would come home, and she wanted to remember it the way it used to be. They all talked at the kitchen table until Maru finally went home. Lanya got ready for bed and curled up, knowing there would not be any nightmares tonight.

Having her brother home was as good as life was going to get, Lanya was sure of that. She tried not to think about what had been lost between her sister and Babu. Plenty of people had lost even more. Lanya wanted to look to the future, not in the past. Mishka went back to the steel plant and was rehired to weld, they were so happy to see him. Lanya and Maru started talking about shows to see and Maru wanted Lanya to try out for a new one. Lanya was not sure. Being on stage in the early days of the war had been good, but all the mess with Ivan was never far from her mind. Should she try out again?

Chapter Forty-Seven

Lanya decided as she walked to the Party office what she needed to do. She would tell Josef as gently as she could that they had no future. She entered and hardly saw the mousy people, waited in line for her ration cards and looked for Josef. He was expecting her, she could tell because his eyes lit up when she caught him looking at her. She felt guilty immediately. She gave him a weak smile as she turned to leave. She left slowly, knowing he would follow. She got outside and appreciated the sun and the green trees and flowers that were filling the gardens. Josef came out quickly and smiled again as he saw her. "Josef, it's so nice to see you again." She held her hand out and he quickly grasped it, not too tightly then quickly let it fall. "I want to talk with you when you are done here; can I meet you after work?" She knew she could not do this now at work while he was at work. He looked left and right and his smile faded, like he knew what was coming.

"I am done here at 5:30. Where can we meet? Would you like dinner?"

"Thank you, but no dinner. Can I meet you right here? Right at 5:30?" His face seemed to sag as she said it.

"That will work, sure." Lanya reached out and squeezed his hand briefly and began to turn.

"See you soon, thanks Josef." She completed her turn and moved away quickly. It was a minute before she heard his steps to go back in. As she walked, her confidence dropped. Breaking his heart, dropping his heart on the floor... why was life so hard? Maru could do it, she had broken up with men time and time again. Lanya never had, so this was new. And hard.

At 5:30, Lanya was in the exact same spot, her fingers fidgeting on her sleeve. Her brain was all over the place, *what if I say the wrong thing? What if I am not clear? What if I am not gentle enough?* As these thoughts zipped around in her head again, she saw him come out the door and she smiled. "Josef," she said quietly. "Thanks for meeting. Can you walk with me?" She decided earlier that walking would mean he would not stare at her as she spoke. That felt smart. He nodded and they fell into step along the empty sidewalk.

"Josef, I wanted to talk to you. You said something the other day that was so genuine and heartwarming, I was not sure how to react. You did not pressure me. But I pressured myself, Josef. You want to go to Moscow and you asked me to go with you." She stopped, not sure why. He looked at her face. She put on her bravest face and reached for his hands. "Josef, you have been so good to me. You have been a great friend in this ugly period. You might have saved my life. I can never repay you. But, Josef, I cannot go to Moscow." She looked carefully at his face but he was showing no emotion, and she was glad of that. "I cannot love the Party. You probably know my parents were taken by the Party years ago." She waited for a reaction but saw none. "You love working with the Party; I am glad for what the Party does for us and I am glad you are being promoted and you will do well in Moscow. But I will stay here in Leningrad. I wish I could feel more; you are a good man. You will be a great husband someday, but it will not be for me." She kept her eyes on him, looking for any sign of heartbreak.

"Lanya, thank you." His voice was quiet but clear. "Thank you for telling me. I thought that would be your response, but I felt like I needed to ask you." He sighed and Lanya felt relieved. "You have been such a bright spot for me through this hell of a war, and I looked forward to seeing you come in. I could never do anything or make it easier. You never asked me for anything, Lanya, when so many others might. I am glad you are so honest." He searched her face but she had no reaction yet. "I did not know about your parents, but I had a feeling, you gave me a hint once. And, I knew you would not go." Again a big sigh. "I will be going in a few weeks, they are setting it up. Moscow will be a big mess. My mom is going with me, and that is good." Lanya smiled. She remembered meeting his mom on New Year's Eve last year and how she doted on Josef.

"Josef, that is good. She will be glad to be with you. You will do well in Moscow. Maybe someday we will hear about you, advising Comrade Stalin on big decisions!" Lanya wanted to lighten things up, but felt she was trying too hard. She took his hands again, "Josef, you will always hold a place in my heart. You have been so good to me. Please send me a letter when you get settled in. If I ever come to Moscow I will look you up."

"Lanya..." he pulled her close and gave her a tight hug. She enjoyed the closeness and could feel what he was feeling. "Lanya... you will always hold a place in my heart, too. I will think of you every day. And I will take you to dinner if you ever come to Moscow." He let her go and she took a step back.

"Josef, thank you. I was so worried and you have made this simple. Not easy," she looked away with a weak smile, "but simple." Was it done? Was she free of this guilt? Should she go off now? Was there more to say?

"Lanya, I see that you are troubled. I will be fine. I did not expect more and I truly appreciate your honesty. I need to go, I have a lot to do. I will see you next week, I hope?" Now, Josef was trying to make it light and Lanya was grateful. She gave one last squeeze of his hands and turned. He squeezed back and they parted quietly in the street. Lanya took a few small steps and when she heard his footsteps she continued on her way.

Her brain did not release its anxiety though. *Did I do the right thing? Was I too harsh? Could I love him if I tried? Would Maru have said the same things?* A kaleidoscope in her brain turned again as she walked home on this sunny day.

Chapter Forty-Eight

Lanya was in the kitchen after a long day at work. They had been back to five days a week for almost a year, and today she felt a bit tired. Dinner was almost done when she heard her brother come in the house. *Good timing* she thought. He walked into the kitchen, Lanya could see he was smiling and felt like a breath of fresh air.

"Hello Mishka, what is going on?"

He grabbed her wrist and said "Lanya, come here." He pulled her out of the kitchen towards the front door.

"What?" She followed, wondering what was going on. She smoothed her hair with her hand hoping she did not look a mess as he propelled her out the door.

"Come with me; there is something I want you to see." This was not like Mishka. He was not impulsive and Lanya quickened her pace to keep up with him. She knew not to tell him no. If he wanted this, she would do it. She took a moment and was grateful that he was even home. So many men came back but were never okay. Physically broken or emotionally shattered, and families had to walk on eggshells in case they cracked. Mishka seemed fine. He led her to a small café near the corner that she had been in once or twice. She saw a few people eating and sipping coffee.

Mishka grabbed her hand and brought her to a table with a man sitting at it. Lanya held back. She did not want to sit with this man she did not know. She looked at him and opened her mouth to say something but Mishka sat down, so she did too, not understanding. Her nerves were on edge as she looked at this man. He had brown stringy hair, a slight beard and a gray shirt, nothing special to see. She looked at Mishka with a question in her eye. Her heart was beating fast but she did not understand it. Did she know this man? She looked down and saw this man was missing the bottom part of his leg. So many were. She looked away, as she did not want to stare. This man was a hero to her.

"Svetlana, so good to see you." His voice was gentle and Lanya looked at his face. He knew her, but she did not recognize him. She opened her mouth but Mishka was quicker.

"Lanya, you remember my friend Aleksander?" Lanya's mouth dropped open. He was dead! "He told me he came to see you at the old apartment." Lanya was speechless. Aleksander? She studied his face and saw some familiarity.

"Aleksander? I was told you were dead!" Her thoughts were all over the place. *Alive? How?*

"Svetlana, who told you that? Was it Boris? He lied about everything!" Aleksander slapped his hand on the table in frustration as he rolled his eyes. Boris.

"Yes, it was Boris. He came to see me and told me you were dead." There was more but Lanya did not want to get into that now.

"He told me you were interested in him! Not long after saying that he got transferred out of our unit and I never saw him again."

Mishka spoke up "Boris came to see Lanya, when I was not myself. He told her about you. He was drunk and attacked Lanya, put his hands all over her." Mishka paused, his voice tight. Lanya could see he was on edge about this story. "I came out and we fought, got into the street and were taken to the police. Took some talking, by my sister, and they believed us. He was a slime of a man!" Mishka felt strongly, even if he did not remember it. He did not need to remember it to be angry that a man would put his hands on his sister. He took a moment and came back to the conversation. Mishka turned to Lanya, "I was going through this store the other day and this man comes along in a rickety old wheelchair. Of course I gave him room. But he stopped right in front of me. And, it was Aleksander!" Mishka was relaxed again and put his hand on Aleksander's arm. "And I knew you would want to see him, since you told me what Boris said."

Lanya had so many things running through her head. Aleksander was alive! Mishka would have a friend around, which was amazing, since so many did not come back. Aleksander! What a world! Lanya remembered how she felt when he came to visit and the hospital visit, a warm, friendly feeling. And here he was! A lead weight dissolved in her heart.

Mishka went to get coffee, and Aleksander reached across the table and touched Lanya's hand. "You do not know this, but you kept me alive." Lanya's mouth again fell open. "When I was worried that I would die on the field, I thought of you. I remembered your smile. It made such a difference. And when I was in the hospital for my leg," he gestured to the stump of a leg. "thoughts of you and when I might see you again are what kept me from hating my life. I hoped that I would find a way to see you." Aleksander had a light in his eyes. "Then, when I got home, I went to your apartment and saw it was bombed. The walls were gone and the whole thing was ready to fall. I thought you might be dead. I left there worried that I would not have a friend in the world." She could see a tear come to his eye. He changed the subject and the tear disappeared. "So many died. This town is such a mess." Lanya's heart was in her stomach. He had a tear because he thought she was dead? There was a lot going on with him.

Mishka returned and sat down, with a big smile. Was he matchmaking? Lanya listened to their talk about the war but did not add anything. What was she feeling? Relief, that he was alive. Hurt, because he was not the man he used to be. Could he be? He seemed very happy to see her, and she felt happy too. But what did it mean? Lanya decided she needed expert advice and that would not happen at this table, that would happen at Maru's house. She made excuses about dinner and quickly left. She needed Maru's thoughts!

She knocked on Maru's door and pulled her back into her bedroom. "I have to talk to you!" Maru was smiling over the excitement she could see on Lanya's face. Lanya pulled them both down onto Maru's bed. "Remember Aleksander, Mishka's friend I went to see in the hospital?"

"Yes, you said he died."

"He didn't!" Lanya was almost bouncing on the bed. "Mishka bumped into him in town and just took me to meet him! He is alive! He lost a leg, but his smile is the same!" Maru grabbed Lanya's hand. "I can't believe he is alive! And we are so lucky that Mishka found him! In a grocery store! And he went to our old apartment, where he came before..." Maru nodded, fascinated. Lanya was full of excitement and could not stop. "And he saw how it was bombed and he thought we were dead! He thought we were dead!" Lanya took a deep breath, realizing she was dumping news by the bucket. "Can you imagine, we both thought the other was dead, but we aren't!"

"Wow, that is romantic. You each thought you lost the other, but somehow you were wrong. What a story!"

Lanya took a moment and ran her hands through her hair. "So what do I do?"

Maru thought for a moment. She knew that Lanya would do whatever she suggested so she weighed her ideas. "You want to know what to do with this man whom your brother likes and you used to have a soft spot for? Did he say anything to you?"

"Yes- I forgot to say it, I was so flustered! He said thinking about me kept him alive. He remembered my smile and it helped him when he thought he might die."

"He said that! Oh, my! No one has ever said that to me! So what do you do now?"

"So tell me Maru, what do I do now?"

"Lanya, this is fantastic! A fresh start!" She paused and looked deeply into Lanya's eyes. "What do you feel?" This question was impossible to answer.

"I am not sure. Hopeful? Excited? Scared?" Lanya choked on the words. "You know, the war killed so much. Not just people. Too many people. But think it killed the idea that I could find a man. That we could find a man. So many are gone." Maru nodded her head but did not want to interrupt. "But maybe?" Lanya went on, "We have seen so much in the last four years. Things we never imagined we would ever see. And here we are. We survived." She squeezed Maru's hand. "We are here, so should we grab any opportunity that comes?"

Maru squeezed back. Their survival was almost a miracle, after all they had been through. "Yes, this war killed so many ideas and hearts. But we are still here girl. We can't give up all hope. This could be something or not. What if..." she paused and put her finger on her cheek, "what if you invited him over for dinner? I would come too, and we could have a nice dinner? Would that be a start?"

Lanya smiled. Again, Maru had the best ideas. "Dinner! Perfect!"

Lanya got herself home with a light heart and ate her cold supper. Dinner here would be just right. Friendly but not a date. And with

Mishka and Maru. Perfect. Mishka came home and Lanya looked at him with a smile.

"Brother, you surprised me today!" Mishka smiled too and Lanya loved him even more.

"That was nice. You took off but we stayed and talked. I am glad to have found him."

"Yes, it is good to find a friend." Lanya wanted to say more but Mishka broke in.

"He is not a friend. He is a brother. We fought together, he is a brother to me. I hope we can do more."

Lanya knew this was the time. "Can we have him over for dinner? It would be nice. I cannot cook like Babu, but I can make something." Mishka smiled.

"That would be great! When?"

"You tell me, when is he free? Tomorrow? Any day is good, I just need to do some shopping."

After work the next day, Lanya rushed to get food, hoping the lines were not too bad. Lanya tried to hurry through shopping to get home, sure that Mishka would not say tonight. He was not home so she put things away and settled in. Her brain had a hard time staying on task, always running back to Aleksander's words "You saved my life." What was she supposed to do with that? She brewed a cup of tea and allowed herself to think. And feel. Her life with men had not been good so far, and at 24 years old, it did not seem like it would get better. Few men her age were alive. If they were, many were injured like Aleksander. *Can I handle living with a cripple? He got around, but there are limits. Can I love him?* That might work; she knew she had liked him years ago. Could he love her? He might. That felt good. She had no crystal ball. But what if? What if she and Aleksander could be a couple? Even get married and have kids? Lanya had never thought like this about any other man and it was heady. Giddy. Maru would have fun with this!

Mikhail came home with a smile on his face. "Lanya, your idea is good. Aleksander would love to come for dinner. He says he is a rotten cook, so he would enjoy any good meal! And he is free tomorrow. Does that work for you?"

"Mishka, that is perfect. I will tell Maru too, so she can come. Please tell him we will be happy to see him tomorrow." Lanya quickly left the room; she did not want her brother to see her feet floating off the ground. He knew her too well.

The next day flew by and Lanya was home from work with a fresh loaf of bread before she knew it. She settled into the kitchen to get the soup and the dumplings started. Babu would have it done in thirty minutes but Lanya scrambled to get it all together. Maru knocked on the door at 5:00, a bit early. She came into the kitchen and saw what Lanya was working on and stirred the soup. "When will they be here?"

Lanya paused and said "I think 6:00. But any time will be good. These cook quickly."

Maru turned to look at Lanya. "Lanya, I am having a problem. I need to talk with your brother. I cannot believe he does not see me, that he does not know I adore him. He is not that dense!" Lanya froze and looked at Maru, but did not say anything. "Is he? Dense? I thought he could understand how I feel, but no. What is his problem? I need to talk with him!" She stopped when she heard the men coming in. They heard them coming before they saw them, the wheelchair squeaking and Mishka's heavy feet. The door opened and Aleksander was first, wheeling himself in with Mishka holding the door. Aleksander's face lit up with a smile. He was dressed in new slacks with one leg pinned up, and his face was shaved smooth and his hair had been trimmed. Lanya smiled. He was trying. Lanya came to the door, trying to stay out of the way. Maru stood nearby. Lanya looked at her and remembered they never met. "Aleksander, thanks for coming tonight. It is our pleasure to have you here. This is my best friend Maru. She and I go way back." Mishka snorted, with a smile.

"Someday, my brother, I will tell you stories about what these two have done. Vodka?" Mishka went to get shot glasses and put them on the table. Everyone started with a shot. Lanya felt good, but could not find any words. She was almost afraid to think too much. *To hope?*

"This is a nice place, I went by your old one and there was nothing there but some tumbled down bricks. What happened?" Aleksander asked. Lanya wanted to rush in with the story but Mishka started. "It was blown up. As so many were." He left it at that. Why? Why not tell him that Boris tried to kill them? Shouldn't Aleksander know how bad Boris was? "We hated to leave it since we had been there so long, but we are happy here." Lanya decided to let it go. No point in bringing up ugly memories. They started with the onion soup blended with cheese and Lanya was glad she had saved Babu's recipe. It was not as good as Babu's but not bad. Aleksander seemed to be savoring each spoonful. The dumplings went well as an entrée, and as they finished they each had another shot of vodka. Lanya had used a few more ration cards than she wanted to, but she could not be less than happy about this dinner.

Lanya wondered what Aleksander did each day but did not want to ask, but Mishka had no worries. "So. Aleksander, do you spend all your time dawdling in the grocery store? Both times I found you, that's where you were!" Aleksander smiled and the creases around his mouth showed that he was enjoying himself.

"No, of course not. But I keep looking for some meal to be already made so I do not have to cook!" They all laughed. Mishka got a deck of cards out of a drawer and they quickly got into card games where each one laughed and tried hard to win. Lanya smiled more than she had in a long time and Maru looked just like she belonged there. At a break, Maru and Lanya took the dishes into the kitchen and Mishka and Aleksander went outdoors for a smoke. Lanya smiled, they knew they could smoke in the apartment, so there must be some important talking going on.

"Lanya, what are you thinking?" Maru rinsed dishes and Lanya turned to face her.

"I am not sure. I feel happy, relaxed. Mishka and Aleksander are so good together."

"No, you. What are you feeling about you, not them!"

"I am not sure. I used to like Aleksander, could I again? Could he like me? Would that work?"

"It would be worth spending some time on. He seems to like you. What would your brother say? I think he would say go ahead."

"You think so? I could trust his judgement."

"Well, the decision about what to do next will be up to you, not him. But I say, what have you got to lose?" Lanya fell silent, thinking about that. *What do I have to lose?*

The men came back inside and Lanya smiled. Maru looked at her and got up.

"Mikhail, can I talk with you please?" Mishka looked puzzled, Maru gestured to the door and they went out. Aleksander watched with a smile on his face as they went outside. Outside, Maru crossed her arms and looked at Mishka.

"What do you need, Maru?" He seemed a bit uncomfortable, and she was glad of it. She decided to distract.

"Well your sister seems happy with Aleksander around. Are you?"

"I am very happy to have him around. Why do you ask?" He looked away, trying to avoid her eyes.

"Well, I think they could have a chance. So many people will never have a chance." He nodded. She pushed. "What about you Mishka? Will you ever have a chance?" He looked at her now, wondering where this was going. "What will it take Mishka?" She let the words hang. He studied her face, trying to read it, but he was not seeing anything. She reached out and took his hand. "Mikhail, I have been crazy about you for years. But you never noticed." She paused again. Maybe he was dense. Maybe his brain still did not work right. Too bad. She was not done yet. "I think you and I could make a go of it, take a risk. You know me; we fit together very well." She paused again and wondered if she would have to smack him. "And we could have beautiful children!" His face cracked into a smile and he seemed to have heard.

"Maru... I um...I am stupid." He looked at everything but her. "Truly stupid. I never thought like that. You are Lanya's friend and for some reason I thought that was off limits. I thought she would hate me if I screwed up your friendship with her." Maru looked at him, with disbelief. But she stayed quiet, He had more. "You are beautiful and I have watched you many times, looking good... wondering..." He touched her arm with his hand. "But I thought I would be a bad brother if I ever made a move. I thought Lanya would hate me!" Her hand went to his shoulder. "Was I wrong?"

"You are so wrong." She playfully punched his arm. "Lanya would love for us to be together. You never asked her did you?"

"No, never."

"So, ask me." Maru was being bold, and she liked that feeling.

"Ask you what?" Dense. He was dense. She waited. And waited. "Oh- sorry. Um, Maru... would you go out with me, tomorrow? Can we date?" Maru smiled. There was hope.

"Yes, Mishka, I will. But it will have to be a few dates. Not just one. We can go back now." She turned to go back inside.

Inside, Lanya and Aleksander were sitting at the table playing cards, and Lanya looked up to see if she could tell what was going on. Mishka was looking sheepish but Maru had a smile as broad as could be. She looked at Lanya and gave a slight nod. Lanya looked at her brother as he turned to talk to Aleksander.

Lanya brought dessert to the table and they talked while they ate. She kept looking at Mishka but he gave no notice of what was going on in his head. Maru smiled a lot, so Lanya was sure what had happened. She grinned. The cards were shuffled and the vodka was poured again. Lanya was feeling like this was good; this was what she wanted in life.

Aleksander said it was time for him to go, and Maru got up too. Lanya and Mishka both walked them to the street and Lanya offered to do it again next week. Aleksander smiled and said he would come any time she would allow. Lanya smiled at that. Maru moved to go and Mishka touched her arm, and said "Tomorrow?" She smiled and nodded and turned to go.

Lanya and Mishka got back into the apartment. Lanya went to the kitchen to do clean up and Mishka followed. Lanya looked up, he never did clean up. He leaned against the door frame. "Lanya, um... would you mind if I dated Maru? She is so pretty and I thought..."

Lanya laughed out loud. "What? Of course I would be happy for you to date Maru! She is crazy for you! You would be the luckiest man alive!" The relief on Mishka's face was obvious.

"I never thought you would like it. I have looked at her for years and thought, but worried that you would be mad at me."

"Mikhail..." Lanya picked up the kitchen towel and flicked it at him. "You are not usually stupid... But, I would love it if you and Maru could be together. It would be the best." He smiled and looked relaxed. "You know that she has been crazy about you for years, don't you?" Mishka had a smile that grew as Lanya talked. "She told me when she first met you and has not given up on you. But I almost did!"

"What about you, sister?" She turned to look at him and waited for him to say more. "Could you be with Aleksander?"

She paused before answering. She did not want to give too much away. "Well, he has not asked me. So it may not be a thing."

"He will. He told me he wants to ask you out, maybe more. But he is a cripple. Could you do that?" Lanya could not answer. That would take some time.

"I will figure that out if he asks. A lot to think about." With that, he left the kitchen and Lanya was alone with the dishes. She filled the sink, dishes were good for thinking.

Can I love him? The old him, yes. He was a gentle soul and seemed crazy about her. That was a good start. The new him, with one leg? He is still a gentle soul. And still crazy about her. Can I care for him as he ages, as he needs more help going places? Is there anything else wrong? Does he have nightmares? Episodes? So many men had long term problems. Can I love him, the whole package? She put dishes away as she pondered.

Yes, she could.

Chapter Forty-Nine

Lanya spent the next few days in something of a fog. Work went well, there was fresh fruit at the grocery store, her little plot of garden was doing well. When she lay down at night, sleep was slow. So much going on. What about Aleksander? She had not seen him since the dinner of last week. But she felt like he was close. *Where does he live? Does he live alone? Any family? If I decide to date him, how does that work? Can a cripple "date"? Will a relationship with him mean years of service to him? Will it matter? What might Babu say?* Sometimes Lanya felt like Babu was right on her shoulder, advising and being cautious, as she always did. Would Babu think a relationship with Aleksander was a good idea? She remembered Babu being friendly when he came to visit. *What if Aleksander does not want me? He may have when he was hurt but what about now?* There were lots of women looking for men. Even without his leg, he could still be in great demand. Should that affect her thinking?

Her sister Valentina jumped into her head. Wild, spontaneous Valentina. She would be grown up now. *What would Valentina say?* Lanya smiled at that. When Valentina was alive, Lanya never went to her for advice, so why should she now? But she was sure Valentina would say, *Jump right in!* Valentina was always ready to jump into things. She thought about Valentina's ugly words, when she told her sister "You are scared of everything". This had come into her mind so often, and she remembered how it felt then. Lanya had been angry when Valentina said that, but time had mellowed that and she acknowledged that Valentina had been right. She had been scared of so much. *Am I still scared?*

This stayed with Lanya all day. *What am I scared of now? I have lived through a war, been bombed, starved, in jail, and had wished for death. Could it be any worse? Can being scared be any worse than living through all that?* She chuckled. No, living through all these last few years means she was not scared of much. But what about Aleksander? *Am I scared of a relationship, a true, grown up relationship with him? Where both sides gave one hundred percent? Yes, I am.*

She admitted she had never had one of those. Her brother had not either. And her parents seemed like so long ago. So she had nothing to compare, no guidance. *How can I learn? Trial and error? What if it went all wrong?* As soon as she said that, she saw Valentina's face and the "scared" word. *This is terrifying. This is why people often avoided it or expected the least. Can I make it work?* She scoffed at herself again, since she did not know what was in Aleksander's brain. How on earth could she make decisions for them both when she had not talked with him? Even Maru could not help on this.

After work, she returned to their apartment, with her brain moving faster than her feet. At the apartment, she saw someone. Aleksander? At her door? She scampered faster, hating to make him wait. He broke out in a big smile.

"Lanya, sorry to just pop in on you. Just getting home?" She smiled back and opened the door. He worked his way in and turned to look at her.

"Mikhail is not here now, but he should be soon. Can I make you some tea?"

"I did not come here to see him, I came to see you." With that, her hands grabbed her skirt and she looked at him. His face was expectant. "I wanted to ask you something. Please do not answer immediately; take your time." He paused and wiped his hands on his pants. Was he nervous too? "Svetlana, I want to ask you to be my girlfriend, my partner. That is asking a lot, since I am in this chair. But, I had hoped, years ago that we might be able to make it work, and I still believe that is true." He paused again and breathed deeply. Lanya did too. She had spent hours wondering this same question. "I will answer any questions you have. and give you my best efforts and my whole heart." She looked away from him but he continued to look deep into her. She twisted her fingers in her skirt. He reached out and took them. "You do not need to worry. I am a simple man with simple needs."

Her fingers relaxed and she smiled. "I am going to leave now. Here is my address if you want to come talk to me. I am trying to find a job I can do with this contraption, but I am usually home. Come talk to me." He grabbed his wheels and turned around while Lanya jumped to get the door. She opened it and he pushed his way through getting through the doorway. He smiled as he left and said "I hope to see you soon." Then he wheeled off.

Lanya sunk into a chair. What? Aleksander wanted her? His strong smile and gentle hands? What was she going to do? Maru would help. But as she gathered her purse, she set it down. This she needed to figure out on her own. Maru would not be part of this decision. She made a cup of tea and went to the kitchen table. Mishka would start with a plus/minus chart. She did not have paper handy so she went through it in her head. Plus, he wanted her. Plus, he was cute. Plus, he was close to Mishka. Plus, he would find a job. Plus, he would always have some sort of income from the government because of his leg. With a deep slow breath, she started on the minus section. Minus, he was missing part of his leg. Minus... she waited. What were the other minuses? Were there any? She sipped her tea and spent a few minutes thinking. She did not know his family, was that minus? Or a plus? He was patient, now. Would he always be? She had not seen him drink, except for a few shots last week. Did he drink too much? She heard that many who came back from the war drank every day. She liked her vodka but not every day. He did not seem like the kind who could beat his wife, she could get away from him. Soldiers did that, too, she heard from the women at work.

She made a second cup of tea. *What about my life on stage? Will he allow it? Will he see that stage was good for her? Will he come to see her shows?* As she wondered and worried, the door opened and Mishka came in, covered in dust from the plant, like he did before the war. The picture of it warmed her heart. Should she tell him about Aleksander's visit?

"Hello sister. What is going on today?" His words were warm and strong. She decided to keep it to herself. Which was new. Not new, she corrected. During the war, she kept everything to herself since he did not understand her much.

"Nothing going on here. Valya at work thinks she is pregnant. I hope so." Small talk was enough.

"That is good. What are you and Maru up to?" He asked about Maru? Good.

"There is a show at the one theater that is rebuilt down by the Tuchkov bridge. Looks good. We are going tomorrow. " He turned and went to his room, he did not care for shows.

For the show, Lanya again wore her new dress and when Maru came by, she had on her new navy also. The daylight lasted well into the night and when they came out, it felt like early evening.

"Do you remember meeting Ivan and Leonid after that show before the war got here?" Maru looked at her and smiled.

Yes, it was exciting." If only she would have known what Ivan would lead her to. She would never have spoken to him! Her stomach clenched up at the memory.

"That was a long time ago, wasn't it? What do we have to look forward to now?" Maru was asking good questions it seemed.

"Well, I saw one of my friends from the first show while you went to the restroom and he told me that there will be tryouts for a new show in two weeks. I want to get back on stage!"

"Of course! If you do that you can quit at the factory... but no, stay with me!"

"I am not going anywhere, but I will look into those tryouts. What do you have to look forward to?"

"One date with your brother is not enough. I need to tell him what I want. He probably wants the same thing. I need to be clear, we need to get married and have babies!" Maru was smiling and her eyes were sparkling. She knew what she wanted. Maru had never said all that before, but she was almost hopping as she said it and Lanya grabbed her with a hug.

"That would be the best thing ever! Anything I can do?"

"No, but if I think of something, I will let you know. What about you? Any men- how about Aleksander?" Lanya knew this question was coming. She did not know when, but she knew it would come. They walked along the canal and dodged the piles of rubble that still littered streets.

"I did not tell you yet, I needed time to sort it all out. He came to see me..." Maru grabbed her arm and stopped her on the street.

"What?"

"He came by the apartment when Mishka was at work. He told me he wanted to be my partner, my boyfriend. He told me to take my time and talk to him when I was ready."

"And what did you do?" Maru would not let her leave anything out.

"Nothing. I have thought and thought. I made a plus and minus list. Some good plusses."

"Minuses? What were the minuses?"

"I only found one, Maru. The only minus is his missing leg. Everything else was a plus." Lanya felt silly. It was so clear. *Only one minus for a man who likes her! Why do I take so long?*

"And you did not tell him?"

"No, I did not. He gave me his address so I could come to him when I was ready..."

Maru was smiling as she grabbed Lanya's hands. "Tomorrow, you will go, tomorrow. Do I need to walk you over?" As they walked, Lanya felt light and knew this was a good choice.

Chapter Fifty

Aleksander's apartment was on a side street off a main road, easy to find. There was a ramp that led to the doorways and Lanya wondered if most residents needed wheelchairs. This would be easy for them to get in and out of.

Lanya stood just off the porch. What should she say? Would a simple yes do it? Or should she explain? What would Babu say? She slowed her breathing and remembered her grandmother, sure that Babu would say go ahead and take this risk. Mishka would say the same, and Valentina would be knocking on the door already. She smiled at that. She was the only one scared. Even Aleksander was brave. She was here. She would be brave too.

She went to knock, but as she reached for the door, it opened. Aleksander smiled and moved aside so she could come in. It was a small place but the doorways were wider than most, probably for the chair. She looked toward the kitchen and could see the counters were lower and they had extended edges so a chair could fit under.

"It looks like this place is perfect for you." she said quietly. He smiled and looked around.

"It is designed for us in these chairs. Better than other places for sure. Can I make you some tea?"

"Oh no, I do not need anything."

"Come sit down." He grabbed her hand, led her to a chair and he pulled up facing her. She sat. Her throat was tight. Why was she not talking? Was there wool in her throat? Maybe tea would be good. "You decided to come see me. I am glad of that." He looked at her.

"Do you have any questions? I will answer what I can. I would have a ton of questions."

She felt better with that. She did not feel so guilty with her questions. "Can you please tell me about your family?" Safe was good. He relaxed and breathed deeply.

"I have a sister; she is 32 and married with kids and lives outside Moscow. I had a brother two years older than me, but Stalingrad killed him." He paused and Lanya could see his pain. "My mom got sick before the war and died in 1940, my dad has been missing since the battle of Moscow. We do not know if he is alive." Was there an easier way to do this? She had ideas racing through her brain. Aleksander went on. "My leg was blown up in a mine search. They sent us through a field and I did not step on it but I walked close to it and my lower leg was blown off. I was lucky, twelve of the men I was with died." He paused and Lanya could see the memory was painful. "I can use crutches sometimes, I cannot dance, but the chair gets me around." He looked at her and there was a twinkle in his eye. "All other parts present and accounted for, in good working order." She gasped and her face turned bright red! *How does he know I was thinking that question? I could never have asked!* She covered her face with her hands and he reached over and took her hands down. "I wanted you to know. I can do all that is necessary to start a family. Does that make a difference?" Lanya wanted to sink into the floor. She said nothing. She hoped her color was returning to normal. "And, I just got a job with the postal corps, sorting mail. I can do it from my chair and it seems simple enough. So I have a job!" He was truly proud of that, as he should be.

Lanya decided she needed to do some talking. "I did have questions and you have answered them all. Thanks." She took a deep breath and hoped she did not look nervous. "I don't know if you know this, but I like to be in the theater, on stage. Singing." He looked at her like she was an angel. "Would that be a problem? If I was out at night performing?" *Oh no, I just jumped in and offered my whole life to him! How stupid! He has not ever said let's get married and spend our nights together! He only wants a girlfriend!* She stared at her shoes, wishing the floor would open up and swallow her.

"Lanya, your brother told me about your voice. How it sounds like angels. If you want to be on stage, I will be in the first row. What you want to do is important. It will be important to both of us." He set his hand on hers and squeezed gently. She felt like she would not sink into the floor. Like maybe this would work.

"I think I would like to try, this..." Her voice was not yet clear, and she choked on her words. "With you." He squeezed her hand again. He picked up her hand and turned it and kissed the back of it. Looking straight in her eyes, he started to sing.

"New beginnings are a fresh start, new beginning for a fresh heart..." She knew the song. It was a classic. She blushed again. "Hope you don't mind me singing sometimes." He smiled. "Will you be my girlfriend. Svetlana?"

"Yes, I will."

With her stomach all aflutter, Lanya stood up, dropping his hand. Girlfriend? She needed to let this sink in.

"I... need to go." Her voice was still shaky. She looked at his face, his eyes. She saw gentleness and eagerness. She smiled and turned to the door. "I will see you soon."

"Goodbye girlfriend." He gave a small wave as she opened the door, she smiled.

"Goodbye." She did not say boyfriend. That was just too much, for now.

She walked down the street to get her tram and was glad that her stomach was not a mess. She had worried about that. Overthinking again. Her fingers did not drum on her skirt as she got on the tram. Was she relaxed? That was a funny thought, she said to herself. Relaxed? After all I have been through? A smile crossed her face and she took a deep breath. Yes, relaxed was the right word.

Back at the apartment, Lanya prepared a small dinner. Mishka was not home, he was out with Maru, so she ate. Her brain was full, but it was a warm full. She had a boyfriend! And not like Ivan, a man who would get her in danger and cared about other things more. And not like Josef, who was a good man but attached to the Party. Aleksander would put her first. She was sure of that.

As she processed this new idea, she wanted to feel Babu. She went to her bedroom where the journals were. As she opened one, she remembered the stability her grandmother had been in her life. She whispered a thank you. She thumbed through and remembered all that she learned. She came across the one thing that had stuck, when

Babu said there is no misfortune without a blessing. For the first time, she could see that this was true.

She let that sink in. She had been through misery for sure. Losing her parents, her sister and her brother being so broken. The bombings, the people who died from starvation and cold, and losing Babu. Then Ivan and jail. Yes, she has seen misery. But, the war was over and a new world was beginning. She was at peace and embraced the new. It was time for blessings.

About the author

Thank you so much for reading <u>Songs of the Siege.</u> It has been a labor of love.

History is like breathing for me. I taught high school World History in Southern California (San Marcos) for 34 years. I have always loved Russia, the depth and breadth of the history and culture. I fell in love with St. Petersburg (Leningrad) after a visit in 2000, and knew the story needed to be told. The Germans surrounded the city and bombed it but never invaded. And the Leningraders survived!

I wrote this after my husband challenged me to do better when I complained about the poor quality of books I was reading. So, I began! I wrote at home in Maine and while I was doing substitute work (thank you Seahawk friends!). I am married to wonderful Tom, and I have two grown children, Maggie and Gavin. With Tom, we have three more.

Lanya and Mikhail will continue in another story soon.

I would appreciate any reviews you could leave on, reviews are important! Thank you for those!

Blessings
Angela Ferguson
authoraferguson@gmail.com

www.ingramcontent.com/pod-product-compliance
Lightning Source LLC
Chambersburg PA
CBHW050015120726
47903CB00006B/1783